Christopher

History isn't only what we inherit, safe and sound and after the fact; it is also what we are ourselves obliged to endure.

'Public Intellectuals', Cynthia Ozick, *Quarrel & Quandary*.

And now the sun had stretched out all the hills,
And now was dropped into the western bay;
At last he rose, and twitched his mantle blue:
Tomorrow to fresh woods, and pastures new.

'Lycidas', John Milton.

And then another problem reared its head. When Miss Gilby had first entered the inner courtyard there had been a great deal of trouble that had lasted quite some time. Eventually, the whole thing had got buried under the routine and rhythms of quotidian life. But soon everything was raked up again; I hadn't given much thought to Miss Gilby's nationality for a long time but now I began to do so. I said to my husband, 'I think you should ask her to leave.' He kept quiet. I said a lot of unpleasant things to him. He heard me out, silent and sad, and then left the room. I sulked and cried for a while. That night, he said to me, 'Bimala, I cannot see Miss Gilby as *just* an English woman and nothing more. Does the fact that you've known her for so long count as nothing? Is her Englishness everything? Don't you understand how fond she is of you?'

I felt ashamed but couldn't swallow my pride entirely and agree that he was right. So I said, somewhat petulantly, 'All right, then, let her stay. Who's asked her to leave?'

from 'Bimala's autobiography', Rabindranath Tagore, *The Home and the World*.

ZERO

There was a queue for electric furnaces at Kalighat crematorium on the eleventh of October. Ritwik did not know how long he had to wait before one became available.

'You have to wait, like everyone else. No corpse is privileged over the other. You can't hurry death, do you understand?' he was told by one of the furnace attendants, as if he had asked to jump the queue when all he had wanted to know was how long it would take. He reasoned he would much rather a longer wait for he did not want to go through that bristling panoply of rituals before the sliding rails carried his mother's body into the heart of fire, in full, cleansing view of everyone. When the moment arrived, he knew he had been dreading it with a cold, randomly clutching-and-unclutching grip in his bowels. His mother's body had been laid out on a criss-cross frame of cheap wood that formed a ramshackle stretcher, secured to it with rough coir ropes and covered with a white, coarse sheet; her head had been left exposed. It nodded and lolled like a floppy doll's as the stretcher was placed in front of one of the three furnaces that would ultimately devour her.

The Brahmin priest was already there, more a harried figure doing brisk business than a sombre religious person. A distracted, infinitely bored look had seeped its way into his

1

stubbly face through years of practice in the death trade: it was an irremovable mask now, his only skin. His eyes were the yellow of mangled fried eggs and he had foul breath.

'Are you wearing any animal products? You'll have to remove them,' he said to Ritwik.

'What animal products? Leather?' Ritwik wasn't sure what he had to remove.

'Yes, leather, wool, anything made with horn. You will have to take off your shirt as well.' From the complete absence of tone, he might as well have been reading out a lesson he had taught every day for decades to a bunch of vapid children.

Ritwik undid his borrowed watch – the strap was made of leather – and handed it to his brother, Aritra. He then took off his shirt and stood there, naked to the waist.

'What about the belt? Is that made of leather?' the priest asked. Those sick yellow eyes didn't miss a thing.

'Yes, I think it is,' Ritwik said, 'but I can't take it off. My jeans are three sizes too big for me; if I remove it, they'll just slip off.'

There was the noise, no, not even noise, but the atmospheric charge, of a dutifully suppressed titter of shock around him. As the priest grudgingly assented or ignored, he could not figure out which, he was handed a bundle of burning faggots and asked to circle his mother seven times and touch the barely burning straw-and-twigs to her grey face every time he reached her head during the circling. This then was *mukhagni*, the fire-to-the-face ritual that initiated the funeral process and without which it was unsanctioned and incomplete, this the very act that had made him shy away from all the ceremonies which were the first-born son's duty at his father's cremation eleven days ago. But now he did not have the heart, or the steeliness of will, to send along his

2

mother without the reckoning, with all the imperfections on her head.

Ritwik suddenly had a suspicion of a supremely ironic design of Things, with a malignant sense of humour, which had brought him to perform what he had so wilfully avoided a few days ago. Someone was laughing somewhere, he thought, as he turned his head away every time he branded his mother's dead face: it left a black, ashy singe wherever it touched. His stomach heaved, letting him know that it had been empty for a very long time, and a malicious spurt of acid moved up swiftly behind his chest bone, his throat, impatient to enter his mouth, but he swallowed the sour fire.

The wooden stretcher with his mother on it was positioned on the rails; it slid shudderingly along them towards the door of the furnace with insides of consuming fire. The body entered it, the door shut all from fire to fire, while he stood outside in his intolerable shirt of flame and a wail went up from a clot of numbed people in front of another furnace, the sound like a refraction in a distorting mirror. This then was the atomised end, the final breakdown into the fundamental particles. *It will take an hour and a half for it to be over, come away now, come.* Ninety minutes was too too long for a human body, wasn't it? Did it burn like paper to an infinitely curling hyaline thinness, his mother escaping out of a flue somewhere upwards and ascending still . . .

Two days after they took her to the hospital, Ritwik's mother died. The whisper everywhere was that his father had taken his mother away. 'Pulled her away to him,' everyone said. Otherwise, how could one explain the abnormally small gap of eleven days, *eleven days*, between the two deaths? To Ritwik,

3

everyone seemed scared at this sign of the workings of a world beyond the here and now, as if their lives had been momentarily lit by a cruel, grand flash of the great unknown, a reminder of something ineffable, then plunged back into their dim, quotidian greyness again. He detected a faint whiff of an 'I told you so' attitude in his uncles, his aunts, the neighbours, or was that just imagined? But there was no mistaking the holy dread at what was being discussed as the bond that worked beyond human life.

On the day it happened – grey, close, the no-time between afternoon and dusk – Ritwik was sitting on the floor of his uncle Pradip's room, indifferently pushing around the cold rice and dal and vegetables on the stainless steel plate in front of him, with relatives and neighbours sitting around, waiting and watching for signs of grief at his father's death nine days ago. This parliament of vultures had been gathering for the last week to circle around that one death when it looked as if it could suddenly, thrillingly, jump up to two. Their piously suppressed excitement provided a tight murmur in the background, like the muffled buzzing of bees: grief offered such a delicious peek into the minutiae of other people's lives.

His mother was in her room, in the customary mourning garb, coarse handspun white cotton sari, being watched by another set of people, waiting, watching, and commiserating. It was then that Mejo-mashi, one of his aunts, ran into Pradip-mama's room and wailed, 'Something's happened to Didi, come quickly, she's slurring her speech and rolling her eyes!'

In one swift swarm they reached his mother's room. Ritwik saw her, awkwardly reclined on the floor, trying to stretch out beside the low bed but failing, her jaw a fluid, mobile line involved in the painful formation of words which kept slipping away from the solid, sharp edges they unthinkingly assumed in healthy people. Her eyes were trying both to shut and to keep open at the same time, as if seeking a fugitive point of focus that kept eluding her. The elastic slippages of the words managed somehow to convey 'pain' and 'head'. Ritwik barked out to nobody in particular, 'Why are you shouting? Why are you all crowding around her? Move away, give her some air!'

It did not take long for the neighbourhood doctor, who had come quickly, to conduct a few basic tests – scratching a key on the soles of her feet, asking her, a bit too loudly and slowly, as if speaking to a retarded child, to focus on the tip of a pen which he held in his fingers and moved from one point to another in a straight horizontal line – and confirm what was already nudging darkly at the back of Ritwik's mind: she had had a massive cerebral stroke ('hemiplegia' was the word the doctor used) and was to be rushed to the intensive care unit of a hospital.

There were no ambulances in Calcutta. Assuming you had a telephone in the first place, there were no emergency numbers to dial either. Although Ritwik's childhood had been dotted here and there with the excitement of seeing fire engines rush past, a standing fireman in an overlarge helmet clanging a loud bell with a stick or pulling the string attached to it, he had no idea how it had been summoned. A phone call or someone running to fetch it? In any case, they did not have a telephone and it would have meant going upstairs to Tabbu's flat to use their phone, so someone had to go to the bus stop, a ten-minute walk away, and fetch a taxi from the rank there.

His mother had meanwhile thrown up the chyme of boiled rice, boiled potatoes, boiled green bananas – a sure sign, the doctor had said, of cerebral haemorrhage. In popular belief it was a 'medical' indication that things were very serious indeed. There was a short, tense debate between Ritwik and his uncles whether carrying her horizontally to the taxi parked outside would exacerbate her condition or whether supporting her two arms around the necks of two strong men and walking her to the taxi would be more damaging. In the end, it was decided she would be walked out, supported by Pradip-mama on one side and Pratik-mama on the other, with Ritwik following closely to offer additional help should it be needed.

There was a crowd now: neighbours congregating in the balconies of nearby houses, trying, and failing, to be discreet as they looked on; the throng surrounding the passage of his mother from the house to the taxi outside (they had to shout 'Make way, make way' several times to ease the obstruction); and the assortment of relatives. There was Ria-mami, married to his oldest uncle, Pradip-mama; their daughter, the three-year old Munu, whimpering, not quite sure of what had happened but, with a child's unerring nose, had somehow sniffed out that her favourite person in the household was going away, perhaps with no hope of return; Nisha, the maidservant; his mother's sister, Mejo, who looked retreating and forlorn, whether from what had happened to her sister or from Ritwik's sharp words a few minutes ago, he could not tell; Tabbu's mother; half a dozen neighbours.

The taxi was one of those not unusual Calcutta ones which had two drivers sharing the business of driving in shifts. There was trouble fitting everyone in: Tabbu sat in front, squeezed between the two drivers, Pradip-mama, Ritwik, and Aritra in the back, with their mother half-carried, half-slumping. Ritwik's three other uncles gathered around, wanting to clamber in, in a display of hectic participation. He came close to pointing out that

6

the taxi couldn't fit any more; besides, there were quite enough people to take care of things, but he held his tongue: it gave them something to do, a kind of focus to an otherwise unvaried stretch of the same day, day after day.

Throughout the dust-blown journey to the hospital, the second driver had his arm out of the passenger window and flailed a filthy red cloth, in all probability the one used for cleaning the taxi. This was the Calcutta equivalent of the warning wail of the ambulance. The hope that traffic in this city would stop or make way for a taxi with an insignificant red rag flapping out of one of its windows was risible and infuriating at the same time. How many people knew that a red rag meant a car carrying the seriously ill to hospital? Ritwik certainly didn't until now.

The taxi went down Anwar Shah Road, turned right at Deshpran Sashmal Road, with its straight, uninterrupted stretch of tramlines, and made its way to Kalighat, its wheels sending up a dense cottony billow of yellow-grey dust that, mingled with the exhaust fumes, kept blowing into the vehicle through the open windows. It snagged in Ritwik's mind as another worry: his mother really shouldn't be breathing in such visibly polluted air at this time. The roads on either side of the tram tracks were dug up in places and it was a bumpy, convoluted ride, all straight lines from one point to another becoming two oblique diagonals taking in a distant, third point. With each jerk, Ritwik feared the clot in his mother's head was oozing out more blood, or her frangible brain-lobes juddering with the impact and disintegrating like some delicate pudding that could barely hold its shape.

At Kalighat, the taxi took a left turn and went past the crematorium – the same crematorium where his mother had performed the last rites for his father nine days ago – on its way to the medical centre in Alipore. It was one of the busiest crossroads in the city. Pedestrians and traffic flowed into each other like indiscriminate waters; there were no demarcated spaces for either, no rules about their separation. A cow stood, calm and transcendent, in the middle of this barely moving, lawless sea of people, bicycles, autorickshaws, lorries, cars, buses, stray dogs and trams. A woman with stainless steel kitchen utensils balanced on her head shouted out her wares and tried to cross over to the other side towards Gariahat. All these registered in Ritwik's head like separate photographs, without syntax. And above all this incessant noise of traffic and horns and human living, he could hear, as an abiding bass-line, the raucous cry of crows. He just had to shift the focus of his ears, from foreground to background, to hear the harsh, continuous cawing welling out over everything, like the slow, silent beginnings of a flood.

And now that it was all happening, how would he live? Throughout his teenage years, he had forced himself to think about his mother's death, as if that willed act could deprive fate of the power at least to seize him with the suddenness of tragedy. It comes to him easily, the line, *Readiness is all.* Lying on the floor, between his mother and Aritra, his father on the pallet, night after sweat-saturated night he had taken himself ruthlessly through the worst scenarios and when it had all played out in his febrile imagination up to a point beyond which nothing, no hope, no solace, no consolation, nothing remained, he went one step further. It became a slowly forged shield through which the vagaries and surprises of events could scarcely touch him for he had already imagined and lived inside the worst.

What *would* life be without her? In some amorphous way he had always thought that all his happiness would come to an end with her death. But what if it released him instead into a terrifying new life, unshadowed by the prospect of her ageing and dying in slow degrees? What if that freedom was given him so early? If he could only push the inevitable away to some unspecified point in the future when he was old enough, a proper adult, he would be able to deal with it efficiently and well, but no, it really was happening now. It wasn't the luxury of a safe mind toying with dark imaginings in terrified fascination any more. At thirteen, he thought twenty-five was the right age for dealing with Big Events like the death of a parent; now, at twenty-one, the notion of a safe age turned out to be a mirage, receding further and further into the distance as one approached a moving boundary. Perhaps there really wasn't any safe age for loss.

And his father had just died, leaving him as the theoretical head of the family. Following the ineluctable laws of Bengali hierarchies, he was now in charge of their family of three, responsible for his mother and his younger brother. It was this that ate at him more than his father's death, this swift alighting of burdens and responsibilities when he was so unprepared, so green. How was he going to provide for them? On that deceptively small question, everything foundered. Families were based more on subtle ties of provider and receiver than on any intangible emotional bonding. If he had been ten or twelve at this moment, he wouldn't have had to think about all this; something would have been arranged by the other adults in the household until he came of age. But he couldn't hope for it now. If he could become invisible, or just cease to exist, be whisked away to a different country, a different continent . . . It wasn't the first time he had had such fantasies but now, looking distractedly out of the taxi window at a group of strutting pigeons pecking at some spilled grain on the roadside, at two slum children just sitting and staring blankly at traffic and passersby, their eyes opaque and unreadable, he felt guilty about letting thoughts of money enter his head. He should be thinking of his mother, her well-being, not costing it down or ledgering family relationships.

All those fears of his mother dying and leaving him alone were really his fears of a parent in hospital with no money to pay for medical bills, doctors, nurses, medicines, tests. But for now his pockets were heavy with borrowed and given money. He had been sharp enough to grab the bulging wallet which his mother had held so close to her in her week of mourning, a wallet filled with money from relatives, his own friends, Aritra's friends and their parents, people who instinctively knew that that would be the greatest necessity now that her husband, the family's sole earner, was dead. Soumik's mother, Uncle Adip, Mrinal, all had come forward with generous wads of cash, which they had embarrassedly pushed into her hands, or had bypassed her altogether and had given Ritwik and Aritra instead. Taking possession of his mother's wallet had come naturally; as soon as the taxi had arrived outside the front door, he had picked it up from beside the bed. If he had been less alert, it would almost certainly have been stolen by one of his uncles and, when asked, they would have denied ever having set their eyes upon it. It was the story of their lives in Grange Road. It had been clever of him to get in there first and prevent the money from going missing. That opportune seizing brought temporary redemption from more begging, more debts (he knew the money would be spent in a matter of days) and more shame. At least for now, he wouldn't have to call on Mrinal for a handout for the first things – the doctor's home visit, the taxi fare to the hospital, the admission charges.

The hospital was new, swanky, and built and run with the dirty money of Marwaris. Everything seemed to happen swiftly and efficiently here, to Ritwik's amazement. He had grown up with news coverage of innumerable hospitals in Calcutta where cats roamed and pissed in the wards, dogs came in and walked away with newborns or wandered around licking the wounds and sores of people lying there with no hope of escape. But here there were silent lifts and the white noise of functioning state-of-the-art medical appliances. The insistent air-conditioning goosepimpled his thin arms, the floors shone with the zing and ardour of the new. Money changed hands as he signed the requisite forms – he noticed there was a clause absolving the hospital of all responsibility should the worst happen and wondered if it was true of hospitals everywhere – and his mother was wheeled away by uniformed nurses and attendants to an intensive care unit on a floor high up in the building.

Tabbu's obtrusive altruism now took the form of an iterative chanting of, 'Nothing's happened, everything's all right, everything will be OK', and Ritwik started counting on the digits of his fingers how many times he repeated the saving formula. Both he and Tabbu were chain-smoking in the car park just inside the entrance of the hospital, as if what had happened had released them into a new permissiveness. For Ritwik, the act of smoking in front of his uncles still carried a minor charge of flouting accepted codes of behaviour: it was almost a dare on his part, a gauntlet thrown down to his uncles. He had already begun to show them that, just because his father was dead and his mother in a perhaps terminal coma in hospital, he wasn't going to be bossed around by them. It was best to make things clear from the very beginning. But the cleanly triumphant feeling he had been hoping to be rewarded with didn't quite arrive. Instead, it was clouded by tiny motes of betrayal: his mother had worked so hard to ensure that the boys didn't fall prey to the bad habits that so characterised her brothers and here he was, indulging in the very thing she had tried to protect him from, to score cheap points. The cigarettes left a woolly burn along his throat and lungs. He had a taste of the futility of her life and his heart turned over.

Ritwik carefully folded away the very short encounter with the doctor the next morning in the hope of deliberately expunging it some day in the future. Everyone assembled at the hospital awaited the doctor's arrival with varying degrees of apprehension. They had all been told who the doctor was and their irritatingly frequent questions – *when will he come down? when will he let us know? will he be long?* – had been answered with exemplary patience.

When the self-possessed doctor did arrive, everyone rushed to him like pigs to the feeding farmer. Ritwik composed his face into an expressionless nothing as the doctor said, 'We can't say anything with absolute certainty at the moment except that we have to keep her under observation for seventy-two hours. She's in a coma and we can't say when she will come around. Obviously, the cerebral stroke she has suffered is huge and extremely serious. Both sides of her body are completely paralysed and even if she does recover, she will remain paralysed, in all probability, for the rest of her life. Of course, that might well change . . . We need to conduct a few more tests – an MRI scan of the brain, a CAT scan . . .' Fluent, articulate, utterly detached.

Ritwik nodded impassively as the onslaught of information battered through his insides. He recalled Dida, his grandmother, another semi-paralysed stroke survivor who had hobbled her bitter way around the flat, skulking in corners and shadows, occasionally beaten up by her own sons, a twisted and hating figure, till her second cerebral stroke had sent her into a two-month coma from which she ultimately never recovered. The doctor's words burnt out a clearing in his head: like all clearings, it contained both ash and space.

The next day, during visiting hours, he took the lift high up to his mother's room. She seemed conscious, her eyes opening wide as if she had just woken up from a long sleep and was having considerable trouble easing herself into the unfamiliarity surrounding her; the world of her sleep still inflected the hospital room. She struggled to get up, looked at her son, and said, 'Home, I want to go home. Why am I here? What is this place?'

Ritwik answered, 'Yes, of course, you'll go home, but you're not very well at the moment, Ma. As soon as you're better, we're going to take you home.' He spoke very slowly, articulating each word separately and distinctly, as if he was simplifying something complex to an inquisitive child.

Buffeted by some barely articulable unease, she tried to raise her head against the pillows again. She looked like a strung-up marionette that hadn't quite come to fluid and easy life because the puppeteer had only just begun and was going through his hand and finger warming-up exercises. One of the monitors attached to her showed a jagged green graph, like a curious, moving snake, forming and reforming, arcanely measuring out her life in electronic signals.

Ritwik, remembering what the doctor had said about extensive damage to the brain, asked her, 'Can you recognize me? Who am I?'

She answered him correctly, an emptiness in her face, perhaps trying to work out if it was a trick question, but the look of blank confusion could equally have been the effect of the stroke.

She tried to lift her hands, in an eerily lost movement, as if they had acquired an unmoored yet independent life, no longer governed by the directing brain. The words came out truncated and random, 'Pain, headache. Here, here, no here' – her hands, nowhere near her head, flailed about, unsuccessfully trying to locate the exact spot – 'please massage my head, it'll go away. Just a headache. And then you'll take me home.'

Her eyes were wide and unfocused; they didn't seem to be registering anything.

Ritwik had to find out if her ability to perceive and recognize objects had been impaired as well. From his sidebag, he took out the book he was currently reading – *The Complete Illustrated Nonsense of Edward Lear* – held it in front of him and asked, 'Ma, can you tell me what I'm holding in my hands?'

She rolled her eyes towards him but didn't manage to fix them either on him or on the book. 'Book, a book', the words tumbled out like an erratic spill of oranges from a paper bag. 'Why are you asking me these questions? If you press your hands on my head, head, here, here' – this time she didn't even manage to raise her arms – 'it'll go, really, it will.'

He said, 'The doctor will make it go away. You're in good hands.' The lie jangled so shrilly in his ears he looked up to see if she had heard it.

She had shut her eyes and was mumbling, 'Like you used to massage my temples, forehead, with Amrutanjan when I had headaches, like that, it'll go away. When you were young. It's a very severe headache, you know?'

He felt as if something had gone through the centre of his torso, entering through his navel and boring its way out back through the spine. The duty nurse came in and saved him. 'All right, that's enough. You mustn't tire her out.'

Ritwik stood up to leave with his back turned to the bed. He couldn't bear to look at the bloodless face of his mother already asleep – or was it comatose? – on the regulation pillows but the need to twist the knife proved too strong. He turned around and a careless calculation, done god knows when, hiding and waiting until this moment for the ruthless ambush, tripped up his entire being: she had been four years older than he was now when she had given birth to him. He gripped the metal rail at the end of her bed and swallowed. When had his own span of life, one he had thought so small that it could be counted, almost totally, on the digits of one outstretched hand, become so large that half his mother's could be circumscribed within it? Half a lifetime, a mid-point reached with his birth: how could time be calibrated with such erratic abandon?

That night he slept in the flat of Aritra's college friend, Sujoy. It was a convenient distance from the hospital and near-strangers offered both anonymity and a hiatus from the pinning focus of searchers looking for information, signs of grief, points of breakage. He was tired but did not want to be subjected to the ruthless time between switching off the light and the tricky oblivion of sleep, so he forced his attention on his Edward Lear.

He didn't know what woke him up in the middle of the night. His mouth was dry, his throat a sore, raspy burn. Did she wake up as well, in an alien, clinical bed, her mind alert and ranging over things with the dreamlike clarity that colours such hours? Was she afraid? Did she think she was going to die? What did it feel like? Did she call out for him, her strangled cry bounding and rebounding off the insulated dark walls, or faintly leaking and petering out in the lowly lit corridors? Did she think of his father's death or her own?

The next morning, the inevitability of going to the hospital gave him a sense of doom that seemed to drag and dredge inside him. There were people there already, his friends from college, and Aritra's, who had offered to do the early morning shift. It was like a vigil, he thought, as he went to shoulder his time. Something in the shadows of Arpit's face while he crossed the main hall already told him. Certain floating pieces of signs and sense, unconnected until now, suddenly came together in a confirmed design, a design he had always known would be, must be, as Arpit said in his infinitely rehearsed 'thus you break the bad news' voice that his mother had 'expired' in the early hours of the morning.

'Expired,' Ritwik thought, 'what an improbable word to use.' He nodded almost imperceptibly, acknowledging the news. Inside him was a breathless hollow, at once spiky and porous, awl-and-threaded through with the fibres of his very soul it seemed; it could have accommodated entire other worlds, other times.

Giving Arpit and others the slip, he went up to his mother's hospital eyrie, perched so safe and high above the torrent of the city, to see what she looked like in death. He wanted to be alone, at least for this first view of his dead mother. A pale face in all its waxy coldness, lips with the pallor of ash, eyes shut: it could have been a deeply sleeping face that rested against the pillows. How could they be so sure that all the beating, breathing, painful life had left that face? He thought he was going to reach out his hand and touch it but couldn't bring himself to move even an inch.

And here the gratuitous tyranny of memory seized him by the balls and no place, no time was safe, and he was a mere nothing to that event he had never, never thought about, never remembered, till now it was everything. He is four years old, and he and his mother board a hand-pulled rickshaw in Park Circus, on a road adjacent to the west side of the big circus green. Even now he feels that momentary precariousness of his position in the slightly scary rickshaw, as if he is about to fall backwards as the puller lifts up the front of the vehicle and the world tilts around him. Suddenly in front of them, in the middle air, there is a whole colony of blue and water-green dragonflies, circling and hovering in their staccato way, sometimes still in the air with just a vibration of wings, a static thrumming, and then off again with a jerky move. *Ma, Ma, look, look, dragonflies! What a lot of them! What are they doing there? Why aren't they landing on something?* That suspension of a large swarm a cause of wonder and his mother with an explanation for a small child: *They have just been born, up in the heavens, and have been sent down to earth right now*, as if heaven were up above behind the canopy of the blue sky, the dragonflies shimmering their papery net-wings, a dazzling whirr in the clear light, having just pierced the blue screen above in their birth and descent. The little boy is delighted at the miracle and his eyes widen with wonder and happiness as his mother smiles and smiles at this benediction of air.

At Kalighat, he was struck by the place's newly found familiarity; it was becoming a dangerously regular haunt, almost known, almost comfortable. There were three or four tea shacks with corrugated tin sheds opposite the main entrance to the crematorium. They looked so fragile, with their rows of smudged glass jars which contained gaudily coloured biscuits, the open coal fire with the huge kettle for boiling tea, milk and sugar together, and the long, leaning columns of terracotta drinking cups. The bit of the road along the shanties was a little drain of these discarded and broken cups, of muddy washing-up water and the red stains of paan spittle.

Eleven days ago he had been here for his father's cremation. It appeared to be a type of puerile radicalism now, the way he thought he had scored points in refusing to perform the last rites for his father. In denying the honourable duties that bound the male first-born in a Hindu family – although his family was that only in a diluted, anodyne way – he thought he had taken a socially meaningful step. This was compounded, although Ritwik could take no credit for it, by his mother's decision to do the necessary rituals. Untraditionally so, because Hindu tradition gave no place to women to atone for the sins of the deceased and see off his soul. If anyone had thought it odd or deviatory, this business of the last rites being performed by the dead man's widow instead of his surviving sons, they had not said so. On top of that, both he and Aritra had refused to go through *ashauch*, the ritual eleven-day mourning, a period of defilement, culminating in the *sraddha* ceremony, where the soul of the dead was finally unmoored from all its earthly ties and sent on its way to purgatory or another birth or whatever.

Just recalling what his uncles had gone through when their mother had died made him furious with the punishing nature of it all: sleeping on hay and straw with bricks for headrests, no shaving or cutting of hair, no meals after sundown, a mind-boggling assortment of dietary rules . . . And then there was the final ceremony that ended it all: all hair was shorn off and shaved, including chest and armpit hair (although not pubic hair), the endless abracadabra with the phoney priest, pour this on fire pour that on fire, make seven or nine or three portions of that sickly mess of rice and bananas and ghee and place it there and there and there while chanting the names of your male ancestors (no one could go beyond a generation, or two at the most), the obligatory mass-feeding of relatives, neighbours, friends, the poor ... *Cock cock cock* he'd spat out *I'm damned if I'm doing any of this when my time comes*. But this death was different. This time Ritwik was going to do what was expected of him. If there really was a soul after all, which needed to be released, he didn't want to take any chances with his mother's.

There was no question of opting for the traditional open wooden pyre, so uninsulated, so barbaric to Ritwik's mind. In those blank hours between registering the corpse for cremation in an electric furnace and the little ritual before it actually happened, Ritwik noticed disparate patches of people strewn around the crematorium. Death sometimes made survivors gregarious. He was surprised that there were so few inconsolable people; he had expected far more than the occasional ones, from whom he glanced away. Every haggard face there looked dry, as if deprived of some essential sap which loss had wrung out of them drop by drop, leaving only dark shadows and a desiccation around the mouth, the unkemptness of dusty hair, the crushed, limp dullness of the stale clothes; Ritwik wondered if he looked like them as well.

The billow and swell of support and advice around Ritwik and Aritra grew. It seemed that virtually half of Aritra's college had come over to stand by him in this hour of need. Information rained down on him, thick and merciless, like a choking Old Testament plague – the time it would take for the corpse to be completely burnt once it entered the furnace; how the ramp automatically rose to advance and lower the 'body' inside; how the gates of the furnace came down to cover the process from human view; the list of things he had to do before and after the cremation. Now that he had to perform all these himself, he was

19

fascinated by the structures and codes of this little world of the business and commerce and rituals of death. It was an alternative world, so inescapably under his own yet so unknown until he had to educate himself in its rules. Who would have thought that such knowledge had to be bought with so much fire, fire that would send his mother somewhere upwards and ascending still, in dispersing, intermittent clouds of elementary particles, so that if he breathed in he could fill his chest with tiny fragments of her being and hold this transubstantiation locked inside his distending lungs.

In Hindu belief, the navel is indestructible, left behind in the furnace as the whole body is converted to a fistful of ash. The last act of the cremation was the retrieval of this undestroyed navel from the maws of the furnace. There was a short walk to the Ganga, which ran right behind the crematorium, to set the 'navel' afloat (or whatever lump of rock or charcoal the *panda*, the crematorium tout, had handed you) following the guidelines of yet another priest or hanger-on hoping for a few rupees.

Aritra's face was flushed, as if one of the walls of the furnace that held their mother's corpse had suddenly slid from its fixed position and the contained fire had licked and blazed too close to the boy's face. A purification, an extinguishing. The dark of his pupils seemed to have welled and inked out in circles under his eyes. He made Ritwik a generous offer, 'Look, if you don't feel up to it, I can do this last bit.'

'No, it's all right; I've done it so far, let me see it to the end.' He paused for a second, then added, 'Besides, I'm the elder son . . .' his voice trailed off to make space for the excuse.

The *panda*s, who ferreted through the ashes with long sticks after the body was fully incinerated, handed him what passed for his mother's navel in a flimsy earthen bowl. They had heaped it with ash and cinder out of an odd sense of decorum. There was a small procession – he, Aritra, Tabbu, a couple of Aritra's friends, Pratik-mama, and a few others – to the dark slurry of putrefying matter which was the Ganga, the holy river, not running but stagnant and stench-bound behind the crematorium. On the way, he was seized by an urge to root through the ashes and earth in the little bowl in his hands (surprisingly heavy) and see if it really contained his mother's rubbery navel and the stump of her umbilical cord untouched by fire.

They reached the slopes of the bank and as he was asked to step closer, almost into that seething shit, he was once again overcome by nausea, afraid that any physical contact with the river would cause some repulsive illness. He stepped forward a few inches, gingerly, steeling himself to disobey any orders to stand ankle-deep in it. There were emaciated dogs moving around the place, materializing in and out of the thick darkness everywhere, sniffing for, he supposed, human limbs and charred flesh. He tried to take his mind off the marauding creatures and perform all that was asked of him. From the slums on the other side of the river, random feathers of Hindi film songs kept getting blown in with the intermittent breeze: *Slowly, slowly we must increase our love, O magician, who has cast a spell on my virgin heart.* The weak electric bulbs, dotted here and there among the huts, looked like static tapers.

The brothers flinched when the priest sprinkled everyone with holy water from the river: for a few moments they were acutely conscious of the exact spots on their bodies where the contaminated water had landed. They must remember to wash with Dettol when they returned home. Ritwik was asked to set the 'navel' afloat. But there wasn't very much water in the river and instead of floating away, as it was picturesquely supposed to do, towards salvation on the other side, the bowl landed with the squelching splash of a hard object hitting clay.

Here, all ends and begins.

PART ONE

I.

Miss Gilby finally succeeds in uniting the name of the man who has written to her with a face and a context. She picks up the coarse handmade paper, with its elegant and educated copperplate in royal blue, from her desk. The red shellac is impressed with the seal of the zamindar of Nawabgunj. Or so she supposes. She reads the letter again.

> *'Dighi Bari',*
> *Nawabgunj,*
> *Bengal.*
> *28th March 1902*

Dear Miss Gilby,

I do not presume you remember me after nearly three years but we met at the Tea Party generously hosted by your Respected Brother, District Collector James Gilby, at his Summer retreat in Ootacamund in June 1899, and to which I was so kindly invited by him. I trust and pray that you are in good health & high spirits.

Since that gathering, I have had the good fortune to find myself a Wife & a Helpmeet & it is my express desire that she be educated in the most Beautiful & Useful English Language & the ways of Ladies of your

Progressive Nation. I would wish her to be able to converse in the English Language, read your Great Writers, play the piano, & otherwise inculcate all the desirable Virtues & Practices of English Ladies such as are practised in both the home & outside. For it is also my great wish that, unlike most Indian Women, my Wife, Bimala, should step outside from the Inner Courtyard to which Women of our Country have been confined for Centuries & see the World at large. True Education consists in Experience & without it, I am afraid, most remain in the dark or the partially lit.

To these ends, I am emboldened to request you to take up the position of Governess & Teacher to my Wife. I have heard, along with Laudatory Reports of your Success as Governess, that you are resident in Calcutta now & therefore I am made hopeful that you can be approached with this suit of mine. You shall, of course, have your lodgings here with us in 'Dighi Bari'. Anything else you might desire, it is yours to command. I shall consider myself fortunate in the extreme if you look on this petition with consideration.

I remain,

Yours faithfully,
Nikhilesh Roy Chowdhury

James's Summer Season tea party in Ooty three years ago. Of course, she remembers it, remembers the subtle rivalry between the wife of the Police Superintendent, the Colonel's Lady and herself, but then, as James's sister, she didn't quite have the airs that the wives of officials gave themselves. Yet, she was the sister of the highest ranking man in Madras

Presidency, and the memsahibs' behaviour had been an oddly balanced mixture of deference and hauteur, one of the many things about the English community here which irritated her so much that it usually brought on a headache and then the obligatory afternoon retirement with drawn curtains and a bottle of eau de cologne.

James's tea party that summer – that great annual event for the Anglo-Indians and those selected natives who thought it was the greatest honour to be included – had gone exactly the way she had thought it would. Mrs Egerton-Smith had preened and frowned; Anthony Sykes's wife had been so nervous that she kept spilling her gin on her dress, at least ten years out of fashion, and then on Mrs Egerton-Smith's; Miss Carlisle wouldn't talk to anyone or come out from the marquee in the fear the sun would ruin her make-up and her yards and yards of taffeta and silk, all watery blue, straight out of the Whiteaway and Laidlaw catalogue from three Seasons ago but almost certainly made by the *darzees* in Madras from the catalogue picture. Mrs Ripon and Lady Headley-Dent, the wife of the Superintendent of Police and the Colonel, respectively, had stood by, all crinoline, parasol, hats with stuffed birds on them and smiles of the most perfectly chiselled indifference; they wouldn't even talk to the other wives but that was normal, even expected, in this community of exiles. The party had divided into the usual six sections: the men; the wives of the three burrasahibs; the other wives; the single women, usually from the 'fishing fleet' of that year, who had come over from home to look for husbands in India and who were well-connected enough to be invited to the District Collector's Summer Season party; the native men; and their wives. Six small castles, moated, granged and walled almost completely from each other. Each deemed the British Empire a grand success.

When Miss Gilby had first arrived in India, in 1891, she had been silently expected to fall into this hierarchy but her very situation had challenged it from the beginning. For a start, she had come to Madras because James's wife, Henrietta, never the most robust of women, had been struck down by a particularly nasty sunstroke from which she never recovered. James had needed someone to look after him and having always been close to his elder sister, somewhat unusually so, he had begged her to come and see to things (it must be admitted, there were things a man couldn't be expected to do, they needed a woman's presence, the feminine touch). Who would organize the household, engage the cook, the cleaner, the other *khansama*s and *chaprassi*s, arrange the parties, see to the social life, deal with the little cogs and ratchets of the everyday which kept life ticking along so silently, so imperceptibly, that you didn't notice it till it was gone, like the air you breathe in?

So Maud Gilby had sailed to India in a P&O ship from Portsmouth in the autumn of 1891. She had been advised to sail at a time that would allow her to arrive in India in the cooler winter months, otherwise the first experience of the Hot Weather in India, straight after landing, would be just overwhelming, indeed dangerous. But Madras had been no cooler than the hottest of English summers, certainly not as hot as it got in June or July, but not cool, definitely not cool. And then there had been the landing, her first touching of Indian soil, or rather, water, the choppy, turbulent waves of the Bay of Bengal which, in a crucial and inexplicable way, had done something to her, what, she cannot name or even put a finger on, but it had given her a sense of freedom, of dissidence even.

Madras didn't have a natural harbour so incoming ships just stopped a few miles from the shore, dinghies were let down and the passengers ferried across to the sand. Often dinghies rowed by the natives met the ship offshore and rowed the passengers in. Ladies and children disembarked first, but only with the bare minimum of luggage – the remaining stuff was brought in after all the passengers had been rowed across. The waves were unruly and high and the flimsy boats swayed with such abandon that it struck fear into the hearts of these ladies who had never ventured beyond the calm of the Norfolk Broads or the mostly well-behaved Thames. To be rowed by a group of night-black natives, who grinned away, not a word of English between them, not a care for the awesome tossing of the bark, would have turned the bravest of souls queasy with terror. On top of this, there were large groups of natives who thronged the beach, some to watch the drama of landing, others to wade out and lift, actually lift, the dinghies and carry them and set them down on the sands, as if they weren't boats but palanquins. Miss Gilby, with the intuitive wisdom of women, realized then, while being borne aloft in a shell of a boat with fearful English ladies, that all her English manners and notions and ideas would have to be thrown out into the heart of the Bay of Bengal because this country was like no other, because it was not like anything she had ever encountered or even dreamed of, regardless of all the stories that circulated in the Ladies' Club of Colchester and the parties in High Season; it was a country where she was going to have to learn all over again. So she set about doing exactly that.

Like every other Raj party, James's party was one where nobody mingled; after all, parties were thrown to show who stood where, immovable, the possibility of mobility a dangerous mirage. Stuck, stuck, stuck, Miss Gilby, defiant and different, had always thought. In her eight years in India, she had attracted a lot of attention and opprobrium – she had been called various things: 'dangerous', 'unwomanly', 'unladylike', 'monstrous', 'unruly', 'unpatriotic', 'traitorous', 'unnatural'. If it bothered her slightly in the beginning, it didn't now. She had refused to play their game, she had refused to live in a little England of these little people's making in the heart of such a big, baffling, incomprehensible country. It didn't come as a surprise that she was punished for breaking the rules, especially that central rule of the Raj – you didn't treat the natives as equals. Of course, you were friendly with them, you worked with them (well, you had to), you invited them to certain parties, although not all, but you most certainly didn't treat them as equals, not after 1857, not after Cawnpore. The natives inhabited a different world from their masters and governors and the space in between was, should be, unbridgeable. Rule set in stone, cast in iron. There was no deflection from that. If you swayed from it, you had to pay.

Miss Gilby made sure that she moved around, talking to as many people as she could manage, especially the Indians and their wives, at every party. James's were no exceptions. She cast her mind back to the Ooty party of 1899 to place Nikhilesh Roy Chowdhury. He had been one of the men who had turned up not in the obligatory black tie but in his dhoti-kurta and a beautiful shawl, the colour of a young fawn, embroidered so delicately that she had wanted to run her hands over the stitches and the fabric. He had been talking to the Major

General, or someone from the Indian Army. When she asked James who the Indian gentleman was, he said, 'Oh, that's Nik, Nikilesh. He's a minor zamindar in Bengal. Jolly nice chap. Knows the Mertons and the Leigh-Fermors. Some sort of Harrow connection, I think, but I'm not sure. Jolly good sort, you know. Not a drunken idiot like the rest of the nawabs around here. Here, let me introduce you.'

Miss Gilby's first impression of Nikhilesh was of gentleness and refinement. He spoke English beautifully, with none of the low louting and fawning and other affectations, which so afflicted the natives, and he spoke it in a soft, gentle voice. Miss Gilby was of the firm opinion that behind all the servile tics, the deep bowing and the ingratiating attitudes of most of the natives, they were mocking the Anglos all the time, in fact using the very customs of the English and distorting them in such a way that it could only be a type of insolent sarcasm. She had first had this feeling when the natives had carried the dinghies of English passengers over the unceasingly crashing breakers on to the beach in Madras, laughing all the time, as if they were having the time of their life, while the seasick, frightened and tired Englishwomen screeched, cried and prayed. She was convinced the men were enjoying their discomfort and behind their '*haan*, memsa'b', '*na*, memsa'b', their begging and their over-eagerness, they were tilting the boats and making it that much more turbulent for the English ladies.

The exchange of greetings was barely over when Miss Gilby had the unshakeable feeling that this was one Indian man, possibly the first in her eight years in this country, who was not secretly mocking her and her countrymen while keeping up an outward show of courteous, even flattering, behaviour.

This may have had something to do with the fact that the nice gentleman did not have any of the twitches of false obeisance and ridiculously exaggerated manners the natives were so given to, thinking this would be of advantage to them. Not a trace of that in this calm, refined man: he held his head high when he spoke, enunciated clearly, balanced the teacup in his hand with poise.

Miss Gilby can only guess how Nikhilesh Roy Chowdhury knows of her move up north to Calcutta from Madras, hardly more than a year ago. For the last year, she has been attached to the household of the Nawab of Motibagh, in the capacity of governess to the Begum – funny how the upper class Indians seemed to call 'companions' to their wives 'governesses', as if they were little children in need of basic education in manners, speech and writing – and it would be surprising if that news did not travel fast in the enclosed world of minor Bengal royalty. An event such as having an Anglo-Indian in the household was like throwing a stone in a tiny pond – the ripples were bound to reach the edge.

If she is to take up this offer of being 'governess' to Bimala – she's sure he means English Teacher and Companion – she will have to give up her position with the Nawab of Motibagh. It will have to be done with delicacy and tact so that the Nawab doesn't think she is leaving them for the employ of a man he is certain to consider his inferior in terms of rank or title. She has not been making enormous progress with Saira Begum. Besides, Miss Gilby has the distinctly uncomfortable feeling that her presence in that household had caused not a few ruffled feathers, that she had been asked to join them in the first place because having a European in your employment was such a mark of distinction. In the face of such petty machinations, Miss Gilby feels soiled, her noble aim of enlightening native women compromised. She would like to make clear her aims and purposes in seeking positions in native Indian families as a teacher but that would only make the men even more suspicious than her race already did. In this, the English and the Indian men were alike and in complete agreement – women didn't need to be taught vast amounts of things. If she were to outline her ideals about how the native womenfolk should interact with their English counterparts, there would be a minor revolt amongst the men, both Indian and English. And then she wouldn't be able to do the very little on which she thinks she has just embarked. Best to keep quiet and get on with things, even give out the impression that she has no purpose other than employment in mind. Miss Gilby has learnt this lesson the hard way: if you want to get your own way, give away nothing, draw attention to nothing, indeed create smokescreens behind which you can hide while moving secretly, silently towards your destination.

She catches herself thinking about that old chestnut again and stops; she cannot dwell on it if things are to move forward. And move forward they will, if Nikhilesh Roy Chowdhury's letter is anything to go by. Here is a different man, here is a peer, a fellow thinker, a friend, Miss Gilby dares to dream. Her decision is made.

She takes pen and paper and writes:

Dear Mr Roy Chowdhury,

How kind of you to remember me from James's Summer Season Party in Ooty three years ago. And congratulations – very belated though they may be – on your marriage. I feel honoured that you should have thought of me in regard to Bimala's Education in English.

I shall be very happy to take up the position of Teacher and Companion to Bimala as soon as it is mutually convenient.

I look forward to meeting you soon.

Yours sincerely,
Miss Maud Gilby

She blows on the paper, puts it in an envelope, seals it and then writes his address on the front. She gets up from her desk, goes to the door, puts her head out and calls, '*Koi hain? Mahesh! Mahesh! Yahaan aao!*' No answer. No sound of movement either. Where has that man disappeared to yet again?

Miss Gilby descends the stairs and decides to take matters in hand. The envelope is held securely between her fingers.

ONE

Ritwik raises the lower sash of the window and leans out, almost to his waist, letting the English rain fall on him on a darkening afternoon. His tiny room is on the top floor of a house on the corner of two cobbled streets. One of them is called Logic Lane; something out of Pope, he had thought on his first day in England, dragging his two heavy suitcases over random cobbles designed to defeat any movement on them except the one for which they were initially made. They ream through the thin soles of his Indian shoes. Walking on them is like wearing acupressure sandals, which have textured soles made of hundreds of raised points, except that *these* raised points are little mounds, and uneven, on top of that.

The room is so small he can hardly move around. It has what he will later come to call a celibacy bed, a row of white shelves against one wall, a desk and a chair, an armchair, a window with fluorescent peach curtains, a wardrobe and an upright wooden box with a glass front. The box contains a coil of thick rope and the glass has a sign, which says, 'FIRE ESCAPE'.

For a long time he thinks, not wholly frivolously, that it is quite radical of his college to provide its depressed and clinically on-the-edge students with the means of escape from it all, till Gavin one day points out that you are meant to swing it out of the window and clamber down, stupid, Tarzan or Indian fakir style, take your pick, when everything is blazing to the ground.

Even the rain, so typical and so patly conforming to a stereotype of England the non-English assiduously propagate, begins to irritate him with its in-between status. It is neither the obliterating deluge of the Calcutta monsoon, nor the obliging short bursts of a life-giving natural force after an arid summer. All those clichés about the English climate trotted out by his friends, their parents, and anybody who knew someone who knew someone who had visited England, had only bored him. He had been prepared to deal with this skewed vision of the perfectly rainy land; after all, he had lived with rain for the four months of monsoon every year, for twenty-two years. After that, the English rain could only be a gentle variation in a minor key.

But nothing had prepared him for this. It is variation, all right, but muffled. For most of the time, it is not the actual physical thing, the element of water, which he experiences, but the intent to rain, a sort of pervasive threat in the dead gunmetal skies. He doesn't understand how it is possible, this excess of wetness without downpour. It is in England he first encounters the infinite nuances of drizzle: soft spitting, a spattering of directionless spray blown by the wind here and there, sometimes a thinning out of even that insubstantial spume till there is nothing but wet jewels in the hair. At times, the stronger drizzle eventually gathers enough critical mass to reach down to his scalp and trickle coldly down. That is an unpleasant moment.

Then there are the changing dramas of the different darkenings of the sky, each one with its own subtle warning of imminent rain. The rain mostly never falls and when it does, the end precipitation is never commensurate with the fear contained in the threat of the changeable clouds. It is all very disappointing, and ultimately irritating, this long play of umbrous forms and shades between the potential and its fitful realization. Part of his impatience lies in the fact that he begins to appreciate this miniature drama of deferral.

As for the rain with which he had grown up, it was less rain than some primal frustration vented on little mortals. From June to September, everyone who lived under the vengeful path of the monsoons understood what rainfall must have been like in prehistoric times. The relentless sheets of water were unleashed unforgivingly. There was zero visibility in this all-erasing elemental fury – you couldn't see beyond the edge of your helpless umbrella – but there was also the euphoria of end and destruction to it.

Ritwik had dissented stubbornly from all notions of the idealised monsoon, which school textbooks and the general culture propagated – all dancing farmers, overabundant fields, frolicking peacocks – for he had lived an infernal one of floods and waterlogging on a miserable scale. Every monsoon, Calcutta became, intermittently, a city that stepped deeper and further into those capricious waters that swallowed towns and villages inch by inexorable inch. The open drains on the sides of the streets invariably overflowed and houses were left looking at their reflections in the muddy brown stream which their streets had become.

As children, both Ritwik and Aritra had played with the idea that this was what Venice must be like – waterways connecting houses – but without the excitement of hopping on a boat from your doorbank to get from point A to B. That was so typical of living in Calcutta, this festering mediocrity: there was neither the cruel extreme of the floods which ravaged neighbouring Bangladesh and made refugees of two million people every year, nor the transforming romance of a Venice-like watercity. In the absence of either, both brothers had sat with their legs dangling out of the railings of the verandah and floated flimsy paper boats, made from the lined paper of their school exercise books, in the stream between the roads and the open drains that formed the margins of the streets in this part of south Calcutta.

Every monsoon it was brought home to him how *little* people were, wading laboriously through waist-deep waters, their roads sunk, their houses leaking, suspended between the dull unforgiving sky and their land which was only fugitively land. What happened to the slums along Park Circus Maidan, in the back streets of Golpark and Rajabazaar, those makeshift tents of plastic and rotting blankets secured from the wind by a strategically placed brick or two? Where did those people go with their blue plastic sheets, their bundles of tatters and rags, and a couple of tin pans?

The flooding at the major intersection at Gariahat was so bad that for the monsoon months two or three buses and a few cars, all stalled and damaged temporarily by the water level, would become fixtures on the road, sticking out like dead relics from a lost underwater civilization slowly surfacing. The water frequently reached up to the waist, all traffic stopped, and people were trapped in offices, schools, homes, shops. Ritwik and some other friends often returned from school walking part of the way, and wading through the rest, satchels held on their heads.

There was anarchic joy in this disruption of normal life as the boys, all headed more or less the same way, giggled, waded and pushed the waters with one arm outstretched for balance and the other holding their satchels firmly on their heads. They swayed like flimsy reeds every time a rare passing bus or lorry generated what seemed like a huge wave in its wake and threatened to knock them off their already wobbling position, half under half above the water. More laughter as someone inevitably lost balance. Sometimes amused warnings, 'Careful, don't step into a ditch', for no one knew what potholes and trenches lurked under the murky waters.

Those trenches were what made Calcutta a place that had leaped out of the pages of Dante and been transposed east. The road from Gariahat straight through to Jadavpur was relatively safe as far as these underwater holes were concerned but it was a different story in central and north Calcutta, in Kalighat, the area around the Maidan, the Monument, Chowringhee and practically all the stretch of the old, decrepit northern part of the city. Work on the metro, an unending labour, had meant large areas of dug-up roads. The trenches were deep; anyone could break his bones if he accidentally fell down one. He had never seen anyone working in them and once the holes appeared, they tended to stay, uncovered, unmarked by danger or roadworks signs, in one seamless connection between traffic, roads, pedestrians, and remain there for years. When sporadic activity on laying down or repairing telephone cables was added to this, the city became a nightmare of ditches and trenches, an eviscerated hell.

Then there was the business of avoiding the bloated, floating carcasses of dogs and cows, the used sanitary towels, adrift, sometimes wrapping themselves around the legs with a bloody will of their own, the daily rubbish of human living which elsewhere got thrown in bins and taken away in garbage trucks but which in Calcutta sat around on almost every street corner, accumulated into largish hillocks, rotted, and then got partially dispersed by the rain in the streets. Eggshells, vegetable matter, food scrapings, bread, fruit peel, paper, rags, bits and pieces of cloth, hair balls, dead rats, rancid food, floor sweepings, congealing vomit, a turd or two, blister packs, bottles, jars, plastic bags, containers. And disease, DISEASE, DISEASE . . . even thinking about it sent that familiar shudder down his spine.

On rainy days like this, nostalgia wraps around him like an insidious fog; it is everywhere, but while inside it, he can hardly tell how enveloped he is in it. Nostalgia, and something else. He won't name it, he won't even think about it because if he lets go for even a few seconds, the grey, sour rain outside will bend him to its own form. This rain, in a different land, slightly over a year after his parents' deaths, can read him. He won't think about them lest the rain reads him again, as it has done for the past two months, and reduces him to its sad, transparent cipher.

It was within his first week of arrival he met another student in the long queue in the buttery during lunchtime: very tall, eyes so blue they were like an electric zap, and hair so golden and curly it looked like an improbable wig. He had a foolish smile that seemed plastered indelibly on to his face and a clockwork sideways nodding of the head. He was like some overgrown animate toy from Enid Blyton, the innocence in his face enhanced by the jerky, toy-like movements.

The queue was a chance to meet people, make friends, introduce himself; he must seize this moment, not wander around, lonely and lost, in the narrow wet streets; *here was the opportunity for a new social life, grab it grab it grab it.* So he smiled back at the blond toy's general smile, 'Hi, I'm Ritwik.'

'Hello, I'm Robert. Hello. Hello.' Nodding, nodding, like it was a nervous tic. 'Have you just arrived?'

'Yes, last week.' *Keep talking, say something, say something about the weather, ask him what he reads.* 'It's so cold here.' He had read somewhere that clichés are clichés because they are universally accepted truths, tried and tested generation after generation.

'Do you think so? It's all right, isn't it?'

'Where are you from?'

The smile found a focus now. 'I'm from a place called High Wycombe. Do you know it?'

Ritwik lied, 'Yes, yes, I do.'

Robert was surprised, 'Really? Where are you from then?'

'India.'

Robert's smile now carried hints of wonder; he answered in clipped, short bursts, 'Wow. Nice. Great. I love India.'

It was Ritwik's turn to be surprised now. 'Really? Have you been?'

Once again, that foolishness. 'No. No. I haven't. But my mother has.'

Ritwik pursued this one. 'So why do *you* love India?'

'It's so exotic, isn't it? And wild, do you know what I mean? And all that mysticism and stuff, it's spiritual, like, isn't it?'

Ritwik flashed his smile-of-finality. He wanted to say, 'Yes, you're right. We have naked fakirs, white elephants and striped tigers on the streets of Delhi,' but held back the words. Perhaps this beautiful boy, his head a furious golden halo in the cold light of the buttery, was trying to make friends as well. Ritwik moved on to something brown and absurd-looking, a sort of stylised representation of a perfectly formed turd contained in its own brown, rectangular casing, with an absurd name: 'toad in the hole'.

The first meeting with his tutor and his group had induced a

41

similar feeling of distance, as if he were watching himself trying to learn the rules of a new game. Dr Elizabeth Carter was ageless, had blue eyes with the incisiveness of a laser beam, and spoke in a kind of breathless and hushed undertone. She was the only person whose words he understood. Her introduction set his ears aflame: 'This is Ritwik Ghosh (she pronounced it 'gosh', the absence of the usual exclamation mark after the word only making it sound worse) who's come from Calcutta to do the BA.' He tried to appear relaxed, knowing, in control. His group consisted of ten others who had been together for a year and were all friends. They gabbled away amongst each other, and with Dr Carter, who they all called 'Liz' or 'Lizzie'. He could never bring himself to use her first name, but 'Ma'am' sounded so horribly gauche in the face of the easy familiarity the others had with her. He couldn't understand a word of what they said.

They murmured polite hellos, thrown somewhere across the room vaguely in his direction, but he didn't feel any of those reached him. They had all been handed glasses of a cloying drink, sherry, which increased the heaviness in his legs. Suddenly he realized he had this panicky vacuum somewhere in his lower stomach, a hollow that pressed his insides intermittently: he did not understand simple English as spoken by true-blood English people. Occasionally, a soothing wisp of Dr Carter's sentences reached him – '. . . about it, it gets better with practice . . .', '. . . the Midlands dialect in which Langland wrote could pose . . .' and then it would be lost in the fizz and crackle of other Englishes.

But surely that guy, Declan Whelan, with glasses and wispy red curls fast disappearing, did not speak English. His voice and words were a sinuous curve of dip and soar; that could not be English, he did not understand one single word of it. God, they must be so clever, they all understand German, they're all laughing at his jokes, falling apart laughing, he thought. He felt small and stupid and, all of a sudden, very lonely and lost, as the small rain tapped on the panes of the little oriel windows and everyone sat around in the low-ceilinged room with walls covered in books, jabbering away, excited and nervous about their Chaucer and Hildegard von Bingen and Julian of Norwich and he, with that small cold glass of pale liquid gold in his hands, wondered how he would go about making friends with these people.

The meeting ended with Dr Carter issuing out reading lists, a set of essay topics, instructions on little college exams during the first week of term, and invitations to her house for tea. As they clambered down the narrow and noisy wooden stairs, winding down and down, the tall one who was called Pete came up to him and shook his hand, 'Hi, I'm Pete. I didn't quite catch your name'.

'It's Ritwik, R-I-T-W-I-K.'

Pete gave a polite wow and repeated his name a few times. 'Ritwik, Ritwik. Is that a common name from where you come?'

'No, not really, but it's not unusual.'

'It's very unusual to my ears,' he smiled.

'It means "he who officiates at a fire sacrifice",' the words tumbled out, heavy and anachronistic in the faultless green of the rain-washed main quad, before he could stop himself.

'Wow.' This time the wonder was real. 'Do all Indian names have a meaning?'

'Yes, they do.' They had entered the main hall now where some of them were beginning to disperse. Someone came up to Pete and he started talking to her before Ritwik had a chance to tell him that his name meant rock.

He went up to Sarah, the confident, friendly girl with glasses and radiating rings of brown, springy, corkscrew curls. 'Is it necessary to know German then?'

She frowned, then laughed and said, 'German? Good god, no! Why do you think it's necessary to know German?'

'I thought you were all joking in German. You see, I don't know the language at all . . . Declan's German, isn't he?'

It took a few seconds for the pieces to fall into place. She cracked up, laughing, 'No, no, you've got it wrong, he's from Liverpool, that's his accent . . . Dec's not German . . . oh, that's so funny, wait till the others hear of it.' She continued laughing. He joined her, weakly and uncertainly at first, then got swept up in it. Maybe he found it funny as well.

The days are loads, bearing him down. The cold has given him an intractable case of dandruff, but for the first time in his life he has money to go into the shops and buy things for himself, superficial and silly things, things that deal with problems such as dandruff. He has heard of the Body Shop; Jhimli had got her delicious lip balms from that place on one of her numerous trips abroad with her dance company. He can now buy those improbable objects that fill him with wonder: is it even possible to have ginger root anti-dandruff shampoo, a *banana* conditioner? How can you get butter from mango? He buys stackloads of different types of products. They give him a sense of control over his life: yes, he's finally grown up, he can choose his own luxury items. He can pay for them himself. They're going to do him good.

But the embers of hyperacidity behind his breastbone, sometimes up in his throat, won't be extinguished; at times they flare up into something more unmanageable (he has a supply of

Pepto Bismol at hand) but most of the time it's just a slow burn inside him. He's convinced it's caused by eating dinner at six o'clock in the evening. Back home, dinner, when it was at all available, was between half-past ten and half-past eleven at night.

After that absurdly early dinner, he lopes back to his cell and reads in the yellow spill of light, gets up sometimes and paces around, thinking of Christ the knight jousting at a tournament and ending up bleeding. Or of Hunger plaguing poor farmers and helpless little men and women battling with the cold and their masters' stubborn land. That acid sting surges and falls, surges and falls. When he's bored and lonely, he looks at the little row of his Body Shop objects, fingers them lovingly, sometimes uncaps a bottle or two and has a sniff. The thought of using some of those things the next day makes him feel all right again. He owns these products. They are bought with his scholarship money and they belong to him. They will protect his face from the legion knives of the February wind, keep his armpits fragrant, free his tangled locks of dandruff. He can have a new body in England, even be a new person. Maybe.

The clock tower chimes out the notes for half past the hour. It's a melody he knows by heart; he knows he has to wait for another incomplete installment before the full tune is rung out at the hour. Unfailingly, every fifteen minutes, this escalating teasing of three-note and four-note unfulfillment. It drives him mad, this knowing what's going to come – so trite and mechanical, so unchanging – but having it deferred. The giant horse chestnut tree outside, across the cobbles, is losing its edges and becoming an amorphous looming shadow. Someone has recently told him the blossom of the horse chestnut is called

45

'candle'. Candles of horse chestnut, he savours the phrase in his head.

He turns around to walk towards the light switch. His mother is sitting in the armchair near the door.

There is a barely whispered presence in this threshold time of the gathering dark. In a thought-swift instant he understands the expression about hairs standing on end – fear tastes like this; it is the opening of the pores of your face, inside your ears, behind your head.

Don't come back like this you're gone you belong elsewhere not here I cannot live on this hinge you've just shown me it's one or the other now or then elsetime elseplace but please please please not me not ever.

He suddenly has an urgent need to piss, but it seems he has grown gnarled, hugging roots into the regulation carpet. How can he bring himself to cross the few feet, past that armchair which is charged with her imagined trace, to the toilet outside? Only by this and by this only:

He must have been six or seven at the time, so it was quite natural to have thought it was a great idea to stick the rubbery gob of chewing gum in his mouth in the hair of Tipshu, the small girl next door. Tipshu didn't notice until much later. They had to cut off some of her lovely, glossy hair as she brought the house down, howling and crying. Her mother came around for the inevitable complaint, serious words about improper bringing up of children, insufficient discipline that let naughtiness such as this run unchecked.

Ritwik's mother was out, tutoring children in a couple of houses in the neighbourhood; this was her way of supple-menting her husband's apology of an income. Dida, his grandmother, already at the door eavesdropping on the loud

46

confusion next door, received the complaint much in the way a hungry dog receives leftovers. Ritwik was warned, darkly, 'Wait till Ma's back. You're in for a bad time.'

There was a sudden manic animation that lit up Dida's eyes like embers from within. She sat in the balcony, keeping a sharp eye out for her daughter, jittery with excitement. No sooner had she spied her at the far end of Grange Road than she limped to the door: she could barely wait for the knock before she opened it and the rush of tales spilled out before his mother had even had a chance to sit down and drink a cooling glass of water, 'You won't believe what Ritwik's done, he stuck a dozen Chiclets in Tipshu's hair, they've had to shave all her hair off. Her mother came to complain to you, she is absolutely livid with rage, shaking with anger, said what kind of discipline is this . . .'

The first kick caught him unawares; it happened in the instant of a blink and sent him nearly flying to the niche where the mortar and pestle stood. While losing his balance and skidding across the floor Ritwik caught, in the peripheries of his field of vision, the blur of his mother pulling a belt from the nylon line on which his father's clothes hung, shabby and limp. He lay on the floor, a foetal quiver of fear, as the first lash from the leather belt cleanly cut a menacing crack through the compact air and landed on him with the sting of fire. The fiery flowers bloomed rapidly across his legs his thighs his back his scalp, now all one clarifying tingle of pain, and his hairs took life in rising to attention to this rain of weals. Maybe he was sobbing maybe crying *please spare me spare me I'll never do it again never again never stop* but this was not just any rain of fire, it was a deluge, which didn't know when to stop, until she put an end to it and instead started kicking his head his stomach his chest then stood on him with her fierce weight of fury. He felt choked and air air was all he wanted to breathe in, air in, not this hollow of nothing of craving to inhale; then there is only dark, only a saving obliterating blackness.

When he wakes up, it takes him a span of viscous, murky time to realize he is in a bed next door, in Tipshu's house. And the story he pieces together to comfort himself goes something like this: the commotion must have brought the next-door neighbours rushing in, Tipshu's mother had carried the unconscious Ritwik away to their flat, called a doctor or given him water to revive him, then put him to bed, letting the heave of his residual sobbing subside to a calm, but he doesn't actually know if it went like that. All he knows is that they can't put him in a plaster cast for cracked ribs; he has to sit, or lie, and wait it out, still as a forgotten stone in a corner, erased, absent.

He lets the liquid heat of his piss comfort him in its trickle down the inside of his legs and, when his saturated jeans cannot take it any more, watches it leak through pathetically in weak, stuttering drops on to the carpet. He is pissing, shaking and sobbing beside his desk, his room now completely in the grip of the dark. He feels he can never stop this trembling as he makes his way out, fumbling, to the bathroom. It is only much later that he notices how walking past that armchair is no longer a problem, no longer a consuming terror.

One cold evening, when his head is badly trying to contain the tumult of words inside it, and with an upper stomach burning slowly, he takes a walk to begin, belatedly, an acquaintance with other streets, other buildings. He starts off with the certainty that he's going to lose his way, stray into badlands and have trouble getting back to the haven of his college. With every step forward he thrills with this little fear. He walks past shops and streets with people bathed in the sick orange glow of sodium vapour lamps till he feels he has wandered well beyond the High Street. It is on a darker side street off an excessively lit road that he suddenly sees the man looking at him. No, *looking*, the kind that tells him in a flash that he has been noticed for some time now.

With that sudden emptying squeeze in his stomach and the drowning out of all noise by the percussion of his heart he knows, he knows he's been followed, he knows this is going to be a pick-up, that he can walk ahead, turning his head around a couple of times to let the stranger know he knows and that he can carry on following him because he's interested too; it's a little courtship dance, like the eight-patterned flight of bees or the choreographed code of birds.

There is that very familiar dryness in his mouth as he plays out this first movement of the suite with a stranger. It has its unerring, delicious shiver as always, but also an inchoate fear of the unknown: who knows, this is not Calcutta, this is the country of psychopathic serial killers, of thousands of AIDS-infected people, of twisted criminals the papers write about almost every day. What if he is one of those? It was only a few days ago he read about how two ten-year-old boys had led a toddler away to a railway siding and battered him to death.

Ritwik absurdly splices together unnamed and imagined horrors with the almost mythical accretions around the names of the Yorkshire Ripper and Jeffrey Dahmer. The thought of disease keeps dipping and circling in his head. He marks how unattractive the man is — short, pale, with small eyes, jowls, and a terrible and impossibly black moustache — and he knows with an almost pathological sense of sureness that he's going to have sex with that man.

And here he is now, on another dark street – god knows how far and lost he is – unsure whether he has led or been led by this man. The man nods, there is a twist of a smile on his weak mouth. 'Hello,' he says.

'Hello,' Ritwik replies and then, almost out of sheer habit, asks him the very first question people asked each other in Calcutta once they had moved into stage one of the game, 'Do you have a place we could go to?' Casual, uninterested, trying very hard not to let the tremor in his knees or the manic thudding of his heart inflect his now slightly phlegmy voice.

'No, I don't.' Pause. 'Do you live here?'

'Yes . . . yes, I do, I'm a student.' He knows what the next question is going to be.

'Can't we go back to yours?'

'No, no . . . you see, I live in college . . .' he deliberately lets it tail off.

That man is just too unattractive, not what he wants, but the game has begun; in fact, they're too far in it. For Ritwik, it wouldn't do to give up now; he'll be left with that uneasy itch which not seeing things through to their end unfailingly gives him. It's almost a feeling of déjà-vu, almost, this illusion of choice which ultimately reveals its hand but always too late, this going through with something to its conclusion out of a misplaced purism. It's a game, there must be closure, must be. The man seems to understand Ritwik's constraints about taking him back to his room in college. 'Oh, I see,' he says. Silence. 'I have a car, though . . .' he adds.

This is it, Ritwik thinks, the standard opening gambit of a serial killer; you're powerless the moment you enter his car. It speeds down anonymous highways as your life flashes past you in its aura of lurid orange glow from the streetlights, till you reach an abandoned barn or a hillside cottage where no one can hear you scream except the cold stars and the gently nibbling sheep. He gets into the passenger seat, the fear so indelibly stained with excitement he can't wash one of the trace of the other.

The car races along what seems too unfamiliar, too far, for a long time. His nervousness mounts, he starts fidgeting, tries to muffle all the edginess out of his voice as he answers all those unimportant questions, 'Where are you from?', 'What are you reading?'. He recognizes the kick in his insides at the less innocuous one, 'What do you like doing?'. Maybe he is a mutilator-rapist: he won't kill but bruise and maim, leave him infected with HIV and he'll have nothing to take to the police, no name, only a description. But descriptions either become fuzzier with time or lose all their sharpness and certainties under close questioning and the faceless requirements of bureaucratic forms. He must note the number of the car and commit it to memory, but it could easily be someone else's car, maybe even a stolen one. He tries to concentrate on the names of streets that slip by in an orange blur. On top of all this, the man is really really unattractive.

He drives down some dark side streets, pulls the car at the end of one and turns off the engine. The street is badly lit and there are some infrequent yellow squares of light where the curtains haven't been drawn in the houses along each side. It seems completely deserted as well. Ritwik doesn't feel comfortable here. 'It's not really safe, is it? A police car could drive in here.'

'It should be OK.'

Ritwik insists, 'Could we go somewhere else? Not a residential street.'

The man turns the ignition again. This time they drive through darker and darker roads till they reach a place where streets end and it becomes a slightly bumpy ride over crunchy pebbles and gravel. That gives out as well and they're soon in the wider dark of open space. The countryside, maybe. It's impossible to make out shapes or contours but it's better to leave the lights out, he supposes. He lets his eyes adapt to the outer darkness; through the windscreen he cannot so much see as sense a treeless plain with the dull mirror of a stretch of water. The darker hulks take on edges and become caravans. Or maybe they are big trucks. It's so quiet the slight chink-clink of the chain and keys still dangling in the ignition switch seems capable of bringing people running from all sides.

In seconds, Ritwik has established that the man is of the type who tries to kiss and stroke and be affectionate first before getting down to business. He averts his face as the man brings his mouth closer to his. In case it appears as too overt a rejection, he puts his arms around his neck and pulls him into a hug. There, no chance of a kiss now.

They pull their trousers down to their ankles. Ritwik's rigid cock springs out, slapping his stomach, while the man's tumescing one just lolls. He bends down sideways, takes Ritwik's cock in his mouth and starts sucking him off with such full-throated ease that had it been at all possible Ritwik would have been taken inside his mouth up to his entire hip. It's cramped and uncomfortable and being sucked from that odd angle, rather than from the front, with the man's bobbing head between his thighs, does not quite make it to his A-list of Top Ten Oral Sex Moments. There is also a subdued whiff of curing leather somewhere; he hopes it's not from the man's body or his mouth. He is jerking himself off as he keeps sucking. As Ritwik whispers, 'I'm going to come soon,' he lets go of his cock, leaving him to finish off, while he starts to moan, 'Oh, yeah ... oh yeah ... come on then, come, come, shoot your load ...' the movement of his hand becoming more and more furious. There seems to be a restless animal in his devouring eyes. Ritwik finds his exaggerated porn-speak so ridiculous that he has to make an effort to subdue the laughter bubbling up from inside, it's in his throat now, it has to be pushed down down, no he can't let it come out, can't come out as he comes all over himself, the little opal pools pearlescent on his dark skin even in the darkness inside and around. He watches with detachment the man bringing himself off, whispering more of those absurdities while eyeing his semen hungrily. Ritwik makes sure he doesn't come anywhere near his jeans or his legs.

As if the release of orgasm has freed his attention on to other things, Ritwik suddenly notices the deeper darkening inside the car and wheels his head in panic. The windows are opaque, they are no longer clear glass between inside and outside. There are bodies and faces outside, looking in. His heart thuds in his throat in slow motion; he has no idea how many seconds or minutes elapse before they both realize the shapes outside are not humans.

'Horses,' the man says.

'What?' Ritwik's voice is a blur.

'Horses. The trucks you see, they carry horses. They've stopped here for the night and let them out on to the meadow. They'll carry on tomorrow morning.'

It takes some time for this to sink in. The animals on all sides are peering in, their noses and muzzle so close that he strains to catch another shade of the dark in a horse's eye looking in through the passenger window. Their snuffling breath has condensed here and there and trickles down as threads of water. The last residue of panic still courses around in him somewhere. He looks ahead, out of the windscreen, and there, in the clotted blackness outside, notices a shuffling dance of firelight, as if a dozen will o' the wisps have suddenly erupted from nowhere. His mind isn't quite working, he can't understand these suspended points of fireflicker swimming about. The man almost senses his confusion. He lets out a little laugh, 'See, they've come out of their trailers now to take them in. They're looking for the horses.'

As if on cue, the silence shivers only a tiny fraction to let a few high up-and-down calls from the searchers escape, then it gathers back again over those truncated shepherds' notes as if they'd never been. The shapes outside the car begin to move.

'We should go,' the man says.

Ritwik nods, unable to speak, but his fear and tension have disappeared. He feels a sense of release, an achievement almost. The man is trying to be affectionate by putting his arms around him and trying to kiss him, again, but only manages an awkward parody of it. He is also muttering some fearful slush in his ears while stroking his hair, 'You're Hassan, my prince, my lovely prince Hassan . . .' Ritwik curls his toes. He starts stroking the man's face to prepare him for his next move: 'Could you please drop me off somewhere in town . . . perhaps where you picked me up?'

'Yes, yes, of course,' says the stranger and then lapses into his fantasy again: 'You're an Arab prince, your name is Hassan—'

'No, I'm not.' His words cut in like the lash of a whip. The man removes his hand as if he's been struck. Ritwik regrets it instantly, 'Look, it's getting late . . .'

'Oh, yes, yes.' He turns on the ignition and cuts out the headlights the second they come on. The revving car is too loud. The horses can't be seen anymore. The searching lanterns seem to have disappeared as well.

It's late when he's dropped off at the corner of Broad Street and Cornmarket Street. It has started drizzling gently; under the sodium vapour lamps it looks like a sad sequin shower without the celebratory glitter. He feels light, not quite happy, but getting there, getting there. While trying to put on his Thinsulate branded gloves, he notices black stains on his palms. He tries to figure out what they can be; they come off when he rubs them hard, and when he sniffs his hand, there is a familiar chemical tang he tries to identify . . . shoe-polish, that's it, black shoe-wax. He doesn't know why he instantly thinks that the man had dyed his moustache with it.

He sneaks back into college, almost tip-toeing to his room. He doesn't want to be seen, or talked to, and then smiles wryly: there's hardly anyone to notice him or talk to him apart from Gavin and he knows Gavin is working late at his studio tonight. He feels both lonely and the utter banality of this loneliness at the same time. Maybe he'll tell himself a story, the story of that blue-clad Englishwoman from a film so ablaze with reds and russets and oranges and flame that she had stood out like its principle of meaning, holding out the slender hope that she was going to shore up all the dispersal and disintegration around her. He has no idea why the film, *Ghare Bairey*, has suddenly come unbidden to his mind, a film he had seen nearly ten years ago in Calcutta, but that fleeting woman, Miss Gilby, who had passed through its frames for all of three minutes, or less, all blue primness and measured politeness, will simply not leave his head. She was so marginal, her presence so brief, vanishing almost before her story began. What if he told her story, which hadn't been written down or filmed?

Before he enters his room he goes to the bathroom, scrubs clean his hands, his cock, his mouth and face at the sink. Quietly, very quietly, so that Zoe and Charlotte, in the adjoining rooms, don't suspect anything. He enters his room, drowning out any surfacing fear of his mother sitting inside and quickly turns on the light. He sits down and writes.

II.

The rains have started early this season. Very soon, the
Maidan is going to become a shallow lake, and Free School
Street, Eliot Road, all muddy little streams and rivulets. Miss
Gilby knows that the rains are going to bring with them ants,
termites, cockroaches, a hundred other unnamed creeping
and crawling creatures, and the incessant croaking of toads
and frogs all night long in the puddles and ponds which
accumulate everywhere during the monsoon. They talk to
each other all night, an amphibian parody of antiphon
and response, and it drills into Miss Gilby's head with
its monotonous regularity. Besides, she hates those ugly
creatures. During the entire rainy season, there are scores of
them in the front courtyard, sometimes even at the bottom of
the stairs leading to her rooms. She had stepped on one of
these inadvertently once. The experience still sends shudders
down Miss Gilby's spine: first of all, she hadn't expected the
creature to turn upside down, exposing its disgusting smooth
white underneath, and then, before she had had time to step
off it in horror, she discovered the resiliently springy texture
of the animal, as if it were a large jujube or jelly. She was
grateful the toad didn't go 'splat' and explode under her shoe
but it disturbed her no end that no sooner had she moved her

foot than it hopped off, springing to life, the weight of Miss Gilby just a minor pressure on its innards of sponge. Ugh!

If Mahesh gets more intransigent this season, Miss Gilby is going to discharge him from his duties. Not a single week passes when she doesn't have to chide him for carelessness or sheer forgetfulness. He still hasn't managed to ask the builder to come and look at the various leaks, one right in the ceiling of the drawing room, which dripped water down on to her floor, inches away from her Steinway. He had put pails and buckets to catch the drips but mostly in the wrong places so that the damage had already begun. When she had taken him to task for it, he had grovelled first and then dared to answer back – how was he to know where the leaks were if they didn't start dripping in the first place. Unconscionable impudence. As if she hadn't spent all of last Rainy Season pointing out the leaks to him over and over again.

She will ask him to get the chairs from the verandah, especially her favourite planter's long sleever, a present from James, in to the drawing room, remove all the cane chairs and tables, and let down the rattan shades so that the rains don't flood her verandah every day. And then there will be the fraught business of packing up, storage, removal and relocation.

Mr Roy Chowdhury had kindly offered to come down to Calcutta in his motorcar and drive her to Nawabgunj, which, of course, will save her a long, bone-rattling journey, for at least part of the way on a *palkee*. But some of her possessions are going to have to go by train and then by God knows what, in all probability a bullock cart; she is sure most of them are never going to arrive in one piece, jolted and shaken as they are certainly going to be on the atrocious Indian roads and the mud and *kunkur* tracks. The very thought makes her feel weak so she sits down and starts making lists. There is great comfort to be derived from lists: they organize life, bring order and method, cut the amorphous business of a messy life into manageable and sizeable chunks.

She leaves at the end of the month to take up her position in the Roy Chowdhury family. She is excited at the prospect of making friends with an Indian woman who has so far been kept in the *andarmahal* but, thanks to her progressive husband, has been brought out of it and given a new world to move around in. Would she have been excited if she had been in Bimala's shoes? Or just plain afraid? Is Bimala enjoying her new freedom, the huge expansion of her world? Mr Roy Chowdhury, in the course of their correspondence, had mentioned that she was literate, and competent in reading, writing, even arithmetic, but almost wholly in her own language, Bengali. She read voraciously, she even knew some English, which he had started her on but now didn't find the time or the regularity that a new student needed. So Miss Gilby wasn't really inheriting a *tabula rasa* – his term – but a compliant and intelligent student, he hoped, except that her problem was chronic shyness, indeed, fear at meeting an English lady and having to converse with her, eventually, in English; she was convinced she would not be able to cross the first hurdle, she would be a tongue-tied and hopeless student, Miss Gilby would give up in despair and leave etc etc.

Miss Gilby knows all these symptoms. They are not just the classic signs of nerves and a sense of inferiority but also so much more. Imagine a woman, kept confined to the *andarmahal*, socializing only with the other women in the household, rarely coming across men, even her own father, imagine growing up with this great sense of awe and fear of men, nay, this sense of the great unknown, of the alien race that the male is to her, imagine whiling away an entire girlhood in games and house-work and feminine chores till she gets married one day, without any consultation or involvement, to one of those very creatures she has seldom met in her life, creatures she has only seen during *jaatra* performances in her house through a chink in the curtains or the *tatti* which separates the women's section of the audience from the men's, imagine growing up in a society where on those very rare occasions when a woman suddenly comes across a man other than her husband she draws her veil instantly to cover her face and hastily leaves the room. Imagine all that. Then imagine her being catapulted into the big, wide, open world. It would be something akin to being thrown into an ocean when all you know is your little enamel bath. Miss Gilby herself would be very nervous in Bimala's situation. She had seen with her very eyes Hindu women from wealthy, privileged families taking their annual dip in the holy Ganges by having their entire palanquin, shut and enclosed, lowered into the waters while they remained inside, and then being carried off back home on the shoulders of the bearers. Because the waters teemed with bathing men, it was an act that managed ingeniously to observe a sacred ritual without endangering any of the sanctions against women being seen in public.

She remembers those painful visits with Miss Shepherd, Colonel Campbell's wife and Mr Fearfield's wife – all members of the Madras Ladies' Club – to the Maharani of Mysore a few years ago. The process leading up to those visits itself comprised a story. For months she had importuned James and Sir George to do something about the Indian women of the Presidency: where were they? why didn't they come, along with their husbands, to any of the events to which they were invited? why did only the men turn up? why were they so rigidly secluded? could the Anglos not do anything to break this down? James had patiently explained to her the status of women in Indian society. Well, then, if men posed so many threats and problems to them, surely the English ladies could do something? Send out an invitation for a 'Ladies Only' at the Club? Once again, James had explained to her, in his very patient and forbearing way, the problems Indian men had exposing their wives to foreigners. But surely they wouldn't have problems 'exposing' them to foreign women? At which point James had thrown up his hands in despair and said if she wanted to so much, why didn't she try, along with the other ladies of the Presidency, and see where they got. There was a stiff little lecture on how damnedest the Raj had tried to do away with barbaric Indian customs like *suttee*, *purdah*, the evils of *zenana*, the way Indian men treated their women as chattel, and if the bloody obstinate men were not going to allow them to meet their wives, he was damned if he was going to allow them to meet English ladies.

Ah.

So Miss Gilby, accompanied by the more stalwart and interested ladies, had set about getting to know these invisible Indian women. As sister of the District Collector, she sent out invitations for an 'At Home'. Nearly no one bothered to reply. The chicken galantine with aspic jelly, cucumber sandwiches, anchovy and salad sandwiches, rout cakes, the proud madeira cake, petits fours, mango and custard apple ices – all the lovely things she and Iris Shepherd had planned so excitedly from their new Mrs Beeton had come to nothing. The most articulate of the refusals was sent to James. 'Dear Sir,' it said, 'as my wife does not know English, she desires me to write this to you, regarding the "At Home" this evening. My wife is extremely thankful to Mr' – and then an 's' added in ink after the typewritten 'Mr' – 'Gilby for graciously extending the invitation to her, but regrets very much that as according to the prevailing custom of the country, no Hindu lady is likely to attend the party, she is afraid to be the solitary exception to it. Moreover, she will feel herself completely stranded in the midst of strangers, and would, I am afraid, make an awkward nuisance of herself as she has never attended a party in all her life, least of all one hosted by English gentlemen and ladies. She, therefore, sincerely regrets that she is unable to oblige and sends her heartfelt apologies etc etc.'

Miss Gilby's first thought was, God, if we haven't given them anything else, we certainly have given them our language of evasiveness, and then, ashamed of this uncharitable and unusual flare-up in her generally kind soul, she began to comprehend the real problems the letter had expressed. How would the English and the native ladies communicate, how would she go about in her crusade of breaking down barriers, if they did not share a common tongue? It was of utmost importance that Indian ladies be educated in English. From there everything would follow, as the night the day.

The goal proved much more elusive than Miss Gilby had initially reckoned it to be. Like a mirage, it kept receding further and further, not just out of her reach but, it seemed, almost a thousand miles away. The problem was this: how did you go about educating Indian women if you didn't get to see them in the first place? But what would be the purpose of access if the two sides couldn't talk to each other? She felt she was being whirled around in a giant cartwheel that had no beginning, no end, only a frustrating, endless going around in circles. James just grunted his 'See, I told you so' grunt and said things were best left as they stood; these Indian women were never going to be let out of their prison by their men. They played by very different rules here and why didn't Maud just leave these things well alone and concentrate instead on other things.

What other things?

Oh, well, the Hart-Davises were having a polo week in Hyderabad, wouldn't she like to go?

And what would she do there?

Well, erm, she could watch, couldn't she?

Well, Indian social traditions and the frosty complacency of the Raj hadn't quite reckoned with the stubbornness of Miss Gilby. She pleaded, argued, debated, threatened, quarrelled, cajoled till she had extracted from her brother a firm promise to write to his friend (well, kind of friend), the Maharajah of Mysore, and wield his influence to get Miss Gilby and a few of her friends into his household to mingle with the ladies.

The first meeting had seen Jane Fearfield, Iris Shepherd and Maud Gilby, excited and nervous as girls on the eve of their stepping-out ball, traverse a distance of more than three hundred miles by train and then received by the Maharajah's carriage to be driven a liver-jostling five miles or so to the palace where the ladies would stay as royal guests for three nights. The ladies could not forget – how could they? they had been told so many times by so many different sets of people – the trouble James, a few other high-ranking Raj officials and His Highness the Maharajah of Mysore had been through to ensure this meeting. Rules had been broken on both sides, and rules, both spoken and unspoken, dense legions of them, had to be observed meticulously in this rare conjunction across the divide. The English ladies were to stick resolutely to the women's quarters of the palace, they were not to drink alcohol or ask for it, there would be one Anglo and two Indian guards escorting them to the palace and staying in the servants' quarters while they visited. The ladies had even been given a short, concentrated course on household customs in both Hindu and Muslim families so that they didn't fall into easy errors, humiliating or offensive, to which an unfamiliarity with the dizzying sets of rules could easily have led them.

The meetings hadn't gone well from the very outset, when Jane Fearfield, the newest and the youngest member of their informal little club, hadn't been able to control her giggling fit at being garlanded with flowers as soon as they had stepped across the threshold.

Not a single lady in the Maharajah of Mysore's family spoke or understood English. This was the first thing they had been told by a palace official – old and elaborately turbaned, with his eyes permanently focused on something an inch or so away from his feet – who was going to double as interpreter during the 'honourable' ladies' visit to His Highness's 'humble abode'.

Never mind, Miss Gilby thought, while watching Jane fidget with the silk and muslin handkerchieves they had been given as honoured guests of the Maharajah, delicate pieces of cloth doused to saturation point with some heavy *attar* – roses or maybe jasmine, but at this concentration it was impossible to tell – which immediately made the head reel and the temples clutch with the slow beginnings of an obstinate headache. Never mind their inability to speak English, Miss Gilby thought; the main thing was to meet, exchange news and views and become familiar, although how this was going to be done without a common language, she did not ask herself, instead choosing to pin her hopes on the interpreter and even on Iris Shepherd who had boasted she could hold a conversation in Hindi and understand some rudimentary Urdu.

The room, or rather, the enormous hall where the meeting was going to take place was similarly perfumed, from a mixture of incense, *attar*, and the rose petals which had been strewn everywhere. The English ladies had tried to imagine what the insides of an Indian palace would be like; they had even read or been told about the ostentation of wealth and artistry in these palaces, but nothing had prepared them for this sumptuous feast of grandeur which made the senses swoon and assaulted them from so many quarters – the viscous fragrances, the monotone of the threnody being played on some mournful stringed instrument by a hidden player, the sea of colours, fabrics, jewels, ornaments, tapestry, curtains, rugs, pillars, chandeliers – that there wasn't very much else to do except to obscure large sections of it in order not to drown in this gilded and marbled symphony of excess.

The Indian women, eleven in all – Miss Gilby had done a swift count while the seating formalities were being taken care of by the interpreter – were seated on piles of velvet cushions and fabrics arranged on the marble floor into a separate section of the room. Two chaise longues and four elaborate *chowpaya*s, all blue silk and gold embroidery and carved wood, had been arranged opposite this so that the two contingents of women faced each other. Between them, rose petals lying like wounds on the white marble, above them, the frozen crystal fountain of a chandelier. And the interpreter, somewhere out of sight, in one of the many shadows which stalked and lingered in the room despite the profusion of mirrors, chandeliers, candelabra, the fractured brilliance of glasswork.

For a while, all of Miss Gilby's attention was taken by the flash and fire of the jewels on the Indian women. Even their clothes were heavy with gold threads and wires, teeth of pearl, their fingers and hands dipped into the heart of Hindustan's treasures and just withdrawn. There was gold around their necks – chokers, collars, necklaces and chains, which fell in solid waves down their fronts, sometimes to their waists. They wore gold flowers on their toes, paisley-shaped earrings that covered their entire ears, and when they moved their hands, diamonds would carelessly catch a stray beam of light and send out an angry flare as if to remind everyone of their presence. And on the dark black skin of the women the metals and stones came into secret lives of their own which they hid from other, paler people. It was almost as if the darkness had put on a special fireworks show for the visitors – the jewellery accentuated their black skin while the fire of stones and metals made the skin a darker shade of night.

Miss Gilby hoped she hadn't stared rudely at these decorated women for that was exactly what they were doing, unabashed, unashamed. Eleven pairs of huge, dark eyes stared unblinking at the English women as though they were exotic or mythical birds they had heard about all their lives and which had just been put up on captive display.

Dazzled, literally, by the jewels, Miss Gilby came late to the realization that one of the princesses, hardly more than a girl, eleven or twelve maybe, was giggling shamelessly at the foreigners while a stately queen, perhaps some dowager maharani, maybe even Her Highness herself, was trying to shut her up.

'*Hanso mat*,' she ordered, her kohl-lined eyes flashing fire. This was a woman born to command, her lazy, cushion-propped body breathing arrogance and majesty through every pore.

'Don't laugh,' the interpreter dutifully translated, either unaware of the parties involved in that short exchange or untutored in the rules of interpreting.

The elderly woman now broke out into her own language clearly directed at the minister to translate. After she finished, he droned, 'Her Highness welcomes the English ladies to her court on this auspicious day. She is honoured that such esteemed ladies are condescending to visit her humble abode and hopes that they find everything to their liking.'

Iris Shepherd replied with the necessary formalities. Quick-witted, that woman, Miss Gilby thought.

Then there was a long silence during which two of the Indian women started whispering to each other. A third joined in, leaning over one of the older women. This seemed to cause no offence to the woman who was being used as a physical support to join, as it were, the two whispering camps. And there seemed to be no attempt to disguise or hide the fact they were talking about the three Englishwomen: they stared and then turned around to whisper; often they looked at their English guests askance while breathing out their words into someone's ear. While this open display of whispering was in progress, Miss Gilby decided to introduce her party.

'I am sure Her Highness has been informed about us but I thought I would take this opportunity to do so ourselves.'

She pointed to Iris Shepherd and said, 'This is Miss Iris Shepherd...'

Before she could finish, a peacock flew into the room from somewhere, stalked a few rose petals, and then, with a harsh scream that made Jane drop her scented handkerchiefs and start out of her chaise longue, deposited unfeasibly large amounts of faeces on the marbled floor and ran to the end of the room that gave out on to the courtyard.

It was mayhem from that point. Miss Gilby and Miss Shepherd properly looked away and fixed their gazes on the Indian contingent, pretending that this was an everyday occurrence that did not merit even the briefest of pauses in the conversation. Miss Gilby continued with the introductions but didn't progress beyond two or three more words because the Indian women had broken into uncontrollable laughter, accompanied by hoots and shrieks. A young girl stood up and ran out, laughing hysterically, the thin music of her jangling chains and bangles chasing after her. Another girl stood up and tried to make loud noises of disgust, shaking her hands as though she was trying to rid them of excess water, but was overwhelmed by mirth and subsided helplessly into the arms of another hysterical woman. Over this cacophony of raucous and uninhibited laughter, the Maharani was trying to summon a seriousness, which was clearly eluding her. Her face was oddly poised between laughter at one moment, disapproving frowns the next. The interpreter had meanwhile moved into everyone's field of vision and was bowing to Her Highness, clearly awaiting instructions from her.

Jane had been stunned into silence but Iris kept repeating her question 'Was that a peacock? Was that a peacock?' over and over again but no one bothered to give her an answer. Miss Gilby suddenly noticed that the tittering and the whispering in the Indian camp hadn't stopped. In between unbridled laughter, the gossipy conversations continued; all the women were now staring, whispering and laughing with such concerted yet easeful candour that Miss Gilby was in no doubt they were laughing at their visitors, so differently attired, so different looking they could be other creatures altogether.

The Maharani at last managed to bark out a rapid string of imperious words. The interpreter bowed low and departed from the room. A woman, presumably an *ayah*, walked in with a boy of about seven or eight, dressed in impeccable white silk and a gold-bordered, feathered pink turban. He halted in his tracks when he saw the foreigners and turned around to hide his face in the voluminous folds of his *ayah*'s clothes. A wave of commotion arose from the Indian women at the sight of this little boy, so reluctant to advance to the centre of the room. There were calls, shouts, cheers and in Miss Gilby's utter inability to understand a single word or read a single exclamation, they could equally well have been cheering the boy on, voicing blandishments, issuing orders or coaxing him.

The interpreter returned with two servant girls who set about cleaning up the mess the peacock had made. He bowed in the direction of the boy, to the gaggle of queens and princesses and disappeared into the shadows again. One of the women said something loudly. After a few seconds' pause the interpreter said, 'Are the honourable English ladies giving birth to any children? Are they having husbands?'

It took a considerable while for the questions and their possible meanings to sink in. During that interim, the Indian women didn't take their eagerly anticipating eyes off their guests. Miss Gilby frowned, she hoped disapprovingly. Jane Fearfield started giggling again, while Miss Shepherd opened and shut her mouth, at regular intervals, like a landed fish.

Miss Gilby cleared her throat and answered, 'If I understand you correctly, only Jane Fearfield here is married. I am the sister of James Gilby, the District Collector of Madras, and Miss Iris Shepherd has just arrived from England.'

The interpreter passed this through the opaque glass of his Indian language; Miss Gilby was certain the reflection was a very distorted version of reality. Another voice, another set of orders, silence from the interpreter, then the slow, gently goading movements of the *ayah* trying to move her charge to the centre of the room. The boy stood with his back to the Indian contingent, facing the English visitors. Someone from the Indian side spoke out – she could have been his mother – and the boy was repositioned to turn ninety degrees, with one group to his left, another to his right and the shadows at the far end of the room in front of him.

The interpreter announced, 'His Highness Prince Krishna Wadiar will now sing an English song in honour of the English guests.'

Another round of whispering and tittering broke out in the Indian camp. It didn't seem to be doing the prince, clearly very nervous and inhibited, any good. The English ladies, their curiosity piqued by the surprise announcement, leaned forward. What song was it going to be? How come the little prince spoke English? Who tutored him in the language? Why wasn't that tutor acting as interpreter today?

A thin, high voice started up, so weak in the cavernous spaces of the room, it could barely be heard. An Indian woman shouted out one word repeatedly. The boy stopped and started again but there was no appreciable difference to the volume. Miss Gilby strained to hear the words of the song to identify it – the tune was practically non-existent – but couldn't make out even one intelligible word. Suddenly the words 'Robin Redbreast' leaped out and it almost made sense: the young prince was singing 'When the snow is on the ground'. But it was obvious the prince didn't know the language; he had learned the song by rote and was eliding and dissecting the words randomly, running three or four words, even a fraction of a word, together, stopping in the middle of one word and joining the rest with the next few ones. It was all dictated by his own aural world; it had no resemblance to English whatsoever.

'*Vendas no nisonda gound, littttil robinwedbest gives / Fornobe ris canbefound, anondatis therenolivs,*' the prince sang in his private language. Miss Gilby looked out of the corner of her eyes and saw Iris looking fixedly at a rose petal near her feet and Jane crumpling a handkerchief in front of her quivering mouth.

She needn't have bothered because two of the younger girls on the Indian side, just a few years older than the performing boy, erupted into rude, loud giggling while the brave boy carried on to the end of the song – '*andenhilliv tilda snowisgon.*' Then he gave a dainty bow and ran into the arms of his *ayah* who had been waiting behind a fluted pillar, away from the sight of the foreigners.

Once again, there was a minor hullaballoo: some of the Indian women started clapping, the English women followed suit, a bit too enthusiastically, while the giggling girls were reprimanded loudly. There seemed to be calls for the prince to come on again. Seemed. For Miss Gilby, that was the central word around which everything during this visit was arranging itself. She felt she had been catapulted onto stage in a play whose characters, design, plot, language were all utterly unknown to her, but she had to remain on stage and play her part, whatever it was, trying to pick out tenuous clues by watching everyone carefully and mimicking their actions. But this was proving treacherous too.

The prince had somehow found his way on to the laps of the queens and was now being cuddled, patted and stroked by three of them while the two giggling girls stood apart, looking on. There was a whole chorus of discordant chattering in progress. Before long, the boy had been convinced to take his former place again. The Maharani shushed loudly for silence, then appeared to speak harsh words to no one in particular in her camp, followed by words directed at Prince Krishna.

The boy began singing again, Jane Fearfield tried to hide her snorting by pretending to sniff into her handkerchief in the most unbecoming manner, while Miss Gilby gave up all attempts to decipher which English song it was this time. Iris Shepherd leaned sideways and rudely whispered, 'Little Star, Little Star'.

Yes, so it was. At the line 'In the pretty sky so blue', which the prince managed to leave relatively unmangled, Miss Gilby realized the truth of Iris Shepherd's recognition. The boy reached the ascendant – 'Little Star! O tell me, pray / Where you hide yourself all day', Miss Gilby giving the words their proper enunciation in her head – when he stopped, gulped, repeated 'O tell me, pray' three times, stopped again, cast around pathetic glances, looked at the floor, took a deep breath and started the song from the beginning again.

He had forgotten the rest of the song.

This time, he reached 'In the pretty sky so blue' and slipped; he was progressively forgetting more and more of the song. His voice had a tremor in it somewhere and the harder he tried to swallow it the more it defeated him. Then Miss Gilby noticed his lower lip quivering, his chin wobbling: the inevitable was about to happen. The boy rushed away, wrapped himself around his *ayah*'s legs and started sobbing. Then, to the courteous minds of the English, the inconceivable happened: a roar of derisive laughter went up in the Indian camp accompanied by what appeared to be the native version of booing and catcalls. Miss Gilby was shocked by this naked display of cruelty. Iris Shepherd stood up in outrage and was evidently composing herself to say something and protest at this bad behaviour. Miss Gilby stood up too. The two girls who had been tittering and giggling earlier were now unimpeded in their laughing triumph.

But before either Miss Gilby or Iris Shepherd could bring themselves to voice their concern, the Maharani and two older women decided to take things in hand: they chided the girls, shouted at the mocking women, demanded silence, even compassion and understanding for the hapless boy, and eventually imposed some semblance of order.

Miss Gilby spoke out. 'We are delighted at the prince's performance. And surprised, too. Well done, young man. It was very . . . brave.' She started applauding. Iris Shepherd and Jane Fearfield joined in with such vigour that after an embarrassing lag some of the Indian women joined in too, drowning out the translation the interpreter was trotting out. There was entreaty for the boy to be brought to them. The *ayah* pushed him in their direction but the prince clung to her legs. She bent down, whispered a few words in his ear, even pointed to the English ladies and pushed him again. This time he ran across, his head held firmly down, ran straight into the Maharani's gold- and jewel-encrusted bosom, buried his head there and refused to budge. The Maharani kissed and coddled him, spoke words in his ear, and passed him around to the other women who all did the same.

At a sharpish rasp of words from one of the queens, the *ayah* too went up to the royal enclosure, gathered up the now puzzled prince and departed, keeping to the shadows at the edge of the room.

Another long silence ensued.

One of the girls said something out loud at which most of the other women tittered and laughed.

The interpreter's voice droned, 'They ask why you have arms which are being so white they look uncooked and what are the funny things on your head.'

In the silence after his words something beyond language passed like an invisible electric current between the three points of contact. Both Indian and British camps realized that the interpreter had translated words that were meant to be private and each was waiting for the other side to react.

The seconds ticked away, each one seemed of far longer duration than normal. Then Miss Gilby held her head up, laughed, and said, 'These are hats.'

TWO

Gavin tries to be dismissive every time Ritwik tells him about his life in Calcutta. Ritwik supposes it is posturing on his part, an attempt to appear cool and unfazed by what he hears. Perhaps that is as it should be. Besides, Ritwik doesn't really tell him everything, only bits here and there; there are a lot of things he elides, mostly out of a sense of shame and embarrassment. He hopes Gavin isn't going to ask him searching questions which would lead to all those things he passes over in silence. Sometimes he is not so lucky.

'Why did they send you to that Catholic school?' he asks one day, after Ritwik tells him about the time Shivaji Jana was beaten up so badly by Miss Lewis, in junior school, that he had a 'dislocated kidney'. Ritwik heard that Shivaji's father had been in to see the Principal, not to complain or rage, but just to say that his son wouldn't be attending that school any more. Ashoke's mother had seen him come out of Father Paul's office. He had gone up to her and suddenly started sobbing like a little child. 'My only son, he's in hospital, Mrs Biswas,' he had said between sobs, and shuffled out.

'It had a great reputation,' Ritwik answers.

Gavin snorts. 'For general buggery and torture! Jeee-sus!' Ritwik notices he says 'Sheeesus.'

75

'No, no, it was a good school. English-medium, as we call it in India. That alone raises it to the first bracket. The education was top quality. These things run solely on reputation, you know. By the time the negative things start making a general mark on public consciousness, the school will have done twenty more years of brisk business.'

Gavin rolls his eyes, as if it were Ritwik's fault somehow that he went to Don Bosco School in Park Circus, Calcutta. 'Did no one complain?' he asks, starting to roll a joint.

'You couldn't. They were too powerful. Anyone whose parents complained would be victimized by the teachers. He would eventually have to leave. Anyway, for every complaint, there would be fifty endorsements from the brown-nose lobby of parents. Or plain scared parents. They didn't want to risk their boys' well-being or even their place in a school of such repute by supporting complaints.' He suddenly feels a wave of fury at this remembered powerlessness.

'God, the Catholics,' Gavin says, with another of his exasperated looks. 'They are the bloody same everywhere. They are a disease.'

'Also, there were sons of police commissioners, businessmen, ministers in the school,' Ritwik continues. 'Those powerful men would have protected the school from any slur.'

The joint is ready. They stand near the window of Gavin's shoebox room and exhale outside. At least Ritwik's room looks out onto gardens and a giant horse chestnut. Gavin's fronts a square of brutalist student blocks built in the sixties. There isn't a thread of green anywhere in sight.

For a few minutes, they are quiet. Gavin instinctively understands this culture of microcorruption and vested interests. 'It's the same in my country,' he says.

76

'They were a subset of Catholics,' Ritwik tells Gavin. 'Salesians.'

'You mean like Jesuits?' Gavin asks.

'Followers of Francis de la Sale. The school's foundation wisdom was "Give me a boy and I'll give you a man."'

'It could be the name of a gay porn film,' Gavin sniggers. They both giggle for a while.

As the dope kicks in, Ritwik invariably wonders whether he really fancies Gavin or whether it's just his generalized hunger for white men. Anyway, Gavin is as straight as they come with a line in Tamil and Sri Lankan women. When he is single, as he is now, he looks at Pakistani and Indian women and goes, 'Oh, sheees, look at her, just look at her.' And if the woman is with another guy, especially one who he thinks is English, he always adds, 'What a bloody waste.' Gavin tries to live up to the cliché of the sexually rampant Latino man. With his balding head, goatee and white skin – his mother is from Brazil but his late father was Scottish – he doesn't quite fulfill the image of the dusky South American stud.

As if in some backhand acknowledgement of this, Ritwik asks him to play that Brazilian song he loves, the one about sexual success. Gavin obliges, laughingly. As the song comes on, Ritwik asks him to translate, although he knows the lines, in Gavin's translation, by heart. He likes to watch Gavin laugh affectionately with his countrymen, or even at their stereotyping.

'What use do I have of money, friends, fame,' Gavin laughs and translates, 'if I do not have sexual success?'

They practically roll around laughing. Ritwik loves the sound of those Brazilian words: *Para quê que eu quero grana, Para quê que eu quero fama sem sucesso sexual*. He likes the rhythm and the cock-strutting masculinity of the song as well. It would be considered ironic here but he is certain it's dead serious in Brazil.

'My country is mad,' says Gavin. But there is no doubt, either in his mind or in Ritwik's, that he loves Brazil, loves it with the indulgent love of a parent for a slightly wayward but basically good child. He belongs to some militant Maoist group in São Paulo and wants to go back there to join in grassroots activism before the next general election. He is convinced they will win and the thought of imminent election fills him with excitement: he raises his arms and says things like 'Long live the Revolution' and wears Castro and Che Guevara T-shirts. He is a great acolyte of Trotsky and he designed an exhibition poster for the Ruskin School's annual degree show – a reproduction of his lithograph of Trotsky in his open grave. It borders on the abstract; the various shades of grey and black just about give the impression of an awkwardly curled-up figure – like some sleeping Pompeiian – lying on the ground, with a stick, or something of that sort, beside it. Gavin explains it's the ice pick, which was driven into his head by the assassin employed by Stalin to hound him out, even in furthest Mexico. Apparently, he died saying, 'Stalin did it.' Ritwik asks him for a copy of the poster and Blu Tacks it to his wall.

Gavin is a clever art student. He makes things which have such a novelty value for Ritwik that he likes them instantly and thinks they're the Next Great Thing. This is not difficult, for Ritwik's knowledge of twentieth-century art stretches up to Matisse and Picasso, Rothko at a pinch. It is centred exclusively on paintings as well; other forms of representation to him are jarringly modern. But there is this one nifty thing that Gavin does with empty plastic bottles which extends Ritwik's horizons in a silent way. He puts photocopies of photographs of people inside empty plastic or glass bottles, along with bits of rubber band, cloth, miscellaneous found objects, and then covers up the mouth of the bottles with cloth and string. He extends this principle to boxes and tins with windows cut out in them, shoeboxes with slits that make them look like barred windows. The effect is one of not only looking in, but also of these objects inside – puppets, statues, photographs – looking out from their confinement on to the free viewer.

Gavin makes one for him with an empty 330 ml bottle of Evian and a picture of a woman's face. He later explains that the woman is one of many whose sons went missing while Pinochet was in power. Ritwik keeps it on his mantelpiece, secretly hoping that one day he can sell it for a huge sum when Gavin becomes a big name. He is confident Gavin is going to become a big name, like the ones Gavin himself thinks are great – Paula Rego, Andrzej Klimowski, and a few others whose names Ritwik doesn't remember. He hasn't heard of any of them, his idea of a contemporary big name is the only name he knows of in the art scene – David Hockney. He doesn't know anything about Hockney, he has just picked up the name from Jonti, another art student to whom Gavin introduced him some months ago. Jonti and Ritwik get on well and sometimes the three of them get stoned in Jonti's room where he talks about David Bowie and Hockney and charges them £2 at the end of the evening for sharing his dope with them. Gavin always says, 'God, the English really are a nation of shopkeepers,' when he comes out of Jonti's room.

Meanwhile, Ritwik tries to bone up on all the names in this new world to which Gavin has introduced him. He remembers, with a hot flush of embarrassment, how he had made friends with Gavin by talking nervously about Piero della Francesca,

Simone Martini and Ghirlandaio after overhearing at a meal in halls that he was an art student, as though all it took to lure art students into friendship was a name or two from his gallery of childhood obsessions. He had culled the names, as a boy of ten, from the *Collins Concise Encyclopaedia*, his first peek into the greater world outside the horizons of his life in Grange Road; it was a book that became a shield, the talisman against his life at home, the very first stumbling, halting steps to his escape. He had doggedly chased those names and their works, hunted them down in bad, grainy reproductions on the brittle pages of out of print, cheap imprints in decrepit, poorly stocked libraries in Calcutta; to utter those names aloud, to hear his own voice articulate them, felt like sacrilege, a breaking of an unimaginable taboo. Gavin, however, knew them and had got excited about having someone to talk to about the various hand gestures of Mary in the Annunciation. Ritwik had been so grateful that he had had to swallow the several lumps in his throat and rapidly blink his smarting eyes as Gavin had talked to him about Michael Baxandall. Six months into his friendship with Gavin hasn't eroded that gratitude. Here, where the past seems more foreign, more unknown to almost everyone, Gavin is a little oasis in a desert of amnesia. He is convinced this is so because Gavin is Brazilian and engages with Europe in a way only outsiders can do.

He envies Gavin his familiarity with the contours of the world he studies but, above all, he envies Gavin his easy acceptance of Maoism, his left-wing activism. He goes to meetings of the Socialist Workers' Party and raises his arm in that characteristic way of his while uttering a joyous 'Yea' when Ritwik tells him how, when the Communists came to power in Bengal in 1979, they changed the names of all Calcutta streets that honoured

British viceroys, governor generals and rulers to names of Communist leaders. Curzon Street, Bentinck Street, Ripon Street were ditched and in their stead there were Lenin Sarani, Ho-Chi-Minh Sarani. The sole exception was Theatre Road; it was renamed Shakespeare Sarani because the British Council was on it.

Gavin thinks this wholesale renaming is important. Ritwik tells him how people in Calcutta still keep calling the roads by the names of their erstwhile British overlords; he has never heard anyone use the name Ho-Chi-Minh Sarani. Rickshaw pullers, taxi drivers, bus conductors, ordinary people, all stuck to Harrington Street and Dalhousie Square.

'But, Gavin, it's all very well to say "People this", "People that", but nothing, absolutely fucking NOTHING works in that state,' Ritwik occasionally splutters.

'You can't have Revolution overnight,' Gavin says. Ritwik can hear the upper-case 'R' in his voice. 'Besides, while you were having a Communist Revolution in Bengal, they elected Thatcher here,' he adds with distaste.

Ritwik knows Thatcher is Bad but does not exactly know why. He asks tentatively, 'Is it because of the poll tax?' He has heard that term mentioned before with disgust and anger.

'I was living in London at the time of the poll tax riots. I tell you, I come from Brazil, and I've never seen police brutality on that level anywhere, anywhere before. It was shocking.'

Ritwik's images of Thatcher are from recycled newsreel on the neighbours' television during the week-long mourning after Mrs Gandhi's assassination. He tells Gavin about this. 'You know, when Indira Gandhi was killed, we had nothing on national television for days on end, except films about her. Documentaries, news footage, films, homage, the works.' He slides over the fact that they had all crowded around the television set next door, in Tipshu's house: he is too ashamed to admit they didn't own a television. 'On one of these newsreels they showed Thatcher and Indira Gandhi chatting, laughing, you know, getting on really well. They always seemed to be together. One of my uncles said, "Look, two women at the top, they're friends. It must be so lonely for them. I suppose it's their mutual loneliness that has made them bond. They both understand how difficult it is." At that time, that thought really struck me, this alliance of powerful solitaries. You know, "Uneasy lies the head that wears the crown" sort of thing.'

The library is like a sombre chapel, a dark redbrick edifice with gothicky spires and a huge heavy door, which not only looks but also feels like the door to a castle, all enormous wood and metal; he has to push against it with his entire body to get it to open. He likes working here: it is cosy, warm and unintimidating, not at all like the central library where you have to wait for more than six hours for the ordered books to arrive and when you go up to the members of staff after the scheduled wait, they sometimes tell you things like, 'Sorry we couldn't find it, it's missing, and we have no idea when it will turn up.' Or, 'The book fell off the trolley and its spine was crushed under the wheels; it's gone to the binders, it'll be six months before we get it back.'

But here, he can see the books on their shelves, go up to them, pull them out, browse, let his attention wander to other books far removed from his subject. At the table next to his, the historian with round glasses, red hair and the area around his nose and eyes marked by a populous colony of freckles has left a pile of books on Indian history lying around. Instantly curious,

Ritwik reaches out for a volume with an incredible title: *Wanderings of a Pilgrim in search of the Picturesque, during four-and-twenty years in the East; with Revelations of Life in the Zenāna* by a Fanny Parkes, an Englishwoman who travelled around in India in the 1820s and 30s. Ritwik tries to dampen the excitement at this serendipitous find as he flicks through the pages: entire sections on a visit to a former Queen of Gwalior at a camp in Fatehpur, a chapter on a visit to a Mulka Humanee Begum married to a Colonel James Gardner . . . Here it is, an outsider, a foreigner, being let in and recording her experiences; he adds the book to his own tottering pile.

He can touch and smell the books in this library, make a precarious tower of a dozen or so of them on his desk and feel secure behind that wall. He can even borrow them and take them back to his room, arrange them according to size on his small desk or his bookshelves and feel the satisfaction of order and method, order and method.

He reads as if his life depends on this reckless rush of words entering him in a torrent; words of different tongues, of other times and alien places all now gone, words which force their own spaces inside him so they can rush in to fill them up.

He reads about a mother who stands under a tree and tells passers-by to look at her for there is no sorrow greater than hers: her son has been nailed through to a tree. He reads of how this son came to her, to be conceived, as still as the April dew that falls on grass and flowers. On another page, the son enters her as the all-comprehending light through a stained-glass window. Another one about a helpless mother crying and watching her son die in a welter of blood and thorns and nail.

He reads about people who are so sleepless with love-longing they have gone mad and driven themselves to the forests where they meet others complaining about their despair in love. There is always someone standing under a thorn tree, singing as they languish in love's prison. And he wonders at Jankin, the naughty church officiant who, instead of chanting *Kyrie eleison*, breaks out cunningly into *Kyrie Alison*, hoping the girl in the congregation is going to show him some mercy.

The strong undertow of his thoughts have pulled him so far away to the pitiful mother that he has trouble making his way back to the shallows again. The poems don't tell him how she survives.

III.

The days pass in anticipation and apprehension. Most of her possessions are packed in large trunks and boxes. Mahesh will see off the first consignment to Sealdah station tomorrow morning. She is taking her first class carriage in a week's time, on the Eastern Bengal Railway, from Sealdah to Kooshtea. Mr Roy Chowdhury will receive her there himself and arrange for transportation from Kooshtea to Nawabgunj, in all probability in his motor car, but he has written that the rivers arc in spate this season, the tracks are either all flooded or swamped with mud, where wheels will invariably get rutted, so Miss Gilby is really not looking forward to that particular leg of her long journey.

These days she spends mostly saying goodbye to people and things. Yesterday, she had farewell tea with her Bengali teacher, the old Sheikh Maqsood Ali, in his overcrowded, dark house, crammed with objects, in Collutolla Street. It had been impossible to read the expression in those nearly blind eyes behind their shield of lenses so thick that they looked magnified like an owl's. Ali-*miyan* had refused to take back the books which he had lent her in the beginning – 'Keep them, Miss Gilby, keep them, consider them a humble gift from teacher to student, something which I hope will remind you of our lessons together' – books of the Bengali alphabet, elementary reading, sentence construction and writing by an eminent Bengali gentleman, Ishwarchandra Vidyasagar; Ali-*miyan* had never stopped singing the praises of that 'great man'. Despite the initial difficulties with such a strange script, Miss Gilby had made not inconsiderable progress: she could read that bizarre and unpleasant moral tale of a boy who had his ear cut off as punishment for being a liar almost without any halting or help from Ali-*miyan*. He had been pleased; for Miss Gilby, his joy had been a welcome change from the almost constant state of his surprise at the rare occurrence of a *memsahib* making the effort to learn an Indian language. Even after three years he still couldn't believe he had an English lady as one of his private pupils and one who came to his house to take her lessons. It was rare, it was unconventional, it was daring, and Ali-*miyan* had both savoured and feared it.

For the last three years, every Tuesday, Thursday and Saturday, without fail, come rain, floods or the unbearable sticky heat of summer, Miss Gilby appeared in her private brougham, from Eliot Road to Collutolla Street, for her Bengali lessons. The lessons had to be terminated, regrettably for both parties, when Miss Gilby was invited to tutor Saira-*begum*: it was an offer she couldn't refuse because the Nawab of Motibagh was one of her brother's influential acquaintances and when Miss Gilby had first moved to Calcutta four years ago the Nawab had extended every possible help to her because she was James's sister. Besides, this was an opportunity Miss Gilby had been looking for all along, this chance to spread the knowledge not only of English but also of a different way of living, the knowledge of a whole new world, to Indian women, to forge a contact with these unheard and dumb creatures, to hear them speak, to hear their lives.

In the balance of things, her lessons with Ali-*miyan*, enjoyable and challenging though they were, and her unfolding relationship with her old teacher proved wonderfully that James, and along with him every single servant of the Empire in India and all the Anglo-Indian community, was wrong wrong wrong about the impossibility of a true, trustful friendship between the natives and the Anglos; the lessons had had to be sacrificed but she had made ,certain that her continuing friendship with Ali-*miyan* didn't suffer. To this effect, she had visited him for tea – an institution to which she had slowly converted the all-too-willing teacher by speaking gloriously of the ways in which her people in England practised it daily – every first Sunday of the month during her time with the Motibaghs.

For her now, there is a valedictory air to everything in this messy city of lanes and by-lanes and road repairs and road building. It tinges her beloved tramcar journeys, which she has taken at least once every week during her time here. She goes down her favourite routes again and again: first, from Sealdah Station through Circular Road, Bowbazaar Street, Dalhousie Square, through Customs House and Strand Road – which, Ali-*miyan* tells her, was under water until 1823 or so – to Armenian Ghat on the banks of the Ganges. Seated in her first class carriage, she wills herself not to think of James's words beating themselves out to the titup-titup-titup of the horses' hooves on the cobbles as houses, temples, churches, people, buildings gently pass by, leaving her desiring the wide open space of the Maidan or the muddy brown water of the river, the sky low over it, and on its broad surface, boats and dinghies, ramshackle things barely held together with bamboos and tattered cloth. She likes the stillness of these boats; they seem to ply the waters in so leisurely a manner that it is difficult to believe they're going anywhere or transporting people on them. It is the very rhythm of the country, this apparent lack of movement, of any forward motion altogether. Time means an altogether different thing to them.

In the autumns, during the Durga Puja celebrations, there are steam engines drawing the tramcar carriages on Chowringhee Road, carrying pilgrims from and to the temple in Kalighat. These ghats are something which Miss Gilby had never seen before coming to Calcutta. They had grown on her so much that in the autumns and winters she and Ali-*miyan*, sometimes with Mrs Cameron, used to take the air in the early afternoons on the banks of the Hooghly, with Ali-*miyan* keeping up a running commentary about the history and names of the scores of ghats which dot the stretch of the river.

Ali-*miyan* guided the coachman as the brougham made its way from Kashipur in the north to Hastings on the Ganges estuary in the south, pointed out the ghats – steps leading down to the water, sometimes half submerged, made of marble or bricks, at other times docks really, for landing, anchoring and hauling of goods – and reeled off their names and explanations that awed Miss Gilby: 'Look, Miss Gilby, that's Ahiritolla Ghat, named so because this was the area where cowherds and milkmen lived'; 'That's Nimtolla Ghat, where Hindus cremate their dead'. Miss Gilby had been disturbed much more by this social ritual of people burning their dead on the banks of a river than by the odd practice of people bathing outdoors. She found the funeral practices primitive and didn't encourage Ali-*miyan* to elaborate on this, quickly diverting him to give her a prolix history of another ghat, Huzurimal Ghat, or the ones with English names – Jackson *sahib*'s Ghat, Colvin Ghat, Foreman *sahib*'s Ghat. Miss Gilby has always found it amazing that the ghats are used for bathing, cremating, as docking and landing points of goods to be transported either inland or on the river. Even though each ghat is given over to only one of these functions, Miss Gilby is still struck by this unusual commingling of cleansing, commerce and ritual as if life, living and death were interchangeable, or all one.

She keeps repeating to herself that she will return to this city, that the appointment in Nawabgunj is only for a few years, but something deeper and unnameable, both inside and outside her, impels her to traverse the lengths and breadths of Calcutta in her brougham or in tramcars as if she were breathing in her last of the place, etching it solidly in her mind in a way only people who know they are never going to return do.

There are letters to write – polite 'thank you' notes, more intimate ones to one or two of her friends here, slightly more formal ones letting acquaintances know of her new address and residence, a more general one to the members of the Anglo-Indian community she knows through Clubs, that sort of thing. These she usually keeps for the mornings. Afternoons are taken up with visiting or, in those rare spare hours, travelling through the city, mostly on her own. It is a little adventure, partly thrilling, partly fearsome, she rations to herself as a treat.

The evenings are mostly taken up, although reluctantly and with much misgiving, by the Club. This is on the insistence of Mrs Cameron, her only true friend in Calcutta. A widow who had been married to the Lieutenant-Governor of Allahabad, she had moved down east shortly after her husband's death. Her ten-year-old daughter, Jane, was in London and her younger son, Christopher, at Summerfield. Sending her children, both born in India, to be educated back Home was the only sign of conformity to Raj society she had shown. Fiercely independent and unconventional, she had cocked a snook at Calcutta's ossified Anglo-Indian society: ignoring the listings in the Warrant of Precedence; setting up schools for the education of Indian women in her own backyard and, in the winter months, in her garden; campaigning for the end of the *moorgi khana* in Clubs – her sins were so numerous that she was practically on the verge of ostracism by the unforgiving Anglo-Indian community. But she was one of life's great irrepressibles, a true free spirit, and Miss Gilby knew that she enjoyed every bit of the controversy attaching to her, down to her outcast status, her lack of invitations to the Governor's balls or the Viceroy's Winter Dances: these were things that didn't matter to her. She laughed at them, laughed at the choreographed dance of folly, which her countrymen indulged in, and held their snobbery in deep contempt. It was she who had recognized a kindred spirit in Miss Gilby and, on her arrival in Calcutta, had tested the newcomer by throwing to the winds the whole mad business of calling cards and appearing on her doorstep to invite Miss Gilby to afternoon tea; Miss Gilby had been utterly delighted. Mrs Cameron had warned her, 'If you are intelligent, try and hide it if you can: a clever woman is not a very popular item in this jolly place.'

Miss Gilby and Mrs Cameron had taken on the might of the Club with glee. While most considered that they had lost, the two women knew they had nothing to lose. Besides, they were financially independent and sufficiently high up the ladder for any of the mutterings and whisperings to really bite. Despite a lot of cold shoulders and frosty behaviour at the Club, they had persisted in socializing there in the evenings when there was nothing to be done – 'Maud, we cannot stop going to the Club, it will be a victory for them, don't you see? If they think they can make things difficult for us there, don't you think we can do exactly the same for them? They are far more uncomfortable with our presence than we are with theirs. We don't care, they do, that's our trump card' – and had even ended up earning a sort of grudging respect.

Gimlets or pegs of whisky and soda on the lawns, a spot of tennis very early in the morning, even swimming sometimes, the endless rounds of gossip and talking about the intransigence of servants: it was amusing how she who had suffered all these obligatory things should now feel herself poised on the brink of missing them, trying to fit them in in her final days so that they were fixed in some future memory.

One advantage Mrs Cameron certainly had over the outraged little Anglo-Indians was the quality of her dinner parties. Here, she was nonpareil, an unqualified social success. And here, too, she broke all the rules. She tore up the Warrant of Precedence and seated guests wherever her fancy or mood took her. At one such party in the early days of her stay in Calcutta, she had seated an army officer in the wrong place, at which the incensed guest had informed her that he was a full colonel; she had chirpily replied, 'Are you really? Well, I do so hope that when dinner is over you will be fuller still.'

Miss Gilby had found in the older woman a soulmate, a mentor who exposed in her the nervous steel to do things about which she would either have thought twice before or, having done it, would have felt lonely in the isolation that committing such a deed would have almost certainly brought her.

Suddenly Miss Gilby feels a pang of sorrow for her impending separation from Violet Cameron. Mrs Cameron is a little surprised at Miss Gilby's insistence on strolling in the Eden Gardens or walking down the Strand as the bands played, two or sometimes three times a week, even during the wet, squally afternoons. Could it possibly be because Miss Gilby is trying to hold on to her company in these last few days left to her? *Solamen miseris socios habuisse doloris*, but could not the same be said of happy people in the joy they took of each other? They will write to each other regularly and, yes, this communication is going to take a lot longer than the scores of chits circulated around the community and carried by the servants to and fro, and it will not have the immediacy and urgency of a chit written half an hour before its delivery to the addressee by a hot-footed servant, but it will have to do.

During one of their dinners – informal, just the two of them, but neither of them forgets to dress up – Mrs Cameron asks, 'So do you have any idea what this woman Bimala is like?'

Miss Gilby says, 'No, what I know of her is what I have gleaned from her husband's letters. He is very well educated: a recent MA from Calcutta University.'

'But Maud, she's not one of those girl brides, is she?'

'No, no, I don't think so. She can't be any older than twenty or so but she is no girl. Or at least that's not the impression I get from his letters.'

There is a pause for a few minutes as the servants remove the empty plates of consommé and bring in the curried prawns.

'Are you not somewhat anxious about living with an Indian family?' Mrs Cameron asks.

'To tell you the truth,' Miss Gilby replies, 'yes, I am, a little.'

'Will they have an untouchable European put in a separate wing of the house, give you servants who will not be allowed to touch or do any work for the other members of the household, that sort of thing?'

'Oh, Violet, I've thought and thought about these practical arrangements and even mentioned one or two of them to Mr Roy Chowdhury. It appears they are a very progressive family. He has two widowed sisters-in-law who live with them and I'm assuming they observe strict religious rules or whatever the norms and mores are in these cases, but I've been asking around about rules and etiquette in Hindu families. One thing I'm sure of is that he doesn't have much truck with the caste system.'

There is another clearing of plates before the leg of mutton is brought to the table. Miss Gilby asks, 'Are you going to carry on with the school?'

'Yes, of course, Maud, of course. It will be difficult without you. God knows, you've been such a great help and I don't know what I'm going to do without you. Miss Hailey – you know her, don't you, Grant Hailey's sister – is showing an interest but she is the timid sort and one harsh word from her brother, or, indeed, anyone, would be enough to make her cower into subservience.'

'You know, Violet, don't you, I really wish I could stay on but . . .' she says, an askance glance picking up the burden of the unsaid.

'No, Maud, you must go where your heart takes you. And if you don't manage to get into all these families and familiarize yourself with their running, get to know their women, your book is going to be a little thin. Have you started it yet?'

'No, I haven't, not yet, but I'm hoping to begin once I've settled in in Nawabgunj. I'm so glad you understand, Violet. Mr Roy Chowdhury says he's very interested in your school. If you need any help from him – talking to people, funds, anything – you just have to ask. He seems to be a very enlightened young man.'

'You are lucky. You could have got yourself into a family that locked the women away in dark rooms and allowed them to do nothing but play with dolls and gossip and bear children.'

'In that case, I don't think I would have been asked for in the first place.'

Mrs Cameron gives orders for the table to be cleared. They have both had somewhat more than their usual amount of claret. Lightheaded, they move to the drawing room. It has started raining again and there are all sorts of flying insects making a beeline for the candles in the room; something drifts down, too slow to be an insect. Miss Gilby realizes it's a feather from somewhere, maybe a wet bird outside, or a pillow. She blows on it and instead of falling down it changes its course and gets wafted in the direction of Mrs Cameron.

Mrs Cameron exclaims, 'Oh, look, a feather.' There's a childish delight in her voice. She moves her head forward and lets out a puff of breath from lips protruding in an O; the breath catches the swaying, falling feather and it swerves towards Miss Gilby. But before it can reach Miss Gilby's blowing range, it loses momentum and starts gravitating downwards again. Miss Gilby gets up, goes down on her knees and before the feather can reach the chairs, she blows on it very hard.

'Quick, Violet, quick, blow it up to the level of the table. Go on, lie down and blow it up, up,' she squeals with urgency.

Mrs Cameron does exactly that – she crouches very low on the floor and, with her neck pointed upward, blows up, moving her head like a cat that has seen a flying insect or bird above it. She tries several bursts to get the feather right in the current.

'You've got it, you've got it,' Miss Gilby shouts and raises herself up to meet the ascending feather.

'Maud, Maud, try and raise it higher so we can do it standing up. No, higher, higher,' Mrs Cameron shouts.

The two women shuffle and parry in an odd, staccato dance while the feather, which gets tossed between them, never seems to lose its light grace.

THREE

Paper covers stone. Stone breaks scissors. Scissors cut paper. Paper cuts him, has always done. Not just those occasional cuts when he is impatiently opening the rare envelope in his pigeonhole, no, not those. It cuts him into new shapes, new forms, until there is no he anymore, but a cipher, a shadow, dependent on other things for his very existence. Sometimes while papers and their resident words slip and slide into him, drowning him under so that he can't take so much life in its burning bright rush inside him, he casually looks up to catch the face of someone in the window opposite his desk. For the space of something not calibrated in human time, only registered by the sudden sway of his heart towards his throat, he does not recognize that the unmoored face looking back at him is his own. He is goosepimpled by his own presence, or a deferred version of himself, as if he is not really there. He chances upon Edmund Spenser's dedicatory epistle to Lady Carey: 'Therefore I have determined to give my selfe wholly to you, as quite abandoned from my selfe . . .' His eyes stop at *quite abandoned from my selfe*. Yes, this is it; he has found confirmation in another page, in other words, of what happens to him. But there is no he left when he reads. So who is it that looks at him from the impressionable glass? Words for him are like the sporing rust on metal – they eat away at him until there is only an unidentifiable husk. He has become nothing.

These presences and shadows scare him sometimes. He has taken to sitting with his back firmly pressed to the corner where two walls meet at right angles. He has become like a cat: at least two sides are covered and nothing can startle him from behind. Whatever encounter there is in store for him will be face to face; he's prepared for it, ready to look it in the eye.

Look her in the eye if she comes back again.

So far, she hasn't come back while he has been in his room, but occasionally, when he returns at night, turns the key in the lock, pushes the door open and, leaning forward, quickly switches on the light with an outstretched arm while still standing outside, he knows she has been in the room. No, nothing has been moved or hidden, nothing has been disturbed. There is no trace, no evidence, only a gathering together of the air into its normal Brownian motion after it has been sliced through and agitated by a recent presence. It is like water restored to calm after the ripples generated by a lost stone have died out but the water still remembers. The air in his room sometimes has that quality of remembrance. That's all. And he's afraid of that memory of air.

He doesn't dare tell anyone about it; he knows they're going to be polite, commiserating, maybe just embarrassed, averting his eye. He certainly doesn't want to confide in Gavin. Lately, he has been getting on Ritwik's nerves. When he's alone with Gavin, the deprecatory humour directed at him, the ribbing, they're quite all right; he takes them in his stride as part of Gavin's affection for him. He even enjoys, up to a point, Gavin's feigned exasperation with him, his attitude of *what are we going to do with a* _____ *like you?* The blank term changes: sometimes it's *rustic peasant*, at other times *phony, charlatan, unsophisticated yokel, embarrassment;* it all depends on his mood, but it's all done in the spirit of fun and friendship.

Maybe.

In public, this takes on a sharper edge. Then, it seems Gavin is intent on pulling him down. Ritwik becomes some sort of a clown-freak for whom Gavin has to apologize even at the same time as he's expected to perform for others. It is quite relentless; Gavin doesn't seem capable of any other mode with him in public. Sometimes it's funny, this *you must treat Ritwik with indulgence, he's a third-world peasant* disclaimer from Gavin. At other times, the sheer unchangingness of it grates on him. Maybe he reads too much into all this because he is touchy and feels insulted. It could all be ironic, all the time, in which case it would be very trendy and in.

So telling Gavin, even ironically, is out of the question. Besides, what could he say? *Oh, Gavin, by the way, my mother keeps appearing in my room. This hash is really wicked, it steals up on you slowly. What were you saying about 'index' and 'icon'?* He doesn't want to dent Gavin's *soi disant* role of educator and civilizer. It's a role that has taught Ritwik to smoothe over the jagged edges of his own behaviour, to learn to observe, ape and conform.

Gavin is full of contradictions in this way; for all his radical lefty politics, he occasionally jolts Ritwik with a type of old-guard parochialism, such as his firm belief in good breeding. On the back of some conversation about women – they are never very far from Gavin's mind – he once said he didn't see why people objected to arranged marriages: at least one could make sure then the girl came from a good family. This is a vital thing in Gavin's book: he sets a high premium on manners, decorum, social niceties, impeccably behaved children. And he's very aware of class. There is this girl he fancies, Miriam; she reads English and plays the cello. He tells Ritwik, 'Wouldn't it be great to have Miriam play the cello naked?'

Ritwik says, 'You know, there's a Buñuel film where a woman plays some Brahms at the piano, nude.'

Gavin's mind is on other things. 'That well-bred personality all thrown to the winds . . . the cello between her legs . . . oooff, I can't bear to think about it,' he rhapsodizes, then adds, 'It would make her poshness *piccante*, you know, the contrast between good behaviour and . . . and . . . shocking, well, shocking . . . WHORISHNESS.' He pounces upon the word.

'How do you know she's well-bred and all that stuff?'

'Oh, I know friends of hers. She went to a posh school in posh North London.'

Ritwik is a bit daunted, although this doesn't last very long for he finds out, in a few months, that Gavin's use of the word 'posh' is a bit loose, that Miriam went to what they call a bog-standard comprehensive, that she does not come from a posh (even by Gavin's definition) bit of north London. But then, he thinks, there are two types of people. The first, his type, is the myopic, narrow sort: they take people exactly as they come – curly hair, glasses, crushed velvet trousers from a Marie Curie shop, plays the clarinet, hasn't heard of Alain Resnais, etc etc. No more, no less. There is no other meaning behind these appearances and facts. They mean to him: curly hair, glasses, crushed velvet trousers from a Marie Curie shop, plays the clarinet, hasn't heard of Alain Resnais, etc etc.

The second type, to which Gavin belongs, is endowed with a shrewd socio-historical perceptiveness. They meet people and extrapolate a whole complex context from their parents' marital status, parents' jobs, area of residence, school attended, etc etc. By themselves those elements are nothing but indices to further extrapolation. So Gavin tells him how Highgate and Mitcham lead to further, different meanings. By itself Highgate, or Mitcham, signifies nothing. It's like a game in which corridors open to further niches and passages that might then lead to rooms. Or might not. Perhaps one day he is going to understand England and its people well enough to have that breadth of vision. He certainly means to.

His fellow-students in the group, or at least a couple of them, are helpful to him. Not in any egregious or patronizing way; they assume that cultures don't translate neatly or dovetail into each other with a satisfying click, so they mostly leave him alone, or ask him questions to satisfy some minor curiosities. In the early days, when he was just beginning to settle in and get introduced to some of the students in college, a standard question was *So is it very different then? Are you adjusting well? Is it a big shock?* His equally anodyne answers were vague mutterings about *No, not all that much, you know, we grew up reading Enid Blyton and, later, Agatha Christie and P.G. Wodehouse,* or, *Well, Calcutta is still such a colonial outpost . . .*

An important question now seems to be, 'How is it you read English Literature in *India* and came here to do more of it?' He surprises them by revealing that English Literature, as an academic discipline, was first taught in India, not in England; English administrators and policy-makers thought that the study of English Literature would have an ennobling and civilizing effect on the natives. They are thrown a bit, even a little embarrassed by this.

Declan is more wide-eyed than most at this nugget of

information. 'Does that mean it's compulsory in schools, like? Are you forced to read English Literature?' he asks, incredulous.

'No, it's not forced, but it's a discipline, a subject offered in universities. You can do a degree in it if you want to. Like Engineering or Maths.'

'It's a strange thought, isn't it, thousands of Indians poring over Shakespeare and Keats,' Declan says. Now that Ritwik has it pointed out to him by an outsider, it becomes unfamiliar, shifts patterns and configurations, like one of those exercises where he sits in his room and tries to imagine if there could be another him, looking in through a window at himself. What would that other he see? He often wants to look into his own room, locked and empty, from the outside; the bed, the books, the posters, all silent and waiting, as if they had a secret life of their own to which he couldn't be privy, but living on the second floor put paid to that fantasy.

He knows where Declan's coming from: how can anyone square a Dr Johnson reader with images of loincloth-clad, emaciated farmers standing next to equally cadaverous cows? Play 'The Association Game' with a white man, say 'India', and pat will come the word 'Poverty'; it's a coupling branded in the western mind, and who can say it's wrong? It's etched in his · mind too.

Sarah, sharp as ever, clothes this in other words, 'So how do you feel about being a post-colonial subject still studying the imperialists' literature?'

'Well . . .' he shrugs and hedges the question. 'It's not quite like that, is it? Or not always.'

The unasked question is *Did you go to an elite expensive school to come this far?* He can almost see the unuttered assumptions buzz and collide like bluebottles against window panes: *rich kid father must be well-connected or influential you know what they say about rich third-world people when they are wealthy they are wealthier than the extremely rich in the first-world privileged boy to have been bought an education which paved his way here.*

But it's not quite like that, not at all.

In Ritwik's mind, there were two types of poverty. One, the un-experienced sub-Saharan type, some sort of a shrine for the western media, with images of devouring eyes; fly-encrusted lips of children; women and men and offspring reduced to bare, forked animals, a cage of awkward stubborn bones barely sheathed in polished skin. The other was the slow drip drip drip which did not decimate populations in one fell swoop but hounded you every fraction of your time, got under your skin, into every space in your head and made you a lesser person, an edgy jittery animal because, you see, it never finished you off but gnawed at you here and there just to remind you it was there and that you were powerless in its half-grip. Gloating and victorious, but sleazily so, poverty not as Death triumphant in a Bosch nightmare but instead, one of his low, seedy, taunting thieves.

This was the poverty that played cat and mouse with Ritwik. It ruled in his world of worn-out clothes, of ill-fitting school shoes that ate into his toes but lasted forever with the help of his father's home repairs, of the tired vegetables sold at cut price when the greengrocers in the daily market were about to pack up and leave for the suburbs, of the hungry delight with which he waited for the treat of gristly and bony meat once in two months or so. It was everywhere, all the time, so much so that Ritwik either did not remember a time when it was not a daily struggle, or his memory did not match his father's nostalgic stories of days of plenty.

When he was four, his parents and their two sons had moved from their rented ground floor flat in Park Circus to his uncles' in Jadavpur. He had never been able to figure out the reason for this. In any case, he was too young to remember except for one somewhat unfocused memory of his mother, in one of her moods, shouting at him while dressing him: *You'll get nothing to eat but salt and rice at your uncles' house, we'll see then how fussy you can be about food.*

Knowledge is a cumulative business, acquired with the slow, unnoticed accretion of information here and there, and when four-year-old Ritwik arrived at his uncles' home, he had neither the tools nor the pile-up of evidence to comprehend their instant economically downward move in this act which, for him, was full of fun and excitement. The word for 'uncles' house' in Bengali is, after all, synonymous with boundless liberty and fun. Instead, growing up in Jadavpur became a growing intimacy with the shame of his father's moving in with his in-laws in *their* home.

A man with a wife and two children was not allowed to do that sort of thing. Whatever a marriage was for a woman, it certainly wasn't an invitation on the part of her family to her husband to extend the household. It was *decreasing* the numbers by giving the daughter away. To leave and then return with a retinue was one of those things which was socially forbidden, almost taboo. And to break that tacit rule was to invite the neighbourhood's tongues and eyes and ears inside the house and give them free play. Which may well have been the case all those years ago but with an important twist: Ritwik's father was silently expected to provide for everyone already living in the flat in Grange Road – a disabled grandmother, four unemployed uncles, one marriageable aunt – besides his wife and two sons.

Ritwik's grandfather had died nearly four years ago, having vehemently opposed the marriage of his daughter to a man thirty-three years older than her. He had apparently relented when Ritwik was born and had gone to see his first grandchild in hospital. With his death, the household in Grange Road had lost its breadwinner. He had left no savings, there was nothing in the way of investments, the flat was a rented one and they had fallen behind with the rent and bills for four years. The electricity had been cut off and one of the first things Ritwik's father did when they moved in was to have it restored.

Since the death of Ritwik's grandfather, his grandmother and uncles and aunt had lived from hand to mouth, sometimes on the charity of neighbours and distant relatives, at other times on meagre handouts and soft loans begged from people. Ritwik's father could not have moved in at a more opportune moment. It was an extended family of ten now, living in a three-bedroom flat, with one tiny kitchen, an equally small bathroom, a balcony fronting the street, and a larger room which was really no room, in the true sense, only an open space on to which all the bedrooms opened.

In some ways, there seemed to have been a barter, as tacit as the social rules his father's move to his in-laws' home broke. It was an understanding that this shameful thing would be tolerated if he took on the mantle of the chief (it turned out, only) earner. So to atone for the shaming move here his father took upon himself the more respectable and empowering role of head of family: head of family who earned money on which nine other people lived. It was only much later that Ritwik unravelled the killing illogic of someone trying to undo his own weaker position by accepting to be hobbled with leaching burdens: it was the Third World Debt principle. It was submerged blackmail, pure and simple. His father was sixty-one when all this was set in motion.

The continued unemployment of his uncles was a central source of tension in the family. Pradip, the eldest of the four brothers, did have a short-lived job as a bus conductor in a minibus on the Garia to BBD Bagh route but gave it up when his girlfriend at the time complained that this was not a suitably dignified job. 'It's a prestige issue,' she said, using that incontrovertible argument of the Bengalis.

Ritwik's childhood was signposted mostly by the frictions between his father, resentful of having four young men in their twenties and thirties living off him, and his uncles, who evaded, dodged and hid from his father and from any sense of adult responsibility. Sometimes this erupted into open confrontations, with his father trying to reason with them, or taunt and humiliate them into some sort of contribution to the running of the household. His uncles swallowed everything in guilty silence, and then slunk away, avoiding another run-in with their brother-in-law by returning home well after midnight. Weeks went by in this careful dance of avoidance, with Dida acting as choreographer, warning her sons off if her son-in-law was at home, or carrying news of the dominant mood to them so they could stay away or time their return home. In their absence, Ritwik's father took out his frustration on his wife with words carefully chosen for maximal damage.

'A bunch of illiterate spongers, that's what your brothers are. Don't they feel any shame, living off an old man? I'm not paying for them anymore; we'll have separate kitchens from now on –

they can fend for their own food. You can tell them that. Parasites, parasites!'

Silence from his mother.

'And your parents, both illiterate, they were good for nothing except breeding. Look at this bloody nest of vipers they've produced. All they did was litter. They didn't provide for your education, they did nothing, as if just animal breeding were qualification enough for title of parent. It reminds me of dogs. That's what your family is, a bloody bunch of strays.'

More silence from his mother. Sometimes quiet tears, or a storming out of the room. Then there were days of non-communication, slamming of doors, badly cooked food, setting down of plates with a crash and clatter. She took her anger out on her two sons, mostly on Ritwik. As soon as his father left the house, she rounded on him on some pretext or the other.

'Have you done your homework? Have you? Why are you wasting time then?' He got a sharp slap across his face, or was dragged by his hair across the room and pushed to the corner where his schoolbooks were piled. 'Now don't dare move until you've done the lesson. If it's not ready in an hour, I'll finish you off, do you understand, finish you off,' she screamed.

Ritwik, whimpering and scared, pulled out a book, any book, and let his eyes swim over random pages: irrigation in Punjab, how plants made their own food, why we should love and obey God. Nothing sank in; the words were just empty black marks on the page held down by trembling hands.

Whenever his father lashed out against his mother's family, Ritwik blindly took her side. There was no doubt that all that he said was true but articulating it so cruelly and corrosively made it an unfair stealth-weapon. As a child, he felt anxious and unhappy when his parents quarrelled: at the merest whiff of it –

something in the set of his mother's jaw, or the menace in her heavy tread – his heart began thudding painfully against his ribs. From a very early age, he learnt to sniff out gathering tension in the air, much like old people who can tell changes in the weather by the feeling in their joints. But this was inseparable from the sympathy he felt for her; he must have sensed how difficult it was for her to be in the middle, riven by divided affections and allegiances. She seemed to Ritwik to be a pathetic pawn in this war. *When elephants fight, it's the grass that suffers*, Dida used to say. Yes, his mother suffered.

Truth was, there was no effort on his uncles' part to make things better. They just grew a thicker hide. They knew they had it good: sleeping in till mid-day, having food waiting for them (when it was there), no rent to pay, no bills to think about. They knew if they left it long enough, a crisis would develop and their brother-in-law would have to do something about it, so they left it to him. The confrontations, unhappiness, the dividing lines that were slowly developing – all these seemed to them a small price to pay for the larger pleasures of laziness and living off someone else.

And if there were occasions when they did not have food waiting for them, they could always take it out on their mother. The whole family was a twisted version of some domino effect. They were all linked by their use of each other as channels of anger and resentment; a pressure on one point in this chain would invariably lead to effects all along the line. So Ritwik's father shouted at his wife; Ritwik's mother screamed and beat up her sons; his uncles either went underground or, when a showdown became inevitable, braved it out and then took out their humiliation on their paralysed mother.

Any excuse would do. Shirt was a recurring one. Pratik had

one decent shirt that he hid zealously away from his brothers. Every time one of his brothers felt the need to wear something special, something other than the one frayed shirt and one pair of trousers each of them had, he stole Pratik's fancy shirt. He either found out the hiding place by coercing his mother or, if she refused to tell, ransacked the whole house till he found it. By some malign law of probability, the shirt would go missing the very evening Pratik wanted to wear it himself. When he found out it had been stolen, his first target was his mother.

'You must have told Pradip. Only you knew where it was kept,' he shouted. (That was another thing: nobody spoke in that house, everyone shouted. Everything was done slightly awry to the civilized norm.)

'No, I didn't. I didn't know where you hid it,' Dida muttered.

'You did. You saw me putting it away under the mattress,' Pratik challenged.

Dida was scared now. 'Nn . . . o . . .' She started limping away.

Pratik saw that chink and pounced. Literally. He clutched her hair, pushed her against the wall and started banging her head against it. 'You did, you did. What am I going to wear tonight then?' he kept on shouting.

Ritwik's mother rushed in and separated them. She shouted back at her brother, 'How dare you do this to your own mother? You're an animal, an animal.' It petered out, aware of its own futility.

Pratik simmered till Pradip returned very late at night, hoping Pratik would be asleep so that he could slip the shirt back in under the mattress. No such luck: Pratik was waiting in the dark like a crouching feline.

Another fight broke out. The sound of two men fighting in a confined space in a tiny flat was like a little earthquake of thuds and crashes; it woke up everyone, even some of the neighbours. In the room where Ritwik and Aritra and his parents slept everyone started stirring. Ritwik's father did not miss this chance of delivering another blow to his wife. 'There, the dogs are at it again. There's no bloody peace in this house.' He made as if to get up and intervene but she stopped him.

'Why do you want to get involved if you hate them so much? Let them tear themselves to pieces, what do you care?' Her voice was like a spring coiled to the point of breakage.

'It's because of my sons. How can you bring up children in this hell? What do you think they're going to pick up from this?' he replied. The boys were wide awake now but they pretended to be asleep; at least they could spare their parents one added concern. Not only was Ritwik's heart knocking painfully against his chest again, there was also something new – a rising and falling column of sharp fire from behind his chestbone up to his throat, then down and then up again. He knew Aritra was awake because his breathing had gone very quiet and measured.

'Why did you come here then? How many times did I tell you, before we moved, don't give up the flat in Park Circus, don't give up the flat in Park Circus. Why didn't you listen to me?' Her words were a jet of acid hiss against glass: they were both trying not to wake up their children.

It was his father's turn to remain silent now, a guilty silence in that pitch dark room, as if she had exposed his complicity in the whole business and he had no reasonable defence with which to counter her accusation.

There was a loud crash followed by a thud in the other room. As one by one the neighbours' lights came on, Dida tried to intervene in the fight taking place right under her nose. She mumbled, 'What will the neighbours think?'

This was all the excuse the brothers needed. It was Pradip's turn to have a go at his mother. Like a feral dog, he turned his attention on her, crouching low beside the bed on which she lay. 'What did you say about the neighbours? What did you say?' he shouted.

She was too scared to answer. This just stoked the fire. He started slapping her face – one, two, three, four, the sound of skin on skin a neat sharp crack each time. 'You told him I wore his shirt. You're behind this.' She couldn't even move away from this assault: it took her a long time to shift her body from one side to another.

Pradip continued shouting, 'You're the bitch behind all this. That's what you do all day – carry tales from one camp to another, play people off against each other. You've nothing else to do all day, you sit in your chair and gossip.'

She was crying now, her mouth a helpless rictus of pain, but no sound escaped from her, not even a sob; it was as if she was trying to erase any sign of life that marked her out as another human being, to reduce herself to an inanimate object, so that her sons could ignore her and vent their fury on something else. At that point, Ritwik's mother entered the room.

'Aren't you ashamed of yourselves?' she said. Her voice was between a shout and a threat. 'What will everyone think?' The brothers loped away like chided dogs with their tails between their legs. It had happened before, it would happen again. Sometimes she tried to scare her brothers by reminding them that violence towards their own mother was one of the greatest sins possible. It was as bad as killing a cow; it would call down certain vengeance from the gods. Surely the gods had already cursed them for such unnatural behaviour: the squalor, the unhappiness, the menace, weren't all these really just effects of their displeasure with the family? This only had a loose hold on her brothers' minds for it came undone, readily and with slick, perfect ease, at the next flashpoint.

And so it went on.

Ritwik never understood what his father did for a living but felt instead a growing anxiety at its irregularity and meagreness. A broker, maybe? An in-between man in deals? A facilitator? As a young boy, when he had asked his father his profession, possibly because he had been set the standard school homework of writing five sentences on 'My Father', the answer had been, 'Engineer'. That had stuck for a very long time, along with other things whose residue he has started to scrape off slowly only now. It had acquired the status of truth. Even to this date, the 'father-as-engineer' picture stole in microseconds before the certainty of its untruth.

So what *did* he do? He really didn't know and not having been very close to his father, especially in those abrasive late teenage years, he hadn't made much of an effort to find out. It was partly to save both of them the embarrassment of having to address an issue which demanded fixed, stable answers in accordance with the fixed, stable structure given to parent-child relations. How would his father have faced up to an answer that was fuzzy, for he really did not have a profession category in which he could slot himself? How would Ritwik have taken such an answer, or shored up against his own uncertainties of childhood the flotsam of an old man's shame and insecurities?

The only established fact he had about his father's jobs was their requirement of his long presence. The regularity of his mother waiting for his arrival home from work, first in the balcony, and then walking out to the bus stop, was a stable cornerstone of his boyhood. There were late nights; eleven or midnight was worrying, especially for a man who had suffered three cardiac arrests. Ritwik remembered a tired man with his head down walking so slowly along the edges of the road, beside the margins of the open drains, that he could have been looking resignedly for something he had lost along the same stretch of the street as he had walked on it in the opposite direction earlier on in the day. An old old old man, thrown in unregarded corners, already half in the shadow of death.

Ritwik had always been, as far back as he could remember, embarrassed by an old and sick father. Until the age of eleven, he had been taken to school – a forty-minute bus ride from Jadavpur to Park Circus – by one member of the family or another. Sometimes, his father took him there and insisted on seeing him inside, seeing him mingle with the other boys before the bell rang for morning assembly. He tried to dodge and parry the growing unease and sense of shame, which set upon him as soon as they neared the school building, by several clumsy strategies – walking faster to create a distance between them, insisting that his father went home once they had reached the main gate and not accompany him inside, *see nobody's father goes inside why should you why don't you go back now I'll be all right*. The truth was that he didn't want to be physically associated with this shabby old man. On a few occasions he had even gratuitously lied to his friends that the man with him was the driver dropping him off to school en route to taking his father to his swanky office.

Although Ritwik didn't understand it then, part of the problem may have arisen from his unconscious reaction to the contrast between the class of boys – from well-heeled, middle-class to upper-middle-class families – who attended that school and his own lot. Always a progressive man, his father had decided that the children's education came first. 'Without knowledge of the English language, you're crippled,' he used to say. If sacrifices had to be made for it, they would be made in some other household department. No compromise was ever to be made with the boys' schooling: that was sacrosanct.

That, and books. Not in any superstitious way that was the general air in his uncles' house, where he had to pick up books, paper, pens, pencils, erasers, pencil sharpeners – anything remotely connected to the world of study – and touch them to his forehead and chest, in the quick gesture of prayer, if he touched them accidentally with his feet. Books and related objects were sacred to Saraswati, the goddess of learning, and to bring feet anywhere near them was a mark of grave disrespect and would bring down a curse from her: she would never bless the offender with the gift of learning. Ritwik did all these things out of fear and, later, out of habit, but his father taught him a different sanctity of books.

It started when he was six. His father bought him a slim, big book, so thin it could be used for swatting mosquitoes with the sound and motion of a slap, a slipper book, as it was called. The title of the book was *Maya of Mohenjo-daro* and it told the story of Maya, also six, who lived in the ancient city of Mohenjo-daro and accompanied her father one morning to the Great Bath and from there to the Great Granary via the paved and clean streets of the town, which were laid out in such a way that the winds cleaned them every day. At the end of the day, both father and daughter made their way back home after he had bought her an orange woollen ball the colour of the setting sun. Happy, Maya returned home and was ready to go to bed when she noticed that her ball was like the sun, now sinking below the horizon in a blaze of orange and red fire.

Ritwik read it over and over again, and asked his father scores of questions: 'Where is Mohenjo-daro?', 'What is an ancient city?', 'How old is ancient?', 'What is civilization?', 'Can I have a fluffy orange ball the colour of the sun?' This last was, of course, the main thrust. In a book almost wholly illustrated in sepia and other shades of brown, the orange ball stood out like a lamp in the environing dark, almost ready to jump out of Maya's dark hands into his. Every time he turned back to the page in which the bright ball first appeared it would seem to Ritwik that an added luminosity had stolen into his room. He stared and stared at the ball as his father told him about things he barely understood – Harappa, Indus Valley, ancient civilizations. In the book, Maya and her father were always smiling serenely. He didn't know it was a strange longing that he felt each time he opened it.

Whenever a book was demanded by Ritwik, it arrived. His father went and ordered it in 'Study', the tiny bookshop in Jadavpur Central Market, paid in advance, and the book appeared, wrapped in crisp brown paper, in a week or two. *Baba, I'd like to join the school quiz team I need General Knowledge books the four volumes of the Bournvita Quiz Book.* Or, *Baba, volumes five to seven of the Bournvita Book are out now can I have them soon.* This was at a time when the landlord, Khokababu, visited the house weekly to demand the back payments on arrears and his father pretended to be too ill to go to work so that Khokababu could extend the deadline on sympathetic grounds. The household subsisted on rice and boiled potatoes for an entire week but there was no stinting with Ritwik's books, no complaints about how expensive they were.

His mother said, 'You're spoilt, you know. Before the words fall from your lips, your father goes out and does your bidding.' He never understood whether she said this with disapproval or pride.

The Bournvita books were hardbound, the size of coffee-table books, with gold lettering on the spines. He guarded them with his life while his uncles looked at them with silent recrimination. On one occasion he heard Pratim saying to his mother, 'All this talk of no money, no money, no money, rents unpaid, electricity bills unpaid, we're constantly under fire from Jamaibabu, where's all the money for these swish books coming from?' Ritwik promptly hid them and only took them out when his uncles were out and when he was sure he could hide from the prying eyes of Dida.

And then one day the *Collins Concise Encyclopaedia* arrived, stout, big and substantial, in its bright red dust jacket, twelve hundred-odd pages of close, compact type on thin, tissue-like paper. It had black and white pictures as well: the bearded Louis Pasteur and Johannes Brahms; a severe yet benign Marie Curie; Keats reading an octavo volume with one hand on his forehead; a Chardin still-life with a vase of flowers; winged seeds that are dispersed by the wind; Byron in Greek headgear. It cost forty rupees and he had gone out with his father to get it from 'Study'. He had beamed all the way there and back while his father cautioned him, 'Don't let anyone find out, especially Dida and your uncles. Keep it in a safe place, it costs a lot of money. . .' Ritwik plunged into it like a fish released from captivity into the waters again.

The excitement of the book never wore off; instead it surprised him with its myriad forms. First, there was the excitement of discovering an entry that was familiar to him. It gave him a little shiver of joy to see on the certainty of the printed page little areas of his mind précised into three or four close-knit lines. He looked up *Tagore, Rabindranath*; *photosynthesis*; *mycology*; *Beethoven, Ludwig van*; *electrocardiogram* with the thrill of seeing known things in unfamiliar and new settings, in the prestige of print. It endorsed his knowledge in some kind of way at the same time as it opened up new avenues in a proliferative dance. So *gene* led to *DNA*, *DNA* led to *double-helix*, from there to *Watson and Crick* through *meiosis* and *mitosis*, *cell division* to *McClintock, Barbara*. It was like the picture of nerve dendrons in his biology book, a web of paths and sub-paths, a familiar road suddenly leading him down unknown ones till he ended up himself as a wide-open space from the initial little cluster he had started off as.

At other times it was a different joy of finding out totally unknown things. There was curiosity, bafflement and, once again, that intense chasing dance, the moves of some of which he could not master for a long time. Someone had mentioned Bach in school so he came home and looked it up. There seemed to be a lot of them, and he didn't know the first names, but he assumed it must be *Bach, Johann Sebastian*, because he had the maximum number of lines to his name. It led him on separate enquiries: a slowly enclosing one from *counterpoint*, to *canon*, to *fugue*, to *suite*; the other, a widening dance: *Bach, Johann Sebastian*; *Rameau, Jean-Philippe*; *Albinoni, Tomasso*; *Vivaldi, Antonio*; *Couperin, Louis* . . . It reminded him of those funny chapters in the Old Testament which went on and on and on about how Shem begat Arphaxad begat Salah begat Eber begat Peleg, theoretically stretching to the here and now, but this one was different: each name, each term was a new world, not a dead proper noun on the page.

There was a lot he didn't understand. When this happened, he committed the thing to memory or read it over and over again, ten times, fourteen times, repeating **counterpoint** *The term comes from the idea of note-against-note, or point-against-point, the Latin for which is **punctus contra punctum**. It consists of melodic lines that are heard against one another, and are woven together so that their individual notes harmonize. In this sense Counterpoint is the same as **Polyphony**,* repeating it in his head as a rapid chant, as though manipulating this stubborn thing and chasing its strewn spores across other pages with such white-hot doggedness would suddenly make it give up its resilient secret. When he shut the book at last and looked around him, at the bare whitewashed walls, the cobwebby mosquito nets in the windows, the gathering dust everywhere, he saw them differently, as though the whole world had been newly named. Was this what Brother Matthew meant when he talked about new heaven, new earth?

Outside, another conflict had erupted. Pratim had been hiding for three days because Mr Malvya from across the street had told Ritwik's mother that he had lent Pratim some money which he said he would return in a week. 'He wanted about three hundred rupees; he said you haven't been able to pay the boys' school fees for over two months now. I didn't have three hundred with me, I gave him a hundred and seventy-five,' he said. He had been clearly embarrassed confronting her with their inability to pay for their children's education. Ritwik's mother had been furious at this unashamed lie; she didn't know which was worse – telling Mr Malvya that Pratim had lied or letting him continue to think that it was she who had sent her brother out to beg for some money. Each was equally humiliating.

As always, it was Dida who had informed Pratim that

everyone knew what he had done. So he had lain low for a few days, but it was a small, enclosed world, and as Dida frequently said, 'The world is round, remember; things have a habit of coming back full circle.' Pratim too reached the completion of this particular circle a bit too quickly for his comfort and faced the wrath of his sister and Jamaibabu.

'We won't be able to show our faces to our neighbours any more,' Ritwik's mother shouted. 'The shame, the shame!' Pratim decided to keep quiet and ride it out; all this was so much bluster and wind, it would blow over soon. After all, everyone knew he couldn't repay the money and, because he had used the boys' school fees as an excuse, Jamaibabu was going to be shamed into paying it back to save his face, never mind what the truth was. Besides, he didn't care. It was embarrassing for them, not for him; he was going to keep himself in the shadows for a few more weeks and everything would be buried under the weight of a new crisis.

Ritwik listened to the shouting outside with horror. His mother had begun crying, deep, wretched sobs of frustration and anger. There was going to be more of this when his father returned home. She would have to tell him; another round of recriminations, bitterness, tension would ensue. That heave and slow rattle behind his ribs was starting again. He didn't want to hear any more, he just wanted the draining thudding inside to stop, stop now. He squeezed his eyes shut, tight tight tight, till there were exploding colours inside his eyeballs, and let his voice articulate the words he had memorized from the page in front of him, to drown out the squabble: **sonata form**: . . . *regular sonata form movement falls into 3 main sections: 1. EXPOSITION (usually containing two subjects, the first subject is in tonic key, the second subject . . .*

'What have you done with the money? WHAT HAVE YOU DONE WITH IT?'

in dominant; there may be further subjects), often repeated and giving way to 2. DEVELOPMENT (here the material from the Exposition . . .

'. . . gambling or drinking? How low can you sink? Did you think about the boys when you did it? Did you? I try so hard to raise . . .'

This time with effort coiled up into a ball: *3. RECAPITULATION (in which the essential feature is the return of the second subject but now in the home key or the tonic, and the repetition of Exposition material, though often with modification). The Recapitulation has a coda, which helps provide a proper feeling of finality. Some composers, including Beethoven, extend this coda into what, to all intents and purposes, is a second Development section. The principle behind sonata form is key relationships.*

Everything fell away. He was left just with a rustling page and the accumulative music of repeated words.

The space between the shit-brown door and the hinge offers him a strip of view, just a thin, long line of fluorescent-lit space. He has to keep one eye shut, though, and one side of his face pressed to the cold metal of the door. If he shifts between the right eye and the left, the view from the crack changes in a parallactic dance. Right left, right left, right left. They don't add up to a seamless whole, there is either an overlap or a gap, he can't understand which.

Luckily, he doesn't have to stand in this position all the time, neck twisted, eyes strained. Because the toilets are underground, he can hear heavy footsteps descending; only then does he get up from the toilet seat and move to his spyline swiftly to catch the man entering the toilets while he passes through that narrow ribbon of vision for a fleeting second. He's cautious and doesn't want to lose the man during that split second so he rushes to the door as soon as he hears footsteps running down.

There are two staircases leading down to the two wide pissoirs, all brushed aluminium and falling jets of water, separated by a long length of mirrors with four washbasins and an open space off which four cubicles open on either side. The cubicle Ritwik occupies, his favourite one, is an anomaly that disturbs this elegant symmetry; it is placed diagonally behind the two small cubicles which open out from one side of the short wide corridor leading to the mirrors and sinks. There is no corresponding cubicle on the other side. If he draws a straight line through the middle of the sinks and corridor, each half of the St. Giles public toilets almost becomes a mirror image of the other. Almost, because his cubicle, the biggest one, breaks this symmetry: it is like a stray, careless note in a perfect fugue.

But he likes it best because it offers him a view of who's coming in, who's going out, without having to get out of the toilet and do all the ridiculous things to signal he was really using the loo – flush, wait two seconds, open the door noisily, get out, head straight for the sinks, wash hands for a long time, shake hands, go to the dryers and spend another five minutes there, pressing the 'on' button each time it stops, once, twice, three times, as if he is really drying his hands.

The hot air dispensers are a stale joke, a cliché: everyone in the trade knows that if the button is pressed more than two times the last thing that is happening is hand-drying. Yet it is allowed, almost lovingly indulged, its loud, whirry drone providing a reassuring matrix of meaning to the game. It is so transparent a guise that it is not a guise any more but a tattered, old, understood code. Ritwik loves it; the sound sends a little surge of camaraderie coursing through him: he knows he is in the company of familiar strangers.

The other reasons he prefers this particular cubicle to the others is because it is so roomy. There is space enough for someone to sleep in there comfortably in a sleeping bag. Three people could fit inside without finding it a squish. This aspect is readily exploited as and when the opportunities and inclinations arise.

There is graffiti on the walls, the door, even some on the ceiling. Most of it seems to be written with marker pens, some with pencil or biro, and some etched and scratched on to the paint of the metal door and the one metal wall with sharp objects. There are the usual ones: 'For cock action call 865974', 'Any horny 18–21y old around looking for 9" cock here every Friday and Saturday evening. Show hard at the urinals', '8 in cock, cut, for sucking fucking Sunday afternoon. Genuine. Leave message below with date and time.'

There is one that can only be described as super-efficient: 'I love to suck young juicy cocks and swallow your creamy spunk. Make date'. And then, below, five columns: name, age, size, date, time. The writer has even taken the trouble of drawing vertical and horizontal lines, so the whole thing looks like a statistical table. There are two entries as well in the columns. The age is always under twenty-one, the size never below seven inches. 'Genuine' seems to be a desirable quality: more than half the messages have that word as its final note. Occasionally, they get cleaned or painted away but some are too stubbornly written with invincible ink, they just fade a bit. Soon others appear and before long it is thick with these urgent, hot words again.

Every night he takes some time to read them: they ease him

into the swing of things and even get him aroused. His favourite one is:

> Batter my arse, three persons at the door
> Who but knock, breathe, rub, and seeke to mend;
> That I may rise, and stand, o'erthrow mee, and bend
> On knees, to breake, blowe, burn and make me new.

The changes to the sonnet are minimal and not especially clever but seeing it in that context reconfigures it for Ritwik in such a way that there is no other way to look at it any longer but as a feverish request for a trinitarian gang-bang. The metaphors, the desire behind the writing, all seem to fall into place with such ease it is as if he has at last unlocked a room to which he has been denied complete access for a long time. He laughs silently for some time at the aptness of the whole thing. He wonders if in his essay on the metaphysicals he could get away with saying that the seventeenth-century religious poet loiters with intent in his prayer closet, cruising god. The final three lines – 'Take mee to you, imprison mee, for I / Except you enthrall mee, never shall be free, / Nor ever chast, except you ravish mee' – when they come, are exact and inevitable. Some marginalia have been added to the sonnet: 'Doesn't scan any more you poof wanker' and 'Posh turd burglar fuck off to your AIDS.'

This is a true laboratory of the senses: all of them are stretched to their experiential limits – the eye at the door hinge; the ears pricked to catch footsteps entering or exiting, the flush of the cistern, the hissing drum of a jet of urine hitting the metal pissoir, running water and gurgling sink, the slightest movement and shift of feet; the nose acclimatized to the acrid bite of ammonia, disinfectant and sometimes the wafting stench of shit.

The way everything is registered on impeccably tuned keys of sight, sound and smell here, he could easily be a hunter in the wild; either that or a beast of prey, sensing out danger even in the slightest change of wind direction.

There are infinite ways in which this game is played out, all set but all indeterminate at the same time. The unchanging basis for all, however, is the checking out of goods, an unillusioned appraisal. The concept of 'goods' varies, of course.

A standard procedure for Ritwik is to stay inside his cubicle if the fleeting slit-view of a man entering the toilets does not appeal. If it does, he still remains locked in; after all, the man could have come in for an innocent piss only. This is either confirmed or negated in the next few minutes by one or more of various signals – not exiting after the standard time taken for a pee, washing hands at the sink for a long time (though this could be any other person in the toilets, but chances are it is the new arrival), that telling hand-dryer business, entering a cubicle *after* his piss and locking himself in . . . it is like a problem in logic: if p, then not q, but only after a finite set of conditions, • {a, b, c . . . n}, has been satisfied.

And yet, and yet, it lacks the fixity of logic because the elements of the set to be satisfied have margins of uncertainty themselves. For example, how can entering a cubicle after a reasonable time spent at the urinal be taken as a *certain* sign of cruising? But even if in these cases the laws of probability work to the advantage of the cruiser, everything could come down like a house of cards if the final checking out doesn't lead to the neat snuggling of two desires fitting each other like identical spoons.

Everything is predicated on that meeting. There are a number of ways leading to it:

1. Standing at the pissoir, his cock out, massaged to erection. He hides it and pretends he has just finished peeing, shaking the last dribble off it if some kosher pisser enters the toilet. Sometimes he just buttons up and enters his cubicle. If it isn't a genuine pisser, and he likes the look of the man, he stands there, making it obvious what he's doing. Chances of a hit on this one: 50–50, 50 for his liking the man, 50 the other way around.

2. If the view from his spystrip really dazzles, and chances of this are low anyway, he rushes out after three or four seconds, making sure he has flushed noisily – just another casual public toilet user emerging from a cubicle to wash and dry his hands zealously. Chances of the dazzling one being a cottager: low. Chances of that click of reciprocal desire: still lower.

3. On some occasions, 2 leads to 1, if he's convinced the newcomer at the urinal is doing anything but urinating, or urinating AND.

4. Then there is the possibility of Ritwik's favourite cubicle being occupied by someone else. In this event, which irritates him immensely, as if he has some proprietary right over that one, he reluctantly confines himself to one of the smaller, inferior ones. Their disadvantages are many, not having a view being the most crippling; he has to depend solely on his ears then. But there is one thing working for them: being adjacent to another cubicle, a possible pick-up might happen without having to go through 1, 2, and 3. After a while it becomes obvious why the man in the next cubicle has entered it. Once that is confirmed, another little game of advancing feet, inch by inch, to the gap under the partition wall begins. Often this is preceded by noises, such as low moaning, or letting out heavy breaths in an overdone I'm-really-horny way. Once the feet touch, at least one certainty has been established. This could be

followed by notes written on loo paper and passed on under the gap: 'Do you have a place?', usually, to start off with. Or just standing on the toilet seat and peeping over the wall into the next cubicle to see what he's letting himself in for. No. 4 is a more prolonged game with elements of a blind date to it. It's more exciting, sometimes, than 2 or 3, or even 1.

5. Several people at the urinals. Sometimes this has what Ritwik calls the 'honeypot effect' – one or two cruising men at the urinals suddenly start attracting practically all the cottagers in the St. Giles toilets until there is a row of men, cocks out, checking each other out, all heads tilted left or right, angled downwards, sometimes craning back to catch the eye of someone at the pissoir across on the other side of the mirrors and sinks. It is a predictable set of movements, but of all the methods, this gives the most direct access to the goods. This is when it becomes most transparently a marketplace: there is no pissing around, wasting time and acting out tired old moves; it is sharp, to the point and immediately effective. Or not, but in that case at least the people involved are not left hanging on, thinking will he won't he will he won't he while doing some more hand-drying and pretend pissing and all that nonsense.

No. 5 is also unflinchingly frank: Ritwik knows quickly who wants him and who doesn't. Rejection, however couched, even if it involves just tucking a penis in and moving away to a position beside another person, is still rejection and potentially bruising. But it's all part of the game, or the logic of the meat market: would a shopper buy maggoty meat out of kindness to the poor lamb which had died or the butcher who didn't have any better? Ritwik himself has learned, a bit too efficiently, to reject: it is best done swiftly otherwise he accuses himself of leading them on and feels slightly guilty about it. Also very pleased, because someone fancies him. To be in the position of saying 'no' to someone and turning him down is one of the greatest luxuries in life, he reckons. He has it here, sometimes.

There are the beginnings of a fraternity here among some of the regulars, of whom Ritwik has become one. He smiles at some of them, or nods and acknowledges their presence and some are glad of this small social gesture. It's not solidarity or anything, just a flickering registration of the commonality that brings them together underground. They don't know each other's names, where they live, or indeed, where they disappear once they reach the upper world. They only exist for each other in this strip-lit netherworld.

Ritwik has had sex with a couple of these regulars. There's Martin who works for British Rail, has short spiky hair and a good-natured leer permanently stuck on his face. And the other man, whose name he doesn't know or hasn't bothered to find out, who takes off all his clothes, every single stitch, and leaves his cubicle door wide open while playing with himself and fingering his arsehole. He shuts it as soon as he hears new footsteps but if he thinks it's safe he opens the door fully again.

There is no rivalry within this set of people; in fact, when a newcomer arrives and shows an interest in one of them, the rest, who know they are not fancied, egg on the lucky one. They keep watch if the people they are familiar with are having sex in the open: it's a give-and-take, this one – they get the pleasure of watching and in return they provide an early warning service.

Sometimes they warn off each other from 'time-wasters', people who come and endlessly tease, hang around, show cock, peep, peer, lock themselves in cubicles for ages but ultimately never pick up anyone. Just as 'genuine' is a high recommendation in this world, 'time-waster' is equally pejorative.

Ritwik is glad to have the more experienced ones dissuade him from running down such cul-de-sacs. It is, of course, a minor corollary of Sod's Law that almost every 'time-waster' is gorgeous.

Ritwik also realizes, in slow stages, that his is a type of minority appeal, catering to the 'special interest' group rather than the mainstream, because of his nationality, looks, skin colour. He keeps pushing the word 'race' away. The mainstream is blonde, white, young, slim. Or, more accurately, that is the desired mainstream. He doesn't satisfy the crucial first two although the last two can influence the swing cruisers.

One nameless man, to whose two-up two-down off the Woodstock Road he goes back one night from St. Giles, tells him how this world divides into two classes: the rice queens – men who fancy Oriental guys – and the potato queens – men who have a thing for white British men. That puts him in a type of classificatory limbo, although for lack of a better taxonomy the latter term will have to do. All in all, if the swing cottagers are taken into account, he doesn't do too badly although it could be better, significantly better.

This cottaging business is developing into a kind of fixture in Ritwik's life. Every evening, or almost every evening, he finds his way here unerringly, like an insect following a pheromone track. Sometimes he does a round at the Angel and Greyhound Meadow under Magdalen Bridge, but it is a less familiar dance, not of the thoroughly rehearsed St. Giles variety. Besides, St. Giles offers solid shelter from the frequent rains and wind. And an embarrassment of riches.

That, above all, is what he finds incredible – the sheer availability at practically all times, the accepted and understood fact that at certain types of places, at certain times, you can get what you want. It's there for the taking; you just have to turn up and wait for it.

But there are good days and bad days. There are cold evenings of nearly frozen feet, the socks like a thick sheath of ice, spent waiting, waiting for footsteps which are few and far between, evenings when the cottaging population seems to have become almost extinct, or when the few available ones do not please at all. To wait is to experience time in its purest form; he understands how viscous, like treacle, it is in its unadulterated state. During these evenings, he paces around inside his cubicle, running to the hinge at the slightest sound. Some of these evenings seem to be jinxed – only the old, dirty-mac brigade seems to be out hunting.

Sometimes he sits on the toilet seat and thinks of how to carry on the essay from where he left off, still lying on his desk under the weight of a bottle of Quink. Sentences flit and hide, like a sudden green flapping and screeching of parrots overhead: *It is the bright and battering sandal of representation that bruises Hopkins, not dark nights of the soul, not theological despair, not the fugitive presence/absence of God. How to hold and contain, how to speak God's grandeur, and nature, His book's, in fallen language, language 'soiled with trade', other than to burn, buckle and bend the old language to forge a new? This straining against linguistic representation is acted out as a personal drama of despair, but, paradoxically enough, the bruising of the poet releases his scent, like camomile or thyme crushed . . .* The rain beats out its peculiar music on the reinforced glass and concrete roof overhead. It lulls and comforts him. All he is waiting for is the sound of the right footsteps.

IV.

The room is enormous and for one which contains such a lot of furniture – an ornate gilt mirror, chairs, a sofa, a divan, a grand piano with its legs resting on small saucers of water to prevent insects from climbing it and building their colonies inside, and books, books everywhere, in glass-fronted dark wood cupboards taking up two entire walls and a large section of the third – it seems unusually full of light. The curtains are not heavy and the two doors are wide open, one to the courtyard, one to the interior, which is also filled with diffuse light on this sunny day, so rare for monsoon. Miss Gilby has time to take in the room and its furnishings before Bimala arrives accompanied by her husband for her first meeting with her English tutor and companion. Miss Gilby tries to steady her hand around her teacup; she is surprised she is as nervous with anticipation as possibly Bimala is this morning.

She moves over to one of the bookcases; this appears to be the one that houses English books only. Complete works of Shakespeare. The collected poetry and prose of Milton. The works of Dr Johnson. There's a lot of poetry: Wordsworth, Keats, Shelley, Byron, Browning, Tennyson. Beautiful octavo editions in brown leather with gold-tooled letters on the spine.

She picks out one that says, laconically, 'Lyrics' only and starts leafing through it. Instantly she recognizes it as the volume of medieval English short poems so beloved of her and Violet, the very book from which they took turns to read aloud to each other on evenings spent in each other's company only. A random poem catches her eye – 'Now springes the spray,/All for love I am so seek/That slepen I ne may' – then another: 'He cam also stille/Ther his moder was,/As dew in Aprille/That falleth on the grass.' She is so stabbed with nostalgia, with a kind of homesickness, that she puts the book back and carries on with the safer activity of reading only the titles on spines. Godwin, Mary Wollstonecraft, Thomas More, Locke. She moves to another cupboard. This contains only Bengali books. She has to bend slightly and crane her neck in order to read the writing on the spines. She can only manage to do this slowly in the beginning. Before she has had a chance to decipher some of the letters, as a little test of her fledgling literacy in the language, she notices an edition of Mrs Beeton. Surely a mistake in shelving otherwise how could it have strayed here, among the Bengali books, she thinks, when she hears footsteps and the swish of fabric outside. Without hurrying, she moves to the sofa, sits and puts down her cup on the glass-covered table in front of her.

As husband and wife enter the room, Miss Gilby stands up. Mr Roy Chowdhury says, 'No, no, Miss Gilby, please remain seated, there's no need to stand.'

Bimala stands at his side, head down, the *aanchol* of her sari lifted up to the back of her head and over it, the rich magnetic blue of the cloth accentuating the deep vermilion parting in the middle. She looks as if she would prefer to be invisible or to hide behind her husband. Dark skinned, slightly built, arms with bangles – gold, coral, the mandatory white shell of the married woman – but nothing ostentatious, the sleeves of her simple blue blouse coming down to her elbows, a plain gold chain around her neck, small gold earrings. She refuses to look anywhere except at the coloured geometric designs on the tiled floor.

Miss Gilby takes in a deep breath – her heart is beating very fast – and says as clearly as she can manage, 'How do you do Bimala. It is such a pleasure to meet you at last,' every word separate, enunciated, crystalline.

Bimala keeps her head bowed. Her husband stands at her side and says something in Bengali, which Miss Gilby cannot quite follow. They advance into the room, she so draggingly that it seems she is willing the floor to open up and swallow her, and take their seats on the divan opposite.

Mr Roy Chowdhury addresses Miss Gilby: 'She's feeling very shy. She's been so nervous about this meeting that she has stayed up nearly three nights in a row.' He laughs affectionately. Bimala whispers something quickly to him. The body language leaves Miss Gilby in no doubt that she is aghast that her husband should reveal this to her English tutor. Which means, Miss Gilby rejoices in her heart, Bimala understands a lot more English than she had been led to believe.

'What is there to be nervous about? I'm here to be your friend.' Miss Gilby tries to make her voice as amiable as possible.

There is no verbal response from Bimala but she lifts up her face and looks at Miss Gilby. The large, doe-dark eyes take in the English lady, perhaps the first one she has ever seen at such close range. There is a hint of a smile in the corners of her mouth. She looks down almost immediately again.

Mr Roy Chowdhury and Miss Gilby exchange glances that are at once amused and protective, the sort of look parents and teachers exchange over a child struck dumb by shyness. He says, 'I think she will speak but it might take time.'

Miss Gilby hastens to allay, 'Don't worry, this is just the first meeting. I'm sure she'll open up with time, won't you, Bimala?' She turns her gaze on the young woman who still continues concentrating steadfastly on the patterns on the floor.

Bimala says nothing then she whispers to her husband. Mr Roy Chowdhury nods enthusiastically, says something back, but Bimala seems to react to it with even greater withdrawal.

Mr Roy Chowdhury asks Miss Gilby, 'Bimala wants to serve you some sweets that she has made herself. She wants me to ask you if you will have some.'

Miss Gilby immediately seizes her opportunity. 'Yes, of course, I will be delighted. But on one condition.' She pauses. Bimala looks up expectantly. Good, thinks Miss Gilby, she's understood every single word.

She speaks slowly and clearly, 'I will be very happy to eat the sweets you have prepared, Bimala, but only if you ask me directly, not through your husband.'

Mr Roy Chowdhury is pleasantly surprised by this move. He looks at the Englishwoman with admiration.

The silence in the room is expectant. Mr Roy Chowdhury turns to his wife and asks gently, in English, 'Did you hear that? Aren't you going to ask her, Bimala?'

Bimala has her hands clasped tightly as if in desperate prayer. She whispers something to her husband and before he can say anything, she gets up and runs out of the room, a flurry of swishing sari and tinkling bangles and anklets.

Mr Roy Chowdhury breaks the surprised silence by chuckling out loud. Miss Gilby joins in too. He says, 'It's all a bit new for her. It's been only a year that she has stepped out of the *andarmahal.*'

'Please don't apologize, I understand how terrifying it must be for her. Where did she disappear?'

'I think she's gone to get you tea. I'll be surprised if she comes back. She'll probably send one of the servants.'

She smiles in acknowledgement. They sit talking for a while – he asks her if she is comfortable, if she needs anything, apologizes for any oversight on his part – he's unfailingly gentle and courteous.

From the sound of footsteps outside, they know that Bimala isn't the one who is approaching the room; there is no music from her bangles and anklets, but instead the gentle tremor of crockery and cutlery being transported carefully on a tray. A servant appears at the threshold. Mr Roy Chowdhury says something, he enters, puts the huge tea tray down on the table between them and departs.

'Good, tea's arrived. Now, Miss Gilby, how do you take your tea?'

There is a great deal of china on the plate, all white, and the teapot is covered in a cosy that has been beautifully embroidered with a motif of songbirds and creepers and roses. Miss Gilby is certain it is Bimala's handiwork, a special object to be taken out for a special occasion, or maybe even made for this one. The tray is laden with small dishes containing about six varieties of sweets, four of each.

'Goodness,' Miss Gilby exclaims, 'is this all her work? There's just far too much of it for two. Won't she be joining us?'

'I doubt very much. But you must try one of each, at the very least. Otherwise, she'll think you don't like her.' He can't help smiling when he says this.

Miss Gilby laughs: she is not wound up inside any more. As she watches Mr Roy Chowdhury pour tea, there is once again the sound of footfall outside and, along with it, the jingle of bangles, the rustling of cloth. It stops suddenly. Expecting Bimala, both Mr Roy Chowdhury and Miss Gilby look up. There is a long pause but no one enters. They look at each other and exchange a conspiratorial smile.

'I think she wants to hear what you think of her sweets. Or what the two of us have planned for her,' Mr Roy Chowdhury whispers.

Miss Gilby whispers too, 'Does she know that we know?'

Mr Roy Chowdhury raises his voice and calls out to her. Instantly, there is a sound of hasty retreat, footsteps, rustling, tinkling, all fading down to the interior of the house. Mr Roy Chowdhury and Miss Gilby fall about laughing as if they've been the ones caught playing children's games.

The house, called 'Dighi Bari', or 'Lake House' – although there is no lake near it, just a big pond with dark, unfathomable water and wet, green woods ringing most of its circumference – is big, not half as big as the palace of the Nawab of Motibagh, but capacious enough for it to be recognized as a local *zamindar*'s house: three storeys, painted a buttery yellow, in a regular quadrilateral shape, enclosing a large, brick-paved central courtyard. All the rooms in the house open out on to this courtyard. The rooms facing east look out on to a garden, big and rambling, which leads ultimately to a track to the village, about half a mile away: this is the designated 'front' of the house. Miss Gilby has her quarters in this section of the house (East Wing, she calls it) on the top storey. Mr Roy Chowdhury must have told the *malee* about the English love of gardens, so he has dutifully brought up dozens of pots of plants and flowers and arranged them on the verandah outside her rooms. There are canna, zinnia, dahlia, rose, even petunia and snapdragon, a couple of ficus plants, a flowering jasmine, which he has lovingly trailed around the iron railings. He comes to water the plants every morning, bows low when he sees the *memsahib*, so incongruous in this house, so conspicuous in this village, which has hardly ever seen a white face.

While this back verandah with the plants, which is also a running corridor linking all the rooms on that floor, looks out on to the courtyard below, she notices that half of the first floor – the two sides on the floor directly below hers – situated to the west-facing back of the house, which should open east to the courtyard, have wooden shutters and stained glass running their entire length, from the floor to the ceiling. The other side of the rooms in that 'West Wing' presumably has a view of the woods that nestle the dark pond that gives the house its name. This is the *andarmahal*, the secluded area of the house where the women live and, until recently, Bimala did too. She hasn't been invited to see that area; it's not that she has been told to stay off, but just that that section of the house hasn't featured in any conversation so far. The open area of that floor is Mr Roy Chowdhury and Bimala's quarters, while the ground floor is given over to a study, the living room, three offices, a 'meeting room' for conducting business, and a smaller library.

It is in the living room that Miss Gilby gives piano lessons to Bimala and conducts most of the English lessons as well. A few lessons have occasionally taken place in Miss Gilby's study upstairs – she knows Bimala is quite curious to see how a *memsahib* might appoint her living space – and it is very likely that they are going to take place in that more intimate room with increasing frequency. One thing Miss Gilby knows for certain is that the passage from stilted, shy formality to an apparently easy companionship in Indian societies is swift, but whether she will be let in to that intimacy is another question. She will have to wait and see.

The first lesson is in the living room. Miss Gilby has requested Mr Roy Chowdhury not to accompany his wife to the lessons: the urge towards dependence on her husband would be too much and, consequently, learning would become a protracted business. He has thought the idea very commendable.

Very shortly after one of these lessons, as soon as Bimala departs and Miss Gilby starts to clear up a little, she notices that Bimala has left behind her exercise book, her textbooks, her pencils, everything she needs for her homework, on the table at which they have been working. She gathers them up quickly, in a swift swoop of her hands, and runs out after Bimala. She sees her bright yellow sari disappearing through a door leading to the *andarmahal*. In her haste, she forgets social rules, what's out of bounds and what's not; she rushes down the stairs, books and pencils in hand, and reaches the floor below. Across from the landing, there is a big wooden door, with coloured glass filling up the space between the top of the doorframe and the ceiling. She knocks on the door then pushes it open and enters. There are three or four low wooden *chowkee*s on the white mosaic floor. It is much darker here than in Miss Gilby's open verandah, but the grass-green and red panes in the glass section above the dark brown painted wooden shutters throw fuzzy gules of coloured light on the white mosaic here and there. A servant is sitting in a corner, cutting vegetables and potatoes on a *bonti*. Seeing Miss Gilby she gasps, shrilly, immediately draws her *aanchol* over her face, runs around one of the corners and disappears. Miss Gilby suddenly stops in her tracks, realizing what she has done. Before she can turn around to go, a woman appears around the corner of the verandah. She wears white, unrelieved, impeccable white cotton, draped around her in a shapeless roll; her head is shaved, her face drawn and pale, there are dark circles under her eyes. She takes one glance at Miss Gilby, shrieks and runs away. A gramophone is playing in one of the rooms, its hissy, scratchy, high-pitched sound almost totally distorting the song it plays. Or perhaps the song itself is tremulous and wobbly. It stops abruptly and, as if to time it together, Bimala makes an appearance, clearly with the maidservant and the shaven-headed woman hiding behind her, but around the corner, against the wall and invisible. Bimala too stops, as if confronted with a mirage whose truth she cannot immediately gauge.

'I'm s-sorry, Bimala,' Miss Gilby stammers, 'I-I just wanted to return these' – she holds out Bimala's books and writing materials lamely – 'I thought how is she going to do her homework if they are left behind . . .'

Bimala comes closer, looks at her with a puzzled expression; Miss Gilby is speaking too fast for her to follow anything. Her eyes alight on Miss Gilby's outstretched hands and suddenly the quizzical expression clears. A smile floods her face.

'Oh, my books. Thank you, Miss Gilby,' she murmurs, taking them from her tutor's hands.

Another woman, also dressed in stark white, but with her black hair tied severely back in plaits, appears behind Bimala. She stands staring, open-mouthed, at this exchange between Bimala and an English lady right in the middle of the *andarmahal*. A Christian lady in the middle of the *andarmahal*. Bimala notices the momentary distraction in Miss Gilby's eyes, focusing on something behind her, and wheels around.

She turns back to Miss Gilby and says, 'My . . . my . . .', searches for a word, 'husband sister, husband sister,' she says, at last, with triumphant relief.

'Yes, your sister-in-law,' Miss Gilby instinctively corrects, 'your husband's sister,' stressing the possessive case. She turns and leaves with rude abruptness.

Once back in her room, she flops down on the nearest armchair and pants, as much with the knowledge of her great blunder as with the physical exertion of running up the stairs. After half an hour, she dares to go out to her verandah, eaten up with curiosity about what her presence in the *andarmahal* might have precipitated, although knowing well that she will not be able to see their verandah. Ten minutes of pacing up and down and straining to hear what's going on rewards her with the sound of excited female voices and the brisk, energetic sound of broomstick against mosaic floor, the splash and swill of water, the sound of meticulous washing of the verandah into which she had mistakenly strayed.

FOUR

Everyone seems to be having money problems. Rachel rigorously limits herself to three pints of lager a week and that too in the college bar because it is heavily subsidized. She tells everyone with disarming frankness, 'I can't afford to go out to the pub, you know.' Ritwik finds the ease with which she talks about financial constraints astonishing: he'd never be able to do it himself. He notices that most of them talk freely about not having very much money, or the need to take up part-time jobs such as waitressing at formal hall dinners, but Peter doesn't ever join this sort of discussion. Declan tells him, sotto voce, 'He gets money from his parents', as soon as Peter goes to the bar to buy a round for everyone. It's impolite to ask others about the details of their finances, so they don't ask him about his, nevertheless he feels guilty that they assume about him what they know of Peter.

Ritwik has worked out that Declan's Catholic – his only visit to the Continent was a bus trip to Lourdes with a bunch of pilgrims – so he tries to avoid mentioning his school past. Declan's a practising believer in a pervasive way, not only in his world of Sunday morning services and prayers sent up to the BVM, but also in tutorials where he talks of *Paradise Lost* as Milton's attempt to make his readers believe in God and the salvation in Christ who pays for the sins of the fallen with His blood. Milton as tub-thumping, silver-tongued evangelist. When he talks about all this, he casts his eyes downwards, a look of utmost reverence settles on his face and his voice goes down an octave or two. He ends by saying that they should all pray after they finish reading the epic. Dr Carter defuses this call to religious communality by agreeing with him but in more sophisticated terms revolving around the seventeenth-century connotations of the word 'justify'. Sarah says, yes, indeed, they should all pray after closing the book but out of sheer bloody relief.

There is this refreshing down-to-earth quality about Sarah; she seems focused too, but not in a manically driven way. She wants 'to do good', as she puts it; to Ritwik, her lack of cynicism, her easy laughter, her feminism are all like a slant of light on the gloom of dusky church marble. She plans to go into education administration because she says Britain's schools are in a parlous state. It is she who explains to him the difference between grammar, state and comprehensive schools, and the cruel misnomer 'public' school. They get on really well and, together with Declan, they form an unusual trio. In another life, he wants to have Sarah's positive force, *be* her even, with her glorious head of ringlets, her candour and freckles and unshakeable faith in radical economic redistribution.

Declan talks of girls all the time, not in the way Gavin does, but with more soul and less hormone. He says things such as, 'Her smile went straight through my heart, you know? I'd like to have her for keeps' or 'She lights up my inner world, like'. There is something so touching in his innocence that the kitsch factor can be easily ignored. But Declan believes in the soul, so within that universe all is perfectly acceptable. But all this talk of girls makes Ritwik anxious: he grips his Guinness a touch more strongly, expecting a casual question about his love life any moment. Of course, he'll lie, but he'll feel guilty about it, especially because he'll be lying to these two guileless people. Beside them, his life is a dark labyrinth of shame and secrets.

Sarah always steers the conversation away from love and relationships when Declan gets into his romantic excesses. It is as though she somehow senses this might be a mined area for Ritwik. This evening she gets up and says, 'Well, I have to be off for work now.'

'What essay are you doing?' Ritwik asks.

'No, it's not essay work, it's work work.'

'You mean work for money?' Ritwik's a bit thrown; he didn't know Sarah had to supplement her grant as well. He feels a surprising, unexpected prick of envy, the envy of the excluded.

'No, no, not that sort of work. I do voluntary work three nights a week for the south-eastern chapter of the NSPCC. Answering telephones, sending out information, stuffing envelopes, you know, all that kind of stuff. A glorified secretary, really. But for an organization with a heart, not for a cheroot-smoking fat cat.'

'NSPCC?' He's thrown again.

'The National Society for the Prevention of Cruelty to Children. It's a charity.'

'Cruelty to children? What sort of cruelty to children?' What he really means to ask is 'Do you have cruelty to children here?', the emphasis sharply on 'here'. His dominant idea of cruelty to children revolves around child labour from where he comes – domestic servants, tea-shack boys, sometimes as little as six or seven, working sixteen-hour days for just two frugal meals and a hole to sleep in, beaten up mercilessly if they break a glass or spill tea.

'Well . . .' she sighs, 'where do I begin? Mostly domestic abuse, you know, people being violent to children, abusing them, physically or sexually, parental violence to children, battered children . . .'

Her words get submerged under the loud pealing of the bells of Magdalen church tower. He has never heard it in this underground cellar bar before, or not consciously, but suddenly it is so loud it seems each ring is coursing through him. Funnily enough, there is no other sound, no bar hubbub, no hum of the other students, no music, just this extreme tolling, as though they are in the suspended moments of a film shot where background noise is eliminated to concentrate on the dialogue between the characters in focus.

'. . . telephone helpline for people to call in to report or seek information and advice, even a childline manned by specially trained counsellors . . .'

Her words toll him back again. Sasha's darts have formed a neat isosceles triangle around the bull's eye but quite a distance from it and Martin has seized up with laughter at the sight. At the other end of the bar, Dave has just finished pulling a dark pint of Guinness and is now moving the glass in slow careful circles to make a shamrock on the foam with the last few drops from the tap.

Sarah continues, 'We're now campaigning for the total ban of smacking in schools. Corporal punishment has long gone, we hope, but even the residue, such as smacking pupils, or children at home, is unacceptable.'

Ritwik moves his left hand from the top of the table and the cold right one from around his pint glass and sits firmly on them: that will stop them from their sudden shaking. His voice is very steady when he asks, 'Do parents not smack their children here occasionally?'

'Well, there's a big debate raging about it at the moment. Most parents seem to be of the view that a firm slap once in a while is no big deal. But we think that constitutes the fundamentals of abuse.' Her words slip into slightly formal institutionalese; not quite jargon yet, but getting there.

'You mean disciplining children counts as child abuse? Isn't that a bit excessive?'

'No, not at all. A child is a person with rights. Hitting her or him is an act of physical violence. It's unacceptable. Besides, there are extreme cases of child abuse that is not sexual. You'll be horrified to hear what some parents do to their children.'

No I won't what do they do tell me tell me in graphic detail tell me what they do.

'These crimes never get reported because children are either inarticulate, accept this as the norm, are too scared to do anything, or just don't know if or how anything can be done about it in the first place. It can be any or all of these factors working together.'

She notices something, just a small shift, something tinily riven, in the air between them, something so small as to be absent.

Almost.

She asks, 'Are you OK?'

Yes, he is. Because he isn't. Because he's survived not being OK.

Bidisha Ghosh was the proudest mother in Jadavpur. Not only were her two boys fair, which drew appreciative comments from neighbours – *Look at your boys, like two little sahibs* – but they also went to an English-medium school, cementing further the comparison with sahib. But above all, they were known to be the two most perfectly disciplined boys around. Or, to shift the focus, Bidisha-di was the byword in Grange Road for good parenting. She ruled with an iron hand, like some furious goddess from the Hindu pantheon, quick to take offence and send down punishment. There was no woolliness about her, no indulgence; it was tough love, love like the grip of a vice. If it didn't constrain and keep the boys within its jaws, they would grow up as spoilt, ill-educated trash like the loafers and *chengras* who hung out in street corners, whistled at the girls, smoked, drank and did no work. Vigilance, constant, unremitting vigilance: if she let her guard down for a split second, the boys would be ruined.

To this end, she had cultivated the persona of the ideal mother who was defined by her readiness to discipline and punish at the slightest hint of wayward behaviour. For what was love if it did not mould and reform? Love spoiled, punishment corrected. The heart could be of gold, but its appearance and expression had to be of tempered steel.

Everyone in the neighbourhood knew that the boys were being brought up in a household with four bums. Their uncles were the worst examples to any child: they hadn't had the benefit of education; they were bone-idle, sleeping in until lunchtime; they were unemployed freeloaders; they smoked and drank; Pratik had a gambling habit; it was suspected that Pratim was on brown sugar; they stole, lied, cheated, beat up their mother, sang Hindi film songs loudly and got into fights. Bidisha had had no choice in moving in here after they had to give up their flat in genteel Park Circus. She certainly didn't have any power to contain her brothers' behaviour and lifestyle, so she decided to concentrate on the children instead – if she couldn't change their environment and make it wholesome for them, she could throw all her energy into making the boys impervious to such malign influences. She built a chinkless wall around Ritwik and Aritra to protect them from the fire all around. In the process, she shut out all the light and air as well.

Being a strict parent brought high marks from everyone who knew them. It was as though this whole act of bringing up the boys were being played out to a crowd of exacting judges and watchers whose every nod of approval, every pursed lip of criticism counted as plus or minus points. She was being watched and marked by this gallery, inside and outside; she had to perform well, win and walk off with the grand prize. So the more she ordered her boys in sharp, staccato bursts, the more this theatre audience approved, the more she barked and shouted, the more they were pleased. She was a hard mother, there was no pussyfooting and mollycoddling, no slipping up or cracks in the performance. She was lean, mean and streamlined; every inch of visible tenderness had been trimmed away like fat off meat. The only person left was the role itself.

Her ordinary tone of voice to the children was like whiplash. *Get your books. Wake up. Go and have a bath* all had the sharp report of a dead, dry twig breaking in silent forest floors. They were always orders, delivered with imperiousness and something approaching distaste, as if the boys had just been bought from a slave market; the spectators approved. And then there were threats articulated through clenched teeth and with rolling eyes: she managed to make ordinary situations a condition of cold, rib-stabbing menace. *It's nearly mid-day, I've been asking you to go and have a bath for the last hour, if you don't go now, I'll tear you to pieces.* Her threats of violence got more and more baroque but they were the common currency of the Bengali household: *I'll batter your face with a shoe, I'll lash you with the broomstick,* or *I'll break every tooth in your face.*

She was always on this edge of fury, like a restrained storm, about to burst any moment. Every aspect of her, every word, every intake of breath, every movement of her eyebrows seemed to have been dipped in an acid bath of anger; in an instant her relatively benign demeanour could change, as if some inner demon had flipped a trip switch with a sudden surge of current. She shouted and raged, the neighbours came out on to their balconies or heard every single word through their open windows and commented, 'Bidisha-di is so scary. The boys fear her as if she were Yama.' It was a commendation of the highest order: it meant the boys would grow up straight.

That was the thrust of Moral Science classes in school as well. The central metaphor was of an upright tree, growing up towards light, growing up tall and straight, because the careful gardener had tended it in its youth, guided its pliable green twigs and branches, supported it with twine, wire, stakes, trained its wayward shoots and tendrils around strong rods. Such was the importance of discipline and correction during the early years, when children could easily go astray, like the crooked plant which no one looked after so it became a jumbly, untidy mess and was uprooted with the noxious weeds and thrown into the flames. No teacher tired of this parable and, at home, Bidisha discovered that it sounded a sympathetic chord in her when she supervised the boys' homework. Practically every week the parable was wheeled out in that storm-cloud tone of voice. Neighbours whispered respectfully, 'Bidisha-di is a perfect mother. Look how well she disciplines her boys. Look how wonderfully she keeps them on the straight and narrow.' Her fame spread, her name was on every tongue.

The incessant shouting became an issue between Bidisha and her husband. He was a kind, gentle, elderly man who believed children should be brought up with love and tenderness, should never be shouted at, and should never, never be hit. Whenever she went on the rampage, he quietly asked her to keep her voice down. 'Why do you have to shout, Bidisha,' he said, 'why can't you just make your point softly but firmly? There's no need to bring the house down.'

This fanned the fire to a mighty crackling roar. 'You keep quiet. You're spoiling the boys; all this business of affection, affection, affection, it's had them dancing on our heads,' she shouted, her voice rising by a few more decibels as her sentence neared the end.

He made another gentle attempt. 'Can't you just speak to them? And how exactly do you see them behaving badly? They seem all right to me.'

She played her trump card. 'You're not helping things by criticizing me in front of everyone. This will later give the boys licence to do the same,' she said. And then she lobbed the little grenade: 'Fine, if you think you know best, you deal with them. You bring them up. You feed them, make them do their homework, take them to school and bring them back, you do everything.' With every clause, her voice rose, till she almost spat out the last word and rushed out of the room. In the kitchen she could be heard handling utensils so noisily that they were afraid she was breaking half of them.

This silenced their father. He gave up in despair; he wasn't combative enough. She could only be tackled by her means:

shouting, aggression, that precarious positioning on the precipice of violence. He didn't have those in him.

Meanwhile, the boys instinctively understood that this bit of friction between their parents was going to take its toll: as soon as their father left the house, she was going to take it out on her sons. They waited in terror and not knowing what she was going to peg her fury on made it worse. It could be a spelling mistake in one of the sets of homework from school; not knowing 'by heart' the last Geography chapter, including every single punctuation mark; or a slip-up in the perfect arrangement of books in the school satchel, the biggest one at the bottom, the smallest one on top and everything in between in descending order of size; an unsharpened pencil in the pencil-box – it could be anything. She could even manufacture something to suit her purpose. They could only wait with churning stomachs and small, dimmed faces, but even during their mother's worst excesses, they prayed and hoped their father wouldn't intervene.

Ritwik was the convergent point of all these coiled energies in her. Her excuse was simple: he was the older of the two; he had to be flawless so that Aritra could follow in the track made by him. That was what Ritwik became, a bit of substantiating evidence around which the flux of daily life was organized. He was the furrow which her cultivating zeal carved out. He was to become her creation, her prize garden, her impeccable son. He was going to be her bulwark against everything that life had ranged in battle against her. *Bend him, buckle him, mould him like wax, like clay, like putty, he's mine, my love will build him anew, I'll show them I've won, the ooze of oil comes only from pressing and bruising, the life in him is going to be the shine of oil, not the dullness of uncrushed seed and I'm going to be responsible for the radiance*, she thought.

The first zone in which this experiment was put to practice was Ritwik's education. Every evening, from six to nine, was homework time: she supervised this, in between cooking dinner for the family, with the sharpness of a predatory bird.

'What subjects do you have for school tomorrow? Take out your diary, let me look at the timetable,' she began, her voice already poised between command and threat.

Ritwik passed the diary to her.

'Why can't you open it to the right page and read it out? Can't you read?' she shouted.

'But . . . but you asked . . .' he muttered.

She cut it short, 'Don't dare answer back, do you understand?' Her voice was beginning to hurt the inside of his eyes and the juddering place behind his ribs.

She took a quick look at the timetable. 'Moral Science, Spelling & Dictation, English Language, Bengali, Science, History & Civics, Math . . .' she read out. 'All right, take out your Moral Science textbook. I want you to learn the questions and answers at the end of the chapter you did in school today. After that, I'm going to give you a spelling and dictation test from the new lesson in Radiant Way Reader, "The Cook and the Crane". I'm going to the kitchen now, I'll be back in an hour. I want both subjects thoroughly prepared by that time. Otherwise you have trouble on your plate.' Every word, every sentence, was a fusillade of command.

She thud-thudded off, leaving the scared boy fumbling with books, having trouble focusing on the words on the page. She returned almost immediately and shouted, 'I want you to read the lessons out aloud, so I can hear you from the kitchen. I want to be sure you're not wasting time.'

149

Ritwik mounted a feeble opposition to this. 'Why can't I do it silently?'

She deigned to reason with this one. 'It's because reading out aloud fixes the work in your head better because you read it and hear it.'

'But I think I learn better if I read things in a murmur rather than aloud.'

'You know better than I do?' That fireform again. He gave in.

For the next half an hour or so, the cheap waxy pages of the Moral Science textbook, with their faint whiff of rancid glue, and the catechism-type exercise at the end of each chapter, became a compact prelude to terror. Its opening chords were so loud and consuming in his ears and his blood that the words on the page were either not fixable or they were meaningless. *Why must we love, honour and obey God? We must love, honour and obey God because He made us in His image and likeness, put us in this beautiful world to enjoy His goodness and generosity, blessed us with life and gave us the chance to glorify Him. He also gave us parents to love and take care of us.* They were in an opaque code, he could have been reading hieroglyphics; he was so scared that willing his voice to give sound to them, one by one, could not give them any meaning. How could he ever learn all this 'by heart' if they never moved from mark to meaning?

He could hear miscellaneous sounds of sizzling and frying and clanking of metal pots and pans coming from the kitchen. And the occasional tremor of her tread as she moved around. Once or twice, there would be a sudden shout from her, 'Why can't I hear you? Why has your voice gone low?' He'd nearly jump out of his skin and increase the volume '. . . *He endowed us with free will so that we can choose between good and bad . . .*'

Some of the answers were quite long, nearly five or six lines;

150

he hated them. Others were short and easy and these he learnt first, leaving the involved ones till later. His attention kept wandering off – he was tempted to look at the final few chapters of his Geography and Biology books, such virgin pages, so far away in the school year. They would do those much later on, in winter, the chapters on tea-growing in Darjeeling and Assam; the north-eastern hill states and union territories; the digestive system; a chapter called 'Coal'. And what was that one about the man being swallowed whole by a huge whale and staying alive in its belly? He couldn't wait to read it all in one quick go. They were new lands waiting to be discovered in the vast sea of this boredom of lessons done to death. He kept sneaking looks at those untouched pages; they were almost forbidden and delicious.

Dida, limping around the flat, came by, stopped at the door and said, 'You'll be put through the wringer if you don't do your work; will serve you right,' and hobbled off. It came out of thin air; no encouragement, no motive, nothing. Did this add some sense of drama to the dead sameness of her days?

Suddenly Bidisha was in the room where Ritwik sat on the floor, amidst the untidy strew of his schoolbooks, pencils, and dirty satchel.

'Are you ready then?' she demanded.

Ritwik froze. 'Nnno . . . I mean yes . . . but . . .' he stammered weakly.

Ritwik desperately wanted his father to come back: in his presence, she shouted and went as far as giving him a slap or two but never let herself go fully. That transformation into a column of fire had to be repressed till he was out of the house.

'Give me the book.' She settled down on the floor opposite him and picked out the wooden ruler. So this was going to be her weapon this evening. It had happened so many times before that Ritwik didn't even flinch but he was scared. Fear was forever new, like spring; nothing ever robbed it of its edge and thisness. She fired quick volleys – 'Which chapter? Which page?' – and then began asking him the questions at the end of each chapter. He was going to have to give her the answer printed after each question verbatim.

'Why did God make us in His image and likeness?'

'God make . . . God make . . .' he whispered, his eyes focused on the slow, irregular brandishing of the ruler gripped in her hand, and almost immediately knew he had made a mistake because she looked up at him with a dull gleam in her eyes and interrupted him.

'God?' she asked in that interrogative tone of hers, which meant that he had got the next word wrong and she wanted to confirm that, or maybe give him a chance to correct it before she brought down the ruler on his exposed arms or legs, he was never sure which.

'God . . . God . . . make,' he murmured, his voice a trembling leaf to the approach of storm. He knew he was getting it wrong but the right word had dried up inside him, gone into hiding.

'God?' That menacing brush of a chance given again, aware that it wasn't going to be availed of.

'God make . . .'

Crack: the ruler on his thigh.

'God?' She was going to carry on the questioning halt at that word till he cleared up the blockage and let the words flow clean and correct.

'God make . . .'

This time there was not one but a whole choir of cracks, neat sharp sounds, syncopated and random, played out on his bare skin everywhere – arms, legs, thighs, a couple on his face and on the knuckles. He tried to dodge and duck but this infuriated her even more. As he half-crawled half-dragged himself to a corner, any corner, she stepped over his books and satchel and wielded the ruler with such abandon that anyone watching this would have thought that it had released something dammed up in her. Whenever she punished him physically, she came into a new being. It could only be called blossoming, as though all the forces in her, concentrated so far in a tight bud, had suddenly unfurled in a terrible beauty.

Ritwik could only feel the rectangles of burn the ruler imprinted on his skin. He noticed that where the thin edge of the ruler had caught one of his knuckles the skin had split in a tiny red gash. Only a tiny one. And there was the torrent of her words, some shouted, some hissed with the spitting anger of an attacking snake, which kept up the continuous bass line to the slap of wood against skin: 'No God MADE God MADE how many times do you need to be told that if you're asked a question containing the word "did" the answer is in the simple past tense so MADE MADE MADE not "make" will you ever make that mistake will you will you say MADE say God MADE.'

'God made, God made,' Ritwik obediently sobbed.

'Stop crying. Stop crying now,' she shrieked. 'I don't want a single sound to escape your lips. I'll throttle you if I hear another sob. Is that clear?'

Ritwik choked and nodded. He was aware of the open wooden shutters of the adjacent house and the squares of fluorescent light visible through their own open windows. He sensed there were people standing near those windows, listening to everything that was going on here. He knew that his mother was aware of the neighbours soaking up the details of this little exemplary drama as well. The theatre inside her head broke into a tumultous applause.

There was an indeterminate gap between the Moral Science and the spelling test. Bidisha strode off to the kitchen after this corrective act, warning her silently crying son, 'I'm going to the kitchen to cook some rice. I want all the difficult words in "The Cook and the Crane" mastered by the time I'm done. Otherwise, what you've just had is going to seem like a picnic compared with what's coming.'

Ritwik had reached the plateau stage of terror. It was only its first installment that rattled and jarred him; after that, it was the physical pain that took front seat while the fear diminished. If there was to be more after a while, he was more or less prepared for it. He took a pencil and started underlining the difficult words in 'The Cook and the Crane': *witty, receive, humorous, kitchen, shoo* . . . The words drew him in and his voice slowly faded until he was reading the whole story silently.

Her appearance at the door took him by surprise; she had come to conclude unfinished business.

'Why can't I hear your voice? Why? Didn't I tell you I wanted to hear every word? Didn't I?'

She advanced on him with huge strides, shouting, 'I can't hear you. Who's taken your tongue?' In the space of an eyelash-flicker she was upon him.

Then she did something she'd never done to him before: she picked him up by his shirt collar, lifted him clean off the floor and flung him, as one would a rag doll or a bag of rubbish, to one corner of the room. She had just extended her repertoire; the audience was on its feet, throwing coins and flowers. The applause was deafening.

Ritwik hit the low bed and the big metal trunk and landed on the little square of space made by the two walls, one edge of the trunk and one side of the bed. She rushed to him, dragged him out of the space and then threw him, again, in the opposite direction. This time he skidded on his school books lying on the floor and fell with his face down, his nose, teeth and tongue somehow hitting the concrete floor, with its patchwork of mismatching loud tiles, all at the same time. It put an end to his scared whimpering, the pain was too much for that. He let out a wail and some torn words, unintelligible, ineffectual, which were like bellows to her fire. While he lay curled on the floor trying instictively to reduce the surface area of contact, she kicked and punched him in between straightening him out so that she could have greater access to his body.

No one in the house intervened to save him. It was necessary disciplining, the rod that taught and educated. Without this just measure of pain, how would a child ever learn to be diligent about his studies? It was an unspoken law of the Bengali household that whatever a mother meted out to her children, it was right and motivated by unconditional love. It couldn't be questioned: everything worked for the greater good of the child.

It was the sight of blood on Ritwik's face that made her stop, or the sense that he was nearly choking, able only to inhale or to exhale but not both, one following the other. Perhaps it was because she had welled herself out empty for the moment. She left the room to go to the kitchen, only returning when the sobbing had given way to an exhausted panting of snot, tears and some blood. There was a very faint air of the truce behind her commands, ever so slightly gentle now – 'Stop crying. Get up, go to the bathroom and wash your face with cold water. I will give you your dinner after that, all right? Go, get up now.'

All of a sudden Dida appeared at the door and whispered, 'So, enjoyed the fun, did you? How did it feel?' From where did the leaking excitement in her voice come? Which bit of it appeared as 'fun' to her? She seemed to be keeping herself on a leash, a little girl trying very hard not to be giddy. Ritwik was convinced that had she, or could she have, let herself go, she would have broken into handstands and cartwheels there and then on the floor.

He whimpered away to the bathroom, washed his face, blew his nose and returned to his books. His eyes scanned the underlined words in 'The Cook and the Crane'. He did not feel any fear. He noted the cunning twists in the spelling of some English words – 'humour' had two 'u's but 'humorous' omitted the second 'u' of 'humour' and added an '—ous'; 'receive', he must remember, had an 'e' before 'i' and not the other way around. When his mother came back from the kitchen and gave him the spelling test, he got all the words correct. He had the uncomfortable feeling that she was somewhat disappointed.

If the cottaging business started off as an unsought adventure and surprised Ritwik by its very existence and possibilities, now, seventeen months down the line, it is a habit. An addiction even. He braves the bone-cutter of the February wind to get to St Giles. No intensity of rain lashing across Catte Street and Broad Street in slanting spears can deter him. In fact, these extremes of weather he constructs as challenges – *let's see who's hunting tonight* – knowing well that he might be the only one, waiting for hour after sleepless hour, listening to the rain and wind, and hoping and waiting for a kind of ashen deliverance.

He gets impatient on summer evenings because the light stays till so late, the darkening blue of the sky never quite reaching the perfect black he thinks is necessary for going out on the prowl. It is a last vestige of some inhibition, this reluctance to go cruising with the residue of daylight stubbornly lingering in the air. He is sure in time it will go although he doesn't know whether that is going to be a good or a bad thing.

He has started questioning himself about why he feels this urge to sit or stand in his cubicle for sometimes three to four hours on wet, icy evenings even when there is no action going on nor any reasonable chance of it. There are more pressing things that need his attention: Miss Gilby has only just made her first appearance at Nikhilesh and Bimala's, *Prometheus Unbound* remains untouched. All those areas in which he thought he had imposed some order and method – books, essays, Miss Gilby – are beginning to escape control. All because, he thinks in a moment of trying to find one monolithic enemy, of that addiction to the adrenaline rush as he steps down the wet stairs into the underworld of St Giles, his heart a slow percussive fist, opening closing, opening closing. There is no denying it is a thrill. And he is hooked to it in the same way a big cat is after its first taste of saltblood. No amount of getting used to it, as he is by now (one of the other regulars calls him 'our Indian chair', he's so much a fixture now in this place), no amount of it totally removes the slight loosening of the sphincter, the vague, peripheral urge to shit, as he makes his way into the toilets. Adrenaline, he notes every time; fight, flight, or fright.

The elements of danger and fear were at the forefront before. Will he get caught by the police? Will anyone who knows him see him in there or going down the stairs? What are the chances of picking up a psycho? What about AIDS? They have all moved back to the shadows, some more, some less. He is now so inured to any sense of danger that if it is there, it is as some complex spicing, present only in the bass notes, resistant to isolation and pinning down.

A particular incident in the toilets one day, at around two in the morning, sticks in his mind. No one there except Ritwik, who had been hanging around, utterly bored yet free and in his element, and another man: short, chubby, small shifty eyes, his skin the colour of bacon fat, tiny scratches on his nose and face, the kind one would see in an infant who has been scratching itself. The man hadn't betrayed any interest in Ritwik at all but it was getting late and all they were going to get that night was each other. So, reluctantly, Ritwik had been making the moves, his mind not really on it, just to tease, just to see if the man was interested. Either way, he probably wouldn't go through with it, he would just tease a bit and leave. The man had suddenly taken down his trousers, flicked out his penis and said, 'If you don't suck my cock, I'll beat you up.' Ritwik had thought how easy it would have been to spit at him and run out of the toilet to the safety of the open public streets above. Instead, though, he had kneeled down and sucked him with greed and had even got the stranger to jerk him off. In the post-ejaculation illusion of rapprochement, Ritwik, a few steps already on his way out while the man was washing his hands, hadn't been able to resist shouting out, 'I have a bigger cock than yours.' Cheap, but it was going to hit home, he was that sort of man. He had shouted back at a hastily retreating Ritwik, 'That's coz you're fuckin' black, that's why.'

It's different tonight. He had had to leave the bar, it was getting too smoky and close in there. In his room, his work had outstared him into defeat. So he's been left with no choice but to trace his invariable tracks to the cottage. Or so he tries to reason with himself. *328665, Tuesdays, Thursdays and Saturdays, from 9 p.m. till 6 a.m.* That information won't leave him alone.

The toilets are fairly busy tonight. Just entering it gives him a temporary reprieve from *328665 328665 328665.* His cubicle is occupied. He waits for the occupant to leave and then practically pounces on the door, lets himself in and locks it. He'll have a tough time keeping this for himself tonight, there are other loiterers like him who want to use it as a base too. There's no option but to stay put in here until the trade thins out a bit. Unlike other evenings, tonight he is not buzzing with the need for action, rushing in and out of the cubicle to check out new arrivals, heading for the viewcrack at the sound of shuffling feet. Tonight he stands with his back against one of the walls and realizes after what seems like a considerable while that he has read all the graffiti many times over without any of it sinking in.

Maybe he can will himself to shut the door that has opened inside him. The unsettling thing is that he did not know the door was there in the first place. No, he has to resist this tug. If he can only force himself to concentrate on the traffic around him, he'll be better; nothing like the tired old game leading to orgasm for a snack of oblivion.

He leaves his cubicle and someone standing at the pissoir neatly moves back and steps in, bolting the door fast. *Bastard.* He'll have to hang around in the open now. He feels exposed and it's not a natural feeling for him, not in this world. Then someone comes out of one of the other cubicles and Ritwik automatically, along with everyone else, looks at him. Very tall and very thin, his exposed collarbones like ridges enclosing two shallow bowls on either side of his neck. *I bet if he takes his trousers off, his hipbones will jut out like promontories in a map*: that is Ritwik's first thought. He marks it with unconscious prescience, for he won't have either the clarity or the luxury to focus on his thoughts about this stranger again. There are dark shadows under his eyes, as if he hasn't slept in a long time. Heroin addicts have such leaking darkness around their eyes, that devoured, consuming look, Ritwik thinks.

They look at each other. Ritwik turns away and moves to the urinal, looking back at him once, making sure there is a lot of space between him and the next person standing and pretending to piss. The stranger doesn't accept the offer, instead he goes and positions himself at the pissoir on the other side of the mirrors. Ritwik's chest has a plummeting feeling inside it. He leans back to look at him and catches him doing the same.

Who dares, wins.

Ritwik zips up, walks over and stands beside him at the other urinal. Heroin Eyes is resolutely looking down, refusing to catch his eye, but he isn't moving away either. Ritwik has become brazen – he is straining to get a glimpse of his cock, willing the man to catch a second of the crackle of electricity that he suddenly seems to have developed around him.

It doesn't work: the stranger buttons up and starts making his way up to street level. Ritwik is unable to let this one go. Almost immediately, he too moves away and follows him outside. The man takes the steps three at a time, bounds up and with enormous strides crosses over to Martyrs' Memorial.

The man looks over his shoulder: Ritwik has nearly broken into a run now. The stranger quickens his pace, crosses Cornmarket Street diagonally and almost runs into the vaulted Friars' Entry, between Debenhams and the Randolph Hotel, just behind the bus stops. Ritwik pursues, running now, desperate, heavy with the knowledge that he has scared him off, is scaring him off right now, by stalking him out in the streets, but he can't stop himself. He runs into the passage too and watches a tall, lanky figure lope away hurriedly, through the uneven patchwork of light and shadows thrown out by huddled buildings, a fair distance from him.

He gives up. His heart is an eel, describing its endless Möbius-strip dance, over and over again. There is no point going down to the loos now; he is suddenly tired and uninterested. He walks slowly back down Broad Street; a keen wind is whipping up little local whirlpools of dried leaves beside a phone booth. Almost without thinking, he walks into the booth, picks up the phone, and the index finger of his right hand – not he, not the entire person – punches in the freephone number: 328665. As soon as the phone starts to ring at the other end, he slams his receiver down on its metal cradle.

He breathes in and out for a couple of minutes, aware of each inhalation and exhalation, then redials the number . . . This time he lets the phone ring. At the fourth ring, a voice answers, 'NSPCC Helpline. How can I help?'

The voice is so familiar he can see the bridge of fading freckles under her eyes and over her nose if he shuts his eyes. He can't answer.

'Hello? Can I help?' Her voice gentle, ever so kind and gentle.

'No.' The word rushes out before he has had a chance to string together other words into a sentence.

'Do you have anything to say?' she asks, slightly coaxing now, but still kind.

'No . . . I mean, yes, yes . . .'

'Yes?'

He is shallow-breathing in fairly rapid bursts now. 'Could you tell me something about about about child abuse?' Pause. 'Please.'

There is nothing in her voice, no sharp intake of breath, no silence left hanging for more than its seemly duration, to tell him that his voice has been recognized and his face mapped on to it. But he knows, in the way the telephone receiver seems to have become sentient in his clammy left hand, or by what he suddenly feels to be a slightly different ordering of the air and signals between the two ends, somewhere deep under the ground, in the souls of the cables.

Her voice is collected, unswerved by the new knowledge. 'What exactly do you want to know?'

Pause. 'I don't know.'

'Do you want to report anything?'

Silence.

'Whatever you say to us is in strictest confidence. If you choose not to identify yourself, that is perfectly all right.' The professional words ring strained in his ears. Perhaps in hers as well.

'It's it's about me.'

'I take it you want to report something about your past?'

Pause. Then a whispered 'Yes'.

'Pardon?'

'Yes,' slightly louder.

'Have you talked to anyone else about it?'

'No, no.'

There is a long silence during which he imagines their words, broken down into constituent letters and then further into electric signals and sound waves, travelling down cables and coalescing into human words again just before they spill out of the earpiece into her ear. He wishes they would remain atomized forever within the cable and get lost in a little black hole along the line and never reach her.

'Do you want to talk about it now?' Her voice has become that of a ministering angel's again.

His throat is a constricted passage of pure obstruction, blocking his words, choking out sound. He is not aware of little guerillas of words escaping this tyranny of his throat. 'It's my mother.'

Silence from her.

'My mother . . .' he tries again.

'Yes?'

'My mother used to . . . beat me.'

'What sort of beating was it?'

Pause. 'Severe.' That'll do, he thinks.

'How old were you at the time?'

He doesn't answer the question. He could be talking to himself as the refractory words tumble out: 'Once when I was six I used some abusive term which I'd picked up from god knows where. You know, nothing very offensive. Roughly translated it would mean "child of a pig". I suppose it has the same heft as "bastard" here.' His voice is reasoned, calm, almost reflective. He is telling a story now in which he is a character; as raconteur, he manages far better, for it could be someone else's story. Indeed, it is someone else's story.

He continues, 'She was making chapatis, you know, flat Indian bread, on a griddle on open coals. She had a pair of tongs and a metal fish-slice sort of thing, which she was using to flip the bread over. As soon as she heard the words, she looked at me and asked me to say the words again, as if she hadn't quite heard them. I gathered that something was wrong, that the words were bad, so I kept quiet. She kept on asking me to repeat them. Then she reached forward and and and . . .'

The barrier of fiction, without any warning, suddenly gives

way. The words become painful pushes against a throat sealing up again. '. . . and she hit me on my thigh with the hot iron spatula.'

Pause. On both sides. He can't hear her breathing. For all he knows, she might have gently put her receiver down on a table and gone away, while his words leak out into a spartan cell, institutional and characterless, and it is only the room that registers the immediate peeling off of a nine-square inch area of skin, like the papery bark of an arbutus tree, the slow seconds of silence and awe watching this wonderful ruching and metamorphosis of blemish, then the deferred shock of pain.

Her voice returns. 'Hello, hello? Are you still there? Hello?'

He doesn't answer; instead, he replaces the receiver, but this time with infinite gentleness, as if he is cradling the head of a newborn, fragile as eggshell, so delicate, so vulnerable to hurt.

Outside, the wind is making ever more furious eddies and edgeless, formless pillars of rising and falling leaves, all atonal brown. At the lit display window of Blackwells, a shy, uncertain Mary looks down from her home in the shiny open pages of a luxury art book at some unspecified spot near his feet. One palm is outstretched and open, pointing downwards, as if she has just finished doling out some grace. He almost looks around him to see if it is still dispersed in the restless air.

V.

'Dighi Bari',
Nawabgunj,
Bograh Distt
Bengal
October the 28th, 1902

Dear Violet,

*I read with great regret and dismay of the troubles you
are facing in your school. If the Bengali babu is not going to
interfere in these petty racial squabbles and take immediate
action against the separatist poison that is choking the
country and which, I am sad to say, our countrymen are
doing nothing to either allay or eradicate, instead
strengthening it for their own petty political games, I am
afraid, Violet, the only way to keep the school running
might be to have Hindoo and Muslim girls attend on
alternate days. I know it goes against our most fundamental
principle of unity but we are both in agreement that the
education of Indian women is of far greater importance
than trying to solve their race wars, which we are too small
to effect. If the Hindoo-Muslim animosity, which, I am
reliably informed (and my readings seem to confirm, too),*

goes back centuries, deflects us from our true task, then we will have lost our battle in bringing the light of knowledge to Indian women. I only wish I could be there beside you at this hour of your need and help you in any way that you might require, or I, in my limited capability, can provide.

You ask of my news. I am very well here and derive considerable joy and pleasure from being part of the Roy Chowdhury family. I have already acquainted you with my accidental straying into the andarmahal last year, haven't I? Well, since that time, I have not only been accompanied and given a 'Grand Tour' of the place by both Bimala and Mr Roy Chowdhury, but I am also invited there occasionally to tea and, on two occasions, to lunch. It seems that Mr Roy Chowdhury has talked sense into his widowed sisters-in-law – he treats them as if they were his own blood – and convinced them, with reason and arguments and affection, that having a Christian lady step into their quarters is not going to defile them or turn them into pariahs. I think curiosity, rather than instruction, has ultimately got the better of them.

Mr Roy Chowdhury has been open and frank about the rituals and observances his sisters-in-law practise, and has told me a considerable part of his, and their, family history. It appears that the older of the two widowed ladies, the one whom Bimala calls 'Naw Jaa', 'jaa' being the Bengali word for husband's sister-in-law, was married off to Mr Roy Chowdhury's brother, a good twelve years older than Mr Roy Chowdhury, when she was but a child of nine, the same age as the young Mr Roy Chowdhury himself at the time of this marriage. They grew up together, as two children, first as two friends in *a family of adults, then the bond between them growing to that between a brother and a sister. When Mr Roy Chowdhury's brother, the girl's husband, died, leaving her a widow at the age of eleven, she had thrown herself into Vaishnavism as succour and consolation – shaving her head, observing extreme dietary laws, such as not eating or drinking after sunset, required by that strain of the Hindoo religion, immersing herself in fasts and prayers and rituals, seemingly in atonement for her sins, which, she was convinced, had caused her husband's death. The bond between her and Mr Roy Chowdhury had only deepened although he had not succeeded in dissuading her from the more extreme aspects of her new religion. If she derives support or happiness from it, if it makes the burden of her tragedy easier for her, who am I to impose my will, he had said to me once, when I was expressing my reservations about the austerity of life for a woman so much younger than I am. Do you know, Violet, she feeds pigeons every morning, opening the shutters of the andarmahal verandah and throwing out handfuls of grain, in the belief that all those cooing birds are a collective incarnation of the little Lord Krishna?*

The other sister-in-law, married to another of Mr Roy Chowdhury's brothers, lost her husband after five years. It seems such misfortune dogs the poor women who marry into this family. She, too, is childless. The second brother's death left Mr Roy Chowdhury as head of family, a role he fulfils with affection, love and a great deal of maturity, with conscientious attention to duty and to every member's wishes and desires. It cannot be easy for him to sustain the roles of brother (for that is what he is to

Bimala's Naw Jaa), beloved brother-in-law and loving husband, all at once, certainly not when Bimala's recent presence in the andarmahal has disrupted, I suspect, former stabilities and precedences. I am also of the opinion, and I haven't mentioned this to anyone, apart from you, Violet, that Mr Roy Chowdhury's gentle prevailing on the matter of Bimala's introduction to the outside world, leaving her seclusion behind, has not been looked upon too kindly by the two other women. It must be difficult for Mr Roy Chowdhury to steer a balanced and peaceful path through a household of women.

But this is all idle surmise. I have more entertaining things to occupy my time here. Now that autumn has arrived, the fields are full of blossoming giant grass, which they call 'kaash phul' here. We, by which I mean Bimala, Mr Roy Chowdhury and I, sometimes go on boat rides on the Jamuna river in Shukshayor. The river is now quite mild, although a very brown colour, and the majhi sometimes sings as he rows us along, very plaintive songs in his cracked voice which make me feel extremely melancholic and long for something but I don't know what. It is a very calm exercise: the boat moves along very slowly indeed on the surface of the water, rocking gently from side to side in such a manner as to induce sleepiness – I was afraid of this soft pitch and swell the first time – while Mr Roy Chowdhury reads poetry aloud to us: Keats and Wordsworth – his favourite – and at times Bengali poetry too. I too read aloud, but from Bengali books – even if I do say so myself, my proficiency in the Bengali language increases apace, thanks to Bimala's expert guidance – graded books called <u>Sahaj Path</u>, which means

Easy Reading, and simple folk tales written for children. Bimala is quite proud of her achievement in this reciprocal education of her tutor and companion. I can only wholeheartedly support this happy arrangement wherein I teach her English, among other things, and she instructs me in her language. I hope I'm not being immodest when I tell you that I can have a reasonable conversation with Bimala and her husband in their mother tongue, while Bimala goes from strength to strength every day – she read out 'A slumber did my spirit seal' last week, beautifully, I thought, only tripping up on the word 'diurnal' in the penultimate line, a word with which she is unfamiliar. We applauded heartily and she took great joy from this little achievement. It is such a sad little poem, we were quite overwhelmed, I can tell you, and I even thought I heard Mr Roy Chowdhury's voice tremble ever so slightly as he explicated the meaning of the poem to Bimala.

Mr Roy Chowdhury has kindly allowed me the use of one of his two horses, a beautiful grey and white dappled gelding whose name is Pakshiraj, which he tells me is the name for the Bengali version of Pegasus, or indeed, any winged horse of myth or folklore. I also have the use of Mr Roy Chowdhury's saees when I go riding and in this delectable weather, I do so quite often, sometimes in the early mornings, when the mist is still on the ground and on the rolling fields, and sometimes in the afternoons, when the delicate autumn light gilds everything orange and gold. It is one of life's more unalloyed pleasures being able to ride for miles and miles, the wind in your face, leaving behind people, houses, habitations, hamlets here and there, just you, the steed and the rush of air and open country passing you by. I pass by rivers and fields, occasionally I ride through villages consisting of no more than a few straggling huts. Everywhere people are polite and friendly, and in our own village, Nawabgunj, a band of young men, whom I often see coming into the offices on the ground floor on, I assume, business to do with the zamindari, have taken to wishing me 'Good morning, memsa'ab', 'Good evening, memsa'ab' when they see me in the village when I go out to take the air or when I set out riding.

Another no small joy in this mild season is Tea on the lawn, or garden, I should rather say, of 'Dighi Bari'. I have been teaching Bimala some of our customs and sometimes I let her practise these during Afternoon Tea on the grass with little folding tables, chairs, parasols. She usually pours for everyone and serves the sandwiches and cakes with such poise that I can tell Mr Roy Chowdhury feels quite proud of her, as I do, too, and no doubt, you would have done as well had you been here, dear Violet. It is at these Teas I miss you most. I speak about you to Bimala and Mr Roy Chowdhury, although it seems he has heard a lot about you and your work from notable Bengali worthies who are his friends and also from the Rajah of Cooch Behar. He always refers to you as 'your eminent friend, Mrs Cameron, who does so much for our country.' I feel very proud of you when he utters your name with such respect.

And now, dear Violet, you will scarcely believe your ears when I impart to you the next bit of information – I have finally embarked upon my book. I have drawn up a *general plan for the disposition of the chapters, the distribution of ideas and the unfolding of the arguments in the first five chapters – there will be twelve in all – and, what is more, I have already started writing the first and the third. I have tentatively entitled it <u>Essay on the Rights of Women</u>. What do you think of the title? I miss your guiding intelligence, our numerous conversations and debates about many of the subjects, which will, no doubt, eventually find their way into the book. I miss your generosity with ideas, your willingness to discuss, correct, argue, modify. When shall we have the opportunity to do that again?*

I have written at length and now I think I should sign off lest this should become more prolix and tax your energies. Send me your news, dear friend, and let me know if you want me to talk to Mr Roy Chowdhury regarding any help you need for your school. My continuing best wishes for its success and smooth running and to you my love and affection. I remain ever

Yours truly,
Maud.

P.S.: Give my love to Jane and Christopher. They must have grown quite beyond recognition now. Are they doing well at school? Think of me.

There is a sudden great influx of men at all hours, but especially during the evenings, in the ground floor offices and study. There are important meetings, some lasting till very late at night; Miss Gilby can hear the murmur of departing voices and, sometimes, their coaches and traps, well after midnight.

There are lots of heated, passionate exchanges, many of them in English, but she hasn't been able to pick out a telling word or phrase to gather the specific nature of these debates. Bimala tells Miss Gilby that it would be better if the lessons were held in a different place, in Miss Gilby's own study, or even in Bimala's room in the *andarmahal*; the piano classes are best left to times when there are no visitors. When Miss Gilby asks who these numerous visitors are, Bimala grows vague and then confesses that they are all involved in business with her husband. Miss Gilby suspects that Bimala either doesn't know the whole truth – for her answer has the ring of incompleteness to it – or she is hiding something from her. Miss Gilby doesn't press her on this matter any further.

The men who attend these meetings all seem to Miss Gilby to belong to the *babu* class – English-educated, wealthy, perhaps even holding government positions. They are attired in *dhoti* and shawls, some carry canes. And where is the gentle Mr Roy Chowdhury in all this? She hasn't seen him properly for over a week, and when she has (only briefly in passing – they have exchanged polite greetings), the time hasn't been right for her to ask him about the sudden spate of late night meetings conducted in his offices. And on those brief occasions, he has had a troubled, preoccupied expression on his face, or has she just imagined it?

Afternoon Teas in the English style, complete with cucumber sandwiches, Victoria sponge, plum cake, scones, lead naturally to Bimala's wish to make Miss Gilby a true lover and connoisseuse of Bengali food. If truth be told, this has been Miss Gilby's secret wish for a long time, not so much the emphasis on the food and kitchen aspects as on the unobvious corners of another country that don't reveal themselves unless one is taken by the hand and shown them by someone who lives and moves there with the ease of one born into them. Besides, the lessons with Bimala have fallen so imperceptibly into such a natural pattern of reciprocity, the two women teaching each other things about their own cultures in such a beautiful and harmonious exchange, that it would be inaccurate to call Miss Gilby tutor any longer. She started off as one but then shed that role to occupy more fully the other, companionate one. Could she have asked for any more? How fortunate she was that the very thing she desired, this immersion into the intimate India, which hardly any one of her countrymen knew or showed an interest in knowing, how serendipitous that such designs should be revealed to her. Maybe she will write a novel, a thinly disguised account of her days in this obscure corner of Bengal, and show her countrymen a true picture of this vast country, which they governed but didn't understand.

So today's morning lesson on Floral Arrangement – not a lesson, really, but just a pleasant way for the two women to while away their time, gossiping about Bimala's *jaa*s, the servants, Mr Roy Chowdhury's MA years in Calcutta, Miss Gilby's Club in Calcutta, Violet Cameron's school, that infamous weekend at the Maharajah of Mysore's palace, while the flowers lie around as neglected decoration – has been cancelled in favour of a trip to the kitchen.

Miss Gilby has never actually cooked anything in a kitchen before: orders were given to servants and they carried them out. In India, this is one thing she has played by the rules. In the morning, she summoned the cook, planned out the day's menu, went into the pantry, measured out everything that was needed – if this duty was left to the servants, they stole from you without batting an eyelid – reiterated the orders and instructions and left everything to the cooks and servants. Bimala, too, worked along similar lines: the cook came to her in the morning, she specified what was to be prepared; another servant went to the market and bought fish, meat, groceries; she issued orders – informed the cook that the fish was going to be cooked in a mustard sauce, that Mr Roy Chowdhury felt like lobster, that it was the season for pancakes – and the cook did her bidding. Only occasionally, as a special treat to her husband or a guest, would she do the cooking herself.

This visit to a kitchen, and a true Bengali kitchen, not one in an Anglo-Indian household run by a *memsahib* and staffed by Indian servants, is going to be a novel experience for Miss Gilby. She is not sure her heart is wholly in this business but it is Bimala's wish and she is, all said and done, curious to know how a native woman runs her household and her servants. Do the servants pull the wool over her eyes as well? Do they steal? Are they recalcitrant at times? Miss Gilby is eager to pick up any useful tips that might, in the future, enable her to get more value from her servants, more peace of mind with them.

The servants have been warned weeks in advance of a visit by a *memsahib* to their domain. Bimala has asked them not to giggle, stare, or worry that the kitchen is going to be polluted by the presence of a Christian. When Bimala and Miss Gilby enter the kitchen, the three women working inside immediately pull up their *aanchol* and cover their heads: the movement is so fast and instinctive, it could be almost involuntary. They turn away, refusing to look, and stare at the stone floor, crushed by shyness. Bimala gives out orders in such rapid Bengali that Miss Gilby is left searching for an isolated word or two whose meaning she might understand

and thereby make some sense of what she has said.

Bimala turns to Miss Gilby. 'We will make something special. A Bengali special food. You will see?'

'Yes, of course, but what is it?'

'You will see,' Bimala repeats mysteriously. One of the women goes to a corner of the kitchen and carries a bucket to the centre. She pulls out a giant fish from it. It is still thrashing, overpowering the woman in whose hands it cannot be contained. It slips out of her small hands and lands on the stone floor with a wet thud, flailing around in that dry, alien world, starved of its own element. An excited chatter breaks out among the servants while Bimala, excited too, moves away a few feet from the beating fish and asks for someone to get hold of it. Two of the servants come forward – one grasps the head, the other the tail – gabbling away constantly. The captured fish still convulses, struggling to get free. Bimala says to Miss Gilby, 'This is *rui*, a favourite Bengali fish.'

The third servant gets out a *bonti*, an enormous sharp curved blade, like a broad, flattened question mark, attached to a wooden stand at right angles, and sets it down on the floor. Bimala shouts out something; everybody is talking all at once, very loudly. The servant with the *bonti* grabs hold of the fish with difficulty – Bimala, standing well away from the centre, shouts again, 'Carefully, carefully' – while another servant fetches her some ash with which she smears her hand while letting go of the fish momentarily, then catches it firmly by its head and neck, leaving the torso and the tail to lash about vigorously all over again. Holding the *bonti* down with her right foot and the fish with both hands she sets its head against the blade and with rapid sawing motions severs it from the rest of the body. A loud cheer goes up, there is blood on

175

her hands and on the floor, Bimala says, 'The head is for you, Miss Gilby. It is our special dish.' She turns around just in time to catch Miss Gilby falling in a faint.

FIVE

He bumps into Sarah two days later in the main quad. They are both on their way to the library and stand around awkwardly for the brief pause of a couple of pulse beats and say 'hello' to each other as if they have been set up by mutual friends at a party, both primed beforehand that they are going to be introduced to a potential date. Then Sarah's social sparkle gleams in into this unease; she starts talking, easily first, and then it builds up to a scatterfire, an excess of things and words that try to keep something at bay with their dense shield.

'. . . and there are times I think is it really worth it, this whole business of being made to hang on, and then he smiles at me in that way he has and my knees turn to jelly . . .'

Ritwik has been so nervous about this encounter with Sarah that all he has looked for is a telling sign of their new knowledge but she is not going to give him any. Why, he wonders. Principle? The rule of confidentiality and anonymity? He hasn't paid the slightest attention to what she has been saying and suddenly it dawns on him that she is confiding in him about her long-standing problems with Richard, her commitment-phobic boyfriend who has been stringing her along for nearly two years now. The whole college seemed to know about it; Sarah's closest friends thought she should end it immediately.

'... sometimes aye, sometimes nay, I'm so confused, but Ritwik, you mustn't think he's bad or anything, it's just that I'm his first important relationship and these are all teething problems, they'll settle down soonish, but sometimes I doubt whether he's in love with me as much as I'm with him. And he's so clever ...'

This gives Ritwik a hook. He grabs it. 'What does he work on?'

'He's doing a DPhil on Wittgenstein. He's very bright. He's now thinking of applying to the US for post-doctoral stuff and I can't help feeling that he's just trying to escape from me, you know, avoiding doing the dirty deed of dumping me and letting it happen the "long-distance relationship petering out" sort of way. God, it makes me so angry sometimes, this cowardice ...'

Ritwik cuts in, 'Sarah, you might be misreading or misinterpreting. I don't know Richard, so obviously I can't say anything useful, and you know your situation best, but have you thought that some people might be like that – non-committal, hedging their bets all the time, leaving all doors open. It doesn't mean they love any less.'

He is talking drivel now, platitudes of received wisdom, but it is the only way he can staunch Sarah's flow. This flood of words, standing in the middle of the main quad, is the only way they both have of acknowledging their knowledge. He is grateful to her for this torrent and now that he has launched himself into it as well, he knows there could have been no better way.

She smiles at his psychobabble, or it could have been a smile of complicity, receiving him into her strategy; from that moment on it becomes what it should have been from the very beginning – an effortless conversation between two friends.

'But Ritwik, what am *I* to do?' she wails.

'You have to make up your mind firmly about what you want, whether you want a man who'll give you all that's conventionally associated with being in love, whatever that means, or someone with whom you're able to negotiate something different.' He gags internally at this shopworn counsellor-talk. *Where did I get all this into my head?*

'Yes, I know all that' – she waves an impatient arm in dismissal – 'but, but what if I'm not *happy* with negotiating? Why do we *need* to negotiate? Why can't we fall into an easy love rather than have this business of having to *negotiate*?'

Ritwik can tell she is getting more and more despondent by the minute; her face is flushed and warm now. He wants to scoop her up in his arms and tell her it is going to be all right, tell her she can lean on him always, but the moment passes.

'Oh, Ritwik, why are all the nice, caring, sensitive *and* good-looking men gay?' she cries out.

They look at each other with something approaching horror and, in that instant, far more than knowledge passes between them; it is understanding, even deep empathy, for Ritwik realizes that Sarah has been telling him about Richard as a reciprocal confiding. This is her way of making them fall together as equals again and she offers him the best she can – not damage, not abuse, but the impossibility of happiness in love. He swallows a few times to rid his throat of lumps then wills himself to spin off the conversation to a superficial chit-chat about the attraction of unattainable things.

'Ah, you see, it's what you can't have,' he says. 'Why do you think nearly all gay men fancy straight boys?' There, he has done it.

Sarah links her arm with his and says, 'Well, we're both a bit buggered then, aren't we?' She lets out a clear peal of laughter and then adds, 'So you've decided to do Milton then? God, you *are* crazy. Shall we go and do some work in the library and then meet later for tea? We can compare notes on who's the bigger bastard – Milton or Johnson.'

He feels so light walking to the library he is almost certain that had she not been there, physically linked to him, he might have blown away like a balloon.

In a few months' time, finals loom like hulking shapes which scare and threaten a child when the lights are turned out. Most of the people he knows withdraw into frenzied revision. Everyone psyches each other out, and there is more than a whiff of tension, fear and rivalry in the air. Jenny Hellman, in the corridor upstairs, sticks unbendingly to her fourteen-hour a day revision schedule – she times her visits to the toilet with a stop watch, adds it all up, then adds that much extra time to the end of her fourteen-hour day. Jo Milne, her neighbour, has all her chemistry formulae, in extra large letters, glued to the ceiling so she can see them first thing every morning; she has grown up with the belief that what you learn in the early hours of waking sticks longest in the mind. She doesn't bother drawing the curtains shut at night so that she can see her formulae in the morning light, first thing when she wakes up. In the college house across the car park, Paul Dunn and Matt Fellowes have discovered this little nugget and it fuels their masturbatory fantasies, which, in the run-up to finals, are a bit more fevered and frequent than usual. Others have taken more austere decisions. Ritwik never fails to be surprised by the sheer tenacity and longevity of the myth of the debilitating orgasm. Students he is intimate with have confided that they have either stopped having sex or given up jerking off, as if the increasing volume of semen in their testicles will directly nourish their brains when they're faced with the question, 'How far are Milton's early works predictive of his later?' Jenny's given up penetrative sex; this from the woman who has had sex in every possible corner of the college – the laundry room, the showers in Staverton Road, the tennis court, the Master's garden, the chapel, the library. There seems to be a secular Lent everywhere.

And then there is the steady rise of illnesses Ritwik's never heard of – glandular fever and ME, chronic fatigue syndrome and RSI. God, these are the very people who take a dozen jabs before they go to India and carry a whole pharmacy with them! At least you get nothing more serious than diarrhoea or worms out there but here you get incurable, unheard of things such as BSE and CFS and ME, the acronyms themselves trying to hide the dreaded nature of the new-fangled confections.

Anti-depressants is the buzzword, stigmatizing in some circles, highly desirable and trendy in others. Mark Pawson decides to opt out of doing finals for the third time in his long stay in college because he can't face it; he is on a record dose. Richard Keene throws himself off a cliff in Torquay, has to be heli-lifted and taken to hospital. Word has it that he is dealing very badly with trying to wean himself off Prozac and the added stress of finals has just pushed him over the edge. The whole college is spooked by it until it is discovered that the helicopter rescue was a creative addition and the only damage Richard seemed to have done was to break his leg when he fell off a boulder while drunk, listening to Nirvana on his personal stereo. The stereo, however, was shattered to bits.

A whole town going self-consciously, safely mad because it was expected of it.

*

Gavin is very busy. Ritwik has hardly seen him this term. He leaves notes outside Gavin's door; a few days later he finds one Gavin has BluTacked on to his. It says how he has been working until two in the morning at the studio and returning there at eight in the morning: the final lap in putting together the degree show is consuming him. But they could meet for a quick tea in his rooms next Sunday afternoon? Yes, writes Ritwik, and sticks the note under the door. He feels both eagerness and apprehension about Sunday – he needs to ask Gavin a few things but he doesn't hope for many answers. Gavin will probably divert it to being facetious and clever-clever.

The cottaging rages like a hectic in Ritwik's blood. It is a habit, an addiction, and he is powerless to break out of its grip. But he hasn't even tried. The pangs of guilt – *I waste so much time down there, I could use it for revision, for plain sleeping, or cracking* <u>Vindication of the Rights of Women</u> – are always mollified, suppressed, or dismissed. So far no one has justified the long waits. Ritwik is beginning to realize that this is the way it is going to be, that no one will come along to save him, but he has the clinical gambler's dopamine-addicted brain, hooked to the tyranny of uncertain and random rewards.

On nights when the sound of footfalls becomes few and far between, sometimes dwindling to nothing for hours, he sits there and thinks of his mother and the lost innocence of the word 'abuse'. The English he has grown up with in India is slightly different from England English; there is a touch of a phase-lag somewhere – they do not superimpose on each other perfectly. 'Abuse' for Ritwik has always meant the hurling of loud, angry, possibly filthy words at someone else – you can call someone a motherfucking bastard and that would be abuse. But to have it upgraded like this, in the casual snap of two fingers, to his entire childhood, to his relationship with a mother who is not there anymore to answer questions or even to listen to him – no, that can't be right. And surely this has happened, more or less, to every child in India? He feels a sudden rush of irritation for this business of other cultures, other countries, renaming and recategorizing things, using their own yardsticks, for other people, as if their definitions were universal. But this fades away as swiftly as it has arrived with the question, 'What if they're right?' The momentousness of the answer is always kept at bay by that classic reasoning: it happens to other people, not to me. He hasn't got his head fully around the cognitive shift 'abuse' has undergone.

At other times he just sits away the hours in his cubicle thinking, 'What would you think if you saw me now? *This*, this stench of urine and disinfectant and cock, this is what I am, not what you wanted me to be.' And he punishes her more by staying on another extra hour when he knows there won't be anyone else visiting the public toilets that night.

It could be any night, it *is* any night, because they are all the same, they all wind down the same way, but not this one. Four pints of Guinness in the college bar, followed by two pipes of hash in Chris Elwes's room, have left Ritwik clouded and dizzy. He can't sit still or lie down for more than a few seconds because everything starts becoming gently, dancingly unstuck and unfixed. The only hope is to keep walking. So he walks down a deserted Banbury Road, northwards, to his dorm on Staverton Road. At this time there are no cars, no people, no bicycles, just a long, well-lit stretch of road with trees on either side dropping blossom intermittently on to the tarmac. The traffic and pelican-crossing lights are desolate; they blink and change for no one at all to the rhythm of some soulless programme they are wired to.

A red car pulls up a few yards in front of him and the passenger door opens. No one gets out. By the time Ritwik arrives next to the passenger door, the driver has lowered his head and is leaning sideways to look at him. He is not thinking, there is a vague feeling somewhere that the driver knows him and is trying to give him a lift. Maybe it is one of the students who lives in his annexe. He gets in, does up the seat belt, slurs out the name of his destination and only then manages to loll his head driverwards to look at him. No, he doesn't know him, but he is nice-looking, nicely aged, a handsome uncle or maybe even a father who'll take care of him. There is a benign smile somewhere behind those thin lips, waiting to break out. Only when the car picks up speed does Ritwik notice that the man hasn't spoken at all, or even asked for directions; in fact, he seems to know where they are headed. Ritwik tries to focus but it is too much of an effort. The motion of the car moving smoothly doesn't do him any good: he longs to move around so that he can keep the imminent sickness at bay.

The man takes the correct left turn, drives into the college annexe – he sure knows the place – parks and turns off the engine.

When Ritwik speaks, what comes out is a slew of words run together, 'J'yoowannoo come up?'

The man nods, pockets his keys and follows Ritwik who is already making his way up the stairs, as stealthily and as silently as he can. He doesn't really need to – there is no one awake at this time. He turns around and puts a finger to his lips, indicating to the man to be quiet. The man nods.

Ritwik tiptoes down his corridor. His is the second room on

the left; there are four on either side of the narrow, fluorescent-lit corridor. He opens his door noiselessly – he is surprised he doesn't fumble with the key and the Yale lock – and steps in. The man follows. There is enough diffused light in the room from the car park outside so he doesn't bother turning on the light or drawing the curtains. He starts taking his shoes and clothes off. The man does likewise, almost mimicking him: first the shoes and socks, then the jacket, the T-shirt, the trousers. They both leave their underwear on.

Ritwik gets into bed and slips under the duvet. The stranger sits on the edge of the bed and takes him in for a while, his face in the refracted orange glow of the room a chiselled piece of shadows. He too gets under the duvet and stretches himself along the entire length of Ritwik, their bodies touching at every possible point. The man's body next to him is all silk and warm honey. And then it hits Ritwik.

The wave, which had been building up for such a long time, which he had managed to avoid so far, now suddenly grabs him up and hurls him against an invisible wall. The whole room spins and nausea crashes all over him.

He tries to lie curled up; his head in the crook of his arm, his eyes shut, and wills it to go away. He thinks of distracting things – *The Parlement of Foules*, the way Dr Carter's eyes had misted up while talking about the moment Pericles recognizes Marina, the day Pradip-mama had dropped a small, heavy metal die-cast on Aritra's head many, many years ago and then run out of the house, fearing Jamaibabu's wrath . . . He is not even willing this random succession of thoughts any more; they are using him as a conduit to flow through, following their own opaque logic. But the room doesn't stop swinging. He lies like an inert log, good for nothing, while the man tries to rouse him with his hands, his mouth, but nothing works. The nausea is so great that Ritwik doesn't have the chance or the luxury to feel embarrassed.

He gets up to go to the toilet to be sick, realizes he doesn't have a thread on him and, anyway, the toilet is too far down the corridor, in the landing outside, so he just lurches out of his room and enters the tiny shower cubicle that two rooms share. He retches at the sink – they are only dry heaves, deep and exhausting – but brings nothing up, only a bit of sour mucus. He decides that if he has a shower he will feel better, so he turns the shower on and lets the hot water sting and lash him while he slowly slides down against the wall to sit on the cubicle floor.

What wakes him up is the cold: the boiler has run out of hot water in the time he has been sleeping under it. He rises, turns it off, shivering from somewhere deep inside him. He steps out, opens the door to his room and there it is, on the floor, as if it has been slid under the door – a white envelope, stark on the dun carpet. Wet and dripping, he picks it up and opens it. Inside, there is a single twenty-pound note. The man has left, god knows after waiting for how long. Ritwik wonders if he tried getting him out of the shower.

He fingers the crisp banknote and a whole new world starts to swim into view like an undiscovered planet caught in its orbit for the first time. So that is how much the man thought he was worth naked but unperforming. And his second thought is – 'food money for nearly a week'.

He doesn't know it now but he is going to look back on this as a watershed in his small life.

PART TWO

PART TWO

SIX

When Ritwik got a two-year scholarship to study in the UK, two months after his mother's sudden death, he knew he was going to leave Calcutta for good. The scholarship was his escape route, the prison door that had been left miraculously ajar. He would walk out of that door and never return. When he flew out of Delhi – strangely enough, on the thirtieth of September, the first anniversary of his father's death – he knew he wasn't going abroad only to study but was also leaving behind one life, permanently, in exchange of another one; unknown, but better. This much he knew – it was going to be a better life, as what wouldn't be, compared with what he had lived for seventeen years in Grange Road?

Ritwik couldn't manage to explain the whole extent of it to Gavin that Sunday afternoon, first, in Queen's Lane coffee house, and then, later, in Gavin's room, when Gavin realized this wasn't any ordinary casual-friendly visit Ritwik had asked for. But he tried. Haltingly first, sometimes embarrassed, at other times, downright ashamed, and then in one scrambled shuffle-dance full of false moves and missteps, he attempted to give Gavin some idea of the terrain he had crossed. There was no order to it, no neatness or linearity, just a piecemeal tearing of the fabric and flinging the bits to Gavin. Let him try and make sense of it, Ritwik thought; where he had not managed well, perhaps someone else, an observer or an outsider, would do better.

At least he started from a kind of beginning: when Gavin asked him what exactly he was escaping from, he said poverty, but what he should have said was the possibility of never escaping.

'I don't want to live in squalor any more. I don't want to go down the way of my father, helpless and exploited, unable to escape. I don't want to become him. If I return there, they will now attach their suckers on to me. Life out there will just carry on running in the same groove, decade after decade. I want a different life,' he said to Gavin. How could he explain that he was also trying to escape the wet sticky monsoons; the blood-drying heat of summer, which made him a drugged, ill, slow creature for six months of the year; the insects that came out in giant colonies and multiplied during the rains; the sheer filth and mud of Calcutta streets, which welled in over the edge of his frayed sandals and oozed between his toes; the thirteen hours of power cuts every day; the chronic water shortage; the smell of paraffin and kerosene oil everywhere; the soot on the glass of the hurricane lamps; the random days without meals, all fanning and exacerbating the tensions in the joint family, year after slowfestering year?

Gavin could very easily have replied, 'Get a grip' or 'Welcome to Real Life', or something equally cutting. And he would perhaps have been justified.

If Gavin was convinced, he didn't show it. He had heard the disjointed, stuttering stories in total silence. For once, he had resisted making comments or ironical facial expressions.

'Is it also . . . also a . . .' Gavin hesitated, 'is it a matter of your

190

sexuality as well that you don't want to go back? I can't imagine gays having a ball in India.'

Ritwik looked up. 'Yes,' he said, 'yes, it's partly that. I can be free here. No, you're right, the opportunity to be myself here is something I value immensely.'

A long silence during which Ritwik fretted at the blatantly unconvincing segue into self-help-book talk.

'Look, Gavin, one runs away from a country because of war, famine, torture, repressive regimes, all that sort of thing. Those are very serious things. But isn't someone justified in turning one's back on unhappiness, just turning away from the end of a road? I'd like the opportunity to start again, in a new place, with new people. Is that so unthinkable?

'Everyone aspires to a better life, why can't I? I've got a chance now . . . if only . . . if only you'd show me an opening . . . you've lived in this country for many years, you came here as a student but you worked and studied and managed to stay on. I'm just asking you to help me go down that way.' He halted. There was a long pause. Then he said, 'Besides, there's nothing . . . no one, actually, to go back to.'

The betrayal was ashy, bitter in his mouth as the image of his brother's innocent face, brimming with the yearning to flee too, stabbed him. But he had to lie now, lie to live; besides, he could console himself with the last letter from Aritra, in which he had written of his imminent departure for Delhi to start his MA. He, too, would escape to his new life, Ritwik thought, trying to console himself, willing himself to believe that Aritra would be fine, would be able to look after himself. He had no choice except to believe in that. What Ritwik had purposefully hidden from Gavin was the sense of freedom into which his parents' death had released him.

His parents had ensured that the brothers got a good education partly in the hope that when the boys grew up they would save their parents from the miserable lives in which they had got mired. Ritwik and Aritra were their one-way escape tickets, their pension fund, their rescue team. They had pinned all their hopes on the boys, counting out their days, waiting, waiting, waiting for the final move out of the hell of Grange Road.

But both boys had been released from that enormous burden of responsibility: from every day being weighed down by the expectation to perform, by the accumulated weight of the sacrifices their parents had made every day. Of course, these had never been made explicit but the silence of martyrdom, an eloquent dumb show of clenched jaws and haggard faces, had become deafening and solid.

The boys had been brought up like pack horses, blinkered to see nothing else but the path straight ahead; suddenly their masters and drivers were gone. The slow grind of the knowledge that they were investments or life-insurance policies disappeared one day, burnt by the same flames that consumed their mother. In its place was a freedom so vast and so dark it was as if they had been catapulted into deep space. No one to look after in their old age, no responsibilities, no waking up in the middle of the night worrying about the ill health of frail parents or the money to pay for their proliferating illnesses, no rope at their neck; their lives were their own at last, no one could lay any claim on them.

When Ritwik had returned from his scholarship interview and told Aritra the good news, his brother's face had first fallen and then radiated the purest joy, the joy of watching your prison inmate escape, knowing you're going to be next through the breach he has made. As children, both of them had been reminded constantly by their mother, 'Doing well in school is the key to everything. You can have everything you want if you're good in studies.' The indoctrination had worked in ways that even she hadn't dreamed of. Both boys had found it easy to do well academically but Ritwik was not so sure if this had come about because it was the only reward he could have given his miserable parents – their eyes lit up when the school report came in or when one of the boys won a prize; they couldn't stop beaming and stopping the neighbours in the streets to tell them about their latest achievement – or if he had been beaten into doing well by his mother. Either way, the key, which she had so incessantly talked about, was miraculously in his possession and he hadn't even known he had had it until he was awarded a scholarship to go and study in England.

It was only now he realized that she had given him both the key and the freedom to do whatever he wanted with it.

The rain was viciously lashing the window, driven wild by a high wind. Something shifted and realigned inside Gavin. Ritwik had almost whispered the last few words, 'Besides, there's nothing . . . no one, actually, to go back to.' Yes, Gavin was going to help him but only just: he didn't want Ritwik to end up as his responsibility. He would introduce him to a few things and a few people and leave him to it. There was no way he was going to become a crutch for this boy who was all set to become a difficult problem. He saw in Ritwik his own early years in London and didn't want that different creature of the immature past, his own green, stumbling self, inflicted on him now, for growing up always entailed a certain degree of embarrassment, a slight desire to wash one's hands of recent history. He didn't want a walking reminder of it in this boy.

Ritwik couldn't have imagined what Gavin was about to hand

him: an old, frail woman living in London who needed care and someone to stay in the house to keep an eye on her. She was too poor to offer any pay but the accommodation was free and he could get a part-time job for other living expenses. Gavin didn't explain how he had met the woman but he mumbled something vague and inaudible about friends of friends among the Brazilian community, or maybe distant relations in North London and left it at that. It seemed to Ritwik that Gavin had stayed at this woman's house, looking after her and working in restaurants, at a time when he needed a toehold in this country but beyond that hypothesis he knew he wasn't going to get any more information from his friend. Besides, he was so thrilled that Gavin had thrown him a lifeline, and that too, so easily, so quickly, he couldn't be bothered prying into Gavin's past; he was sure this old woman was going to shed more light on it.

When the practicalities – convenient time and dates, packing up stuff, storage, finals, phone calls – were all worked out, Gavin asked him, casually, 'You do have a permit, a visa to stay on in England, don't you?'

Equally casually, Ritwik lied, 'Oh yes. Yes, I do.' And then added, for verisimilitude, 'For another two years.'

'But you don't have a work permit?'

'No, but it won't be a problem to find people who'll hire me on a loose-cash-at-the-end-of-the-day basis, will it?' He was willing Gavin to say oh yes, no problem at all, London is brimming with such people.

Instead, he got, 'Strictly speaking, that's illegal. If you're found out, there'll be trouble' – he pronounced it 'trawbble' – 'rules about immigrant work and stuff are very strict and complicated.' When Ritwik looked confused, Gavin added, 'But there are thousands, if not hundreds of thousands, of people working in the black economy. You'll certainly not lack company.'

Ritwik couldn't bring himself to think that far. It was enough for now that he should have found a place to stay, a place for free. That had been shaping up as the most consuming problem in his head and now that it was solved he was going to savour it for a little while before that other big problem – a job – occupied all his thoughts.

He looks like a boy, Anne Cameron thinks. He can't be more than a boy, surely. He is so thin he looks like he hasn't been given a square meal in his life. Dark, gangly, bones everywhere. The first thing she notices about him is the way his sharp collarbones jut out. The Brazilian man – or is he Scottish? She doesn't remember but if he is, he speaks English funny, like a foreigner – sits making introductions, which have long passed their need or usefulness. She is not listening to them, anyway. She is thinking of the big sparrow she had seen that very morning, trying to balance on the swinging birdfeeder at the end of her long garden. Anne Cameron is convinced that any smaller bird, say a robin or a tit, would have managed just fine. It is the size of the sparrow that is suddenly bothering her. It was, frankly, enormous, the size of a builder's fist; she hadn't seen anything like it before.

'. . . couldn't really have guessed it was a sparrow if I hadn't tiptoed closer and watched it for a while.'

The Brazilian man has stopped speaking. The starved boy has looked up sharply at her. The Brazilian man – for the life of her, she can't remember his name – asks politely, 'Pardon?' *And to think that he used to live here for, for . . . oh many months . . .*

'Many months, didn't you?'

195

'Pardon?' he says again.

'You lived here for how long? Many months, wasn't it?' she asks.

'Yes, nearly a year,' he says.

Nicholas, that's it, that's his name.

'Nicholas,' she fairly shouts.

'Pardon?' Again.

'Your name's Nicholas.'

'No, Gavin.'

Gavin? She doesn't recall anyone called Gavin staying with her. In fact, she doesn't know anyone of that name. She furrows her brows for a moment but the name doesn't click or light up. Most of them don't nowadays.

'You were saying something about a sparrow?' he asks hesitantly.

But she has already seen the two men exchange knowing glances. She is not going to tell them. She is going to punish them for thinking she is scatty by depriving them of the morning's marvel, the fat sparrow. She doesn't care very much at this moment that she has been speaking her thoughts aloud again.

'No, I wasn't,' she says with cold firmness. That conversation is now closed.

'What did you say your name is, again?' She looks at the thin boy.

He says something that sounds suspiciously like nitwit.

'You'll have to speak up, I'm getting a bit deaf.'

'Ritwik. R-I-T-W-I-K,' he says.

She takes a few moments to visualize the spelling and then repeats his funny name. 'Ritwik. Ritwik. What a . . . an . . . unusual name,' she says. 'What colourful names you have. Do you know, the woman who lives down the road, I think she's from your country or thereabouts, she once told me that all their names mean something, like . . . like . . . Lord of Fire or . . . Direction, or something. I'm sure she said direction, someone in her family has a name which means direction. You know, north or south, that sort. I can't remember the names, and they're all so difficult, anyway. Do you know the Indian word for direction?'

The boy struggles for a while and then says, 'No, I can't think of one particular word. There are so many languages in the country, so many different words for one thing, that . . . that I can't give you one right answer.'

'But you *are* from India, aren't you, not from Pakistan or Bangladesh?' she asks.

He looks up sharply again. 'Yes, that's absolutely correct,' he says.

Nicholas is quiet, sitting with something approaching a smile on his face. He would so like to interrupt but she is not going to let him: he is in disgrace at the moment for being naughty about her miraculous sparrow.

'You know, you' – she moves and lifts her head towards the dark boy – 'you'll have to keep reminding me of your name. I'll get it slowly, but you'll have to help me. I'm not very good with names, I'm getting on in years . . .' Her voice stops abruptly.

The boy remains quiet.

'If you tell me what your name means, perhaps I shall be able to remember it,' she says.

'It means a priest who officiates at a fire sacrifice,' he answers solemnly. He is embarrassed as well, as if he has said it many times before, with a predictable range of effects, none of them the one he wanted. Nicholas rolls his eyes heavenwards and thinks she hasn't seen him do it.

'Ooooh, how grand, how grand, a priest at fireworks. What fun. Do you have religious fireworks in India? You shall have to tell me all about it.' She has been trying to get out of her battered armchair ever since she decided to punish the impudent Nicholas but hasn't managed so far. She hopes that if she keeps on talking she can distract them from her failed attempts. And then, halfway through some boring old conversation about laundry and bedpan-cleaning and locking all the doors and not letting the cat out, she will rise like an elegant bird, all grace and brilliant plumage, and flit out in one seamless curve, out of the door, up the stairs, glide glide, swoop balletically into the bathroom and only after she has sat on the toilet will she let her bladder go . . .

But, no, she is doing it now on her sofa, the hot, comforting trickle, the gathering wetness under and around her like a leaking amniotic sac; she hopes the men will not notice, or at least not until later, not until she has sat on her piss long enough for it to be absorbed by her skirt and the armchair cover and the thick cushions, but, oh dear, it has somehow managed to be rebellious and trickle over the edge and fall drop by drop at first and then in a halting dribble on to the carpet. She waits for a few seconds, debating whether she should draw attention to it and then has no choice but to ask that Nicholas over there to help her; at least he knows the ropes and where things are. No use fretting over spilt milk. Or spilt piss. She cackles out, 'Spilt piss, ho ho ho ho, no use crying over spilt piss.'

The priest boy doesn't seem to react to her words. He stands up, along with Nicholas, when she at last manages to do so herself. Nicholas comes forward to hold her hand and support her brittle steps, crooning, 'It doesn't matter, doesn't matter at all. Now let us go upstairs gently, one step at a time, one step, one step.'

She feels irritated at being treated like an invalid; after all, she has only pissed herself, not fallen down the stairs and broken her hip or her neck or anything silly like that. She says, a shade too brusquely, 'I know, I know. You know, I can climb the stairs on my own and wash myself and change into fresh clothes without *your* help,' while clinging to his arm. She stresses the 'your' spitefully as she strings out these lies. No use scaring off that pretty priest boy at the first meeting; he'll find out what's what soon enough. She is going to tell Nicholas that the boy can stay and have him explain things to him.

In her state, the only illusion she can hold on to is that she is letting the boy stay out of generosity, not necessity. As she and Nicholas shuffle out she marks that Nicholas doesn't turn around to give the boy another significant look.

Almost the first thing Ritwik notices about Anne Cameron's house is the decrepit state of its interior, as if everything in the house, all the objects and furniture and fittings are sliding, along with their owner, through old age to the final and inevitable stopping and shutting down.

Almost.

Because the first thing that strikes him is Anne Cameron's age, the imprint it has left on her fragile and crumpling face. The furrows of the skin on her face remind him of the folds of clothes and the way they hang in neat, realistic undulations on old statues of the Buddha from Gandhara that he had read about and seen pictures of in history lessons in school so many years ago. He has never seen skin that reminds him of drapery, never seen anyone look so old. When he touches her hand, it is like a weightless claw sheathed in a loose, papery integument; he could have been touching a bird with light, hollow bones. But her blue eyes are clear and bright, with an occasional tendency to go rheumy. It is Ritwik's belief already that they don't miss a thing even when her mind is ballooning far above her immediate physical surroundings. She is so senile that she can't get Gavin's name straight but Ritwik has this uncomfortable feeling that she marks every single significant look Gavin gives him throughout the time they are in the living room with her while her mind is doing opaque leaps and arabesques about fat sparrows and being impervious to what he is called.

Ritwik doesn't know London at all. This is his first visit to the city so he takes Gavin's word for everything but only provisionally; he knows he will revise the co-ordinates Gavin has given him with time. But that bit about Brixton being a different country strikes him, at first glance, as not wholly untrue. Nothing could be more different from the England where he has spent the last two years. That was a beautiful, pale, homogeneous thing out of every second book written in English, the age of its migrant population stuck eternally in the very early twenties, a white white white town. Compared with this clash and colour, it was Life-Lite; this is life with all the dampeners thrown to the four winds. This is populated by another people, mostly Caribbeans, Gavin tells him, with a smattering of African diaspora here and there. He also helpfully adds that it is the crime, drugs, mugging, stabbing and race-riot capital of England: it was the scene of the *most shocking, most brutal* race-riots in the country a mere ten years ago. From the way Gavin says it, Ritwik can't figure out whether this gives the place extra street-cred or lots of negative points.

The people here speak a different English, if English it is at all in the first place, for Ritwik cannot understand a word of the loud conversation, punctuated by effervescent laughter sliding to the outright cackle, that takes place between two enormous women on the seat behind him in the bus. It is the sort of laughter that makes everyone within earshot smile and think nothing can be very wrong with the world, after all; there is the chaotic music of life about it. He suddenly realizes that he is letting out, very slowly, the breath he has held in for two years. Doesn't the notion of feeling at home have to do, first and foremost, with this uncoiling?

The illusion takes a knocking as Ritwik and Gavin walk up Ganymede Road, one of a set of nearly identical roads off Brixton Hill: it is a genteel, late nineteenth-century, redbrick-and-stucco terrace, each house exactly the same as the next one, with only the ascending and descending numbers, and the different coloured front doors, to distinguish them from each other. Road after road, with names such as Leander and Endymion, of this bland sameness: step off the clash, mingle and patchwork of Brixton Road and you are in white, middle-class suburbia. But only *mostly* white and *mostly* middle class – Asmara Eritrean Restaurant, Miss Nid's Jamaican Take-Away, Lion of Judah Take Away, The Temple of Truth, a clutch of hairdressers with names such as 'Hair Today, Gone Tomorrow', 'Hair Apparent' and 'From Hair to Eternity', all keep redrawing the contours of this amazing pocket of England. To Ritwik this indicates that there are other such delicious and defiant dissonances scattered all over this country; he will have to keep his ears open for them from now. They were not something he had heard here before, but now they speak to his blood with an intimacy he finds almost embarrassing, as if he has been exposed as unfaithful, disloyal.

Nothing has prepared Ritwik for 37 Ganymede Road. First of all, it is a detached house in a terrace: it stands out so starkly that Ritwik can't help reading it as some sort of a coded sign trying to tell him that life in number 37 is not going to resemble the broad flow of other lives around it. It is narrow and tall, like a slice from a thick, round cake. When they step in and walk down the narrow passageway to a landing, there is a staircase leading upstairs and five steps leading down to another landing off which open a living room, set back from the front of the house, and a huge kitchen, beyond which there is a big space that could have been a conservatory once but the glass roof is so smeared and dirty now that it is dimmer than the walled rooms. Beyond that, Ritwik can see a long garden, dense with knee-high grass and lush, tangled nettles: it is really a scaled-down forest. He could never have guessed, from the thin outside, that the house would open up like this, room after room, widening from the bottom vertex of a V to its open mouth at the top, much like a wedge.

And then there is the matter of dust. It lies in a thick patina on all the surfaces, sofa covers, bookshelves, tabletops, armrests, mantelpiece, on all the objects in the house – framed photographs, pictures, the leaves of the spindly weeping fig in the living room, the window frames, bric-à-brac, everywhere. There are dust balls, loosely assembled around hair and fluff and lint, in the corners of the filthy linoleum-covered kitchen floor. Dust is slowly invading and taking over the entire place. It is like being in a first-world version of the flat he left behind in Grange Road for a better life, a place where dirt is slowly edging out humans from their space. Everything here is shabby and fading, as if all the colours of things were slowly abandoning a sinking house. It is a drab, battered, leached affair, with all energy extinguished, a space imploding on itself with neglect and inertia.

And if Gavin hadn't told him about the cat, he wouldn't have known what to make of the orange hairs on the sofa covers and cushions, sometimes lying in loose tufts on the carpet, which can only be described as not neutral, not regulation, not snot-beige, but acoloured. At the same time as his heart sinks to think he will have to live here, he feels so much pity for old Mrs Cameron in this dying house that his eyes prick with tears.

The last shreds of any doubt Ritwik has about living in this squalor are dispelled when Mrs Cameron pisses in her armchair. He has no idea what has happened and when the old lady gives off her frightful cackle while wittering on about spilt piss, he thinks her mind has gone down another unknowable alleyway. Even when Gavin gets up to support her upstairs, he wonders briefly about the abrupt departure and the sharpish tone of her voice when she tells Gavin she doesn't need his help; he can't make any sense of it. He sees the darkish, wet patch at the foot of the armchair but doesn't notice it.

Suddenly all the pieces fall into place. It must be because he has been trying to work out subconsciously for some time the characteristic odour of the house. The smell seems familiar to Ritwik but he can't quite pin it down; it is somewhere just outside the edge of his mind, refusing to come in. Initially he thinks it is just the sour and musty smell of unaired old age and its attendant detritus, maybe even stuff rotting in the kitchen bin or something similar. And then ammonia, piss, cat, wet patch, *I can wash myself and change into fresh clothes without your help*, *no use crying over spilt piss* all fall together in a pattern.

There is no one in the room now so he doesn't have to check his tears. Once again, they are not so much for this woman who has nearly arrived at the end of her days as for an imagined future his mother didn't reach. It is not a future he wanted for his mother but he thinks this is probably how she would have ended her days had she been alive. And yet again, a decision has already been made for him: he is going to stay on in 37 Ganymede Road and look after Anne Cameron. He will clean up the place, he decides valiantly. He might not manage to make everything unfade, but he will certainly deal with the dust, dirt, stench and urine-sodden carpets on a war-footing.

One final thing about the haven he has left behind.

He had Heroin Eyes in the toilet cubicle one night. It was a brief, edgy coming together, he remembers now with a dry mouth and a tautness in his gut, an encounter slippery with saliva, semen and fears. He was so grateful for it that the next time he met him there, weeks later, he was bold enough to whisper, 'Do you want to come back to mine?'

Gently, gently, don't rush it, he's a twitchy butterfly, anything sudden will make him flit. But the desire overwhelmed the caution.

Heroin Eyes hesitated; through the crack of that pause, Ritwik pushed in, 'It's safer than here.' There was a desperation in him that made him play on the other man's fears so unscrupulously.

'OK, then. I'll leave first. You follow me out to my car.' Everything in hot muffled whispers.

Ritwik followed him outside, his chest in a tight knot; he would either come back to his room or run away like he did the first time. There was no telling which one it would be. He was going to have to play it very carefully.

They got into the car, a clapped out white Renault, which made a clattering racket as it moved along, and Ritwik gave him directions. His name was Matthew – he wouldn't give his surname – and he seemed uncomfortable with this sudden intimacy that sharing an ordinary, unsexual space with a cottaging pickup had brought between them. It was somehow a more revealing and skinless interaction to negotiate.

Ritwik tried to make the odd reassuring comment – 'Don't worry, my neighbours are all fast asleep at this time', 'I very much have my own privacy' – but they petered out in the shallows of his own unconviction. Matthew, meanwhile, drove steadily, giving away nothing except a pheromonal charge of his deep discomfort. Ritwik didn't dare look at him sideways or in the rear view mirror in case he upset the fragile balance that had brought this beautiful stranger his way. He had been chosen: that fact alone caused an unpleasantly effervescent cocktail of euphoria and anxiety inside him. He had to keep a firm lid on the bubbles of helpless, nervous giggles trying to rise to the surface.

Once past the parking lot and the staircase, in which Matthew behaved like a jittery cat, things seemed to ease out a bit. Matthew even smiled as Ritwik drew the curtains first and then turned on the bedside lamp, twisting it to face the wall so they had only a dim, diffused refraction in which to love.

He was too tall to fit into the bed, which was also too narrow; both of them kept bumping their knees and elbows on the wall against which the bed was pushed as they moved and changed positions. They tried to make as little noise as possible and spoke in whispers, afraid that they were going to wake someone up in the adjacent rooms. At the end of it, Ritwik hoped Matthew had got out of himself and felt a little bit of what he had felt.

Afterwards, Ritwik didn't dare ask him to stay because he was afraid his raw need for this lanky stranger would become so transparent if he spoke out the words; he would surely take fright and scuttle off. Instead, he arranged the single duvet over both of them as best as he could, draped himself around Matthew and nestled his head in the hollow of his shoulder blade and collarbone.

'So what do you read?' Ritwik asked after a while.

'Math.' The knot had loosened somewhat. There was a new languor about him; they could almost be friends talking.

'Where are you from then?' Ritwik immediately regretted the question: two consecutive questions after sex could only seem to be an inquisition to an Englishman.

'Blackpool. Do you know it?' Ritwik could feel his self-deprecating, apologetic smile as he named his hometown, as if it were a private joke he wasn't supposed to get.

'No, I don't. Is it nice? Isn't it near the sea?'

'No, yes, in that order.'

'Why isn't it nice?'

'Have you ever been to an English seaside town? They are havens of the most unimaginable tack.'

Ritwik kept quiet, then casually asked another question, hoping Matthew would not latch on to this crude strategy of extracting information by spacing out and strewing the vital questions among the innocent ones. 'So did you do finals this year?'

Ritwik expected a stark 'yes' or a 'no', which would have made his work slightly more laborious but not impossible. Instead, Matthew, who seemed to have no idea what Ritwik was leading to, answered, 'No, I'll do schools next year.'

OK, second year then. I just need to find out his college.

'Are you going home for the long vac?'

'Yes.' Long pause. 'I need to. I have a summer job waiting for me.'

Why isn't he asking any questions? Why hasn't he even asked my name? Or what I read? He reached his hand backwards and turned the light off.

Ritwik wished he had kept a firm bolt on his mouth seconds after the next question came out but the cumulative effect of Matthew's escape through dark alleyways, his refusal to give out normal information, his wound-up, nervy demeanour, could only have led to this. 'So you aren't out, are you?'

Surprisingly, Matthew appeared to be relaxed about this too. 'No, I'm not.' Brief but untense. He added, 'I did join the Gay Pride march last week though. Along with all of Wadham.'

Ritwik's mind did silent whoops of joy; the last piece of the puzzle had been handed to him on a plate. He refused to let Matthew realize this so he persisted with the outing questions. 'You know, this could be the most supportive town to come out in.'

'Yes. I know. But it's my parents, you see.'

'But parents almost always come round to their children's point of view, don't they? Eventually.' *What do I know about that one?*

'Yeah, but my parents are very . . . very . . . what can I say . . . conservative.'

'You might try testing the waters.'

'You don't know how old-fashioned they are. I was watching telly with them one evening and there was this shot of two blokes kissing – I forget what programme it was – and they freaked, kind of. My mother kept muttering "Disgusting, disgusting", while my father stood up, spat on the telly and turned it off. Then they just sat there, silent and shaking, with . . . disgust. I suppose.'

There was nothing to say after this. Ritwik curled himself

closer around Matthew. As he drifted off, he lost the restraint not to say, 'Stay. Please.'

Matthew remained silent and awake beside him.

The film of sweat, which joined and divided them where their skins touched, was the only indication to Ritwik how much time had elapsed between falling asleep and Matthew's swift leap out of bed on to the floor to get hurriedly into his clothes. He didn't even have time to assimilate this uncoupling before his eyes adjusted to the bending shape of Matthew pulling on his socks. By the time he got the words out, Matthew was at the door.

'Wait. What's wrong? Why don't you stay?' The words come out paratactic, congealed.

'No, I've got to go. Goodnight.'

And he was out of the door, shutting it closed after him with not so much as a scrape or a creak.

Somehow the room seemed to amplify the sounds as Ritwik, wide awake now, listened to the front door slam shut, and then the cough of ignition, once, twice, before Matthew's Renault kicked into its purring life. A narrow beam of car headlights swept flawlessly along the ceiling in a neat, brief arc through a crack where the curtains had not quite joined.

His heart was an eel again, doing its infinite loops around the same elegant path.

VI.

There it is, her name, in the respectful and prominent upper case customarily afforded to the author: VIOLET CAMERON, appended to the essay 'Some Thoughts on Industrialization in Bengal: A Reply to Nikhilesh Roy Chowdhury'. And that juxtaposition is what stops Miss Gilby in her tracks as she is walking along the verandah, idly leafing through this latest issue of the *Dawn*, dated October 1903. It is no secret that Violet has been a member of the Dawn Society from '97 or '98. In fact, Miss Gilby collaborated with her on an essay on the education of Indian girls, which was published in these pages in '99 along with articles by Annie Besant and by the Irish lady who went under the name of Sister Nivedita, and which went on to have far-reaching effects in the Anglo-Indian community not the least of which was the final excommunication of both Mrs Cameron and Miss Gilby from the society of their 'own kind', as James didn't fail to point out repeatedly. But this coming together, this dialogue conducted at a distance between two people who have never met but have heard so much of each other through her, this sudden discovery of her inadvertent role of (of what? catalyst? channel? conductor?) medium, a role she has been so comprehensively ignorant of, this sends a thrill down her spine. It is as if all the coincidences of her worlds were chiming together in a big, resonant harmony.

She rushes into her study and takes in the article in one sitting. There are half echoes and muted soundings in Violet's words: Miss Gilby has herself heard similar ideas from her and has had long discussions with her about self-government and that area forbidden to women – economics. The article appears at once familiar and strange. Violet seems critical of an unthinking and wholesale transplantation of Western industrialism to India, arguing that this will lead to similar problems faced by the West as a consequence of industrial capitalism – the stark division of the wealthy and the poor, class conflict, the gradual erosion of moral values and traditional modes of life and living.

One has only to cast a passing glance at the reports of the various commissions and blue books, which investigated the state of industrial life in the factories, mines and workshops between 1833 and 1842; or to read the pages of Engels's 'State of the Working Classes in England in 1844' to convince oneself of the truth of the total degradation and suffering of the English working classes brought on by the Industrial Revolution, she has written.

The implied position of Mr Roy Chowdhury appears to be in favour of economic independence from British rule by a steady process of industrialization, which would then also become a remedy for the growing poverty of India. Miss Gilby's head swims in the attempt to reconstruct his position from Violet's essay. She is so fired up with curiosity that she immediately writes a note to him and summons Lalloo to deliver it.

Dear Mr Roy Chowdhury, Imagine my pleasant surprise

when reading the latest copy of the Dawn*, which was lying on the table in the drawing room, I discovered my friend Violet – Mrs Violet Cameron – to be the respondent to your article in a previous issue of the same journal. Having now read Violet's article, but missing yours, I am greatly interested in reading it and conversing with you about such matters. Will you be so kind as to let me have the earlier issues of the journal? I gather you are very busy and occupied with a great many things of late but would Afternoon Tea next Wednesday suit you at all? I await your reply. Yours etc.*

It is during the blotting of the note that understanding dawns on her. Part of the answer has been staring her in the face for some time now and she hasn't been able to see it. All these meetings, this thronging of 'Dighi Bari' with strangers and important-looking men at all hours, these late nights, this air of resolve, conspiracy almost, of action and planning and conference, why, Miss Gilby thinks, this is all towards social and political ends. Economic self-determination, alleviation of the country's chronic poverty – these were the noble aims they were working towards. Miss Gilby feels caught up in the great arc of political movements and it is not without its slight tinge of fear – what if these men are plotting a Revolution to overthrow the Raj? Where does she stand then?

She pushes the questions away as figments of her overactive imagination, so prone to creating scenarios of disaster and calamity when there are none on the horizon. She decides to write to Violet and chide her affectionately for not letting her know in advance of this correspondence between herself and Mr Roy Chowdhury in *Dawn*, but she doesn't go ahead with it for she has written to her only a week ago, besides, who knows, Violet may have written to her and the post had been delayed

211

unreasonably, as it was so frequently. She will wait to hear from Mr Roy Chowdhury.

Mr Roy Chowdhury's note, in neat, firm copperplate, arrives next morning, with a pile of *Dawn* back issues going back to 1897. It is brief and warm:

I shall be delighted to take afternoon tea with you the following Wednesday. I apologize for my negligence and absence – there have been too many things demanding my attention of late and I have been inundated by these pressing duties. If you so desire, we might even go for a ride by the river. Will you kindly let me know? Yours ever, etc.

Miss Gilby opts for the ride and sends a note with Lalloo who has evidently been instructed to wait for her reply. The rest of the morning, and a large part of the afternoon, is taken up with *Dawn*. What Miss Gilby assimilates during that time – and it is only a tiny fraction of the surging sea around her – makes her head spin. She reads about English-educated Indians raging about the contrast between the prosperous West and destitute India, about how this is no fate-ordained thing but a deliberate tool of British policy. She learns about the premeditated destruction of Indian handicrafts leading to an overwhelming dependence on agriculture, which in turn has been ruined by an excessive land tax. And then there was *the wealth drain in the form of first investment and later home charges, which India was meeting only through a harmful and deceptive export surplus. India had thus been reduced to the status of supplier of raw materials and market for British-manufactured goods.*

Page after page she is taken through the need for industrialization, the promotion of technical education, demands for the government to abolish its anti-Indian tariff policy. She learns of self-help, boycott of British goods, increasing reliance on home-produced things, all of which constitute *swadeshi*. She uses her burgeoning knowledge of Bengali to translate it as 'of one's own country', 'native', 'indigenous'. She even knows its antonym: *bideshi*, foreign. She reads Bholanath Chandra's rallying cry to dethrone '*King Cotton of Manchester*'. *It would be no crime for us to take the only but most effectual weapon of moral hostility, left us in our last extremity. Let us make use of this potent weapon by resolving to non-consume the goods of England.*

Amidst the long names of Bengali intellectuals – Satishchandra Mukherji, Jogindranath Chattopadhyay, Motilal Ghosh, Kaliprasanna Dasgupta – she notices the flash and shine of two familiar names, Violet Cameron and Nikhilesh Roy Chowdhury, dart through the thicket of words like gleaming fish through dark reeds.

Miss Gilby feels the oppressive heaviness that comes with such a deep and total immersion in a field hitherto largely unknown to her but with it also comes, paradoxically, a liberating lightness conferred by that very activity, for it has resulted in an intellectual endeavour that initiates the long but ultimately victorious battle with ignorance. From now on, she will involve herself in the thick and press of this germinating revolution. No sooner has she made up her mind than another, more nebulous, feeling assails her, a feeling for which she fails to find either a name or a phrase. She feels oddly divided, melancholy, as if her loyalties were neatly riven and have been called into question, as if two equal forces were pulling her in contrary directions. The sense of implied betrayal she feels is already enormous.

At lesson the next day, Bimala and Miss Gilby toil over an English translation of a Rajput story – the one of Queen Padmini, reputed to be so beautiful that when she took her early morning walks in the arbours and waterways of the palace in Chitorgarh lotus buds refused to blossom lest she put their collective splendour to shame. The Bengali is very difficult for Miss Gilby. There are problems with the language – simultaneously both poetic and innocent, intricate and childlike – the metaphors and the idioms that don't quite translate, but as Bimala, slowly and surely, unfurls the story, shaking it out open from its neat, compact folds into a dazzling fabric sewn with every colour and skill imaginable, Miss Gilby falls under its spell.

They have reached the point at which Alauddin Khilji, Emperor of Hindustan, hears of the famed beauty of Padmini, hidden away in the proud and unassailable Rajput stronghold of Chitorgarh, a land that has stubbornly resisted the steady Muslim incursion throughout Hindustan, holding up its militant head defiant and high. The Sultan of Delhi marches towards Rajputana with five hundred thousand soldiers, razing and laying to waste everything they pass, intent on reaching Chitorgarh and abducting Padmini by sheer, brute force. As news reaches Chitorgarh that the Muslim army is advancing towards the town, Rana Lakshman Singh orders the seven iron gates of the town to be shut to the invaders.

Alauddin had thought it would be a child's task to march into Chitorgarh and grab Padmini. But arriving at this hilltop town he found that just as the cage of ribs enclose and hide the heart, in a similar way Padmini was protected by the bristling swords of the brave Rajputs, Bimala and Miss Gilby translate together.

Crossing the tempestuous seas was easy compared with crossing those seven iron gates of Chitorgarh to get to Padmini. The Pathan emperor ordered his troops to set up camp at the base of the hill.

At night, when Padmini and her husband, Rana Lakshman Singh, are taking the air on the crenellated parapets and terraces of the castle, the night air of the desert biting, the moon a bright, bitten nail in the clear black sky, she suddenly points a finger down to the vast desert outside and exclaims with delight, 'Rana, Rana, look at those waves! It's magic, the sea has arrived at our doorstep.' The Rana replies sadly, 'Padmini, those are not the waves of the sea but the tents of Alauddin's army laying siege to our town.'

The following morning, the Rana sends his messenger to the Emperor. Alauddin's wishes are simple. 'I have no bone to pick with the Rana,' he tells the messenger, 'I'm here for Padmini. Hand her over and we'll depart peacefully.' The messenger replies, 'Your Majesty doesn't seem to be very familiar with our Rajput nation. We would rather give our lives than surrender our honour.' Alauddin interrupts, 'The mind of the Sultan of Delhi is unswerving – Padmini or war.' The messenger bows and leaves.

The army of the Delhi Sultanate continues with its siege of the fortress of Chitorgarh for a year but there is no sign of the Rajputs relenting or asking for a truce. Alauddin's hopes of starving the besieged Rajputs have, by the turn of the year, turned to ashes. And he still hasn't set eyes upon this fabled beauty. Meanwhile, his soldiers are getting restless and bored: they murmur against their lot, the desert country they find themselves in, the obstinacy of these Rajput warriors, the lack of comfort and luxury they are used to in Delhi. Alauddin takes *note of this growing disenchantment and hits upon another plan to get his way.*

He sends word to Rana Lakshman Singh that he will return to Delhi with his soldiers if he is granted the sight of Padmini in a mirror: just a reflection of her will satisfy him. And while he is inside the fortress, the Rana shall be held personally responsible for the Sultan's safety. The Rajputs agree readily to this compromise. Alauddin silently congratulates himself on his shrewdness: never in his wildest dreams had he imagined that this race of hardy warriors could be duped so easily.

The day arrives. The Pathan Sultan bathes in rose water, adorns himself in silks, pearls and emeralds. He departs for Chitorgarh castle accompanied by two hundred of his toughest soldiers, men who laugh at danger and death. Alauddin takes the steep, narrow road up to the fortress while his horsemen hide in the forests at the bottom of the hill. By the time he reaches the fort, another dark, chilly desert night has descended.

Rana Bhim Singh, the queen's brother-in-law, leads Alauddin to the white marble palace of Padmini. It is lit with thousands of candles, some of which, flickering and winking through the latticework windows, cast shadows and grids and nets that move and seem alive.

The Sultan is seated on a gold and velvet couch. After a while he says, 'Why the delay? Let's have a vision of the Queen so I can depart for Delhi in peace.' Rana Bhim Singh removes the covering from a huge Aleppo mirror placed directly in front of the Sultan. In the depths of that glass, dark and flawless as the doe's eyes, Padmini is reflected like the light of a thousand suns. The Sultan cannot believe this creature is human. Incredulous, he rises out of his cushioned seat and reaches out his hands to touch this shadow in the lonely depths of the mirror. Rana Bhim Singh cries out, 'Beware, Sultan, don't touch her reflection.' From her hidden place, Padmini reaches for a heavy goblet, picks it up and hurls it towards the mirror with all the strength in her body. The glass shatters into hundreds of little bits and her reflection instantly disappears, like the mirage that it was, with the harsh, brittle jangle of breaking glass, leaving only the blind, dull back of the frame. Alauddin is so startled that he steps back three paces. There are only empty shards of glass everywhere, jagged points of cold light. It is as if she was never there, as if the Sultan had dreamed everything.

The horses move at such a slow canter, side by side, that Miss Gilby can hold the parasol in her left hand and the reins with her right with no degree of effort or stress. The morning mists have disappeared and it is another fine and golden autumn day. There is a light breeze, which sets the bamboo groves shivering with their rustling music, a sound Miss Gilby finds so comforting that she is convinced this particular tree is planted by gardeners not for the usual pleasures afforded by garden vegetation – its appeal to the eye, its fragrance, benevolent shade, fruit or flower – for none of those, but for its sound. As far as possible, she tries to direct her horse through these bamboo thickets to listen to their soothing papery rustle. Mr Roy Chowdhury seems to be in complete agreement with her about the music of bamboos: he calls it Nature's Aeolian harp. Miss Gilby savours the felicitous comparison as the horses move along gently, past flooded rice fields with their eye-hurting green, past fragile mud embankments, past vast, watery fields of jute.

The conversation starts with talk of Bimala, as usual. 'How is she coming along, Miss Gilby?' he asks.

'Wonderfully, just wonderfully, I must say,' she answers, throwing a smile in his direction. 'We're in the middle of learning a song – *Long, long ago* it's called. Perhaps you know it, Mr Roy Chowdhury?'

'Yes, I do. Bimala seems to hum nothing but English airs nowadays. Whatever it is she might be doing – folding clothes, cooking, arranging flowers, sitting with me while I eat – there is an English tune on her lips.' He chuckles gently.

Miss Gilby's smile broadens. 'Well, we are a success then, what do you think?'

'Oh, an extraordinary success. She's so much more confident now, so much more, more – what's the word? – outgoing, I think, if that's not too literal or punning. Did you know that Bimala's *naw jaa* refuses to go to sleep nowadays unless Bimala reads out to her from one of her English books?'

'Really?' Miss Gilby is very surprised.

'Yes, that's the exact specification – a story from an English book. Bimala reads out every sentence in English – that's part of the order, too – and then translates it for her. It seems to have become a daily ritual.'

Miss Gilby laughs with sheer pleasure at this achievement.

'It's just as well that Bimala has someone to talk to these days: I've been occupied with so many things that I've hardly had the time to sit and have leisurely conversations with her.'

'I have noticed there are some demands on your time of late. I've been wondering about all these meetings and this crowd of gentlemen who are around the house of evenings. Do they have anything to do with what I've been reading about in *Dawn*?'

He remains quiet for a while, then lets out a sigh before saying, 'Well, Miss Gilby, it's a long story and I do not know how acquainted you are with recent political developments. I'm afraid I would just bore you to tears if I launched into it.'

'On the contrary, Mr Roy Chowdhury, I shall be very glad to be enlightened. As it is, I feel somewhat in the dark, left out of great happenings.'

'There are no great happenings. Just a gathering of Bengali men very concerned with the destruction of our industries, our country's steady downward spiral into poverty. We're trying to work out ways and means to address the issues and do something about them.'

'Are government policies to blame for some of these ills?' Miss Gilby wants it straight from the horse's mouth.

'I'm not going to lie to you or beat around the bush, Miss Gilby. You must know about things such as the abolition of cotton import duties more than twenty years ago, or the imposition of the countervailing excise fifteen years later. It seems that our country has become just a supplier of raw materials to Europe. We grow cotton, or silk, it's all shipped to England to be made into cloth, and this cloth, grown by us, on our soil, is sold back to us. Who does it benefit? Who makes the money? We have become a huge market for Europe. What is effectively erased is the need for industries in this country. Our production, our manufacturing, our sectors are all being wiped out. But it is our produce that powers British export.' He pauses for a while. 'I'm sorry, Miss Gilby.'

She is silent, sensing that he hasn't quite finished. If she hadn't read about it beforehand, she would have been very shocked.

'Do you know British traders are buying increasing quantities of foodgrains and agricultural raw materials for export? This is forcing up prices and causing periodic famines.' There is another long pause. They take a turn at a narrow mud track running past a field of unidentifiable vegetation, thick, lush, and somewhat menacing. The track leads to the village: Miss Gilby can see the straggle of huts, the minarets of the small mosque and the market square, which is nothing now, now that there are no traders or farmers selling their wares here, but just a clearing, empty, deserted.

'What is the solution, Mr Roy Chowdhury? Am I wrong in thinking that the changes you want, the establishment and flourishing of science-industries in Bengal – and all this I gather from my very recent and, I'm sure, very rudimentary and incomplete reading – this beginning of technical education, the revival of traditional and indigenous crafts, all of this huge venture, is impossible without some radical political changes?' She's not going to bring herself to utter the momentous word.

'You're right, Miss Gilby.' He pauses again. Something in the air between them tells Miss Gilby that he is going to say the unsayable.

He does. 'All this could really be a preparation for the larger agitation for an independent India.'

There, it is out in the open now, Miss Gilby thinks, relieved and concerned at the same time. There is a loose group of five or six men walking towards them. One of them is carrying a large basket on his head and another, two ploughshares. There is an enormous coil, like a rolled up garden hose, of what Miss Gilby used to think was water-lily stem in another man's hands. She now knows it is an edible aquatic plant called *shaapla*, which bears beautiful pink flowers. The men look scantily dressed to Miss Gilby. This is one thing about India she has never come to terms with, this sparsity of attire of its people, the general and constant sense of dirtiness of the little they wear, as if those were the only articles of clothing they had and washing them would mean having to go unclad for the duration of washing and drying. The men's clothes look threadbare and soiled even from this distance. They are probably poor farmers.

Mr Roy Chowdhury obviously knows them for he gets off his horse with an 'Excuse me, Miss Gilby, these are some of my tenants. Do you mind if I have a word or two with them? You can carry on ahead if you wish.'

He dismounts as Miss Gilby says, 'If you don't mind, I'll just wait, shall I?'

The men greet Mr Roy Chowdhury with long *salaam*s. He, in turn, takes each man's hand in his, individually, and lowers his head briefly. Miss Gilby is struck again by the respect with which Mr Roy Chowdhury treats everyone, his unshakeable sense of the dignity of every human being. The men cannot stop staring at her. She gives them a general smile, trots off a few paces ahead and waits while Mr Roy Chowdhury and the men exchange words, which sound to her agitated, concerned. At one point when she turns to look in their direction, she sees one of the men in what she can only term a supplicant's position – arms outstretched and held up, palms open, much in the way Muslims pray to their Allah. Mr Roy Chowdhury speaks with both his hands clasped and held against his heart. From this distance, she cannot hear very much but it wouldn't have made much of a difference even if she could for the local dialect is all but incomprehensible babble to her.

After several minutes, Mr Roy Chowdhury joins her, his arms now laden with the bundle of *shaapla* stems; half a dozen or so of those stems end in delicate flowers. His brows are furrowed, his eyes shaded.

'Not very good news, I'm afraid, Miss Gilby. The salt factory I started last year is making heavy losses. It seems unfeasible now to keep it running for much longer. These men say that because locally produced salt costs more than British salt, they're finding it difficult to sell it to customers. They are suffering losses too. They want me to shut down the factory and let them sell foreign-manufactured products.'

'Did you agree?'

'I never asked them to sell *swadeshi* products only. For the very brief period they did, their losses were so heavy that I immediately reverted. These men are very poor, they have to make a living somehow.'

There is a long silence. Mr Roy Chowdhury sighs again and attempts to introduce a lighter tone into the conversation. The effort is obvious. 'Miss Gilby, I shouldn't be heaping my petty concerns and burdens on you. I do apologize.'

Before Miss Gilby has a chance to protest, he continues, 'You know, my late brother, Hrishikesh – he was the husband of Bimala's *naw jaa* – he used to be part of this secret society called Sanjibani Sabha in the '70s, when he was a teenager. The members tried to set up a match factory and a handloom. When I was a little boy, he used to tell me stories of how the matches refused to ignite and how the handloom produced just one towel, one towel only, before it had to be shut down. I used to find it funny. I still do, but in a different way.'

Miss Gilby is trying to think of an appropriate response when he points to the *shaapla* stems and says, 'Shall we ask

Bimala to get the cook to prepare this for lunch? Have you ever had this before? It's usually added to a *dal*.'

They have reached the gardens of 'Dighi Bari'. Miss Gilby understands that conversation on politics is terminated for the day. Bimala is supervising the *malee* at the flowerbeds and greets them with a radiant smile.

'The Magpie',
Wellesley Lane,
Velloor,
North Arcot,
25th September 1904

Dear Maud,

Where have you come across what you call 'dark mutterings' about the division of Bengal? Why are you concerning yourself with such matters? What exactly you hear – and I cannot, with any confidence, assert what it is you have gathered by way of gossip and unsubstantiated rumour – I do not know for you do not tell me. Instead you ask a lot of questions about an imminent partition of Bengal. I understand that His Excellency Lord Curzon, during his short tour of Bengal earlier on in the year, might have given out to be understood that ambitious schemes for a larger readjustment of Bengal were being considered. The Indian newspapers have been full of this, beating it up into a froth of meaningless frenzy so that their narrow partisan interests are served at the expense of the Government.

What I have gathered – and this might not be very much more than what you have gleaned from your own readings in Indian newspapers yourself – from conversations with people who might be involved with that burdensome and prickly project is already public, for the troublemakers in the Indian National Congress and various loose but no less seditious factions within Bengal have not ceased to trouble Her Majesty's Government of India with petitions, letters, conferences, a veritable barrage of sound and fury, opposing the partition plan. The Bengalees, always a thorn in the side of the Government, like the Mahrattas, like to think themselves a nation, and dream of a future when the English will have been turned out, and a Bengalee Babu installed in the Government House, Calcutta. They will, of course, bitterly resent any disruption that will be likely to interfere with the realization of this dream. If we are weak enough to yield to their clamour now, we shall not be able to dismember or reduce Bengal again; the result will be a cementing and solidifying, on the eastern flank of India, a force already formidable, and certain to be a source of increasing trouble in the future.

The diminution of the power of Bengalee political agitation will assist to remove a serious cause for anxiety: it is the growing power of a population with great intellectual gifts and a talent for making itself heard, a population which, though it is very far from representing the more manly characteristics of the many races of India, is not unlikely to influence public opinion at Home most mischievously. I notice even now that Bengalees, with their genius for intrigue, have already found their own advantage and are indulging their instinct in stirring up strife, so everything has to be done as <u>arcana imperii</u>. From a political point of view alone, putting aside the *enormous administrative difficulties – which are better left to men who understand them best because they are complex, intricate and too difficult for women's gentle and delicate minds to comprehend – that an undivided Bengal continues to present, partition is most necessary.*

The Bengalee race, and most predominantly, its power-hungry and overeducated Hindoo population – for it is the Hindoo population that constitutes the political voice of the Presidency, the Mohammedans having remained inactive so far – is given to conspiracies and endless schemes to consolidate its power and dominance over that Presidency. Bengal united is a power; Bengal divided will pull in several different ways: that is the current wisdom among us and almost wholly justifies any scheme for division. It is uniformly accepted and acknowledged, although no one will put it down on paper, that one of our main objects is to split up and thereby weaken a solid body of opponents to our rule.

What the exact lines of division are going to be, which areas and districts will constitute the new Province of East Bengal, these are unknown to me for they are still in a state of flux and subject to endless discussions, but I gather that the district of Bograh, along with Rungpoor and Pubna – all your neck of the woods, as it were – are going to be transferred to the new Province. Simla might change all that. There seems to be a great air of secrecy and furtiveness about the whole business.

Don't worry yourself too greatly with these matters, the Bengalee Babu is wont to see tigers behind settees when there are none, and accordingly create comparable frenzy and frantic politicking. As with all these things, the

division, if and when it happens, will pass peacefully:
Bengal will make a noise for a few weeks and then
acquiesce.

How is our very own Bengalee Babu responding to all
this? Does he not have any views that he might have
communicated to you? I shall have to leave the story of
the persistent Daisy Ampthill for another occasion for it
is too long to relate now; she grows a menace apace and I
fear for my peace of mind and sanity sometimes with her
around, always hiding in some piece of shrubbery or
behind a tree, waiting to pounce as a tiger on its prey. I
shall leave you on tenterhooks. I promise to write with
more news from Velloor.

Your loving brother always,

James

SEVEN

The November morning briefly toys with the idea of frost but settles for bruised sunshine instead. If it holds, the afternoon is going to be one of those autumn ones, glassy air blazing with burned gold till the dark comes down like a swooping cat, sudden and swift. In their separate rooms, both Anne Cameron and Ritwik, sleepless and still, think of cats.

It wouldn't do for Ugo to get that fat sparrow, no, it wouldn't, but she knows of no way to prevent cats from stalking birds. He would probably come and offer the half-dead bird to her one of these days, purring and wrapping himself around her ankles. No, she couldn't have that. Ugo himself was one of those offerings, although an unintended one. The Pakistani family five doors down, with three children, one of the kids, what was his name now, Saleem or Osman, one of the boys, certainly, but beyond that she cannot be any more definite, one of the boys had come in with seven kittens one day, spilling out of his arms and shoulders and hands, and dropped them one by one in her front room.

'You like? Amma says we can't have them all. You want one? Please.' The boy, hardly more than six, was pleading.

'No,' she said firmly. 'No. Who would look after it?' Best not to get attached to creatures, and at such a very late hour in life too.

'You,' the boy said, with perfect, unassailable innocence.

'I'm not very good at looking after things.' The words hurtled out, as if her faculty of speech itself had become incontinent. What was she *doing?* Very soon, she'd actually start telling this little boy, with such lovely dark eyes, like a forest lake, about how she could never look after things. People. Richard. Clare. Christopher.

'Please.' That word again.

In the end she didn't know how one had come to be left in her house. But she had got the nice and ingratiating Mr Haq, the boy's father, to install a cat-flap in the back door leading to the garden. That way, Ugo could go in and out as he wished; that was more than half the problem taken care of. But the boy, was it Osman or Saleem, she doesn't see any more.

She lies. She saw him once, huddling in a corner of the road with half a dozen other boys, when she made an extremely rare sortie from her front door to the end of the road one day, just to see if she could make it unattended, just to see. The boys had fallen silent when she had emerged from the house. A few foreign words, opaque and derisive, tinged with cruel laughter somewhere, had leaked out from their close cluster. And then, 'Bag lady.' More laughter. Of course, they thought she wouldn't be able to hear.

Maybe it wasn't Saleem or Osman at all among those boys.

Ritwik is obsessed with Ugo. Never having shared a living space with an animal before, his first instinct was to feel slightly repelled by the whole idea. The cat hair everywhere didn't help. And he was convinced he would catch some disease off the fat marmalade animal, diphtheria or something equally terrifying. He doesn't know when that gave way to this rapt adoration, watching Ugo and thinking how he was perfect, pure form. Nothing that he did – the way he moved, yawned, curled himself, stretched out in the slowly moving quadrilaterals of sunshine on the carpet, head-butted Ritwik's outstretched hand, ran his jawline along the human knuckles – nothing was less than infinite grace.

And then there was the disdain, the utter unimportance of taking anything else except his own wants into account. Pure form, yes, but pure selfishness as well. And why not? Why should animals conform to human ideals or indeed be made to behave in human ways? That is why Ritwik hates dogs, their slavering, adoring excess, tailoring their lives to human expectations and emotions. No such rubbish with cats. They do things on their own terms; you like it, fine, you don't, you can fuck off. There was a letter in the *Guardian* a few weeks ago that reminded readers: 'Dogs have owners, cats have staff.'

He is becoming a staff to Anne. No sooner does he think that than he cringes at the bad pun. Oh, well, anyway, he *is* a support, there is no denying that. In the beginning, while Gavin had explained his duties to him, it had all seemed neat, contained, a job more than anything else: making sure that Mrs Cameron used her stairlift all the time; keeping the bath dry *at all times*; locking and securing all doors and windows because who knows what miscreants might be targeting the house, knowing a brittle, eighty-six-year-old lady lived there with only a part-time help; feeding the cat; changing Mrs Cameron's sheets; giving her a warm sponge three times a week; chamber-pot duties; cleaning her after she had messed herself; heating her soup; collecting her winter fuel allowance; trips to the Post Office for monthly collection of state pension . . . The list grew, like something organic, with a breathing, spreading life of its own, but it was manageable. It could be boxed under the broad title of 'duty' and that itself limited it.

What he hadn't been prepared for was the little ambushes tucked away cunningly between the spaces of these boxes. Like the time Anne walked into his room, without knocking, her powder blue nightdress clinging to her bony form like a helpless sail trying to clutch on to something before it was blown away by the lawless winds. In the kind, low light of his bedside lamp, which he always kept on, he noticed there was a conspiratorial look in her hollow eyes, a gleam that could only have been called naughty. And mingling with her normal doughy odour was something else, something floral and sick . . . juniper berries, yes, that was it.

It took him another few seconds to nail down the smell to gin and that too after he had noticed her teetering on the soles of her feet while saying, 'Boy priest, story time. Story time.'

Almost without thinking, Ritwik looked at the watch on his bedside table. Twenty past two. Did the old bat never sleep? Over the last few months, he had gradually trained himself to be woken up like this, with as little gap as possible between the meshy drag of sleep and awareness, sharp like an instant shard of glass. You couldn't have the submerging luxury of drowsiness when there could be an eighty-six-year-old lying in a crooked and impossible heap at the bottom of the stairs. But to be woken up by the drunken old bat demanding to be read a story? There were limits. Besides, where the fuck did she get her hands on a bottle of gin?

He swallowed his annoyance. 'It's very late. Do you know what time it is?' It was pointless asking her anything, or having the to and fro of ordinary human interaction through small talk with her. She never answered. In most cases, she probably never even heard the questions from the other side. In the radical innocence of old age, the horizons of her world had become that of an infant's: very close and devoid of everyone in it except her own self.

'Priest boy will read a story now. You can choose the book.'

'How generous of you. Thank you.' The acid crept up his throat. If Anne heard it, she didn't say anything. There was always the danger that she registered far more things than she ever let on. Ritwik had found out that Anne clocked things with the beady-eyed sharpness of a bird, bringing them out later, at unexpected and sudden moments, seemingly without motive, but they never failed to unsettle Ritwik deeply. It was like having your bookshelf suddenly break into speech one morning, 'You don't really have time for a wank now, why don't you go down and make Anne her tea?'

So he did exactly what he was told: he chose the book. He got out of bed, went over to the bookshelf and picked out his Arden edition of *Hamlet*. *Teach her a lesson, this one; let's see if she ever asks me to read again.*

'Shall we go to my room? Richard shot himself in here. It was his study, you see,' she said.

Just like that. No warning, no advance preparation, nothing. As if it were as trivial as saying, 'This room is too dusty, let's go sit somewhere else.' Ritwik knew that the questions which swarmed into his mind, like humming locusts, a huge drove of them, would receive no answers, not even the basic one, 'Who is Richard?' He filed the comment away, heavy, dangerous, like a bullet, in his head. Like Anne, he would bring it up when least expected, see if surprise led to a chink in this wilful wall.

'I removed all the pictures and drawings of birds from the house after that. The bloody lot. Gave them away, drove out to a landfill and got rid of the rest,' she keeps talking to herself.

'OK, let's go to your room,' he said, his voice perfectly modulated, normal. Overnormal. 'Do you want me to take your arm?'

When they were settled in Anne's room, with its musty smell of dust, sourish yeast and the new liquid detergent Ritwik had bought last week, he opened the book at random and started reading, his delivery flat, expressionless, as deliberately droning and undramatic as he could make it.

> *O Hamlet, speak no more.*
> *Thou turn'st my eyes into my very soul,*
> *And there I see such black and grained spots*
> *As will not leave their tinct.*

To this, Hamlet then says,

> *Nay, but to live*
> *In the rank sweat of an enseamed bed,*
> *Stew'd in corruption, honeying and making love*
> *Over the nasty sty!*

Something in the words, some feathery whisper behind this son chiding his mother, his disgust oozing out from the fascinated, sick lump of words he had so lovingly chosen to pin her down, lulled Ritwik into stressing the right syllables, even doing different vocal modulations for Gertrude and Hamlet. He left out his tags, 'This is the Queen', 'Now Hamlet says', and let the drama tug him away.

O speak to me no more.
These words like daggers enter in my ears.
No more, sweet Hamlet.

Anne's head was lolling. There were bubbles forming and breaking, accompanied by the rhythmic drone of slight susurration, on her lips. Ritwik stopped, reached for the edge of her counterpane and tried to wipe her mouth. At that very instant, she opened her eyes, pin-sharp, unreadable, and said, 'Christopher died in India. Malaria. A severe type, they said. That's why I came back. Richard was in school here. I could hardly live there on my own.'

What on earth was she saying? She was in India? When? Why wait for four months and then mention it? Why not in the very beginning when an *Indian* person was moving in? Who was Christopher? Which bit of India? When? Why? Was Richard her son? Was Christopher her husband? Would Gavin know? Why hadn't he said anything?

He continued his reading, leaping over lines because Anne's words had made him miss pages and he didn't want to waste time finding the line where she had lobbed her explosive: he didn't want to give her an excuse to think he was unduly curious about her life.

Mother, for love of grace,
Lay not that flattering unction to your soul,
That not your trespass but my madness speaks . . .

'We lived first in Delhi and then in Almora. Christopher was with the Forest Commission. You're not from there, are you? You look different.'

'No, I'm from Calcutta.'

'Never went there. I went out there when I was your age. Came back ten years later. Changed something in me. Didn't like it there, not to begin with. Not even while I was there. But after I came home, for years I went around missing something, not sure quite what. Felt a bit empty. Pale. Make no mistake, I was relieved to be back here. But then, over time, I got bored, I suppose.'

Ritwik kept very quiet. It was like watching a very rare animal come out to drink; if you so much as exhaled, it would immediately bound off, never to be spied again.

'One of Christopher's officials was eaten by a tiger. Fancy that. Hoo hoo hoo hoo.' The laugh was like a high moan of a malicious wind in the pliable top branches. 'Shouldn't laugh. But it seems so unbelievable now. Tigers carrying off people. They were doing track repairs to the railway lines, I think.' Pause. 'No, I think I'm confusing it with something else. Heavy rains and the whole rail track got flooded. They had to take a boat from Ranikhet. A boat on the railway lines.' Her voice was becoming faint, she seemed to be losing the thread of her story. She looked distracted.

'Christopher was born there. Son of an army bigwig, Lieutenant-General or something. His mother was a very unconventional woman. Must have had a lot of steel in her to have broken all the rules in that society. Ran a school for Indian girls. Unimaginable at that time, really. Loved India. Passed it on to her son. You know what they say, India rages like a hectic in your blood' – the way he started and looked up sharply, the allusion could have been a jet of ice-cold water between his eyes – 'you have to go back. It does something to you, to your senses, your blood, Christopher used to say. So he went back. Joined

236

the civil service and went back to his first love.'

Ritwik was speechless. He let this torrent of information seep in slowly, then asked, 'What happened then? Did you meet him in England? And his mother?'

Long pause.

'Could you keep an eye on the fat sparrow and see Ugo doesn't go near it?' There, the curtains had come down again.

'It will be difficult to do that.'

And then, like the curl of a whip lashing out, 'You don't have a mother, do you?'

Nothing will wrongfoot him, nothing will make him pause. 'No.' Brief, like the truth.

'So he's going mad and making all sorts of wild accusations about his mother. Go on then, why did you stop?'

O Hamlet, thou hast cleft my heart in twain.

He says,

> *O throw away the worser part of it*
> *And live the purer with the other half.*
> *Good night ...*

His voice was a straight, grey road, monotonous and vistaless. He read the words without managing to get to the meanings behind them. When he lifted up his burning face next, at the sound of a gentle purr, Anne's head was twitching on the pillow, gently pumelled by unknown dreams. He sat there for a while, waiting for the rhythm of her snoring to calm him down, and then turned the light off. Ugo had come in unheard and was rubbing himself against him, purring so loudly that Ritwik was half-convinced he had some pulmonary illness. He picked the cat up and gently left the room. Ugo could come and curl up on his duvet while his fingers gently kneaded the creature's thick orange pelt.

He turns off his bedside lamp: the sky outside has lightened enough. Another twenty minutes of snoozing, then he will have to go about his morning duties – tea and biscuits for Anne, cleaning out the chamber pot, washing her. As he is about to drift off, there is a shuffling outside his door. Seconds later, Anne walks in – she never knocks – and asks, 'What does "enseamed" mean?' She gives the word three syllables.

Ritwik flails about in his head for a bit, then remembers exactly what she is referring to. He says, 'Greasy. Drenched in animal fat and, by extension, disgusting things exuded from the body.' He toys with the idea of saying something more about Hamlet's obsession with his mother having sex but decides there is no need.

She appears not to take notice of what he has said. 'Come into my room, I want to show you something. Come. Don't make any noise.' She beckons with her right hand, like a witch trying to lure a child into her cottage.

Anne leads him to the window looking out into the garden. 'Look at the horse chestnut tree. Somewhere in the middle. Do you see what I see?'

Ritwik has spent a lot of hours in the summer disciplining the garden – weeding, uprooting, cutting down and even burning the more recalcitrant unwanteds, mowing the grass down to a stubble with the lawnmower borrowed from Mr Haq. It doesn't look good – it is still not a garden – but it isn't a contained bit of jungle any more. The three trees – the ceanothus, the lime tree and the horse chestnut – look grand and imposing in the bare space. Right now, the tops of the two big trees are beginning to get tipped with the morning.

In the wet, pewtery light, it takes Ritwik a few seconds to find the exact area that has drawn her interest but when he does, he wonders how he could have missed it. Sitting on the middle branches are a pair of improbable birds, each no bigger than a small pigeon but with red breast and stomach and a regally curving swoop of lustrous green fantail, long, elegant and utterly out of this world, Ritwik thinks. They couldn't be real. And then he notices the small sparrowy head of one of them move jerkily. As if in response, its companion shifts clunkily sideways on the branch.

Anne is speaking and when he manages to listen to her equally improbable words, he doesn't know which amazes him more, what she is saying or the presence of these magical birds. 'Quetzals, I think. Though I may be wrong, my eyesight isn't exactly perfect. Trogonidae. The genus name is *Pharomachrus*. Found only in the mountain forests of southern Mexico and Panama.'

Ritwik is rooted to the ground, unblinking in his gaze. He wants to let the images of the birds sink into the deeper lairs of his head and hold them there forever because he knows they are going to disappear soon, very soon, but this sudden discovery of the ornithologist in Anne distracts him. He is ashamed to discover his unquestioned assumption that an eighty-six-year-old should have no interests, should remember nothing from the heydays of her life, but should be content only to count the last hours off in infirmity, dependence and mindlessness.

Anne breaks the rapt silence. 'They are never found in these parts of the world. What are they doing here?'

She has put her finger on the other nodule of unease in Ritwik. These are not British birds. Of course, he doesn't *know*, but creatures such as these don't perch on trees in south London gardens, that's for sure. Call it a prejudice but *England* cannot harbour these birds.

'You know, they were sacred to the Mayas and the Incas. I think it was first described for Europeans by Francisco Hernández in the 1570s.'

Ritwik is so amazed by this sustained focus, even narrative, that he turns around to face her. 'How do you know all these things?' There is astonishment in his voice; it comes out hoarse and unsteady.

'Oh, it's one of those things I was interested in. I wanted to become an ornithologist but in those days women didn't go to universities. So I kept reading, collecting books, pictures . . . I even started an album of Indian birds of the foothills of the Himalayas. The Garhwal region.'

The world is unfolding in tiny furls of amazement for Ritwik. It is not the sight of the bird that has made him speechless, it is this hidden maze in Anne, this gradual illumination of the penumbral spaces he didn't know had existed.

'I met this quite remarkable woman out there. Ruth Fairweather, her name was. She had embarked on this ambitious project of compiling a comprehensive account of Indian birds, region by region. Much like your Audubon in the United States. I learnt so much from her,' she continues.

'I wanted my son to become an ornithologist. He did.' Pause. 'Richard loved birds.' A longer pause. 'Ruth loved him, treated him as her own son. She taught him how to look, how to listen, how to hold the pen and brush and pencil to draw birds.'

Ritwik's mind is jammed with cogs whirring away and

turning, turning unceasingly. When the right clicks happen, and one cog locks into the groove of another, he holds back all reaction, even to the new knowledge of Anne's son, an ornithologist, having killed himself in the room where he is staying at the moment.

Anne is silent for the longest time this morning. Ritwik senses that a door has been shut. He will have to wait until it opens of its own accord. He turns around and looks out of the window again. He is not surprised to see the quetzals gone. Has he dreamed the whole thing? The morning is brightening but the lower reaches of the trees are still in a mothy gloom; it is only the top branches that hold today's light.

The Haq house was a teeming, heaving slice of the subcontinent, filtered through first world glitz and polish, in a south London street. The throws on the sofas were Indian, a couple of chairs, a low wooden table, a hookah centrepiece on it, the red curtains with mirrorwork, the three framed mirrors with gold Urdu lettering on them, presumably passages from the Koran, all reeked of a home the Haqs had left behind and studiously tried to recreate in a foreign country. The predominant effect was of density: cupola-like curves instead of straight lines, intricate and busy craftwork, *zari*, mirror, colour. The wallpaper, an electric pink, was picked over with golden stars and the gold was repeated in the picture rail, which ran the length of three walls.

Two girls, noses running, had come downstairs and were now standing at the doorway to take in the stranger who had just entered their house. They had chubby cheeks, wore nearly identical salwar-kameez, and looked very similar. Ritwik guessed one was about five and the other, six. He smiled at them and said 'Hello.' One of them, the one who looked slightly older, turned her face away and ran upstairs, barely able to contain her shy smile. The younger one stood staring at him. Mrs Haq – or so he assumed – chided her in Urdu, 'Now, say "hello". Don't be rude.'

The girl ignored this with perfect insouciance and continued staring. The older girl now reappeared, peeped into the room, and said, 'Ma, can you please turn on the CD player again?' Perfect South London English, down to the splayed out vowels in 'again'.

Mrs Haq replied in Urdu. 'No, not now. Look, we have a guest. We'll talk to him now.' She turned to Ritwik and ushered him into the living room. The English she spoke was heavily accented. 'Sit down, sit down.' She made a moue of mock-exasperation and added, 'There's not a moment's rest from these children. Mr Haq's helping Saleem with his homework. He'll come soon.'

Ritwik's first impression was of a woman who seemed very much in control of her household. She chattered on, 'It's good to know there's someone looking after Mrs Cameron. We've always been worried about her. She's so old. She should be living with her children and grandchildren. Why does she live alone? I always ask her, Mrs Cameron, you must live with family, that is what they are for, to take care of you in your old age, but she says nothing, just smiles. You tell me, would this have happened in Pakistan or India? The English like to live alone. Only their own self, that is what they think about all the time. Not mother, not father, but just own self.'

Someone had managed to switch on the CD player upstairs without the help of Mrs Haq. The garish Hindi film song, all overblown strings and a superfluous flute, flooded down. Every word of the shrill female voice was audible: *A ring on my finger, a serpent in the ring*. Mrs Haq ran upstairs. There was the sound of a rapid stream of Urdu and English, a brief wail, a thud and then the abrupt end of the song. When Mrs Haq came down to the living room again, the younger of the two girls was with her. She had put on a headband and some glass bangles. She stayed nestled against her mother but couldn't take her eyes off Ritwik. Mrs Haq started saying something about her children when Mr Haq, bluff, portly and garrulous, walked in. The girl immediately switched allegiances and jumped on her father, who scooped her up, all the time keeping up his bonhomie talk.

'Ah, so you're new boy, heh heh heh, we are curious about you. We find out as soon as you come here, someone from our part of the world is here to look after Mrs Cameron. You're from Pakistan, no?'

Ritwik hesitated before he said, 'Well, very close. India.' He didn't know why that question made him so defensive.

There was a brief blink before he launched into his camaraderie again. 'India. India. Well. We're neighbours. Practically the same country, no? Before they divided us, we were same, all together, Hindu Muslim living as brothers.' He got more and more animated during the course of his benign politics. 'Yes, we live in harmony. We live here in harmony if we can't live there. We are still brothers.' He extended his hand to Ritwik. As Ritwik shook it, Mr Haq chuckled and said, 'And you are young enough to be my little brother, no? Heh heh heh.'

In the course of the next hour, in between glasses of tangy and sweet *nimbu-paani* brought in at regular intervals by Mrs Haq, who had disappeared into the innards of the house on the arrival of her husband, perhaps on kitchen duty, Ritwik was given a filleted history of the Haq family. Mr Haq's father came to England in the early 60s, as part of a wave of subcontinent

243

immigrants England was opening its doors to at the time, partly to salve its colonial guilt, partly to fill its depleting labour market for the jobs the natives wouldn't touch. His father had been a young boy when the partition of 1947 had unrooted the poor cobbler family in Aligarh. It had taken them two years to reach Pakistan, the new Muslim homeland, along with millions of other Muslim families who had made the journey to a new home, new hopes, to the company of equals in faith. But everything had turned sour in the new country. Yes, true, there was no danger of their village getting torched by Hindus on the rampage, but Sindh and Baluchistan were arid dustbowls, Karachi a collection of ragged slums. There were no jobs, no food, just swarms of refugees trying to build homes. When Mr Haq's father was invited by a distant uncle to help him out in his grocery store in Leicester, the family had pinned all hopes on the twenty-one-year-old and borrowed money to put the young man aboard a ship and send him off to a country full of possibilities. He left his wife and their year-old son behind in his village and sailed away.

The young man had done well. By the time he was twenty-seven, he was managing the original store in Leicester, while his uncle had opened two others. Business was good, the Asian community in Leicester was booming and the demand for goods from home was on a dizzyingly upward curve. Mr Haq's father and his uncle rode it. And compared with the price they paid for the goods brought over from Pakistan, even a 100 per cent mark-up meant that the things they imported and sold in their shops were nearly three times cheaper than native English goods. A child could realize that the pound-rupee exchange rate worked heavily in their favour but it required a certain amount of business nous to exploit that to their full advantage. The young man learnt, hands on, the meaning of profit; Zulfikar Haq became a partner with his uncle. The first time he went back, in 1967, his son Shahid was seven years old. He distributed gifts among the family – razor blades, soaps, plastic toys for the children, shirts, a watch for his ageing father, all from England, to show that he had made it and his family wouldn't want for anything any more – and returned to England after three months, promising he would come back every year. He didn't manage to go back every year; the booming business made it more like every three, but he regularly sent money orders and drafts back home. Once again, the rupee-pound exchange kept him a winner.

In the next ten years, Zulfikar Haq and his uncle cracked export licences, cheap sourcing from Pakistan, ship and land delivery, local transport, warehouse logistics, networks of traders from India and Pakistan and, above all, the unarticulated need of an immigrant community to create a little home on foreign soil. They set up the first cash and carry shop in East London in 1970, the year Zulfikar's uncle died, three months after the inauguration of 'Manzil Cash and Carry: For Best Products and Cheapest Value', leaving him in charge of everything. Zulfikar moved to London, delegating the little empire of shops in Leicester and Birmingham, now all his, to a loosely knit assortment of relatives and friends, and travelled to Pakistan to bring back Shahid, now thirteen, to England. He had made it here so he was now going to bring his family over from Pakistan – his wife, whom he had seen only four times since they got married, his three children, Shahid, Salma and Nilufer – and have them ensconced permanently in the good life.

Sitting on his sofa and sipping his wife's lemonade, Shahid Haq told this rags-to-riches story with evident pride, even with a gentle urge to Ritwik that he should learn from this example and do something worthwhile with his life. Or maybe Ritwik imagined that.

'I work for my father. Father says school and university, all useless. Look at him. He didn't have much learning but he was successful' – Ritwik noted the 'was' and wondered if the entrepreneur father was no longer alive but Mr Haq's tenses were not conservative – 'He brought me over to help him in business and then, one day, *inshallah*, take over from him when he gets old. That is what sons are for, to take care of their parents.'

Ritwik did some quick arithmetic: Mr Haq would be in his early to mid-thirties now, although he looked a good ten years older with his greying hair and the paunch overhanging his belt. Zulfikar Haq would be about fifty-five.

'Where is your father now?' Ritwik asked abruptly.

'They go back to Pakistan, my parents. They build big house in Lahore. They go back because they say they want to die in their homeland. The house has become quiet since they left. They want to be with their grandchildren but I tell them, we go back every year to visit them, so they know we're well with Allah's blessing.'

Then Mr Haq, with a sudden narrative pirouette, launched into talk about his business: the chain of cash and carry stores, twelve in total, almost all of them delegated to a team of store managers, all of them Pakistani, trained hands-on in the job; how he had sold off the string of cornershops and larger Asian stores in the Midlands to other businessmen and begun to dedicate himself totally to his London ventures; how with increasing profits and enormous growth of the business, the responsibilities, the workload, the nitty-gritty of management, everything had become staggeringly, dauntingly large.

It wasn't really a hook, but Ritwik decided to use it as one; *now or never*. 'It seems the business has grown too vast for you to run it all yourself. You must need a considerable amount of paid help in the less important aspect of things. Don't you?'

'Oh, yes, we need people to stock, shelve, do the accounts, sell, deal with transport, all that sort of stuff.'

'Would it be possible for you to give me a part-time job in one of your shops? Nothing fancy or high-powered, just a few hours a day, three or four days a week.'

Shahid Haq looked both triumphant, as if a minor suspicion he had harboured for some time had been confirmed, and slightly embarrassed, because he would have to wheel out the tired, old excuses again to turn down this young man, excuses which would doubtless ring false in his ears.

'We try to hire people from families we know, you see, other Pakistani families who are in England.' His words came out halting, with pauses and a breath of a stutter, as if he were making it up as he went along.

Ritwik found this so excruciating that he decided to put Mr Haq out of his misery. 'Oh, don't worry about it. I was just asking.'

It was Mr Haq's turn to do the empty politenesses now. 'No, no, I'll see what I can do. You see my problem with our Pakistani brothers . . .'

'That's absolutely all right. Of course, I see your obligations. Please don't think about it again, Mr Haq.'

'Do you have a work permit in the UK? A National Insurance number?'

'No. I don't.' Something flitted across the dark pupils of Shahid Haq. Ritwik briefly entertained the idea of telling him the whole truth but didn't dare. He lied, 'I'm on a student visa.'

'Oh, I see, I see. Let me think about it for some time.' Then he gave a particularly oleaginous smile, which extended to a grin, and slipped into his man-of-the-world mode. 'Heh, heh, heh, we have to help each other out, don't we? In this country, we need to stick to each other and have our own community.'

Ritwik wasn't sure if that was a hope held out or a discouraging reminder that he stood outside the community.

The Hindi film songs had resumed playing upstairs. There was no sign of Mrs Haq. The voice of one girl was briefly heard over the song and then, silence. The younger of the two girls came into the living room; there was a large red bindi in the centre of her forehead, a few more bangles on her thin arms, a *dupatta*, presumably her mother's, wrapped many times around her child's body and a hair clip in the shape of a butterfly, pink, spangled and enormous, poised precariously on her head. She went to her father, not walking, but with the stylized movements of a Hindi film actress in a song-and-dance number, all the while her eyes fixed on Ritwik. There was a loud call – 'Ameeee-naaa' – from upstairs and she swiftly hid behind her father. Ameena was going to be in trouble with her mother for dressing up to the nines. Ritwik left the house with a strange, lonely feeling of unbelonging and perhaps, just perhaps, envy.

VII.

'Dighi Bari',
Nawabgunj,
Bograh Distt.
Bengal.
May 1905

Dear Violet,

There is Swadeshi on everyone's lips, in the food we eat, the clothes we wear – I feel we are breathing it in with the very air. The papers here are full of the impending Partition, the towns and villages resounding with meetings resolving to boycott English goods. The papers call them 'monster meetings' and 'mass meetings' and 'giant rallies'; there are tens of thousands of people gathering everywhere to protest against the division of Bengal which must surely happen soon so why this public furtiveness on the part of Simla I do not understand. My head is full of this accumulating dissatisfaction against the Government, so eloquently expressed, so ubiquitous – meetings in Khulna, Pubna, Rungpoor, Chittagong, Rajshahi, Dinajepoor, Cooch Behar, Presidency College, Eden Hindu Hostel, Ahiritolla. The *head reels with the sheer number of these protests – it seems everyone has taken to the streets.*

Is it as hectic and mad in Calcutta as I understand from the papers? Are people congregating everywhere? They say here that the boycott of English goods is beginning to bite in Manchester, in Lancashire; even salt from Liverpool has come under the sway of Swadeshi Boycott. The traders are an odd combination of revolutionary euphoria and apprehensiveness, the Bombay cloth mills I read are gearing themselves up for a steep rise in production, while there is the usual division and debate about the comparative merits and demerits of Manchester dhoti versus the Swadeshi dhoti; it is widely acknowledged that Swadeshi cloth will never be able to rival Manchester products in quality and niceness, while the more patriotic allege loudly that Swadeshi cloth is far more durable than English fabric. The Bengali babu is in a quandary: betrayal and luxury on one hand, righteous patriotism and discomfort on the other. I have, of course, politely expressed my desire to Mr Roy Chowdhury that I shall be more than willing to try out Swadeshi goods if that does not extend to my soap: I shall remain loyal to my Pears forever.

Mr Roy Chowdhury explains the complicated business of Trade Boycotts and Surplus and other well-nigh incomprehensible things to me: I sit and nod sagely. He is getting more and more pensive by the day; it has been over a year now that I haven't seen him without furrowed brow. Bimala has announced her decision to forsake all things foreign: needless to say, she's having great difficulties – her piano, her silk blouses, her combs, her dressing table, her mirror, her perfumes, her knitting needles, everything is 'foreign' – but is putting on a brave face and continuing to wear dull, white cotton saris. I hope her new decision doesn't extend to me or to the English songs on which we've been making such wonderful progress.

Dear Violet, write to let me know all the news from Calcutta: it must see much more than our share of the gathering storm. Will you tell me all about it? I wait with equal parts dread and excitement.

Ever your loving friend,
Maud

Mr Roy Chowdhury comes in during a lesson one day, unannounced and apologetic. 'I'm so sorry to interrupt your ...' he begins, but Miss Gilby interrupts him, 'Not at all, not at all, please sit down', before he has had a chance to finish his sentence.

'Bimala here was telling me,' she continues, 'that in the true spirit of *swadeshi* we should be reading only Bengali books and translating from them as part of our language exercises rather than reading English-language books. I was just on the point of mentioning to her whether asking you to adjudicate would be a fair move. And you walked in, as if you had read our thoughts.' Miss Gilby smiles, but there is a hint of reserve somewhere behind the thin mouth.

The information gently inflects his question to Bimala. 'Bimala, is this true?'

This is the first time Miss Gilby has heard him use a language other than his mother tongue in conversation with his wife. Bimala remains tongue-tied and her gaze is steadfastly fixed on to the floor, whether out of the novelty of having to speak to her husband in English or out of the incipient conflict implied in the situation, Miss Gilby cannot ascertain with any degree of sureness.

Mr Roy Chowdhury speaks again, 'Well, Bimala, I'm sure Miss Gilby thinks it is a good idea but will you abandon playing the piano, or singing your favourite English songs as well?'

Before Bimala has a chance to answer, Mr Roy Chowdhury turns to Miss Gilby and adds, 'Did you know, Miss Gilby, our Bimala has become a veritable revolutionary. *Swadeshi, swadeshi, swadeshi*: she doesn't seem to think of anything else. Even while humming English songs, or asking her *darzee* to design a new blouse from a Dickins and Jones catalogue, she thinks and speaks of *swadeshi*.' His voice cracks with good-natured and affectionate laughter. Miss Gilby and Bimala, too, follow suit after a few seconds' hesitation.

'So I've said to her, by all means, do as much *swadeshi* as you feel like, but you might have a few problems making your lessons with Miss Gilby follow such lines, not unless you give up your French perfumes, too.'

Bimala pretends mock anger and accuses her husband of exposing her little failures in front of Miss Gilby, but it is all a joke, all playacting, and the little cloud that threatened to settle overhead passes swiftly.

'Now, Miss Gilby, I do not know whether Bimala has already mentioned this to you but I wanted to let you know that my friend, Sandip – a childhood friend, we go back a long way – will be coming to stay here with us for a while. I was wondering if we could talk about it when you have some time to spare?'

'But of course, Mr Roy Chowdhury. What about teatime

this afternoon? Bimala can sing one of her lovely Bengali songs, while I accompany her on the piano. What do you say, Bimala?'

Bimala nods enthusiastically. Mr Roy Chowdhury is so surprised at Miss Gilby's sure, swift ease with the Bengali world that he remains speechless for a few moments.

18th OCTOBER 1905

Despite the earnest protests of millions of people, the Government has gone through with its insidious and deplorable partition of Bengal on the 16th of October. In anticipation of large-scale rioting and disorderly protests, an unprecedented number of policemen were deployed on the streets of Calcutta but it gives us great satisfaction to report that the infamous day passed peacefully in the city and hundreds of other towns and villages all over undivided Bengal. The people turned this most egregious of political offences into a day of brotherhood and friendship by tying *rakhis* on to the wrist of their brothers and fellow men. And it was not only on to each others' arms that the Hindus and Mohammedans, united in love and common destiny, tied *rakhis*, but also on to the arms of bemused policemen and soldiers, thus showing that the Bengali race will not be provoked or broken by the divisive policies of Lord Curzon. We will turn all actions against us to our advantage, our silent and peaceful resistance will be our biggest victory. This was the day when Lord Curzon went down in the annals of history forever but not for the reasons he understands: for this was the day when the clock started ticking for the English Government in India and the man who set it ticking was Lord Curzon.

Throughout the city shops were closed, businesses shut, schools, colleges, transport, everything on strike. Every single Bengali had taken to the streets, now a sea of heads, from early in the morning until 9 p.m. It was a show of unity and harmony, of peace and love, of strong determination. In the following days, we shall be reporting to you the spread of swadeshi throughout undivided Bengal.

The Bengalee, Calcutta.

PARTITION DAY PASSES PEACEFULLY

With Lord Curzon, the infamous architect of the partition of Bengal, hiding in England after having drawn out a ridiculous drama of resignation, the division came into effect from the 16th of October, a day celebrated – for what other word can be used for this day? – by a massive general strike and a public *rakhi bandhan* ceremony. Every factory, mill, school, college, court, shop, business was closed for the day, a unified cry of protest against an act on which the people it affects most were not consulted. The partition, let us repeat, was done over the heads of the people and in this the Government at Simla showed that peculiar mixture of arrogance, evasiveness and tyranny, which has come to characterize it so singularly.

But if the Government was afraid, indeed expectant of any violence or disorder that was being predicted, the disciplined Bengalis took the very wind out of their sails by turning the day into one of pride in the unity and brotherhood of all Bengali men, Hindus and Mussulmans, scholar and worker, farmer and lawyer. The streets of Calcutta were thronged with people from all backgrounds, singing *Amaar sonar Bangla* and *Bande mataram*, the sky resounding with the sound of proud nationhood.

We can only thank Lord Curzon, for the act which was meant to divide Bengal, administratively, geographically, racially, has brought us all together as brothers. The strength of the Bengali will has been put to the test and we have come out triumphant. History will have more to show. Simla, take note.

Amrita Bazar Patrika, Calcutta, October 18, 1905.

EIGHT

They talk of burnt bridges. Sometimes it is a choice, at other times, enforced, but more often than not the fall of the die takes in both. There are documents, stamps, official insignia, computer-held records, databases, monitors of exits and entries, date stamps, place stamps, ports of entry, records, papers, hard disks, officers, institutions, regulations, limitations, hedge after hedge, wall after wall, moat after moat regulating movements in and out, out and in. Life is calibrated in signs, the swift impress of inked rubber and metal on paper, the brief clatter of keys, a few hits of the return key, information stored in chips. That is all. There are no events, only records. To give all this the slip is to drop out of official, recorded life, of validated life. It is to move from life to existence. On the 21st of December, Ritwik Ghosh will do exactly that: he will silently let his leave to remain in England expire and become a virtual prisoner in this new land. He will not have access to banking, medical care, foreign travel, proper jobs, the welfare state, benefits, nothing. Not even an address, which can be used by other people to write to him, in case the post office people are alerted to his name. The vast grid of the impeccably ordered and arranged first-world modern democratic state will no longer hold him. He will become a shadow behind that grid, a creature with a past but no future, only a teased out mirage of a present. A ghost in limbo. Imprisoned forever but with infinite freedom.

And all for a better, a new life.

The die lands on crossroads. What determines things? The shift in wind direction? The fall of a russet leaf? An ordering of air atoms that makes the die fall that face up and not another?

There are no answers except for that fall of a die, the unshaping of clouds, the head turned around at crossroads, a door ajar, another closed. Choice and chance.

If he is asked, he will reply, 'I didn't want to go back to India because it is too hot out there. I would like to live in a cooler land.'

Choice.

What makes a presence illegal just because another set of keys haven't been touched, another sheaf of papers marked and moved around?

Three weeks after Ritwik's conversation with Mr Haq, Saeed Latif rolled up outside Mrs Cameron's door at three in the morning and sounded his car horn – dash dash dot dot dash style – just as Shahid Haq had said he would. Ritwik had lain awake most of the night because he didn't want to miss the signal. That would have meant ringing the doorbell and waking up Anne who, for all he knew, was wide awake anyway, god knows, that woman seemed to survive on no more than three hours a night.

The car shocked him. He didn't know what he was expecting, perhaps a dirty, scraped, dented, secondhand one, but certainly not this long, beige obscenity, a tired Freudian joke suddenly come alive and purring outside his front door. The low-slung Mercedes had a left-hand drive and a swish leather and wood interior. It was either very new or Saaed Latif spent a lot of time everyday lavishing love and care on his machine. He opened the passenger door for Ritwik and asked, 'You like car?'

Famous first words.

Saeed Latif could have been any age from twenty to thirty-five, had very pale skin, and was probably Middle Eastern in origin but Ritwik wasn't very good at placing people. In fact, it was only recently that he had started thinking about where people came from originally because everyone in London seemed to have arrived from somewhere else.

'Yes, I do. It looks very splendid,' Ritwik half-lied, getting into the soft and yielding passenger seat, which hugged his bottom so eagerly.

'I like, too. Come, we go.'

Before the car started rolling, Ritwik took in Saeed briefly. He wore a shiny blue Umbro top, a thick golden chain around his neck, the links heavy and gleaming even in the halogen-lit night of south London streets, a similar bracelet around his right wrist, and rings, chunky molars of metal, on practically every finger of both his hands: he could have been a magpie's secret dumping ground. The impression was confirmed when Saeed smiled and showed a brief gleam of gold in the region behind his canines.

New to London, Ritwik was eager to figure out how the gargantuan beast was pieced together in its parts by looking out of the window and have Saeed give an intermittent commentary on the different areas of London through which they would be passing. That thought was killed quite early on when, driving down Effra Road, Ritwik noticed the road sign, turned to Saeed and said, 'Look, Effra Road. Do you think the river Effra flowed through this area once?' Saeed briefly turned his head towards Ritwik, then carried on driving, not bothering to reply. His silence seemed to have drawn some conclusions. Ritwik regretted saying such an incongruous thing but couldn't shake off thoughts of Walter Raleigh sailing the river four hundred years ago down this very road, who knows, which now ended with the jostle and tumble of McDonald's, Ritzy cinema, Pizza Hut and Barclays.

'Mr Haq say I take care of you, OK?' Saeed said after a longish silence during which Ritwik studiously looked out, willing Saeed to say at least the names of the areas he was driving him through, but no such luck. After the blankness, which followed the misjudged statement about Effra river, he didn't dare ask Saeed the simple question, 'What's this place called?' Anyway, what did he expect, a history and psychogeography of the various layers of London?

'What Mr Haq say, we do, OK? He say I look after you, give you best job, not construction site job.'

Ritwik didn't have a clue where he was being taken. Mr Haq had reassured him that he was going to be in safe hands. Saeed was a trusted old hand at helping him out with things, both a troubleshooter and a facilitator, Ritwik wasn't to worry at all, after all, he, Shahid Haq, was like his elder brother, wasn't he? And he needed a job, didn't he, an underground job where they didn't ask questions, didn't ask for numbers or bank accounts or other official things, just gave you cash in hand at the end of the day and that was it. Ritwik was looking for that kind of thing because the official type would be difficult to find immediately, he could start doing this over the summer and then Shahid Haq would try and find something else for him, was that OK for now?

Ritwik had nodded to everything Mr Haq had said, although what the 'this' he would be doing over summer was never explained clearly, except for wispy comments about helping out in a friend's farm in Hertfordshire. Ritwik didn't object to fruit-picking, did he? No, of course not, fruit-picking, how wonderful, how how . . . rustic, how pastoral. It was typical of Ritwik to think first of Virgil's *Georgics* at that point rather than hard details of location, hours of work, pay, duration of employment. If he noticed how consummately Mr Haq had read his situation – the unrevealed, messy business of black employment, lack of permits and illegal stay – he didn't raise the issues with Mr Haq; images of bee-loud glades and nectarines and curious peaches reaching themselves into his hands were too much in the foreground to worry about insoluble and irreversible problems. Well, irreversible in a few months' time.

At last Ritwik gathered enough courage to ask, 'Do you know the name of this area we're driving through?' when they crossed a bridge beside which stood a huge abandoned brick building on the further bank, to their right, with white columns at the four corners, resembling an upturned table. The river was dark and oily, the bridge on their immediate left festooned with lights. For a very brief moment, if he kept his head turned left, it looked like a deserted toy town. But only for a moment. If he turned his head to the right, it shifted to an industrial wasteland where shadows stalked the dark outlines of buildings, all spooky warehouses and silent wharves.

Saeed shrugged. Either he didn't know, or he didn't under-stand the question, or he couldn't be bothered to make small talk. The dark blue night was fading to a lighter shade around them almost imperceptibly: Ritwik could see inside the car more clearly now. That, and smell Saeed's fetid breath.

'Where are you from?' Ritwik asked. This was going to be his final attempt.

'London.'

'You mean, originally?'

Silence. 'London. East London.'

Ritwik knew he was lying. He dropped the matter and concentrated on the view smoothly slipping past. Row after row of detached white houses, grand and elegant. There was a big walled garden along the entire stretch of the road.

'Buckin Ham Palace,' Saeed said.

'That? On the right?'

Once again, no answer: conversation was going to happen strictly on Saeed's terms.

Suddenly there was a spacious roundabout, with monuments and victory arches, a hint of a large expanse of green, which soon broadened out to what Ritwik considered the countryside, yet along the other side of the green-bisected road, there was a series of swish, ritzy hotels, Hilton, Park, Dorchester.

'Rich place. Is called Park Lane. Rich people and rich foreigners here,' Saeed said, being surprisingly chatty.

'Is that Hyde Park?' Ritwik asked.

Saeed nodded, driving past another arch and into a long road. Instantly, the scenery changed, like a swift, rumbling movement of theatre backdrop ushering in a new time, a new place. The shops, cafés, restaurants, juice bars, grocery stores, takeaways were almost without exception Arabic – Lebanese, Egyptian, Middle Eastern.

'Edgware Road,' Saeed said, laconic as always, but there seemed to be a trace of light somewhere in his tone, almost a joy, an ease.

'You are Muslim?' Saeed asked as they drove down this stretch of well-heeled garishness, the shop signs too big, the lettering too flash, the sound of new money a whisper too loud.

They all aimed for a type of conspicuous affluence and hit it, ever so slightly awry, by being vulgar.

'No.' Ritwik could guess where this was going.

'What you then? Christian?'

'No, no. Actually, I have no religion.' He felt slightly ashamed to say this. 'I was brought up in a Hindu family but I went to a Catholic school.'

'So you Hindi and Christian?'

'No, neither.'

Saeed absorbed this in silence as Ritwik felt disapproval wrapping around him but this could have been inside his head. He attempted to turn it around by asking Saeed questions instead.

'So you are Muslim then?'

'Yes. I am from Libya. You know?' It seemed that Edgware Road had liberated Saeed into a new honesty and openness, even a pride, about his origins.

'Yes, I mean no, I know *of* it, but I've never been there. Is it a nice place?'

'Beautiful. My country is beautiful. You go one day?'

'Yes, I would like to.' Pause. 'So why did you come to England?'

Saeed didn't reply, which was just as well. He shouldn't have asked that double-edged sword of a question.

Instead, Saeed said, 'All this shops, all Arabic. From Iran, Lebanon, Egypt. They all speak my language.' It seemed that, away from Libya, Saeed had found a corner of wet, vast London, which approximated what he was at ease with.

'They seem to be mostly food places.'

'You eat Arabic food? You like?' An enthusiasm flared up in Saeed like the brief flash of a match.

Ritwik, who went partially hungry most days unless Mrs Haq called him over and fed him or sent him little tupperware boxes of kebabs, *dal bukhara* and *bhindi gosht*, replied feebly, 'No, I don't know Arabic food but I'd love to try some.' His curiosity and greed for food, especially unknown cuisines, was unbounded and haunting.

To Ritwik, the conversation had become a parody: here he was with an unknown Libyan man, who was driving him to an unknown destination, and he was sitting politely and giving quintessentially English answers – 'Yes, please', 'No, but I'd love to' – non-committal and unrevealing, while the real questions bobbed and swelled inside him, his curiosity still sharp and unsatisfied.

How did Saeed meet Mr Haq? What sort of work did he do for the older man? Why did Saeed drive such a flash car? What *did* he do by way of earning money? Why did Ritwik get the impression that whatever Saeed did, it wasn't wholly conventional or licit? Why did he have an uneasy sense that Saeed's money wasn't white, clean or regular?

The blue had lightened to the pre-dawn grey, which held the promise of another unbrokenly cloudless and hot day. Outside, the scene had changed radically again. Ritwik was going to discover this abiding aspect of London: with one corner turned or a side-street stepped into, the whole landscape could change, from Georgian terrace to postwar prefab, tree-lined red brick suburbia to outbreaks of high-rise council estate rashes with cruel names to their buildings: Ullswater, Windermere, Grasmere, Keswick. The demarcations were sudden and jagged. Even the immigrant quarters changed, as Saeed pointed out driving down Finchley Road, 'The Jewish people live here.' This was his first voluntary statement, after Buckingham Palace, about an area of London; Ritwik wondered if the two held equal, not identical, significances in his mind.

'We come near the place,' Saeed volunteered. They passed an underground station: Willesden Green. He drove on for a few minutes, turned left on Anson Road and parked his car.

'We go out.' Saeed leaned forward and sideways to open the door for Ritwik, a gesture he found touching and old-fashioned. It was nearly light and the dawn was cool; Ritwik was glad of his thin jumper.

'We walk there. Not far, five minutes. We don't take car there.' Saeed was becoming almost talkative.

They went back to the main road, Chichele Lane. After a few minutes, Ritwik noticed disparate groups of people. It wasn't as if the journey here had been through utterly deserted streets, but after their relative emptiness, this seemed positively crowded. Men, mostly, standing in little groups, chatting, smoking, huddled, as if sharing a secret or a shame. A few were standing on their own. There were even two women, one with a sleeping baby wrapped around her front in folds and folds of cloth, another one, standing with a pale man, both smoking.

'We stand here. No, not so far,' he said, as Ritwik tried to go further on, right in the middle of these stray clumps of people. 'Here, here is OK.'

Without even thinking, Ritwik marked he was the only person there who was not white. He didn't have a clue from where these people, standing around disjointedly at this unholy hour of the morning, came, or why they were all gathering here. A queue was forming of men who seemed to speak to each other in the same language. Some of them appeared to know each other. Three men stood out. Like Saeed, two of them wore branded clothes and shoes, either real Nikes, Pumas and Filas or fakes. They had heavy chains around their necks and wore bracelets and rings. One of them had thick golden hoops in his earlobes. They smoked and patrolled the street and the people. Most of the people gravitated to these three men who were more loquacious, more confident than the rest: they were like teachers with their group charges on a school trip. The men chatted, laughed occasionally, sized up the two women. There was a tense furtiveness in the way people looked, or refused to look, at each other, an uneasy expectation, a hairline crack of suspicion and something else Ritwik couldn't quite place.

Before Ritwik's questions tumbled out, Saeed started speaking. 'They workers, look for work here every morning. This place Job Street. From many places. Russia, Albania, Romania, Croatia, Montenegro' – Ritwik noted both his surprise and his prejudice at hearing Saeed reel off the names of unusual countries – 'Yugoslavia.'

But that country doesn't exist anymore. A red double-decker bus passed by, bringing the scatter of people together on the pavement. As soon as it was gone, they started unravelling to their former loose alignments. Every time a car or van went down the road, the men stared at it, poised on the edge of some anticipation, almost willing it to stop. A man, darker than the rest, came up to Saeed and spoke to him. The language was unknown to Ritwik but it was obvious what it was from the opening *Salaam aleikum*. They carried on talking seriously, the language oddly guttural and glottally stopped, with its halting music of sibilants and aspirants joined together. Saeed nodded, the man walked off and returned two minutes later with one young woman, a girl really; she looked as if she was still in her teens but with a precocious air of composure and resignation about her. She didn't look up or acknowledge anyone's presence. Saeed didn't bother speaking to her; he continued talking to the man. After a while, the man nodded, shook Saeed's hand and walked off.

Ritwik didn't know how these axes were forming in the first place but it seemed to him that Saeed was now in charge of two people, the girl and Ritwik, just as the three flash men had gathered together their individual groups. Two more young men, obviously known to Saeed, came and joined their growing cluster. Saeed spoke to them in English.

'Hello. We wait for them now. You work in East Anglia or Cambridgeshire today?'

One of the men, lean, blotchy-faced, with gnarled, veined hands, replied, 'They take us. We don't know. We go where they take us.' His English was heavily accented but in a very different way from Saeed's. Ritwik felt frustrated he couldn't place any one of these people but if he were asked to guess the origins of the two new arrivals, he would have put it down to the eastern fringes of Europe, or one of the former Soviet dominions. Some of the men waiting here were so astonishingly beautiful that his eyes kept wandering. Dark hair, fair skin, lean faces, and unreadable, opaque, dark eyes with long lashes. A few others were bony, with spun straw hair, or dark curls, high cheekbones, a throwaway grace to their movements.

Suddenly there was a stir as some men ran forward to a white truck, which had appeared cruising slowly along the road. Saeed said, 'Not our work, not us. Stay here.' The men, seven or eight of them, who crowded around below the driver's door were scrambling and jostling with each other. Two of the bejewelled men were trying to hold them back and talk to the driver at the same time. From where Ritwik stood, he could neither see the driver nor hear what was going on. After a few minutes of conversation between these men, punctuated by one thickset man trying to push his way to the front and put his hand up through the driver's window, the leaders stepped back and picked out three men each. The truck driver opened his door, jumped out, and spoke to the leaders. Three of the men who had joined in the scramble when the truck had arrived on the scene went around the front of the vehicle and got in through the passenger door. The driver did a high five with the man with earrings, got into the truck and drove off. Two minutes later, a large white van came up and stopped as the other leader indicated to it, waving his hand. There was a brief conversation with him, the driver stepped out, opened the back door and let the three other men in. Before he drove off, he reached into his pocket, took out a few notes and gave it to the man who had stopped his van.

The remaining men hung back, some chattering to each other; a couple of them were loud and almost mirthful. The two men who hadn't been picked up by the trucks were remonstrating with the two leaders, but it seemed in a kind of resigned, humorous way. There were other men who had meanwhile arrived and joined the waiting groups.

Ritwik turned to Saeed and asked, 'What's going on?'

Saeed said, 'The men here, they wait for work. When truck arrive, they pick people, one, two, maybe three, maybe more. Depend on the truck. Then they go and work.'

'But what work is it? Where do they go?' He tried not to let the whole flood of questions spill and drown out whatever willingness Saeed might have to enlighten him.

'Construction. Building work. Some in London, some outside. Some farm work, you know? We do farm work. They come soon. You wait.'

'And who are those three men? Do you know the ones I mean?'

Yes, he did. 'They help these men find job.'

'Do these men come here every day looking for work? The same men?'

'Some. Some get work for one day, two day, more, two week maybe. They come again when they finish this job. Some get job only for a day. They come every day.'

A dark knowledge was slowly beginning to take focused shape in Ritwik's mind. Saeed's short, staccato sentences were chiselling out new edges and lines; the picture wasn't altogether clear, or finished, but Ritwik guessed the flashy men were brokers and the people who gathered here in the morning, a bunch of floating labourers, unemployed, perhaps even unemployable, who lived on this day-to-day basis, their horizons bounded on all sides by nothing more than the eternal repetition of nightfall and break of day, sunset and sunrise. 'Bring the day, eat the day', as the Bengali idiom had it.

A white van drove past slowly and Saeed ran after it, managing to thump against one of its metal sides. The van stopped and Saeed went up to the window. He evidently knew the driver.

'I have three, maybe four today. How many you need?' he asked the driver.

The driver got out. He was short and stocky, with legs like tree trunks, and bare arms tattooed heavily with a strange device; the overwhelming impression of those drawings on the skin was of dirty, indistinguishable blues and greens. He wore a singlet, a pair of faded cut-offs and heavy, soiled boots.

'Which ones?' he asked Saeed.

Saeed pointed to Ritwik, the two men he thought were from

Eastern Europe and the young girl Saeed's Arabic friend had consigned to his care.

'They strong. They work.' And pointing to Ritwik he added, 'He speak English. Good English.'

'Look, mate, I need three. For a week, maybe, give or take a day or two' – for Ritwik, the sounds 'myte', 'tyke', 'dye' stood out – 'strawberries now, and other stuff, you know.'

The girl had moved behind the gathering of these five men, reluctant to join them.

'They go where?'

'Cambridgeshire. Twenty pounds each for the day's job. OK?'

'Twenty-five.'

'Twenty, that's what I'm giving, not a penny more. If you're not happy, I can have my pick from any of these people out here.'

There was a growing interest in the groups of waiting men in this negotiation but it was dispersed by the arrival of two more slow trucks on the road.

Saeed did some swift calculation in his head. 'You take?'

'Wha'?' the driver asked.

Saeed repeated, this time gesturing towards each of them.

The driver looked at them slowly, taking them in for the first time, but somehow without any real interest.

'What about the girl and this Paki boy, you Paki aren't you, I think two will do, you can keep those other two' – pointing to the east European men – 'my mate needs some hands in East Anglia, he'll be coming along in a while, why don't ya send them over his way.'

Saeed nodded. 'OK.' He turned to the girl and broke out in swift Arabic. It sounded harsh and peremptory and there were a lot of words, certainly many more than he had spoken to

Ritwik in the course of the morning. The girl kept her head down, still refusing to make eye contact, yet there seemed to be an odd defiance about that gesture, an insolence that Ritwik couldn't quite square with the situation she was in now.

Ritwik turned to the driver and asked him, 'Will you bring us back here from Cambridgeshire at the end of the day?'

'Wha'?' That aggressive hurl of a single word, again.

Ritwik felt intimidated repeating what he had just asked. He rephrased, 'Do we come back to London at the end of the day?' Everything hinged on that. He couldn't go away for the night. Who would look after Anne then?

The driver looked immensely uninterested. 'That depends on you.'

Ritwik steeled himself to ask the original question. 'Will you be coming back to London?'

'Could do.'

'Could you please give me a lift back here?'

'What d'ya think I am, your fuckin' taxi service?' But he said it in a humorous tone. 'Why d'ya speak posh?'

The question threw Ritwik. 'I suppose, I suppose . . . well, I don't know. I didn't think I did.'

Saeed meanwhile was trying to get the driver's attention by hovering around the edge of their conversation, fidgeting. 'You take this guy,' he said, pointing to the wiry young man.

'OK, we leave the girl behind then. Only two today. We'll see tomorrow,' the driver said. He turned to Ritwik and the thin man and gestured them to follow him to the back door. He opened it for them and said, 'In ya go.'

There was a dirty canvas sheet on the floor and an odd assortment of pails, tins, a large tool box, a hoe, a couple of spades, a few rags, a rolled-up oilcloth and a spare pair of heavy-duty boots. It was dark in there and the only view they would have would be through the glass windows on the back door, if they half-crouched and half-knelt like dogs.

'We don't have all day, y'know. Get movin'.' The driver was obviously used to ordering people around.

Ritwik and the thin young man clambered in and sat down on the canvas. Saeed and the driver exchanged more words: Ritwik couldn't make out anything from this trap. The van revved up and started moving. Ritwik lurched towards the back door windows and held his palm against the glass in goodbye to Saeed. Saeed hesitated before he put up his hand to wave. The clear morning sunshine had caught his face and turned it a shade of pale gold.

Anne's wrinkled parchment-and-bone claw sticks out of the contained pond, clutching the white edge, a parody of some still from a crass Hollywood chiller, while the water laps at the scum-ringed sides in soundless mini-ripples, which are not ripples really, not the ones neatly, concentrically circling out, but only erratically agitated water. The scum ring acts as a sort of Plimsoll line for Ritwik; he always fills the bath a few inches below that rectangular mark running the entire perimeter, always thinking he needs to give it a good scour but it acts as a guideline. He doesn't want Anne to drown or get water in her mouth or nose when she reclines her entire length during the twice-weekly bath.

No bath oil, no foam, no gel, nothing but the spartan bar of ivory Imperial Leather. Sometimes her flailing claws miss the edge and clutch his immersed hand instead. He sits outside, sometimes on his knees, at other times on his haunch, one hand under her armpit – a texturally disturbing combination of dewlap, down and solid rods all holding each other, just about, in a fragile balance – the other hand always free. The hands change roles all the time.

These are Ritwik's first experiences of the naked female body: breasts hung down like meagrely weighted crushed leather bags, the weight low down, like a couple of lonely stones at the very bottom of a sack. They remind him of the sad balloons, deflated and shrivelled, at the end of a child's birthday party. The aureoles are like leaking stains. Everything in her body, the intricately scored map of her skin, her stomach, the pouches under her eyes, her breasts, seems to be having an affair with gravity and cannot resist its pull any longer. Maybe it is the ultimate call to the earth, the flesh impatient to reach where it knows it is destined. He doesn't dare look at the space between her legs; only in the unwilled and involuntary periphery of his vision are snatches of a sparse, sad, grey tuft to which he always shuts his mind as if the sight is going to bore holes into him and also diminish her.

Anne is a submerged bird, a creature of hollowness, all air and insubstantiality, the broken doll of her body accentuated grotesquely by the way the bath water refracts her limbs and shrivelled dugs and torso into slightly skewed sizes and perspectives. The Barbour-green inflatable pillow props up her head because she often dozes off in her bath. Sometimes Ugo comes in, sniffs around, sometimes he jumps on to the edge of the bath and sits watching the movements, of water, of hands, with beryl-eyed curiosity.

Today, Ritwik takes the cream-coloured bar and starts soaping Anne under water, an act he has always found frustrating and futile: the soap doesn't foam or stick to the body because the water dissolves and disperses it instantaneously.

What is the point of soaping if you can't build up a lather, rub and clean yourself with it, and only *then* wash it off? Wasn't it a bit Sisyphean to have it all washed away even as you started? He tried to explain the point to Anne once but she didn't get it at all. Slowly, the water turns into a milky suspension: dirty grey flakes of scum eddy about and move to the margins in a community. Ritwik hates the oily scum, this stubborn refusal of foam.

Anne is lying with her head resting on the pillow, her eyes shut. Ritwik is unsure whether she is asleep but he is used to her abrupt tunings out now. If she wants to speak she will. What he is not used to, not yet, is the feel of her crumpled tissue-paper skin against his hand. It is like touching a creature made up only of folds of hide, with the life taken out of it. That, and the pervasiveness of bones. When life wages war, it is as if these two last foot soldiers hold out until the end, stubbornly fighting a losing battle till they have to succumb to the inevitable as well.

'The water's too hot.' She hasn't opened her eyes.

'Why didn't you tell me when I asked you to dip your hand in?' Ritwik asks.

'That's because it felt all right to the touch.'

It is a logic Ritwik understands, so he asks, 'Do you want me to add some cold water now?'

'No, it's fine.' And then, after a while, 'You'll take that cloth and rub my back, won't you?'

'Yes, of course.'

'That Haq woman has come looking for you a couple of times.'

'Oh, yes?'

'She seems very curious about you. Asks me all sorts of questions.'

'What questions?' There is a slight edge of anxiety in his voice.

'Oh, you know. Your parents, your family, what you do, where you were before this, what you will do in life, that sort of thing.' She opens her eyes; there is laughter in them. 'But I tell her nothing. That's because I don't know anything, do I?'

'Well, Anne, if you ask *very* politely, I might, I *just* might tell you a few of the things you are *dying* to know.' He is laughing now, a clear and teasing sound in this enveloping miasma of steam.

'Oh, *I* am not curious,' she rushes in mock-huffily, in a little parody of his italicized speech. 'I wonder *where* you get all these self-important ideas from. I was just making an *observation* about that nosy Pakistani woman.'

They are both laughing now, she, in a bass guffaw, he, taking the top notes above this line. Ugo appears, looks at them, sniffs the air and lopes away. By a tacit arrangement, they always leave the bathroom door open during bathtimes, as if closing the door would confer on the event an unwholesome intimacy, which neither of them desired or knew how to negotiate.

Ritwik rubs the lemon yellow flannel along her back in slow circles. More grey scum, which had come to rest along the points of contact between water and flesh and water and bathtub, swirl about, as if alive, like plankton.

'I think she means to ask you to do something for her but can't quite bring herself to do it. Probably doesn't know how to put it. Maybe she wants you to be her mouthpiece,' Anne says, leaning back against the pillow and closing her eyes again.

'What do you think it might be?' Ritwik feels slightly apprehensive. He knows Anne is right, as always; she has an uncanny ability to read people like an easy, accessible book.

'I have no idea, but she is quite meddlesome, don't you think? She keeps asking about my family, my children, my grandchildren, as if she hasn't heard the gossip. I've always found this Indian curiosity about other people's lives a bit disturbing. Not offensive, mind you, just a bit difficult to get used to. I found it difficult to cope with when I was living in India, the constant staring, the personal questions. I suppose it is natural in places where there is a strong sense of community.' She slides down a few more inches in the water as if this longish speech has exhausted her.

'What gossip?' Ritwik asks, unsure whether Anne is going to take this as substantiating evidence of the infamous Sub-continental inquisitiveness.

'What gossip?' Anne echoes.

He breathes in deeply and says, 'You said Mrs Haq pretends as if she hasn't heard the neighbours' gossip about you. So I asked what gossip.'

One, two, three . . . Ritwik measures the pause in heartbeats; it is impossible to predict which way Anne will go.

'There are a couple of people who've lived here for almost as long as I have. This place has seen a lot of new people, you know, some moving out, some coming in. The ones who died here, perhaps they passed on gossip to their children, friends, neighbours. I've always waited for the time when I would be the oldest person living in Ganymede Road and everyone who has known me for years and years either dead or long gone to a different place. There will be only new people on this street, people with no idea of who I am, how long I've lived here.' She is visibly tiring after this torrent of words, but it is not over, not yet. She sits up a bit, opens her eyes again and says, 'But gossip's a weed, it keeps coming back. There is no way one can start with a clean slate.' She shuts her eyes, cackles, 'Not at my age. Yours might be a different case.'

Ritwik doesn't fail to notice how she has evaded his question, fobbed him off with a non-answer and seen straight through his apology of a life, all in one seamless stream of words. But he won't give up this time. He repeats, 'What gossip?' This has become a game now and he wants to have at least one won set behind him.

Did they say *bad mother failed mother* she is sure they did, they still do for all she cares, but is there anyone left from, god, when was it, sixty-six, or was it sixty-eight, no it must have been sixty-six, yes, she is quite sure, but it might just be sixty-eight and they're not far from wrong for what sort of mother forgets the year of her son's death, here she is wondering whether it was sixty-six or sixty-eight, shame on her, his brains blown out, a leaking dark jam everywhere, on the desk at which he had sat while doing it, on the wall behind, spattered with blood as if a naughty child had had an accident with a bottle of ink he had been forbidden to touch, no letter, no note, nothing except a *forgive me, mother*, in the refrigerator a day later when she had gone to look for milk for her tea and the police inspector no constable maybe a curl of paper or is she making this up there was no note nothing only the faint metallic whiff of blood and the tinny smell of internal organs her son's brain her thirty-six year-old son's brain her thirty-six-year-old son who had torn out of her one August afternoon with the monsoon coming down in unforgiving sheets outside the bungalow and the Indian midwife inscrutable dumb in her foreign language and Clare's *ayah* all crowding around thirty-one hours for a little head to come out but all tangled up inside and Dr Higgins despairing too *unforeseen complications* the child who made the beginning and the end unendurably difficult while her contractions racked her as if there were no end and no end to the deluge outside waters breaking everywhere this child who would almost take her life with him while receiving his and then who took his own and a bit of his mother's forever so there is nothing anymore except that note or did she imagine it to save herself because there was no one else left to do it?

A difficult child a different child a child who grew up on his own needed very little almost self-enclosed no not the self-enclosedness of a selfish person but of an independent one needed no one needed nothing till the last day when he unravelled everything that everyone had ever thought about him unravelled his assumed self-containedness like a washed skein of recycled wool taught her the last lesson that he too had needed love like everyone else perhaps more for who but the weak among us need love because the strong have everything and she had read him her son her ripped flesh her near-death with the demented Indian monsoon howling outside wanting to carry them both away she and her tangled child she had read him wrong all along misread his silences misread his secrecies his opacity the frequently shut doors the increasingly haunted look a hunted animal looking back on it now she had misread everything and shut the book but the book was now gone taken away irreversibly from her and returned to its sender she would never have a chance to read it again and say yes I understood some of it only now she lives with the abiding incomprehensibility of what she had been given because she didn't see.

But she did give him something no not love not the obliterating love he had wanted oh yes she felt it love in pores and arteries and her leaking nipples and in the pit of her stomach but she could never show it to him never for love is a weakness too isn't it an admission of helplessness so she didn't not obviously but it was always there and if he was so all-comprehending why didn't he see it and save his mother why didn't he so she gave him birds instead those creatures of the air hollow insubstantial through which they communicated their love no she's wrong again she never *communicated* anything otherwise he would still be here and she would comfort him in his isolation saying it didn't matter what he was who he was he was in the end the child who had ripped her apart he was hers always and forever and nothing was going to change it but they had kestrels and oystercatchers and snow eagles and macaws and hoopoes instead. So much love such a lot of air air everywhere for these creatures to live and move and swim in the same air, lower, through which Richard, no more than five, glides through across the green lawn in Simla with a feather clutched in his baby fingers *Mummy, mummy, is this a pigeon feather or a dove's and what are these lovely things at the bottom* pointing to the tuft of down feathers a couple of inches from the base of the quill, her bird-loving son a little blond ornithologist angel with who knew a Civil Service career stored up for him all history between then and now gone like a twinkle in the eye a breath a vapour that is the life of man all of it untying loosening free to scatter in the moment when her son's brains her own innards slither down and crust over a wall and she not knowing what had happened for an uncalibrated moment in time thinking Richard has fallen asleep at his desk and is going to turn around at the sound of her entering the room and say *Why don't you shut the door . . .*

'Why don't you shut the door?' she suddenly mumbles, startling Ritwik out of his reverie. He was certain she was taking one of her cat naps, mouth open, eyes pressed shut, head lolling on the air pillow, everything in the house still, very still, with only the sound of his hand moving occasionally in the water, accentuating the silence. That barely discernible liquid sound and Anne's dream-soaked words – 'brain' and 'feather' were the only two he could make out and even those he is not sure about – escaping from her subterranean world out into this alien space.

'Are you cold?' Ritwik asks her.

No answer. No movement from Anne.

'Look, you will have to sit up a bit if I get up to shut the door,' he says softly.

She moves, an amphibious crab, graceless and pained. Ritwik stands up, shuts the door and sits down by the bath again.

'What do you say to letting out some water and turning the hot tap on for a bit?' he coaxes her gently back to life.

She remains resolutely contained in whatever demesne she has chosen to wander in now. Ritwik releases the plug for a minute, replaces it, turns on the hot tap, swirling his hand in the bath all the time to keep the temperature equable. When the water feels right, he turns the tap off, soaps the yellow cloth and lifts up Anne's breasts and rubs it gently under them, under her armpits, on her shoulders, her thighs, the join of legs and torso, all remnants and residues of what they began life as. The ribcage feels like a very precarious cage, about to unconfigure and lose whatever tired bird it was imprisoning inside, letting it free at last. He is especially shaken, every time, by the craterous area where her breasts started life. He takes up her arms, one by one, puts them on his shoulders and soaps them. Anne wakes up. Her eyes are clouded with a distance that Ritwik can never traverse. When she is in one of these moods, she won't talk, or interact; she will cocoon in on herself and walk away till she readmits him in her own time, the time dictated by the metronome marking the rhythm of the world she has suddenly slipped into.

'That's enough, don't you think?' she asks. 'Give me your hands, so I can get up.'

This is an extremely delicate operation; one false interlocking of fingers on arms, one slippage in any of those myriad surfaces of contact, would spell immediate, even irreversible, disaster.

'OK, take your hands out of the bath so I can dry them.'

She complies like an obedient child.

'Now leave your hands out.' She puts them up on her head. Ritwik dries his own hands and arms thoroughly so that there is not a trace of wetness on which Anne's clutching hands can slither. He puts both hands under her armpits and lets her grip his upper arms: he is a vice, a ball of white-hot concentration. He almost lifts Anne out of the bath, positioning her on to the bath mat, still holding her close, in a near-embrace, till she finds her feet and feels secure enough to disengage herself partially so that Ritwik can towel her dry. He kneels, so that he can do her lower half more efficiently, with a slight quickening of his heart: he must not look, he must not be caught stealing furtive glances at that great unknown. He wonders what Anne feels at this indignity. Does she resent it passionately yet holds her tongue because she has no other option? Does she simply not care? Do you reach an age when things such as enforced nakedness, help with toilet paper and with sluicing the stubborn corners and crevices of the body, count for nothing anymore, the impulse to inhibition just a trivial expression of a long-gone vanity? Would he ever have the courage or the effrontery to ask her directly in one of her more readable moments, perhaps when he is sitting by her bed and reading out *The Little Prince* or *The Owl Who Was Afraid of The Dark* to her as the dark congeals outside the windows and a new bird shatters the silence?

They had peacocks last week, a flutter of cumbersome feathers and raucous shrieks, a sound that still shivers up and down Ritwik's spine in the same way the scrape of fingernails against chalkboard set off shudders in him. The birds had strutted around on the grass, sending out into the innocent December air their abominable cries as if they had been done an injury, which nothing could reverse or recompense. And then they had flown off or disappeared, leaving Ritwik astounded and Anne, stoical and mysterious, with a vague unsmiled smile playing around her bunched mouth, as if she not only knew the answer to this phenomenon but had in fact brought it into being herself.

'I want my kimono,' she announces, breaking what seems to Ritwik an interminable silence, for they have each slipped into their unreachable worlds.

'I need to put some powder on you first, don't I?' Ritwik slips back into duty.

'All right then, but hurry, please, it's cold in here.'

Ritwik reaches for the tin of lavender talcum powder, hesitates a few seconds trying to decide whether he should pour it first on his hand and then smear her or whether he should sprinkle the talc on her directly and then spread it around more evenly. He opts for the latter and realizes immediately that he has made a mistake; he comes to this particular crossroads every bathtime and every time he makes the same mistake, for the talc falls and inhabits the pouches and folds of her skin, stays trapped there, much in the way a powdery drift of snow fills up rills and gullies first. Once again, a bathtime ritual becomes an almost insurmountable logistical problem for Ritwik.

'Hold on to my waist while I do it, OK?' It is like talking to a child, except the position they are locked in now could be that of lovers.

She complies again. When the ritual is all over, Ritwik wraps her dressing gown around her and says, 'Let's go and look for your kimono.'

She refuses to take the stairlift and wants Ritwik to help her upstairs. On the way up, an immeasurably long move and somewhat irritating to Ritwik, partly because his desire for pure order and neatness had been scrambled by the foamless scum and the powder in the ridges of Anne's skin, she asks, 'How is your job with Mr Haq going?'

Fucking clairvoyant psychoterrorist. Of course, he does not voice it.

The lone and level strawberry field stretched far away, but not so far that Ritwik couldn't see something different at the far end, where it met the horizon, another field of a different crop. In the very far distance there was a disparate bunch of what looked like abandoned ricks and sheds and an outmoded combine harvester or some such farming machine. What took his immediate attention were the acres and acres of green which, on closer inspection, appeared somehow straggly and weak, an anaemic shade of the colour, but he had never seen a strawberry bush before and had assumed it would be a tough thing, more like a sturdy, clipped rosebush and less like this semi-climber. Row after long row of bushes, laid out like disciplined armies, thick with red berries. The berries were not obvious at first but when he first spied them, among the low foliage and on the straw bedding, which had been laid down lovingly under the plants along the entire length and breadth of the plantation, he couldn't see anything else. *Like little red lanterns in the green night*, he had paraphrased and then felt immediately ashamed at his cast of mind. And where was this place? Cambridgeshire? Hertfordshire? Berkshire? He had no idea but he wasn't going to ask in case they thought him snoopy or too inquisitive for his own good. Something told him that too many questions, or even revealing some fluency in English, wouldn't go down too well here.

The journey out here had taken slightly over an hour. During the first leg of the drive, Ritwik had frequently clambered up to the back window to get a glimpse of the world outside. As the road had ribboned out in a track of macadam grey, with houses or occasionally fields on either side, he had thought that this was what it felt like to be a prisoner, literally, being taken away in a prison van, watching the other side unspool in relative reverse. Along with this, the jerkiness that came with being in the back of a van had given him a slight sense of motion sickness so, after a while, he had stopped looking out of the window and concentrated instead on dispelling the little waves of nausea.

He had introduced himself to the young man, his fellow passenger. There had been a difficult and halting conversation, Dusan – that was his name – was taciturn and almost hostile at first and then plain inarticulate, his English still rudimentary. Ritwik had persevered; when 'Where are you from?' proved too difficult for Dusan to follow, Ritwik had broken it down to 'Country?' and, pointing to him, 'You'. In the volley that followed, only 'Albania' seemed decipherable. When Ritwik asked him to slow down, Dusan kept pointing to himself and saying, 'Albania, Albania', and then, 'Home: Macedonia, Live: Macedonia'. An Albanian from Macedonia, Ritwik decided. He found it difficult to place: that was a very fuzzy area of the world map. The interaction jolted along, an erratically dotted movement to the more or less smooth onward motion of the van. At one point, Ritwik asked Dusan his age by pointing to himself first, showing ten fingers twice and then four fingers, then pointing to Dusan and making a vague interrogative gesture with his upturned palm. After two tries, Dusan cracked it and answered, without resorting to counting with fingers, 'Fifteen.' Ritwik was sure he hadn't been able to keep the shock off his face: Dusan looked at least twice his age. His eyes were the eyes of someone who had seen things about life which most wouldn't want to be shown, a small bunch of lines already making their forking ways out from the corners, his hands gnarled, his mouth lined. The hinterlands behind those eyes contained dangerous terrain, a whole map of misery.

Over the next three days, the map unfurled a tiny bit for Ritwik to have a fleeting glimpse.

Dusan and Ritwik had first been taken to a hut and Tim, along with two other men, had explained to them what they were supposed to do. There were instructions about filling up punnets and barrows, returning picked fruit to the shed, the workings of the twine machine, the sizes of fruits to be picked, different sizes in different baskets – Ritwik hadn't known that fruit picking – so simple, so . . . so . . . *pure* – could be hedged in by so many rules and dos and don'ts.

'You work until seven and then come to the farm, it's a mile up that road; one of us will come back with you here and have a look at what you have done. You'll get paid then. Is that clear? Another thing: don't eat the fruit. We have a very good idea how much fruit you can pick in twelve hours, between the two of you, and if the weight is any less than our estimate, you get the money taken off your wages. Clear?'

The question of returning to London had assumed such huge proportions in Ritwik's mind that he hadn't even taken in most of the instructions. But he hadn't dared to speak out.

Just half an hour into picking strawberries – larger berries in one basket, smaller ones in another – Ritwik had realized why the farmers didn't do it themselves. You had to either squat or bend, moving like a crab, awkward and hobbling; the first applied unbearable tension on the thighs, the second broke your back. After the first hour, both Ritwik and Dusan had tried crawling on their knees and moving on fours. By the time it was ten o'clock, they had worked out that the optimal thing to do was a combination of all these movements, each sustained until it became unbearable, then switching to another one. The sun was becoming fierce, Ritwik had forgotten to get a bottle of water, and his body was being tested in positions and configurations it wasn't used to. He hadn't wanted to think what the aches would be like after a night of sleep.

Where am I going to sleep? In London? How will I get there? In the shed here? What's going to happen to Anne?

Before midday, Ritwik felt as if he would never walk straight again, his back hunched, the stoop taking its own time to relax and let him ease, very slowly and painfully, up into erect position again. Dusan, either made of more resilient stuff, or used to such work, had doggedly carried on, needing fewer rests and fewer stretches of the body to its natural and original postures.

When the dehydration headache kicked in, first a slow contracting behind the eyes and then the drilling at the temples and at the back of the head, Ritwik decided that finding water couldn't be put off any longer. They walked to the shed only to be disappointed. Dusan explained to him, in broken English, that there was bound to be a source of water somewhere nearby otherwise how would they water their crop? Ritwik accompanied Dusan, the Albanian boy following some arcane and invisible track understood only by him but he led them, after a meandering walk for about three-quarters of an hour, to a lead pipe sticking out of the ground with a tap at its mouth and a huge hose of green plastic coiled near it. They drank, mouths to the tap, as if there were no tomorrow.

As the day wore on, Ritwik realized that Dusan's English was not as minimal as he had first taken it to be. Perhaps it was nervousness that had inhibited him, perhaps the company of strangers, but he told Ritwik that he had read English in his school for three years, a school in a small, small village next to a town called Bogovino near the foothills of the Sar mountains, on the border of Macedonia with Kosovo. Dusan spelt out, like a child learning his first alphabet and getting the vowels jumbled with each other, the names of the town and the mountain, and then inscribed them on the earth with a hardy point of a piece of straw. When Ritwik asked him what had brought him to London, with a shrug his English disappeared once again. Different variations on the question, from several angles, only brought shrugs, silence, apparent incomprehension and a subsequent immersion in work.

The other thing Ritwik noticed about Dusan was that he never smiled. Not that there was much to smile about when your body was contorted impossibly, like a whimsically bent metal clothes hanger, and the sun got more and more ruthless, but normal people smiled when they introduced themselves to each other, or said 'thank you', or did any of those unthinking little acts of civil courtesy or politeness. No trace of those in Dusan; he wasn't rude or anything, but it felt to Ritwik that there were vast dark clouds moving inside him all the time, darkening his eyes. For all he knew, he had never learnt to smile at all.

In the numerous silences that marked their fruit-picking, Ritwik battled with discomfort bordering on pain, hunger, headache, curiosity, anxiety and, the biggest of them all, boredom. Who would have thought that ten to twelve hours in a field of strawberries would become so viscous after the first two that they refused to budge? He filled up the vast spaces between his intermittent conversation with Dusan thinking about the ways in which Miss Gilby was getting knottier by the day, opaque and locked in her world, a world that often refused him entry. Every time he thought or wrote of Miss Gilby now, the face of Anne occupied his mind, ludicrously so because his Miss Gilby was stuck at what, forty-five? Fifty? Fifty-five even?

At other times, he populated the emptiness with musings on the politics of the country house poem; the georgic versus the pastoral; the famous English countryside, written and talked about so much, extolled, loved, and there he was in the middle of it, unable to construct a broader canvas of 'Countryside', stuck in a strawberry field which could only be a tiny detail in the huge picture of the literary construct. Where were the gently rolling green fields, the fields of barley and rye, the hills clothed with forests? And why was it all so close to major roads, so that the sound of traffic, a steady sea-roar, was always its music, not birds or crickets as the books and poems and essays had deceitfully promised? And what was Dusan thinking about? Where was he?

The next three days gave some sort of an answer to where Dusan went inside his head while his red, sore fingers plucked strawberries, his head bent, his body splayed and hunched at the same time. But only a type of answer and one, Ritwik felt, he himself had much to do with piecing together into a coherent fabric from the disparate shreds and rags Dusan threw at him.

On the second day, as Ritwik stretched his whole body out on the ground, racked with currents of pain and brittleness and warnings from his lower back and neck, Dusan asked Ritwik who he lived with, whether he had family in England, if he had lived in this country all his life. Ritwik answered with accurate facts, not a word more than he deemed necessary, but they were all true, if not the whole truth. There was silence for a long while as Ritwik tried to gather enough courage to ask him reciprocal questions but he hesitated too long and the moment went.

That day Ritwik had come prepared with a two-litre bottle of water, two sandwiches – white bread and cheese and tomatoes bought with the previous night's twenty pounds – and two apples, one for himself, one for Dusan. When he offered his food and water to Dusan, the boy looked at him with a dumb surprise, then took them from Ritwik without a word of thanks but with a touching lowering of the head, as if he were being offered grace by an angel. He also volunteered information about himself, which Ritwik had not dared ask for. He lived in a house with his mother, two sisters, two brothers, three uncles, two aunts and five nephews and nieces. Full house, absolutely crammed, thought Ritwik, reminded of the hell of Grange Road. When Ritwik mentioned that he too had lived in a joint family, although not in one as large as Dusan's, the boy painstakingly explained to him that they all lived in one *room*, not one *house*, one room in a place called Barnet. The men, all of them, went to work, if they could find some. His uncles worked exclusively in construction and building: there was more work in that field than in farming and, anyway, this was seasonal, not really a regular job. They did not have proper papers in this country so it was difficult but between the six of them – Dusan, one of his brothers, the three uncles and one nephew – they managed to survive. Dusan's mother and her sons and daughters were waiting to go to the United States because she had an uncle in a town there and he was going to arrange for papers and a house, maybe, who knows, even schools for his sisters and himself, because he would like to be a doctor.

They had waited in England for fourteen months now and, before that, two months in Albania, from which they had had to flee because the police came to their village once, with guns, went knocking on every door and asked everyone to get out and never come back again. And there was no work to be had in Albania, you could die of hunger and thirst and even a dog wouldn't come and piss in your mouth to wet your throat. So they had taken a ship to Bari and then a bus from Bari to Rome and then things got fuzzy and out-of-focus for Ritwik because Dusan wasn't very clear about how he and his family had come from Italy to England. There were vague mutterings about relatives in the UK, an Albanian community, promise of work but the narrative ran into the sand. At this point, Dusan stared hard at the ground and went red-faced and silent. Maybe it was just the sun and the racking pain from fruit-picking. Or maybe Ritwik didn't pay enough attention, for the sound of his own blood rushing around in his ears blocked out this boy's story, a story that exposed his own as thin and tinny. His lot, which he had escaped, appeared as luxury compared with Dusan's. He felt small and ashamed and couldn't make eye contact with the Albanian boy for the duration of their farm experience. Which was all of three days, because he wasn't picked up by Tim's van on the fourth day as he stood on Chichele Lane with loose newspapers and the debris of last night's kebab wrappers and take-away cartons littering the morning road.

And there had been no Dusan either. When Ritwik had asked Saeed, he had answered that he had no idea where the boy was, what his name was, where he came from. Like everyone out here, he was part of a floating population, here today, gone tomorrow, looking for better work, more pay. It was possible that he had found some place else, somewhere less temporary and less short-term than fugitive tasks like fruit-picking. Or, Ritwik thought, his uncles had found him something more stable in a construction job, leaving Ritwik with all those questions he had never asked about Dusan's father and why he had had to leave Macedonia – was there violence? Was his village burnt down as the *dalits*' were in India? Did he watch members of his family killed? – never had time to ask him about his country and if many people escaped or only a few. In the end, it came down to Ritwik's own ignorance of the world, of his willed innocence about what was happening in it: he couldn't look beyond the boundaries of his own shadow.

Over the next month, Ritwik worked for Saeed in the hope that he would bump into Dusan somewhere. Sometimes, he worked stretches of ten days at a go, at other times there were three to four consecutive days when he returned to Ganymede Road after an hour or two of futile waiting in Willesden. There was more fruit-picking and promise of more by a farmer, or his friend, called Jack, in the autumn, in his apple and pear orchards in Kent.

There was the odd bit of packing fruit and vegetables in a giant warehouse off the M25. He met Kurdish and Turkish men and women there and first heard the term 'refugee', whispered, hot with stigma, almost unspeakable. It fell from the lips of the supervisor in charge of their packing unit as he was doing one of his inspection rounds. A baby, bound to its mother's chest, was making an unbearable noise: Ritwik thought it was wailing because it was hungry but there was no stopping it and in the high-roofed cavern of the warehouse the acoustics seemed to conspire with the crying to make it more high-pitched, more insistent. The supervisor was doing his rounds and Ritwik understood that if the woman took time off to feed her baby, she would have the time clocked by the man and deducted from her wages. From all of twenty pounds for a nine-hour day. There was no altercation or even irritated sounds of 'shhhh' and 'tssk' from either the supervisor or the other workers but the air had been heavy with tension; there had been a greater concentration in putting lettuce in cling film. As the supervisor passed by Ritwik, he clearly heard him mutter, 'Bloody fucking refugees and their fucking children', then looked at Ritwik, rolled his eyes upward in a gesture that was meant to draw them together in their mutual irritation at this screaming, and said, 'Why can't they leave them at home? This god-awful racket.' Ritwik had lowered his eyes. The appropriate reply – 'Where should she leave it? At a crèche?' – came too late, as the man's back was receding down the far end, towards the double doors.

In any case, he wouldn't have had the job any more if he had answered back. There were all sorts of talk and gossip in this warehouse – how the workers couldn't be absent even for a day, how all the time they spent in there was costed down to the last second, including visits to the toilet, how lunch breaks fell outside the number of hours at work, how talking amongst each other was discouraged. Nearly every day some of them had a few pence deducted from the cash they queued for at seven o'clock on some excuse or the other. Ritwik wondered if there was a

CCTV, keeping watch on them, hidden away in a strategic corner, or if the management just took it for granted that the workers would be either too intimidated or too lacking in English to protest.

As soon as they emerged outside, everyone would lope off to his specific destination, mostly on his own, but a few in groups of two or three, which made Ritwik think they were either related or they lived in the same neighbourhood. It didn't take him very long to discover that most of these groupings were made along ethnic lines: the Polish men clumped together, the few Kurdish women stayed close to each other because they were returning to the same council estate or bedsit.

Then one evening Ritwik noticed Mehmet, a young Kurdish man, sitting on the ground outside with his back to the warehouse wall, sobbing his guts out, surrounded by four or five other men, presumably all Kurdish. Ritwik edged closer to the group, eaten up by curiosity. Something had happened to Mehmet's sister, but what exactly it was, no one would say. Perhaps they didn't have enough English between them to articulate it. Or it could have been they didn't trust this outsider at all, this thin, young boy who looked starved but could speak fluently in English, so what was he doing here among them when he could so easily have got a better job anywhere else?

Mehmet stopped coming to work. Ritwik worked himself up for three days to ask one of his Kurdish friends, as he was leaving after being paid, what had happened to him. All he got initially was a hooded look of mistrust; some shutter seemed to have come down, leaving Ritwik outside. Two men joined them and spoke rapidly in their tongue. One of them tried to speak to Ritwik but after a few stray words – 'sister', 'police', 'beg' – all flung out without joins and syntax, he gave up in frustration.

What on earth *had* happened? Had Mehmet's sister been caught begging on the Tube and arrested by the police? Did the police then discover she was staying in the country illegally and deport her with her entire family? Other lurid scenarios played themselves in Ritwik's mind: was she a prostitute who was caught by the police in a raid? What was the begging all about? Was she begging the police to let her go? It was still light outside but the traffic whirling around them in the highways and flyovers had become denser and all the vehicles had switched on their head and tail lights. The sound was that of a steadily churning sea.

VIII.

Miss Gilby has taken her seat along with the rest of the *andarmahal* in the balcony of the first floor. The dark green blinds are still drawn but the slats have been opened so that the women can see what is happening in the courtyard below. Bimala, her two sisters-in-law and Miss Gilby are all perched on *moraa*s – cane pouffes with leather seats – while the *andarmahal* cook and the new maid stand behind a pillar in a corner. Bimala has procured a pair of opera glasses, which she passes to Miss Gilby and her sisters-in-law regularly so that they too can hone in on a face or a head in the crowd below.

For there is nothing short of a milling crowd gathered in the courtyard this morning, all waiting to hear the *swadeshi* leader Sandip Banerjea address them and direct the next phase of the movement. There are men from the village, men who have come all the way from Calcutta, men from surrounding districts, a large number of *swadeshi* activists – nearly all of them young students, hardly more than seventeen or eighteen years old – in their customary orange garb that makes them stand out like a bright flash in the dark sky. Mr Banerjea was supposed to have started at ten; he is more than twenty minutes late and although punctuality is something which the Bengali man can never be accused of, Miss Gilby cannot help feeling that the *swadeshi* leader had an actor's cunning sense of timing: he was whetting the appetite of the crowd by making it wait for him.

When he does appear, borne on a wooden board held on the shoulders of four young disciples – Miss Gilby cannot shake off that mildly objectionable word – her feelings appear to be confirmed in an irrational and unverifiable way. Loud cries of *bande mataram* go up, especially from the energetic orange youths, all flashing eyes and revolutionary ardour. The neatly bearded and fashionably attired Mr Banerjea soaks them up with the benign and effortless public smile that comes so naturally to gifted actors and politicians; after a few moments he signals with his right hand – it is a cross between a holy man's gesture of blessing and a signal for the crowd to allay their enthusiasm for a little while. When the crowd has gone so silent that one can hear a reed moving in water, he begins his oration.

Miss Gilby understands only the first sentence – 'The Viceroy, Lord Curzon, has divided Bengal' – and the rest is just a few lucid words here and there in an opaque sea: *swadeshi*, obviously, appears a lot, and *atmasakti*, self-reliance, too, along with 'boycott' and 'English'. But a considerable amount of the sense can be inferred from the tone of his voice, its modulations, the gestures, the blazing-bright eyes, the confidence in his own consummate performance, the timbre and fluidity of his baritone: the man is such a skilled orator, thinks Miss Gilby, that he could easily, at the end of his speech – during which every mouth in the crowd remains half-open, every face rapt – have commanded his audience to do anything, anything, and they would have willingly rushed out and done it. Bimala forgets to pass on the lorgnette after his first few sentences, even *naw jaa* slips off her *moraa* a couple of times, so keen is her eagerness to get as close to the speaker as her confinement in the *andarmahal* will allow.

It remains in no doubt to Miss Gilby why this man is one of the leaders of the *swadeshi* movement: he certainly appears to have been born to such things. He seems to be whipping them up into a fervour of *swadeshi* activity, spreading his message of the boycott of English goods, carrying everyone into the vortex of protest against the unjust division of Bengal. Mr Banerjea is a creature of fire and wind, working together in a dance of fury; for an unsettling moment she sees a childhood illustration of the prophet Elijah in his chariot of fire. Miss Gilby feels like a traitor, sitting and listening to him, but she would be hard-pressed to answer which party she felt she was betraying.

When the speech is over, there is a long moment of silence, in which the radiance and intensity of the blaze the crowd has been exposed to are registered and assimilated, before it breaks into applause, yet more fervid shouts of *bande mataram*, a general clambering and stampede to reach out and touch the speaker who has now acquired in almost everyone's minds the status of a demigod. The orange boys appear delirious and possessed as they move around the crowd, fists balled, arms raised, shouting their mantra. The flock of pigeons, which had settled peacefully along the edges of the roof, perhaps also mesmerized like the humans gathered below, have their spell broken and flutter up in a group. Their departure too sounds like clapping hands. Miss Gilby turns sideways to find all the women in the balcony dabbing at their eyes with the *aanchol* of their *sari*s.

Bimala seems distracted and restless but Miss Gilby does not rule out the possibility that she may be attributing to her charge her own feelings of a sudden and inexplicable diffusion of focus and concentration. Bimala makes three mistakes in the very first two bars of 'Roaming in the gloaming', an unusual thing because she knows the piece so well. She ignores the metronome, too, resulting in Miss Gilby having to stop singing and remind her, indulgently the first few times, and then rather sharply, that her innovative tempi are doing no favours either to the piano or to the spirit of the tune. Bimala sulks for a while and tries to concentrate but it seems that they might have to write off music lessons for the day.

Miss Gilby tries a different tack. 'Why don't we leave music for another day, Bimala, when you've practised some more?'

Bimala jumps at the bait. 'Yes, Miss Gilby. Can I sew for a bit and we can talk and practise Conversation?'

'All right, then. What are you embroidering?' Miss Gilby hopes this form of subtle and covert correction has the right effect on Bimala.

Bimala picks up her embroidery: it is a very large piece of blinding white cloth, with the area to be worked on picked out and stretched like the skin of a drum by the frame, showing the beginnings of Bengali letters in blue.

'*Banglaar pakhi*,' Miss Gilby reads, much to the visible delight of Bimala. 'The birds of Bengal.'

'Yes, yes,' Bimala nods excitedly and unravels more of the cloth lying in folds and soft heaps on the sofa, trailing on the floor. 'I make a bedspread with the different birds of Bengal all over it. Yes?'

Only two birds have been embroidered on to that pristine field of white but they are creatures that could set a cat stalking. Miss Gilby's heart leaps when she sees them – a sparrow in shades of brown and ash and fawn, its eye a dark bead, its legs the colour of dun, dried leaves, and a kingfisher in its blue blaze, the beak a miracle of poised coral red. They are a rapture of finger and thread and needle: who would have thought such a miracle to be possible from those ordinary objects of commonplace life?

Bimala notes Miss Gilby's pleasure and admiration in her sharp intake of breath. 'You like this?' she asks, somewhat redundantly.

'Yes, very, very much. It's so . . .' she searches for a word, 'so . . . lifelike, so real. Did you have a model to work from, a picture or a drawing or something of the kind?'

'Yes, yes, I get it now.' She puts down the spilling cloth, frees herself from its clinging folds and runs out of the room. In a few minutes, she is back, bearing a giant book, which she passes to Miss Gilby.

The Birds of the North-Eastern and East Gangetic Plain by a Ruth A. Fairweather. 1902. Published in London. The brief note about the author says that after twenty years in Bengal, Orissa and the foothills of the north-eastern arm of the mighty Himalayan range, she is now a resident of Almora where she is at work on a companion volume on North Indian birds. The name doesn't ring a bell but there aren't very many Englishwomen in this vast country who have scientific interests and write about Indian birds; surely someone Miss Gilby knows must know her.

As she turns the pages, Miss Gilby cannot make up her mind whether Ruth Fairweather is an artist first and then a scientist, or the other way around. Page after page of luminous plumage, limpid, waterdark eyes; the birds look ready to fly out in a flash of colour and escape from their papery imprisonment to the green and gold outside where they truly belong. Miss Gilby is so hypnotized that she doesn't know how much time has elapsed before she turns her attention on to Bimala who seems to be lost in a daydream.

Miss Gilby gives a slight cough. 'They're extraordinary,' she manages to say at last.

'My husband gives it . . . no, no . . . gave, gave it to me, no?'

'That's correct.'

'He knows I like birds very much. So I sew this for him,' Bimala says, and giggles nervously, not sure whether that homophonic assonance was quite correct or not.

'That is very nice of you. You are a wonderful artist yourself.'

Bimala smiles shyly and starts picking up her embroidery. Miss Gilby tries to get her to talk more; she asks Bimala, 'Why don't you tell me what the fiery Mr Banerjea's speech last week was all about?'

A hectic flush races up Bimala's face and reaches her hairline. She drops her embroidery and makes a great show of picking it up, then gets down on to the floor to look for a lost needle. As the search progresses, a touch excessive and theatrical, Miss Gilby infers from the sudden blush that Mr Banerjea and Bimala, against all prevailing custom and social rules, have been introduced to each other by Mr Roy Chowdhury; the revolutionary must be the first man she has met apart from her husband and she hasn't quite got over the novelty, the sheer transgressiveness of the situation.

When the little charade is over and Bimala settles down again, having failed to find the missing needle but otherwise composed as before, Miss Gilby repeats her question. 'I could not follow a lot of Mr Banerjea's speech in the courtyard. I thought he was speaking a very chaste and purified Bengali. What was he saying? I could gather it was about *swadeshi* but not very much more.'

Bimala looks straight at Miss Gilby, holds her gaze and says, with utmost seriousness, even awe, 'He speaks about Bengal as the mother goddess.'

Miss Gilby involuntarily adds, 'Spoke, Bimala, spoke. He spoke last week; it's in the past.'

Bimala lowers her gaze, smiles embarrassedly, and corrects herself. 'Yes, sorry, spoke, spoke, he spoke.'

'Anything else, apart from the nation as mother goddess?'

Bimala doesn't answer the question. Instead, she expounds similar themes to her tutor. 'You know *bande mataram*? We say *bande mataram*? Yes? It means "We pray to you, mother goddess". Bengal is mother to us. It was written by Bankimchandra Chattopadhyay. He is great writer.'

Miss Gilby at last understands the rallying cry of *swadeshi* leaders and activists. 'How wonderful. I didn't know that. It is Sanskrit, isn't it?'

'Yes, yes,' Bimala nods.

Their effortless and easy interactions now seem to be developing intercalations of uncomfortable pauses and silences. There is one of those now, which Bimala breaks by asking, 'Do you want to learn names of Bengali birds and you teach me English birds?'

'That is a very good idea', says Miss Gilby with something approaching relief.

And then one day, very soon after their Conversation Session spent talking of birds, both British and Bengali, Bimala stops attending lessons.

NINE

He had saved nearly two hundred pounds, all in loose cash and coins, in the Kashmiri wooden box, which he had found in one of the shelves in his room when he had first moved into Anne's house. It had gorgeously drawn peacocks and herons on it but the colours had lost their sheen and turned matte and the patina of dust had proved much more stubborn than he had expected when he tried to brush and, eventually, to scrub it off. Could it have been a relic from Anne's final days in India, nearly sixty years ago? He must remember to ask her about the box. One hundred and ninety-two pounds, eighty-six pence, he counted out. More than a month's subsistence money, maybe two, if he was very careful. And then he would have to start all over again.

He met Saeed one dawn on Chichele Road. Of the increasing queues and groups of peoples, Ritwik could now identify about half a dozen nationalities. He walked up to Saeed and said, 'Can I have a few words with you? After you've seen off your people?', looking briefly in the direction of the few people gathered loosely around him.

'You don't work? We find work for you today.'

'No, no, I'd like to take today off.'

'You speak to Mr Haq?'

'No, I haven't seen him for a long time.' He hadn't been to visit the Haq family ever since Saeed had picked him up from outside 37 Ganymede Road. There had been no need; besides, he wouldn't have been able to look Mr Haq in the eye or talk to his wife and children as if the last two months hadn't happened.

'You wait here. I take you back. OK?'

Ritwik nodded. For the next ninety minutes, he was audience to the drama he had been an actor in not so very long ago: floating groups of people, all trying to edge their way into a better life, get the briefest of toeholds on this dizzying escarpment of what they considered a better world, by becoming ghosts and shadows, the unseen and non-existent workers behind most things which made this ravenous, insatiable monster of a city live and breathe and keep consuming. If he had believed in a loony strain of religion, which asserted that the world was supported by invisible spirits and angels holding everything together in a vast safety net, here was its real objective correlative. He winced at the indelible term, product of such a different world altogether. There was fur in his mouth and Chichele Road had never looked so squalid and seedy as he realized quietly that work was never equal, never levelling; instead, work created the greatest tyrannies.

Saeed saw off his charges, two by two, then stood around for a while, smoking one Benson & Hedges after another, waiting to see if anyone else would need his services. Then he walked back to Ritwik who was sitting on the edge of a pavement. 'I take you back now?'

'Yes, please, if it's not too much trouble. I can always take the Tube but I wanted to ask you a few things.'

His car was parked, as always, in the genteel redbrick terraces of Heber Road. It was not till they were nearing Kilburn Park that Ritwik spoke. He knew Saeed wouldn't until he broke the silence. 'Saeed, I want to take a break for a while.'

Saeed was concentrating on negotiating an intersection off Maida Vale: it was morning rush hour and buses and cars appeared to fill up the streets.

'I mean, just stop working for a few days.'

Saeed nodded. He kept darting surreptitious glances at Ritwik in the rear view mirror.

'I was wondering if I could come back to you later if I needed more work.'

'You go away from London?'

'No, no, nothing of the sort.' Then, after a few seconds' beat, a sliver of the truth came out. 'I've never done this sort of work before and I feel very tired most of the time, you know, physically tired. I just want to rest for a week or so.' He wondered if he sounded convincing enough, for the beginnings of the truth had imperceptibly shaded into a white lie.

There was no immediate response from Saeed. Just before going under Marylebone flyover, he asked, 'You hungry? You eat something?'

Not knowing whether it was a question or a statement, Ritwik hesitated for too long but Saeed had already decided for him. 'We eat something here, OK?'

They went to Al-Shami, a cross between a café and a restaurant, teeming, even at this hour, with Lebanese men and a sprinkling of tourists. There was Khaled playing loudly on their music system but two juicers were going full time, making a great deal of noise and trying to drown out the warm bustle of voices, the usual clatter from the kitchen and the eaters, even the music. The strip lighting, however, made Ritwik feel down, as it invariably did, reminding him of those dingy, shadow-cornered rooms in Grange Road. The air was heavy with unfamiliar smells that made him salivate.

Saeed was clearly in charge here: he led them to a table beside a chunky square column with mirrors, went up to someone he evidently knew and had a brief chat while Ritwik seated himself and looked around. He returned to the table, sat down and asked Ritwik, 'All right?'

Ritwik nodded.

'We get good food here. I order.' He signalled for a waiter, brushed away his offer of two giant menu cards and broke out into rapid-fire Arabic with him. Ritwik obviously wasn't going to be consulted about the food, but he didn't really mind; it was clear that Saeed knew what was good so the decisions were best left to him. The incomprehensible conversation featured a few waves of Saeed's hand in the direction of Ritwik, probably telling the waiter what he thought should be got for him. As the waiter left, Saeed pulled out his packet of cigarettes from the back pocket of his jeans and started smoking.

'You eat at home?' he asked.

'Yes, of course I do,' Ritwik answered, trying to weave a casual laugh in there but failing.

'You look ill. Weak. Nobody take you for heavy job. They think you too weak.'

'No, no, honestly, I eat lots. It's my . . . my metabolism I suppose.' He didn't want the conversation going down this road at all.

There was a lapse as Saeed smoked and looked for words in a language so evidently foreign to him while Ritwik couldn't think of anything but the imminent arrival of food.

'There are rules, OK?' Saeed suddenly announced, leaning forward, as the waiter brought to the table two large tumblers of pincapple and mango juice, one foaming at the top. They had been freshly squeezed, realized Ritwik, as he took his first sip from the pineapple, and hadn't come out of a carton of concentrate. For a moment he thought Saeed was talking about rules governing the eating of this food because that non sequitur had coincided so perfectly with the arrival of the juice.

'Always rules for everything. Every world its own rules, rules in Libya, rules in England, rules in football, rules here we eat,' Saeed continued. There was a fierce concentration in the frown lines on his forehead and in his eyes, a stubborn determination to articulate properly, but Riwik had already lost him. What was all this talk of rules? He hoped it was going to become clear in time.

'You understand?'

'Yes, yes,' he lied.

'Your world there are rules, my world there are rules. The two sometimes different. The world of workers in Willesden, all the immigrants, also rules there. Many rules where you go. You see them OK? If you see them, you OK. If you not see, problems, you unhappy.'

Was this an ominous, circuitous warning that Ritwik could never leave the world he had had a brief glimpse of, that he had to do whatever Saeed asked of him? There didn't seem to be any other signs that this was a threat, apart from the indeterminacies of Saeed's truncated words, but they could equally stand for a kind of consolatory explanation for what Saeed took to be his unhappiness at the shadowy world of refugee workers, Ritwik thought.

Suddenly Saeed leaned forward and caught hold of Ritwik's hand and with his other hand reached for his shoulder across the table and held him there. The food arrived and Saeed let go.

There were stainless steel plates of two kinds of paste with swirls of olive oil and sprinklings of herb, a basket heaped with large, warm segments of flatbread, an oblong parcel wrapped in greaseproof paper, which Saeed indicated to be put down in front of Ritwik, another plate of a herb-dense salad flecked with grains, koftes. Ritwik asked Saeed to name everything for him; Saeed obliged: houmous, moutabbal, sujuk wrapped in flatbread and then toasted, tabbouleh.

For a while the spread pushed away Saeed's enigmatic words and his unexpected gesture to the back of Ritwik's mind. He bit into his sandwich and the hot, spicy juices from the Lebanese sausages ran down his fingers and the back of his hand. He closed his eyes in a moment of pure bliss: the whole world was circumscribed inside his mouth.

Saeed interrupted with, 'You like?'

Ritwik nodded weakly. There was so much pride, he thought, on Saeed's face: he was like a little child showing off his achievements to a parent. Why had he touched him like that? Was it a gesture of camaraderie? Of assurance? Or just an appeal that Ritwik should try and understand him even though his words were not the most perfect carriers of his sense?

What was the sense?

'You do different work for me?' Saeed asked while shovelling food into his mouth. There was no daintiness about his eating, no acknowledgement of the effete etiquette that governs polite eating together, only a functional, self-enclosed approach to his food, almost animal in its own and immediate needs.

'What work?'

Saeed seemed to be too busy eating to have heard so Ritwik repeated the question.

'You speak English. You talk to people I make work. Woman.

Some woman work for me. There is more woman want work. You be between us, you talk, you deal, OK? You my . . .' – he flailed around for a word – 'my . . .' He clenched his fists in frustration.

'Go-between? Liaison officer?' Ritwik offered helpfully. He almost smiled.

Saeed's face lit up. 'Yes, yes, how you say it?'

'Go-between?'

'Yes, yes, go-between.' Saeed repeated the words a few times, savouring their newness, their power to give him access, however tiny, into a different world. 'You be my go-between?'

'Between you and who?' Ritwik asked, miming out the three parties with his hand.

'Many woman. Kurdish, Serbian, Czech. They come to London, look for work, make money, lot of money. You take 5 per cent, 7, maybe 10, OK?'

Ritwik got it but he wanted him to say the words, spell out the trade, right here in the restaurant, in front of the busy waiters and the small throng of eaters. He toyed with some leftover flatbread and moutabbal, ate another forkful of tabbouleh, sipped his pineapple juice and kept his eyes resolutely on the water rings and spattered food on the faux-chrome table top.

'It is OK for you?' Saeed repeated, reaching for his crumpled packet of cigarettes and lighting up.

'Can I think about it for some time?' To fill out the silence Ritwik padded out his evasion, 'It's not every day that I get offered a job, so let me have a think and I promise I'll get in touch with you as soon as I can.' He spoke very fast in the hope that Saeed was deceived by his fluency into thinking that he was not putting him off.

It worked. Saeed nodded for a while – Ritwik detected a

glimmer of respect, or awe, in his eyes, or maybe that was what he wanted to see – and said, 'OK. You touch me by Mr Haq, OK?'

'No, get in touch, not touch.'

'What you say?' Saeed's face had a puzzled look on it.

Ritwik reached out and touched Saeed on his arm, exaggeratedly. 'This is touch.' Then he mimed a phone call and added, 'And this, getting in touch.'

A broad smile cleared away the confusion. 'OK, OK, I see, touch, getting touch.' He chuckled, then added, 'This English, very difficult, very difficult to me.' He laughed again, moved his hand across the table, clutched Ritwik's hand in his fist and said, 'You teach me English, OK?'

Ritwik didn't know if he was in earnest, so he smiled, once again taken aback by the ease with which Saeed touched him in public. Saeed repeated the question, lifting Ritwik's hand off the table and holding it in the air, a gesture of commitment about to be made.

'Yes, yes,' Ritwik stammered, 'if you want.'

'Good. OK. We go then.' With a final squeeze he let go of Ritwik's hand. He signalled to a waiter for the bill that he didn't bother looking at when it arrived. He pulled out a twenty-pound note from a fat wallet, extricated some loose change from another pocket, weighed down the paper note with the coins neatly and got up. His eye caught someone and he went over, all bonhomie and smiles, to an extremely fat man seated behind a table next to the kitchen door, a pile of paper and a calculator in front of him. The men embraced and, for the entire duration of their conversation, they held each other's hands in a clasp. They embraced again before Saeed made his way out. He put his hand on Ritwik's shoulder once they were out on Edgware Road, as men in India do, or men elsewhere, not here, but Saeed seemed oblivious to this. The stalled and swelling traffic on Edgware Road sometimes moved, a few inches at a time, like a lethargic snake.

On fruit-picking days in the summer, Ritwik and Anne saw each other at what Ritwik used to consider 'duty hours', such as bathtimes, or the time allotted to cleaning and changing her, explaining painstakingly what was in the fridge and in the kitchen. He left yellow Post-It notes around the place so that Anne wouldn't forget where the bread was, where her calcium tablets were, or the fact that she had to switch off the burner after the soup had been heated – the house became a paper trail from a treasure hunt. After a few days into it Ritwik realized that Anne, or any other person for that matter, would have a hard time reading, assimilating and remembering all the notes and then acting according to them, so he put up a big note next to Anne's bed reminding her to look at all the notes, very soon saw the absurdity of the whole thing and, bar a couple, took most of them down.

One evening Anne drifted into the kitchen and said, 'Looky here, there is no need to feel guilty that you are away most of the time, so stop leaving these ridiculous notes everywhere. They are no substitute for your presence. I have a hard time remembering to look at them in the first place. If I don't remember to eat then I shall hardly remember to first locate and then look at a note saying what I should have for lunch.'

The logic was so impeccable that it threw Ritwik off wondering if there had been an implicit recrimination in her words. He sat at the kitchen table, held his head in his hands and bleated, 'What else can I do?'

'For a start, you could stop walking around as if you'd been buggered by the entire squadron of the Queen's Horse Guards and their horses.'

'I wish, Anne, I wish. And you should wash your mouth out with carbolic. Look at you, at your age, using language that would make a sailor blush,' he said, in between sobs of laughter.

Anne couldn't stop giggling. Ritwik never disclosed what it was that was making simple, unquestioned things such as sitting down, bending, turning around, climbing up or down the stairs so painful and stiff, as if he had just been put together by a hamfisted joiner. And anyway, he thought, it was just lack of regular physical exercise; he would be fine after a week or so.

Those nights, with sleep coming down on him heavy and seductive, the very sight of the sheaf of papers containing Miss Gilby's unfinished story set him afloat on a deep ocean of exhaustion. How would he ever find the time or the energy to finish it? On those nights he told Anne, in installments, the story of Duo-rani, the wicked queen who, wanting to divert the king's attention from his favourite wife, Suo-rani, pretended to be ill with an incurable bone disease by putting light, hollow twigs of birch and willow and broom under her mattress so that when she tossed and turned it seemed that her very bones were snapping loudly into bits and pieces. Anne lay awake, her thoughts inhabiting god knew what world; Ritwik was certain at times that Anne's attention couldn't be farther from the story he had spliced from his childhood folk tales on to the current aches in his lower back, thighs and legs.

He stopped abruptly in the middle of the story one night, kept quiet for a few minutes, then said, 'I leave all these notes because I don't want to come back one evening and find you lying in a heap at the bottom of the stairs just because you forgot to take the stair lift or misplaced your stick.'

He wasn't really hoping for an answer – it was spoken more to himself, as a kind of summing up, rather than addressed to the drifting woman – so he was surprised when she whispered, 'Yes.'

And then the cold jolt of being read with such ease again: 'What story is it that you keep scribbling down all the time?'

'How do you know it's a story? It could be letters, or anything,' he said, too tired to ask her if she has been going through his stuff.

She didn't reply. After a while, she said, 'You could read that out to me, couldn't you?'

Why not? 'Do you know who she is?'

'What do you mean who she is? Isn't she the heroine of your story?'

'Yes, she is, but she exists elsewhere. She is a very minor figure, appearing for all of four or five paragraphs in an early chapter in a Tagore novel, *Ghare Bairey*. Did you know that? Then Satyajit Ray made it into a film in the early eighties and, in keeping with the book, she was a fleeting, walk-on figure there too.'

'No. But you could still read it out to me, what do you think?' Adamant and tenacious as always.

'Yes, yes, I could. Do you want me to start from the very beginning or read the latest installment?'

'Whichever is easier.'

So Ritwik reads to Anne the chapter in which the great ferment outside enters, in an unsuspectingly malevolent form, the home of Nikhilesh and Bimala:

IX.

First, she doesn't show up one morning. Miss Gilby waits, unworried, not even registering the delay for half an hour because their arrangements are so informal and fluid; after all, one doesn't need appointments and rule books and enslavement to the hands of the clock among members of the family. But after an hour has passed, without any sign of Bimala, she decides to send Lalloo to look for her. Lalloo comes back and says Bimala is not in the *andarmahal*. Miss Gilby leaves a brief note for her saying that if she needs her, she will be in her study upstairs. Bimala doesn't call that day.

The next morning, Bimala is on time. She says, 'Miss Gilby, I'm sorry I wasn't here yesterday. I have important things to do in the *andarmahal*. I couldn't leave.'

Miss Gilby says, 'That's all right. Shall we start by practising scales this morning?'

Next week, she is absent again, once more without any advance warning or subsequent explanation. Miss Gilby's note gets ignored. This time she asks Bimala the reason for her absence because none seems to be forthcoming on her part, not even an apology.

Bimala replies, '*Naw jaa* is not well. I look after her all day.' She refuses to meet Miss Gilby's eyes when she says this.

The next day Miss Gilby asks after *naw jaa*. Bimala says, '*Naw jaa*? *Naw jaa*?' before awareness strikes and she stammers out, 'Yes, yes, she's well.'

That week Bimala is listless and restless in turns, if such an apparently paradoxical condition can be imagined. But there is also something else, a hint of insolence, a defiance some-where struggling to manifest itself but too weak to come into being. She makes flagrant grammatical errors and when Miss Gilby corrects her, she doesn't incorporate them into her next sentence, instead repeats her mistake stubbornly. She expresses a desire to read only Bengali books and sing Bengali songs. Her vocal accompaniment gets more and more careless to the extent that Miss Gilby wonders if Bimala is deliberately doing all this for some unknown reason.

The following week, Bimala doesn't appear for two con-secutive days. This time Miss Gilby doesn't leave a note for her; she waits for Bimala to contact her. When Bimala eventually knocks on her study door, after two days, she tries to pretend as if there has been no hiatus in their daily lessons. Miss Gilby patiently enquires if anything is wrong. Bimala, once again refusing to make eye contact, says something about helping out with *swadeshi* business.

Three days after this, when Bimala doesn't turn up for three consecutive days, Miss Gilby decides that enough is enough; she has no option but to write to Mr Roy Chowdhury about the predicament.

Mr Roy Chowdhury has such prominent dark circles under his eyes that Miss Gilby is moved to asking after his health even before the formalities of greeting have been completed.

'I'm afraid I've not been sleeping very well. I have a number of things weighing on my mind, but, Miss Gilby, I'm so sorry to hear of Bimala's . . . what should I say . . . truancy . . . except I had no idea of it . . . you must excuse me, please . . .' He gives up before he can complete the sentence.

'I'm sure it is something very minor, something unimportant, which she feels she cannot tell me. I'm not even very certain that something's bothering her,' Miss Gilby tries to reassure.

'She seems well to me, if a bit fired up about *swadeshi*. I expect she's told you all about it. She seems quite obsessed with it, doesn't talk about much else.'

'Oh, yes, that must be it,' Miss Gilby says, unconvinced. 'She has appeared to be somewhat careless and distracted of late. Her mind is elsewhere. I was wondering if there is anything in particular which she feels she could tell you but not me.'

'I can't think of anything at the moment. I've always thought that if something was on her mind, she would be far more likely to tell you about it. If it is not a language problem, that is.'

'Ah, that might be it.'

'And . . . and . . .' he hesitates, uncharacteristically dithering and insecure, 'I've been so inattentive, and absent . . . the situation in the village worsens daily . . .'

'What situation?'

He appears to think for a long time before answering, weighing up his words, ordering his thoughts before summarizing an immensely complicated issue.

'How do I even begin to tell you about it? You know that my childhood friend Sandip, Mr Banerjea, is staying here with us. He's using 'Dighi Bari' as his centre for *swadeshi* activities in the neighbouring villages and districts. As you may have noticed, he's a charismatic man, it's difficult, no, impossible, to say no to him. What he wants, he usually gets. He arrived with hardly more than a dozen activists, mostly students. Now it seems that every young man in eastern Bengal is part of his movement.'

Miss Gilby looks up sharply at the use of 'his'. '*His* movement? I thought *swadeshi* was something to which every Bengali had dedicated his life.'

Mr Roy Chowdhury gives a wan smile. 'If only, Miss Gilby, if only.'

'Are you saying that it is not as unanimous as it appears to be?'

There is a long silence, so long that Miss Gilby is about to rephrase and repeat her question but before she has had a chance to do that, Mr Roy Chowdhury says, 'Do you know that all my tenants are Muslims, that the villages here, most of the villages in what is now East Bengal, are comprised of a Muslim majority?'

'Well, I hadn't thought about it but now that you mention it, yes . . .'

'You have been reading the papers, following the whole crisis with this partition for some years, haven't you? It won't come as a surprise to you then if I tell you that one of the biggest motives behind the division of Bengal was to drive a wedge between the Hindu population and the Muslims.'

Miss Gilby involuntarily straightens her back and moves forward to the edge of her chair. It sounds familiar, she has come across this somewhere other than in the newspapers, but she cannot quite put her finger on it at this particular moment. Outside, the luminous winter afternoon is dying in a final blaze of pink and gold.

'The infamous "divide and rule" policy?' Miss Gilby asks lamely for want of anything more substantial to say.

'Yes, basically it is that. When Lord Curzon was on his short tour of Bengal nearly three years back, he gave a speech in Dacca which declared that the partition – still more than two and a half years into the future – would invest the Muslims in eastern Bengal with a unity they had not enjoyed since the days of the Mughal rulers. It was a carefully calculated speech, designed to shore up Muslim support for the division of Bengal.'

She clears her voice and asks, 'But surely it's in the interests of the two races to stay united?'

'One would have thought so' – that dry smile again, hardly visible in the gathering dark inside – 'but it's been considered before. The troublemakers – troublemakers according to our English rulers, that is – in Bengal are the Hindus. They were solidly opposed to the partition, still are, they are also the better educated, the more eloquent. In short, they are the noisy opponents with a political voice. There is no such equivalent in the Muslim community.'

Miss Gilby interrupts, 'So if Bengal was divided along Hindu-Muslim lines then the opposition could be fragmented and therefore weakened?'

' "Bengal united is a power; Bengal divided will pull in several different ways." Famous words,' he says wryly. There is another long pause. 'Well, the plan seems to be working. Despite isolated shows of Hindu-Muslim unity in rallies and gatherings here and there, the truth is quite different. The Muslims have always been poorer, their interests always neglected, their education overlooked, their voices ignored. It's not surprising they don't think very highly of the Hindus who are their landlords, or bureaucrats or government servants. So if a separate province is promised them where Mohammedan interests would be strongly represented, if not predominant, how can we blame them for falling for it?'

'But I still don't understand how this relates directly to your village.'

'You see, because the Hindus of Bengal have been traditionally the political voice of the region, for obvious reasons of class and education and opportunities, the Muslims think *swadeshi* is another Hindu conspiracy and therefore they look on it with great suspicion. They are not wholly wrong.'

Mr Roy Chowdhury moves in his chair to get more comfortable. The last light of the sun, amber dark, catches his glasses and makes them into bright, blind mirrors. 'If it's a choice between the Hindu *babu*, who has traditionally been known to be indifferent to Mussulman interests, and the English governor, who dangles the idea of a predominantly Mohammedan province, I too would choose the chance for a change. My villagers now see these Hindu boys, clad in orange, going around the place, calling for boycott of English goods that provide these poor Muslims a livelihood. Is it that extraordinary they should think this whole *swadeshi* business as another Hindu ploy to keep them poor and downtrodden?'

This is the first time Miss Gilby has heard anger tint his voice; it is a cold, reasoned fury, disciplined and measured, like the rest of the man.

'Sandip's boys are getting a bit carried away in their enthusiasm. It is pointless asking Sandip to rein them in because he clearly believes in what his activists are doing. There is talk of forcible seizure of English goods and burning them, even talk

318

of burning down shops and houses of those who stock or sell English goods. This is terrorism, not revolution. I cannot stand by and see this happen.' His voice nearly breaks.

Miss Gilby is appalled. 'But, Mr Roy Chowdhury, to appear divisive myself for a moment, this is your house, you are letting him use it as a base for his activities.'

'And that seems to be the reason why my tenants, my villagers, with whom my forefathers and my family have had cordial relations for the best part of two hundred years, now appear to think that I am behind all this. They think that without my sanction these Hindu nationalist boys wouldn't have dared go so far.'

The encroaching dusk collects in pools in the room; Miss Gilby can hardly see him put his head in his hands. The mosquitoes have started arriving in whining droves, circling above their heads in little vicious columns.

Miss Gilby continues her train of thought, 'You can surely ask him to leave?'

There is another silence, a long, weighted one. There is a catch in Mr Roy Chowdhury's voice when he answers, 'I cannot do that. I cannot.' The words are barely a whisper. For some reason, the servants have forgotten to bring lights into this room. It is so dark now that to anyone who entered the room it would be impossible to tell if it was inhabited at all. Miss Gilby wishes she could have seen his face, his eyes, to read more, to understand more, because she cannot ask him why and because she has a sharp hunch that there is more going on than is revealed to her.

Bimala starts attending lessons again and this is exactly what their morning meetings have now become – duty-bound, obligatory lessons. When Miss Gilby had first arrived at 'Dighi Bari' years ago, it was like that – a tutor-student meeting – for the first few months but that had changed subtly, giving way to a much more intimate and informal meeting of two friends who lived under the same roof. The lessons had become subsidiary, the company of each other, the principal. Sometimes there were no lessons at all for long stretches, just gossiping, looking at books, exchanging recipes, games in the garden. All that has suddenly reverted to the dry, strictured atmosphere of the classroom now, a chore, not spontaneous pleasure.

Bimala's first appearance after Miss Gilby's meeting with Mr Roy Chowdhury was startling. She had red, swollen eyes, she wore austere clothes – monotone cotton sari, an unremarkable shade of blue, white cotton blouse – she had no bangles on her wrists, no jewellery in sight anywhere, even the vermillion mark in the parting of her hair looked dull. The spartan air must have had to do with Bimala's more active endorsement of *swadeshi*, thought Miss Gilby; she had at last abandoned all items of foreign-manufactured luxury or ostentation.

Miss Gilby's interest in Bimala's book of birds has mounted to an obsession now. With Bimala listless, uncooperative, sometimes passively truculent, it is that part of the afternoon when they go through the books on Indian birds (although Bimala only dutifully so, for she doesn't seem to share her English friend's burning interest in birds anymore) that Miss Gilby looks forward to most. Indeed, two mornings ago, her first thought, after she had woken up, had been not of Bimala, or the new song they were learning, but the delight of 'Birds of the Ganges Estuary Mudflats and Mangroves' and 'Birds of the North Eastern Hill Ranges' awaiting her in the book she had so surprisingly discovered in Mr Roy Chowdhury's study next door.

This morning Bimala has been set a composition exercise – one page on the goddesses of Bengal, something that Miss Gilby thinks might inspire a spark in the jaded Bimala. Her head bent down on her book, Bimala passively fulfils what has been asked of her, occasionally asking the odd question on translation – 'What is this?' she asks, drawing an instrument that the goddess Durga holds in one of her ten hands and for which there is no translation in English except for the awkward and wholly unrepresentative 'spinning discus'.

Seeing that dark head bent over paper, that slender hand forming the foreign letters slowly, much as a child does when it is learning to write, Miss Gilby feels a tightening in her chest. So pressing and sharp is the feeling that ignoring hundreds of years of refinement and social norms and rules, rules, rules, she moves over to Bimala, sits beside her, touches her shoulder and asks that enquiring, surprised face, 'Bimala, if there is anything wrong, you know you can talk to me, don't you?'

Bimala bursts into tears while Miss Gilby leaves her hand on the woman's sobbing, heaving shoulder. Hot tears drop like candle wax on to the paper she has been writing on. With a rare clarity, Miss Gilby notes one smudging drop on the inverted word 'learning' and another poised between 'lion' and 'demon', about to spread out on either side and start disfiguring both.

Late that evening, a perplexed Miss Gilby, hearing the 'rhubarb, rhubarb' murmur of collected voices, looks out of her balcony to see scores of men gathered outside the front gate of the house. She at once guesses, rightly, that they are villagers demanding an audience with Mr Roy Chowdhury. She is both curious and concerned, but it wouldn't do to look at these men from her vantage point two floors above them. Nor would it be right to try and find out what is happening by going downstairs. In any case, if she were to 'accidentally' eavesdrop, she would understand very little of the proceedings. She would have to stay in her quarters and be alert to the sounds and movements, or go down to find Bimala, possibly in the *andarmahal*. After half an hour of such deliberation, she picks up the book on birds she had found in Mr Roy Chowdhury's study and prepares herself to go downstairs with it, on the fragile pretext of returning it to the collection.

By the time she reaches the long verandah off which lie the meeting room, Mr Roy Chowdhury's study, the drawing room and the offices, the sound of voices has grown so loud – sometimes a single voice, at other times, many voices together, all talking at the same time, and occasionally, a veritable cacophony, with what seems like the entire gathering shouting – that there is no doubt this is an altercation, not just a heated debate or the deplorable Indian habit of talking loudly. Miss Gilby takes fright and turns around to mount the staircase up to the second floor but someone emerges from the meeting room and, in hasty confusion and the desire not to be caught loitering in a place where it could easily and naturally be thought she has no business to be, she does a double take and hurriedly crosses the courtyard, her heart thumping with guilt and relief at having avoided shameful exposure by the skin of her teeth. She reaches the verandah parallel to the one in which she was so nearly caught out. The rooms off this one are all dark, except one, which has such feeble candlelight emanating from it that one would have to let one's eyes become dark-adapted before realizing that the room was a significantly lighter shade of the thick darkness everywhere. Miss Gilby decides to rush past that room and quickly take the stairs from the other direction.

As she passes the room, something, perhaps just natural human curiosity, or the bare hint of a sound, not so much heard as sensed, causes her to turn her head. What she sees roots her to the ground and makes her hair stand on end. In that dim firelight, more dark than light, with giant shadows flickeringly eager to devour the little of the room that is in the dirty yellow tallow light, Bimala and Mr Banerjea, the *swadeshi* revolutionary, are entwined in an amorous embrace, their mouths joined together in a communion of unspeakable passion.

TEN

Boarded up windows invariably remind Ritwik of gouged out eyes. A large number of houses in the back streets around King's Cross look as if they have been forcibly blinded, with cheap plywood squares nailed into where windows once were. Abandoned buildings with broken windows; bold, swirling graffiti, mostly unintelligible, sometimes pure, riding form; detritus-blown streets: newspapers, empty cartons, kebab wrappings and takeaway boxes; train sheds with more graffiti in places one would have thought unreachable – in a different country, with different building materials, this would have been called a slum. This is a dead appendage of the urban monster, awaiting amputation or, as they call it here, regeneration. Every building and warehouse along these streets seems to have conspired with the other to induce instant depression and exude an unnameable threat. This is their only resounding achievement. Under the dull, gunmetal London sky, Crinan Street, Delhi Street, Randell's Road, Bingfield Street, Goods Way, Camley Street, Earlsferry Way, all make suicide seem sensible, natural, even desirable.

At night, the drama changes. The dark hides the cracking plaster, the details of the decrepitude, and the emphasis moves from desolation to fear. These are the streets that everyone has learned to call 'soulless', 'dangerous', 'crime hotspot', but no word approaches the shadowy menace always out of the field of vision, always imminent, but never realized. Add to that the impoverishment, this interminable locked-in dance with squalor, and the mixture explodes in little tingles in the skin's pores as you walk down these streets.

Of course, like most of the others who hover here, those who do not hurriedly walk down, Ritwik has learnt to live with the fear, at times finding it somewhat erotic, a conditioned reflex from his cottaging nights. The creatures here dart in and out of shadows. They are creatures of fishnet stockings, high heels, cigarette smoke, impossibly short skirts, the careless glitter and dazzle of sequins and tawdry shiny stuff – fake *zari*, he thinks – and garishly applied lipstick, eye make up, concealer. Or so he imagines, because he has never actually come close enough to *see* their Otto Dix faces and their harlequin make up, except for split second glimpses of mouths, which look like bleeding gashes in the unforgiving light of the intermittent sodium vapour lamps that cast more gloom in a pool right at their bases than light around them.

The stretch off York Way on which Ritwik usually walks is called the 'Meat Mile'. Not that it has got them hanging off hooks, but if one is minded that way, there is plenty available, provided a police car is not cruising by at irregular intervals, or another crackdown on kerb-crawling not taking place. The main thing is knowledge, adherence to codes that to the untrained eye might be invisible. A certain type of aimlessness thrown into one's gait, being seen on the same alley or lane more than once, a few glances sideways and backwards – Ritwik knows all of these with practised ease. It's what they say about swimming, that you never forget it, that it's muscle memory; these codes are written into his veins and arteries. He can read a customer, either his kind or the more numerous and more frequent other type, from the sound their shoes make on the pavement, from the shadows they cast on the occasionally syringe- and ampoule-strewn streets.

And then there is the other fear, the fear that he is a freak here, the break from the norm expected in the 'Meat Mile'. Two weeks ago he had heard a fat woman, all skimpy shawl and enormous breasts almost totally exposed except for a precariously tied piece of glittering cloth on her nipples, spit out the words 'Fucking queer', her gobbet of spit landing with a loud 'splat' near her, before disappearing into the darkness that is always stalking one here.

Ritwik stopped going for about a week or so. During that time, he stayed up sleepless, worried nights, imagining attacks, assault and other unthinkables. Besides, there was the big question of market, supply and demand. Would anyone in his right mind go shopping for clothes at a grocery market? Where was the financial sense – and let there be no mistake, this is all and only about money, about the need to buy food and clothes, not about the more elusive search during his student years in public toilets – in walking the streets here of all places? He would have been better off walking Hampstead Heath or taking out an ad in *Boyz* or *Thud*.

Then, by that very logic, he decided in favour of the 'Meat Mile': surely, the only clothes shop in a grocery market would thrive and prosper. Monopoly, no competition, that sort of thing. As if in annoyance at its unintelligent dilution, bad economics later took its revenge. Ritwik hadn't done well so far: three clients in three weeks. Sixty pounds in total. The money in the Kashmiri wooden box was dwindling; if things didn't pick up, he was going to have to rethink everything.

The first was a dismal blow-job, his back against a dark wall on Gifford Street, his knees on wet grit, the man looking constantly over his shoulders and at one point even saying, 'Hurry the fuck up, will you?', as if his tardy tumescence was all Ritwik's fault. An occasional train or two rumbled past behind him somewhere, shaking the wall. Ritwik had pushed his head back at the first signs of the man's approaching orgasm and asked for the twenty pounds then. He had reasoned that if this infuriated the man, there was little he could do except zip up and walk away. It was only because they were out in the open that Ritwik didn't feel threatened by any potential violence. It was fortunate the man had complied for it could so easily have taken another direction.

Then there was Frank, the man who looked like an insect with his fragile and overgrown head, wet mouth, and beady, non-human eyes, which reminded Ritwik of beetles; he couldn't shake off thoughts of Gregor Samsa. Frank who had wept afterwards in his car parked on Boadicea Street, with its lights off and reeking of poppers, because his wife had left him for his business partner after twenty years of an impeccable marriage: he had come home and found them in bed together.

Ritwik felt bad taking the forty pounds from him and had tried to cover up both his hesitancy and shame by sniffing, coughing, rubbing the edges of his nostrils and saying, 'God, those poppers were powerful, I think I may have burnt my nose. I'm going to have an awful headache soon,' and then, 'Thank you,' to the rustle of crisp notes. Ritwik hadn't known what to do, watching a grown-up man cry so helplessly with his trousers and boxer shorts still around his knees. He had asked an insensitive question – 'Did you love her?' – and then practically kicked himself for letting those words out when Frank had looked him in the eye and said simply, 'Yes.'

Frank had asked for his number and, in relief and delight at the hope that at least one customer was possibly going to become a regular and save him that much trouble, Ritwik had given it him and added, 'Call me anytime you want to meet up.'

But nothing had prepared him for the encounter with the builder-type man who called himself Greg and carried a big carrier bag in the boot of his white Ford Mondeo. He had stopped the car in a very ill-lit back street, got out and retrieved the bag from the boot. Ritwik had been so scared he had had trouble articulating the words, 'What's in that bag?' Greg had asked him to strip completely naked and when Ritwik had refused he had said tersely, 'Don't think you're going to make any money like this.' The menace in his voice thickened the stale air in the car.

'OK, but tell me first what's in the bag.'

He brought out stilettos, a black nylon bra, transparent black panties and then gripped Ritwik's hand. 'I want you to take all your clothes off, put these on and walk outside.'

'Walk outside? In the street?' Ritwik's eyes opened wide at the sheer audacity of the request.

'Yeah.' As if this were the most natural request in the world.

'You must be joking.'

'You want the money or not?'

'Not at this risk.'

'All right then, get out of the car,' he said, starting the car to life.

'Wait, what if I do it in the car?' He had no idea why he was bargaining with this man.

Greg appeared to think for a few seconds. 'OK, but you'll have to move from the front to the back seat.'

Once at the back, Ritwik started taking his clothes off. For a moment he forgot that this was not a sex pickup but a money one, so he asked, 'Aren't you going to take your clothes off as well?'

'What for?' Ritwik had never imagined that so much derision could be packed into those two words.

The bra and panty were about three to four sizes too big for Ritwik's body; he couldn't fasten the bra, which flopped like a loose sail on his chest, while the underwear was kept only in place by Ritwik's back pressed against the seat.

'Now put the heels on.' It was an order that had the glint of a knife blade hidden somewhere in the spaces between the words.

'But you can't see them like this, my feet will be . . .'

Before Ritwik could finish, he barked out, 'Do as you're told. Put them on, lean back and stretch out your legs over the gearbox.'

The shoes were too big as well. At least, Ritwik just had to put them on, not hobble around in them and possibly break his ankle. As he wriggled and manouevred in the cramped space, he was suddenly seized by an intense curiosity to see himself in a mirror, wearing oversized women's knickers and bra and wriggling around to stretch out his long, thin legs on to the front seat through the narrow gap between the driver and the passenger seats. But there was no light anywhere and even if there had been, he would hardly have been able to see anything in the sliver of the rearview mirror.

'Turn around.'

'What?'

'Turn around. Lie on your tummy. Go on.'

Ritwik tried to do as he was ordered but the space was so limited that it was all awkward elbows, knees, shins, metal, leather. Without any warning, Greg got out of the car, moved into the back seat and wrenched Ritwik's legs from the front to try and bundle him into a recumbent position stretched out over the back seats. Food aid sacks were usually handled like this, Ritwik thought. He let out a yelp as his arm got twisted in the process.

'Shut up.' There was an altogether different tone – saturated with hate – in Greg's order now.

With one seamless movement of his strong arms, he had Ritwik crouching face down and knees bent on the seat. He unzipped his fly, bent down on his knees and attempted to mount Ritwik from behind, all the while trying to clamp his hands over Ritwik's mouth. Ritwik struggled furiously to free himself and Greg kept hissing, 'Stay fucking down or I'll really hurt you.' Ritwik managed to say, 'No, no, condoms', before turning himself on his back, using a split second's let-up of pressure from the man's arms. Greg was looming over him, his face twisted with hate and rage. He hit Ritwik twice; the confinement and awkward positions took away some of the impact of the blows but he could taste the salt-metal tang in his mouth immediately. As he lifted his arms to shield himself, his hands hit the glass of the window and caught the door lock. In a reflex action of survival, he pressed it and headbutted the door open, pushing his head out of the car.

The inverted world swung for a few seconds, the dull reddish night sky rimmed around with the tops of buildings. He pushed with his feet and tried to get his shoulders and torso out of the car. Once his hands were out in the open, he half turned on his waist, put his palms on the wet ground, and made an effort to crouch out. In the process, the stiletto heel caught Greg in his groin; with a sharp, loud 'Fuck, fuck', he pushed Ritwik out of the car with such force that his whole body fell out, contorted and heaped, arse on gritty road, elbows scraped, the bra hitched up on to his shoulders, and the lacy underwear now loosely tying his ankles.

All this took place so quickly that it surprises Ritwik now, more than three weeks after the event, that he had had the presence of mind to stand upright, naked except for a bra dangling from his shoulders and a pair of knickers held to his groin with one hand, rush to the front of the car, one stiletto in hand, and shout, 'I have your registration number. If you don't throw my clothes out, right now, I'm going to break your windscreen with this shoe.'

Greg threw out his clothes one by one. Jeans, T-shirt, jumper, no underwear, no socks and only one shoe. Before he had a chance to pick them off the road, Greg moved to the front seat and drove off, his tyres screeching out his rage. What an utter waste of an evening, he had thought; not only did he not get any money, but he actually lost some in the form of a new pair of shoes he would now be forced to buy.

Ritwik didn't go back to King's Cross for nearly a month.

The car is so ludicrously classy that it brings out the skeletal girls – underdressed children, really, all gangly arms and bones and the shadow of night under their eyes – the fat ladies and the lost, indeterminate ones in between, one by one, like victims of famine emerging from bushes and rocks and clumps of scrub. Something in the way these creatures appear, as if from nowhere, and take their positions along the pavement with such premeditated casualness at the smell of possible business, brings to his mind pictures of starving people weakly emerging from behind a crag until what was barren ground becomes magically populated with the remnants of human beings. This could be business, although he assumes, from the car and its obviously unseasoned driver (who else would cruise these streets so brazenly, and in such a car, if not someone utterly unfamiliar with the area?), it is probably not going to be for him.

So he decides to get out of the competition by making his way through to another, darker sidestreet. The car moves in his general direction. Ritwik takes a right and then a left. He succeeds in shaking off the car only to find, a minute later, that it is directly in front, moving slowly towards him. He turns 180 degrees and re-enters the street he emerged from minutes ago. The car follows him into All Saints Street. By now, there is no doubt the driver is tailing him. His heart lifts – money, at last – at the same time as there is the old, familiar grip in his bowels.

He stands against a postbox, staring insolently at the car. It moves past him – it is too dark to make out the person inside – takes a right turn at the end of the street and disappears.

Everything inside him deflates.

He moves in the opposite direction, towards York Way. He toys with the idea of going to Central Station and picking up the sad leftovers at closing time.

And then the car is right ahead of him. He pretends he hasn't seen it and walks past it. The passenger door opens, the driver bends down, cranes his neck and gestures with his hand for Ritwik to climb in.

The man is probably of Middle Eastern origin, Ritwik takes a guess as he belts up. Late thirties to mid forties, spreading middle, moustache, salt and pepper hair, and the twilight of a stereotypical Arab handsomeness dying with a final flourish. His first words, in his flawless English accent, are impossibly absurd, 'What's a nice guy like you doing in a place like this?'

Ritwik, incredulous, looks at him to figure out whether this is self-conscious parody. There are no clues to read. His laugh, which would have been open had he been able to ascertain the nature of the chat-up line, is slightly guarded and nervous. He says, 'I could ask you the same question.'

'Well . . .' he shrugs.

'Where are we going?'

'Aren't you going to take me some place?' This time, the man's eyes are smiling.

Ritwik is thrown by the question. He stammers out, 'I . . . I live some distance away, and . . . and . . . it's not really . . . suitable.'

'Then we can go back to mine. Is that all right?'

Ritwik nods. This is going all wrong, certainly not according to the interactions he has been used to or expecting. Since when did clients ask him his opinion? Since when did they behave like polite and gentle pick-ups in a somewhat fast-tracked dating scene? As the car – a Bentley, he learns later – negotiates its way south through Gray's Inn Road, he regrets having said yes to the stranger's offer of taking him back to his place. The familiar fears and misgivings of getting into a stranger's car darken his thoughts again. At least in the back streets of King's Cross, he is on his own territory, more or less. But now . . .

'Penny for your thoughts.'

Ritwik notes the archaism; presumably, the man was brought up in a former colony, like he was, on staples such as Enid Blyton, P.G. Wodehouse and Jennings, Biggles and Billy Bunter.

Before he can reply, the man throws him again by extending his left hand sideways to him. 'Zafar. Nice to meet you.'

Ritwik shakes his hand and adds his name.

'Say that again?'

'Rit-wik.' It hasn't occurred to him to use something concocted, something easier, less unfamiliar.

The next few predictable questions are avoided by a tricky traffic move. Once past that, Zafar says, 'I'm taking you to my hotel.'

'Oh. Which one?'

'The Dorchester. Do you know it?'

'No, I don't.' It sounds as if he should know it, that single word thrown so nonchalantly. 'Where is it?'

'Park Lane.' Pause. 'Do you live in London?'

'Yes. In Brixton.'

'Ahh.' It could have meant anything.

Ritwik is getting more and more nervous with every passing minute. This interim conversation between first sight and business is a great dampener: the rules of this game do not include superficial familiarity.

Zafar seems to be intimate with London streets and traffic. As the car gently glides into Park Lane, Ritwik realizes with a sharp intake of breath which part of the world he is in.

'Wait, stop. Look, I think it's a bad idea to go to the Dorchester.'

'Why?' Zafar knits his brows.

'I'm . . . I'm not dressed for . . . for such a place. I think they'll stop me at the entrance. That's going to be embarrassing.'

'You're going as my guest. It'll be fine. Don't worry.' His voice and answers are calm, reassuring and supremely confident.

It has been decided for him, not so much by Zafar's authority as by the accumulated nudge the car, the hotel, Zafar's clothes, all give to Ritwik's greed: he could probably get away by asking for an unthought of sum from this man.

Zafar leaves his car to be valet-parked and gently ushers him into the lobby of the Dorchester, bowed to by doormen in regalia. Ritwik feels so out of place that he registers this opulence – the crimson carpet, the light fittings, the floral arrangements, the depersonalized friendliness and judiciously measured fawning of the staff, the gleam and polish of perfect maintenance – only as something that shines by in the margins of his field of vision.

'Do you want a drink in the bar?' Zafar asks him solicitously.

'No . . . no . . . I'm fine. Thanks.' He feels intimidated and tyrannized by the interior and his knees wobble slightly as Zafar leads him to the lift.

He has a whole suite to himself: the John James Audubon suite on the sixth floor. The bird prints comfort him somewhat but not enough for him to feel that he wouldn't soil anything he touched or sat on. He tries very hard to concentrate on Virginian partridge, Louisiana tanager and scarlet tanager, black-bellied darter and a remarkably amusing solitary trumpeter swan, craning its neck backwards and contemplating an insect very close to its parted beak: the swan itself looks tickled by the proximity of this silly insect.

'A drink now?' Zafar has moved to the bar.

'No, thanks. Do the windows on the other end look out on to Park Lane?'

'Yes. Do you want to have a look?'

'Yes, please.'

Zafar draws the curtains. Hyde Park stretches outside like a landscaped parkland in an eighteenth-century print. The traffic below moves by in complete silence. Zafar stands beside him, taking in the sweep, tinkling the ice cubes in his tumbler of whisky.

Ritwik decides to make the first move. He bends down to untie his shoelaces. The business of unmentioned money is bothering him intensely: what if Zafar thinks this is just a casual pick-up and sends him away unpaid? Did he have any inkling in the first place?

'Take your clothes off, everything, and then walk up and down. I want to see you.' It is clearly a command from someone at ease with issuing them yet, at the same time as it is impossible not to recognize it as such and act accordingly, it lacks both urgency and firmness. Ritwik does as told.

'Come into the bedroom.'

Ritwik follows. Zafar sits down on the four-poster bed and takes his shoes, socks and trousers off.

'What about the rest?' Ritwik asks. 'I want to see all of you as well.'

'Come here.'

Ritwik joins him in bed. Zafar pushes him down and pinches his nipples really hard. He winces in pain and tries to push the man's hand away. His breath is hot on his face. Onions, overlaid with whisky. And then before he can move or touch Zafar, the man rises on his knees and pushes his crotch on to Ritwik's head propped up on the oversize pillows. He does what is expected; in less than ten seconds Zafar comes in a bloom of hot, salty liquid in his mouth, rolls off him and subsides on the softly billowing mattress, his hairy legs splayed, his arms akimbo. Ritwik discreetly takes a tissue from the bedside table and silently spits into it, hoping Zafar doesn't notice.

He lies staring at the ceiling for a few minutes, worrying about his next move. Zafar solves it by saying, 'Stay for a bit. I'll drive you home.'

Ritwik instantly relaxes. He turns on his side to face Zafar and tentatively puts an arm and a leg around him. He pushes Ritwik's head on to his chest – the shirt is silk, he notices – and runs his fingers through his curls.

'Even your hair is like my son's,' he says.

Determined not to let the words throw him, he asks in a high, bright voice, 'Oh, I didn't know you had a son. How old is he?'

'Your age, or slightly younger. Seventeen.'

Ritwik leaves Zafar's illusion about his age unpricked. 'Only one son?'

'No, three daughters. All younger.'

'Where are they?'

'Riyadh. Saudi Arabia.'

'Is that where you're from?'

'Yes. But I spent many years in this country.'

'I can tell from your English. Were you educated here?'

'Partly. But tell me, where are you from?'

'India.'

'Ahhh. I was thinking Algeria, Turkey, Jordan, those areas.' Pause. 'So you're . . . Hindi?'

Ritwik doesn't correct the mistake. 'Nothing, actually.' He quickly fires off another question in order to avoid becoming the focus. 'Are you an oil man?'

'What do you mean, oil man?'

'Well, you're from Saudi Arabia' – *and you appear to be loaded* – 'so I thought you had something to do with oil.'

Zafar gives a dry laugh.

Ritwik is well into this familiarity game now. 'Just tell me if you come from one of the Saudi oil families.'

He can feel Zafar smiling. 'You're asking the wrong questions. But, to use your terms, no, I don't come from an "oil family", but yes, I have some dealings with that industry.'

'What do you do?'

'Oh, just bits and bobs. Nothing very much.'

'I would very much like to do the nothing very much that pays for such a lifestyle.'

Zafar laughs briefly again. Ritwik starts playing with himself and Zafar; he doesn't want a single spare second in which to think of the easy link this man has made involving his teenage son. This time the sex is slightly more prolonged but Zafar remains resolutely locked in his own, limited needs. The taking type, rather than the giving, Ritwik thinks as he concentrates on timing and almost botches it up. He can't push away from his head deep-etched prejudices about the unenlightened sexual habits and attitudes of the Arab male. Zafar plays into this conveniently.

The issue of money has now become enormous: because he has not mentioned it right at the outset, he doesn't know how to broach the subject now and is consumed by thinking of moves and countermoves that would bring it up not too egregiously or offensively. He tries to play for more time. 'Look,' he says, 'I'll have a shower, then I need to get going.'

Zafar doesn't reply. Ritwik looks at him and catches him on the verge of dozing off. He touches the man's face and says, 'Do you want to come and have a shower with me?'

The shower is an exercise in awkwardness and unsynchronized movements. Ritwik steps out of the black marble bath a few minutes before Zafar, who leans against the tiles and shuts his eyes with pleasure. Or exhaustion. As he dries himself with a red towel big enough to wrap all of himself in several times over, he tries not to look at Zafar's extraordinarily hirsute body, his growing paunch, and his dangling testicles, which look like used teabags.

Then he notices a thin line of blood stretching along one side of his glans and cries out, 'Oh my god, blood.'

Zafar turns off the taps and steps out onto the bathmat. He asks, 'Really? Where?', peering down, the fear just beginning to form, when Ritwik realizes it is just a stray red thread from his towel.

'No, it's all right, it's just a piece of thread,' he says, grinning in relief, and holds it up for Zafar to see.

'Are you sure?' His face still bears traces of the dissolving fear.

'Yes, take a look.'

Instead of looking at the thread, Zafar inspects his cock, turning it around in order to leave no doubts hanging. He dries himself in silence then disappears into one of the rooms in the suite, presumably to dress. Ritwik has the sense of some unnamed reverie being broken. When Zafar emerges, in a silk dressing gown, it is obvious that he is not going to drive Ritwik home. Before he can ask, Zafar says, 'Why don't I call a taxi for you?' He reaches into a pocket and adds, 'Here, here's some money for the taxi.' He hands Ritwik four crisp fifty-pound notes. 'Keep the rest.'

'Thank you very much,' he says lamely.

Zafar waves his hand dismissively. 'It's nothing. Let me call the people downstairs and let them know you'll be down now.'

'All right. Thank you. Bye.' He brushes against a sudden melancholy: maybe it is just exhaustion. He reaches out his right hand towards Zafar who takes it, gives it a perfunctory, businesslike shake and says, 'Give me a call. I'm here for the week. Take care. Will you be able to see yourself out? Just take the lift downstairs, it shouldn't be too difficult. Turn left and then left again.' The words have something of his handshake in them, too.

He accompanies Ritwik through the enormous living and dining rooms to the mahogany door. 'By the way,' he says, 'was that enough? You can have some more . . .'

By the time Ritwik has found an embarrassed stammer of 'No, no, that's more than enough', the door has shut behind him.

That night he lies awake in his narrow bed, with his bedside light off for long periods so he can watch the rare London moonlight slant along the carpet in an elastic parallelogram, thinking of a small boy with unruly curls being flung up in the air by his father and then caught again in his sure arms amidst delighted squealing and laughter.

Three days later Ritwik is back walking King's Cross again on a raw evening threatening rain. He has the momentary luxury of telling himself that if he doesn't get lucky in the next fifteen minutes he will go home; he doesn't need to work for the next three weeks at least. An emaciated girl with a black eye and scabby lips imperfectly disguised, even in this light, by loud lipstick comes out of the shadows and crosses the street into another set of shadows. He can hear stray words from a murmured bargaining going on between a man in a car and a busty woman leaning and resting her elbows on the window edge, showing her extraordinary cleavage to full effect. They are about ten metres away from him. He decides to take a left turn and walk down to the narrow canal between York Way and Caledonian Road.

Two men are standing a few metres apart on the street. Something in the way that both of them hold themselves and turn around simultaneously to look at Ritwik sends off alarm signals in his head. Before he has the chance to do an about-turn and seek the safety of a main road, the men are beside him. Fear explodes in a starburst inside him. One of the men touches his arm and pushes him gently towards the towpath. 'Come with us. Don't make noise.'

Foreigners, Ritwik thinks. They are both young and good-looking in a footballer stud sort of way. They push him against the wall of a sealed-up public lavatory and stand very close to him. They say something to each other in their language – Albanian, perhaps, Ritwik guesses wildly, not only from the sound but also from their looks – and one of them lights a cigarette. In the brief flare of the yellow light of the lighter they look like textbook criminals.

The leaner of the two asks him, 'You come here every day?'

'No. Only very rarely.' His voice sounds unfamiliar to his own ears.

'What you say?'

Ritwik speaks slowly, 'No, I don't come here every day. Once a week. Maybe less.'

The smoking man takes something out of his pocket, flicks it open, shuts it and then repeats the motions several times over so that Ritwik is left in no doubt as to what it is. No ordinary clients, he thinks, as his mind races through the worst scenarios – unprotected gang rape, torture, mutilation, death, another statistic found by a dirty canal path in London.

The speaking man puts his hand around Ritwik's throat and lifts him clean off the ground while keeping his back against the wall. Halfway through it, his jacket, jumper and T-shirt get hitched up and the exposed brick scrapes the skin off his lower back. He chokes and coughs. The man loosens his hand and lets

Ritwik fall. He is still coughing uncontrollably when the man says, 'You lie. You here every day. We know. We see you.'

Ritwik protests, 'No, no . . .'

A fist pummels into his stomach. He doubles over, choked with pain. After what seems like hours, his eyes focus on the man's shoes, right next to his face. He feels he can never rise up on his feet again. He lies there, his mind concentrated by the pain, waiting for it to run its course. Even the fear of having more blows inflicted on him is displaced by the pain.

The man lifts him up on his feet, steadies him against the wall and asks, 'Who you with?'

Ritwik cannot answer the question because he doesn't understand it in the first place. He thinks the blow to his stomach has done some damage to his rational faculties. He tries to lean sideways and retch but the man is holding him straight by the scruff of his neck. After a couple of dry heaves, he hears the question repeated.

'Who you with?'

'No one.'

'You want hit again?'

'No,' Ritwik cries out, 'no, I don't . . .' The man cuts him short by clamping his iron hand on his mouth.

'Don't make one noise.' The hand seems to churn his jaws. He lifts it and wipes off Ritwik's saliva on his jacket with disgust.

The man turns to his partner, breaks into their own language again, then returns his attention on Ritwik. 'Who your boss?'

Ritwik doesn't understand, yet again, and foolishly answers, 'I don't have a boss.'

This time the other man takes out something from his pocket and hands it to the interrogator. It looks like a small glass flask. Ritwik's mind is whirling.

'You take business from here. You tell who your boss. This is not your boss streets. This not his ground. You don't come here again. You see this?' he asks pointing to the glass bulb.

Ritwik nods. Slowly, clarity is dawning, but it is so scary he wants to remain in ignorance.

'This acid. You come here again, we burn your face.' There is no trace of anger or any other emotion in his voice, not even violence.

'You understand?' he repeats.

Ritwk nods again, vigorously. The pimp lets go of him and has another brief conversation with his friend. They give him one last look and move away. Suddenly, the interrogator wheels around and throws the glass bulb against the wall on which Ritwik is still leaning. He starts and jumps a few feet away, in a saving miracle of reflex action, as the glass explodes with a sharp noise, followed by the smoking hiss of the acid splattering and eating into the wall.

He runs blindly, along alleys, lanes, past houses, dark buildings, empty stretches of wasteland, the backs of railway sheds and only stops when he almost collides with a car moving towards him. The car brakes to a halt and Ritwik, winded and breathless, stops for a second, enough time for him to recognize the dark blue Bentley. Zafar gets out of the car – he has seen and recognized Ritwik a while before Ritwik has him – and looks incredulously at him. Without asking any questions, he says, 'Get in. Now.'

Ritwik cannot have asked for a greater salvation. He obeys meekly, straps himself in and shuts his eyes to taste the sweet relief flooding him.

He doesn't know how many minutes or hours elapse before

he opens his eyes to the question, 'Why were you running? Are you in trouble?'

Ritwik answers disjointedly, 'This pimp beat me up. They threatened me with an acid bulb. My stomach hurts, it hurts if I breathe in or out. The acid, the acid, they threw it, it missed me by a couple of inches. Some sort of turf war between competing pimps. The crossfire, I think I got caught in it. I don't know . . .' he stops and starts again.

'I . . . I . . .' he falters, trying but failing to start at some fixed point.

'You're in some sort of shock. Come back with me. A drink will do you good.' The words are sensible, even caring, but the tone seems to be hooded, unreadable.

Ritwik surrenders to the indifferent care of a stranger and shuts his eyes again. Zafar is silent throughout the drive to Park Lane and, he senses, oddly tense with the weight of unsaid things.

Zafar pushes him into his suite. Ritwik almost stumbles, then steadies himself and turns around in surprise at the unexpectedness of the gesture. Zafar's face is a roiling mask of rage.

'Why did you go there again?'

It takes some time for the question to sink in.

'You didn't get enough money for one night from me? You want more?' Zafar continues, now pacing up and down the dark burgundy carpet of the living room. 'You want more? All right, here's more,' he says, taking off his watch and flinging it across the room to a stupefied Ritwik, who dodges and cowers to avoid getting hit by the heavy metal. It hits the wall, makes a dent in the impeccable wallpaper and sinks with a cushioned thud on the carpet.

Zafar takes off his belt and holds it like a whip in his hand. An image of his mother flashes through Ritwik's mind just for a split second before he cries, 'No, Zafar, no, please, no, not that.'

'Answer me, why did you go there again? Did I not ask you never to do what you do? Did I not repeatedly say, don't go back to King's Cross?'

Ritwik is so taken aback by this fiction, by the delusional questions, he can only answer simply, 'No, you never did.'

'Don't lie,' he shouts and drops the belt.

'Zafar, you're mistaken. Look, calm down, please. You never mentioned anything about it last time. This is what I do for a living.' Ritwik seizes the momentary silence from Zafar to press ahead with a barrage of information. 'I'm an illegal immigrant in this country, I have no working papers, no permit to stay, to work. That's what pays for my food and clothes.'

'Do you work for anyone?'

'No, I don't,' he says firmly.

'Are you sure?'

'What do you mean am I sure?' Ritwik lets his anger leach out into his voice. 'You mean if your hard-earned pennies are going to someone else? No, let me assure you, they're not. I stuff them in a little box at home. I can't have a bank account, obviously. If you don't believe me, why don't you come along with me and see where and how I live?' There is acid in his words now.

Zafar looks away and goes over to the bar. He pours out two drinks and brings one to Ritwik.

'Try downing it in one go.' His voice is distantly caring again, as if nothing has happened to ruffle the placidity of general life.

Ritwik sits and stares at the oily swirl of the ice and whisky in the heavy tumbler. He has never had to articulate his position of no exit to anyone before and now that he has somehow let it slip out in a moment of weakness, of defence, even, it becomes enormous and all-consuming, the sound of it so deafening that there is nothing else but this roaring by which he is defined, against which every other note in his little life is sounded. The room shrinks to the size of a grain of sand within which his whole body is compacted.

Ritwik lies on the bed and finishes the last bit of his hot, sweet milk that Zafar has ordered from the invisible people downstairs. He briefly imagines himself with a milk moustache, licks his upper lip and subsides in the soft sea of linen and silk. He is so tempted to close his eyes and give in to sleep right here but the thought of Anne alone in Ganymede Road nags at him. Zafar has once again had his brief and imperative pleasure from Ritwik before rolling off him and disappearing into the living room with a thrown away, 'I have to finish some work before tomorrow morning. Urgent stuff. Why don't you have a nap here and then I can drive you back later.'

Ritwik can hear the shuffling of papers, the snap of opening and closing of briefcases, a low-voiced telephone call, as he dozes desultorily and wonders whether he can ever ask Zafar if his, Ritwik's, pleasure is not important to him at all. Even in his blurred world of half-sleep he keeps trying to remind himself that this is business, not an ordinary pick-up; questions of his pleasure here are irrelevant, even presumptuous.

He chooses not to think about Zafar's naked display of proprietoriness an hour or so ago. Like all things that dredge the murky depths inside his head, he lets it sink down; he knows its disturbing demands on his attention will resurface later. While he is musing on such imponderables, Zafar pokes his head through the bedroom door and says, 'I'm going to have a shower. Why don't you get dressed if you're feeling better and I can take you home?'

As soon as Zafar is gone, Ritwik gets out of bed and walks into the living room. Zafar's papers lie strewn on the polished dark walnut table. There is a laptop with a winking light amidst the pen, the slimline leather briefcase, the papers and folders, and a couple of video cassettes. The briefcase is open and lazily, uncuriously, Ritwik glances inside. There are four passports. The desire to know Zafar's surname is immediate. He picks one up – it is a Jordanian one – and opens it. Zafar abu Bakr al-Aziz bin Hashm. Born 1947, Amman. The photograph shows a cruelly handsome man in his twenties. It is only when he looks at the other passports that Ritwik is woken out of his passive and blunt curiosity. The remaining three are all issued by different countries – Syria, Saudi Arabia, and the United Kingdom. In each, the date of birth, the name, the photograph and the place of birth are different.

Something unknown begins a slow ticking inside his head. Initially, he identifies it as a vague and intangible envy for someone who has not one, but four travel documents and, therefore, such freedom of travel as four nationalities might allow: Ritwik correlates number of passports to ease of entering and leaving borders. But it doesn't explain a more smoky unease building up in little wisps and grains inside him. He takes a perfunctory glance at the spill of papers everywhere. A fat and battered filofax lies open, but before he has had time to have a quick, furtive browse, some sixth sense in him registers that the sound of the shower has stopped and urges him to move away. He tiptoes into the bedroom, sits on the edge of the bed and starts putting his clothes on.

Zafar enters the room and asks him, 'You feeling better?'

'Yes, much, thanks.'

Zafar ruffles his hair in a surprise gesture of affection before starting to dress. 'Let me put some clothes on and we'll be on our way.'

In the car, he is unusually friendly, asking Ritwik questions about his family, his origins, his education, how he came to England, questions which Ritwik tries to evade, some successfully, others not. Zafar even puts his hand on Ritwik's thigh a couple of times and leaves it there. He decides to frame a careful question.

'So, Zafar, you never told me what you did for a living.'

A long silence during which it seems Zafar is trying to make up his mind whether to give an honest answer. At last he says, 'I work for some departments of the British government.'

'What does that mean? You're a spy?'

Zafar laughs. 'You've been reading too much Le Carré.'

'What then?' Ritwik persists.

'Oh, I'm a sort of business broker. I get international clients for British-manufactured stuff.'

'What sort of stuff?'

'You know what happened to the cat who was curious?' Zafar asks, laughing, but there is no hiding the deterring emphasis behind the words.

'Yes, I do, but you also know what brought it back, don't you?' Ritwik adds, with feigned innocence.

Zafar doesn't reply. After a while, while they are on Vauxhall Bridge Road, he tries again.

'So when are you going back to your country?'

'In a few days.' He has become laconic again.

Ritwik decides to hold his tongue; Zafar is unreadable and

besides, what does it matter to him what the man does for a living?

As the traffic starts moving, Zafar seems released into another short burst of affability. 'You know, maybe you shouldn't go there again.'

Silence.

'In fact, I'm asking you not to go there. If it's money you're worried about, I can see to that, it's no problem.'

Ritwik's senses prick up, like a cat's ears, but he remains quiet in the fear that any word might break this delicate spell of generosity and make Zafar retract everything.

'I can settle something on you. I come to London quite often and when I'm here, you can see me. What do you think?'

Settle. What a strange word. Dust settles, memories settle, agitated liquids settle, but money for exclusive access to bad sex? Does that settle too?

'You must be joking.' Ritwik cannot believe what he is hearing.

'You can be my friend, only mine.' Once again, Ritwik is thrown by the slippage in such an innocuous word.

'Why are you doing this? You don't know me at all.'

'Do you mean, *you* don't know *me*? Is that what is bothering you?'

Thou turn'st my eyes into my very soul . . .

'Trust me. I just want to make your life a bit easier.'

'But why? I don't understand it at all,' Ritwik fairly shouts.

'Let's call it a whim. Or maybe it's because I would like your company when I come to London. Which is often. I would like to have someone to spend some time with, talk to, you know, when I'm here.' The words are tentative and feel as if they are being spun out unrehearsed.

Ritwik is a whirl of flattered ego and utter bafflement. A Bengali proverb, much used by his mother, comes to his mind but inexactly, something along the lines of not pushing away a smiling god.

They are nearing Brixton, so Ritwik starts giving Zafar directions. Once outside number 37 Ganymede Road, Ritwik asks him to stop.

'This is where I live. With a very old woman. I'll tell you about her some day. Her entire family died – her husband, her son, her daughter, too, I suspect. All at different times in her life.'

Zafar makes a noise of regret with his teeth and tongue. 'You'll come to my hotel tomorrow?' he asks.

'What time?'

'I can come and pick you up from here. Say eight o'clock. We can go and have dinner somewhere.'

'All right. See you tomorrow.'

Zafar smiles – this is the first time Ritwik has seen him smile gratuitously and it makes him look like a child who has just received a cuddle – and cups Ritwik's face in his palm, gives it a light squeeze and says something in Arabic.

'What was that?'

'I'll leave you to find out. All right, then. Till tomorrow.'

Ritwik gets out of the car, bends down, gives a wave and lets himself into the house with a very gently tripping heart.

In the next four days, Zafar takes him out to dinner twice – he doesn't see Ritwik on the second and third days; he is busy with other, business, things, 'client dinners' – and invites him to his suite after dinner. The sex is unchangingly swift and one-sided and Zafar retreats into an aloof and impenetrable world of introspection after each time. It is as if Ritwik starts fading for Zafar

350

during the sex and disappears completely afterwards. It is as unintimate as physical contact gets and is always preceded and followed by a shower, in an attempt, Ritwik supposes, to sluice off ritually not only semen, sweat, the touch of another body – there is no saliva, for Zafar never kisses – but also the bigger intangibles that he perceives to come with this paid sex.

The 'settlement' is not mentioned by him again and Ritwik drives himself neurotic thinking about it all the time and being unable to broach the subject in fear of appearing grasping and greedy. On Zafar's final night in London, he slips Ritwik a piece of paper with numbers and letters written on it in green ink before they step out of his bird suite to drive to Brixton. Out of a misplaced sense of politeness, he doesn't read what is written on the paper, he just folds it up and shoves it into the back pocket of his jeans.

'Call this number soon. He's a friend and looks after some of my stuff here. I've spoken to him already and told him you will be in touch, so he'll be expecting your call. Just give him a ring when you need any money, any time. He's very reliable. You can either have him give you a lump sum at a given time every month, or you could get in touch with him as and when you require money. Does that suit you?'

Ritwik is overwhelmed by this casual generosity and feels belittled by the stubborn suspicion about Zafar's motives that will not let go of him. Too many questions are muddying this, too many bad films and stereotypes and myths are in the way. He nods, unable to say anything that will not appear flimsy and hackneyed.

Outside Ritwik's house, Zafar turns off the engine.

'Is there any way I can get in touch with you?' asks Ritwik.

'Why?' The question is as instantaneous as Zafar's regret

for letting it slip out. 'I'm sorry, I didn't mean it like that, I just wanted to . . .'

'No, that's all right. Thank you so much for your generosity.' The whipcrack of Zafar's question has turned on all the harsh lights; even the brief illusion of soft focus images is now gone irreversibly.

'You know my address, you have my phone number,' Ritwik continues, 'you can contact me when you're in London next.'

'Yes, I'll do that. And . . .' Zafar hesitates.

'What?'

'Don't go to King's Cross again. That's our deal, all right? And don't for once think I won't find out if you do it. I have eyes everywhere in London.'

Ritwik finds the image much more startling than the naked threat. Once again, he wonders what Zafar does for a living that gives him such wealth, such a smooth acceptance of the role of imperious master. He doesn't respond immediately to this. When he speaks, his words are of a doormat's.

'How long will it be then before I see you again?' He hates himself for being such a pushover, he finds his own voice whiney and needy.

'Soon,' says Zafar, evasive again.

Ritwik reaches for the door handle. Zafar leans forward, touches his hand and says, 'You give me your word, don't you, you are not going to go with other men?'

Ritwik isn't sure the unidiomatic nature of Zafar's words is real or imagined inside his prejudiced head. He nods and even manages a smile as Zafar holds his face and says something in Arabic again.

'You never said what it means.'

'I will, one day,' he whispers.

*

The rest of the night is sleepless for Ritwik. He writes for a bit, for company, nearing the end of Miss Gilby's story. At other times, he lies in bed and stares at the objects in the room with a fixed gaze, hoping it will induce first a meditative trance and then sleep. No such luck as he discovers that the hoop of the small lock on the metal trunk stowed away under the table doesn't go through the clasp of the bolt. Which means the trunk is not locked but just gives the impression of being so. He leaps out of bed and starts ferreting, unsure of what he is going to find.

Bills, some dating back forty years, house deeds, vehicle registration forms, leasehold papers, brittle yellow pieces of paper, foxed and aged, letters, bank statements, a bundle tied with faded blue silk, a post mortem report from Southwark Coroner's Court for Richard Christopher Cameron, died May 26, 1966, by his own hand, a single gunshot wound to his forehead.

The hands that open the report are not his, they are guided by someone else, someone at once inside and outside him.

Entry through glabella, entry wound consistent with contact wound. Shattering of the crista galli, the collection of the frontal sinuses. Grazing of the corpus callosum. Slower trajectory through the lateral ventricle, which is entirely shattered, along with similar damage to the posterior ramus of the lateral sulciss. Grazes edge of the parieto-occipital lobe, just missing the occipital lobe, exiting through the occipital bone, two centimetres above the superior nuchal line.

Ritwik forces his eyes from this to the doctor's illegible signature, its very scrawl a feeble attempt to restore normality, but foredoomed and drowned by the preceding jargon, at once emotionless and violent. His head is a carillon of one question – why, why, why – increased in amplitude by the belief that never in his or Anne's lifetime will he be able to bring himself to ask her about her son's suicide.

A loose leaf of paper has fallen out from the single fold of the post mortem report. He opens it: a crabbed, ungenerous hand, faded blue ink. It is the last page of a letter: *my view that neither any good nor any remedy can come of what you suggest. I am sorry if I appear to be somewhat inflexible, but our griefs are different. While not wishing for one moment to detract from your great loss – and what can be greater than the death of a son – I would like you to understand that I too have lost someone, and my loss is made more painful by the fact that I have to carry it around secretly like a mark of shame, hiding it from public view, from any acknowledgement of it to even those nearest to me. Your laudable move to sanction my relationship with your son – and perhaps there is something of an attempt to lighten your irredeemable loss by sharing it with someone similarly afflicted – comes too late. Let us mourn, individually, each to his or her own self. What could not be in life, cannot be in the absence of the one who could have bound us. I wish you forbearance, strength (but you have those already) and send you my prayers.*

Yours sorrowfully, James.

P.S.: I am attaching a photograph of Richard and me in Maine two autumns ago. Richard wished you to have it one day.

There is no photograph. Ritwik upends the whole box, shakes out everything on to the floor, goes through every fold and sleeve of paper, but he cannot find it. He feels so hollow and shaky inside that he holds on to the edge of the table before slumping on to the bed. He watches, unmoving, the night lightening to a grey dawn outside his window. He doesn't turn off his bedside lamp.

Next morning he discovers that the tiles on the side of the bath have come loose. As he kneels down to examine the damage more closely to see if he can manage a temporary repair, they fall onto the floor, exposing the dark cavern under the bath and half a dozen bottles of Safeway gin nestling in there. He debates whether to confront Anne with this or simply hide them away silently somewhere out of her reach and decides on the latter; she is so brilliant at evading, stonewalling and plain not listening that the first approach would get him nowhere. What baffles him most is how she has been smuggling it in. Mrs Haq? No, she would never do such a thing. Mr Haq? Equally unlikely. Did Anne herself go out of the house to get it? Impossible. The nearest Safeway is in Balham and Anne doesn't have a car.

He gives up in despair; he can forgive her anything. He paces the garden for a while with his hands on his hips. As he slips his hands into his back pockets, he comes across a folded piece of paper. He takes it out and opens it. On it, in green ink, are an 081 London phone number and the name of Zafar's contact. He cannot believe the name written on it in Zafar's hand so, to have his fears confirmed, he rushes in immediately and calls the number. No one picks up the phone and there is no machine. He tries every twenty minutes, nervous, impatient, puzzled. Seven hours later, at around five in the afternoon, the phone is answered. The voice and accent are unmistakable: they are Saeed Latif's.

X.

Fires have started in the village of Nawabgunj. Little armies of saffron-clad youths, some of them hardly out of their teens, are rushing around the village like the lawless winds, seizing foreign goods wherever they are stocked – cloth from Manchester, salt from Liverpool, stainless steel implements and utensils from Sheffield, sugar from Leicester – dragging them out into the open, pouring kerosene over them and torching them into bonfires. Their zeal is incandescent, the air above the conflagrations redolent with the ardour of their mother goddess mantra, *bande mataram*. No door can remain shut to them, no English goods, however tiny, hidden from their righteous rage. The handful of Muslim traders who have resisted have had their houses set on fire too. Some of them have fled the village, others have voluntarily surrendered their secret stockpiles of tainted English goods to avoid greater dangers.

Miss Gilby has seen for herself the heaps of black ash left in the market square, the aftermath of some burning ceremony. On one occasion, she had even seen the dying embers in one; a little child had picked up stones from nearby and flung them on to the residue of the fire, sending up little flurries of black ash, like insects disturbed, in a shower of red sparks.

Gossip and rumours arrive at 'Dighi Bari' by the hour, spreading like bushfire, accompanied by whispered excitement that can barely be kept in check. *Did you know they have set Faizal Mohsen's warehouse on fire? He was hiding a whole consignment of foreign cloth, planning to pass it off as swadeshi fabric in the market.* Unable to go out, the women in the *andarmahal* gather news from the servants and embellish it with untrammelled freedom. Bimala's *naw jaa* has already started packing her boxes and trunks in preparation for moving to Calcutta. Miss Gilby is no longer certain how much of that possible move has been actually discussed in the family and how much of it is in her fervid imagination. But the sight of those fires made Miss Gilby realize that not all was rumour and fabrication.

Mr Roy Chowdhury holds long, agonized meetings with the elders of the village. He is advised to send his friend, Mr Banerjea, packing. The village grows mutinous against the depredations of these imported youths. The elders advise Mr Roy Chowdhury to placate the Muslim population of the village who are now convinced that it is a Hindu plot to drive them out; they are not going to keep quiet for long and watch these thugs set their lives and living on fire.

All this Miss Gilby finds out when she accidentally crosses Mr Roy Chowdhury's path in the morning while he is on his way out and she on her way to the drawing room for the first of the morning lessons. In a hurried exchange of words in the verandah, marked by great anxiety and foreboding, he warns her of the dangers of going riding unaccompanied at such a volatile time: anti-English sentiments are running high and unchecked and she would do well to be extra cautious. She thanks him for his solicitude; more than that she cannot say because she is robbed of her usual amiability by the haunted and gaunt look that has settled like a mantle of darkness on him.

Then one day the fires outside come inside. On the day the local bank is robbed – it remains in no doubt that *swadeshi* youths have done this for even revolutions need money; besides, the young men who committed the deed didn't bother to mask themselves – that same evening, Robin *babu*, Mr Roy Chowdhury's accountant, is set on by a mob of rabid men and beaten so severely that had Rakhal Sardar not passed by fortuitously, on his way to fetch water from the well, and heard his piteous groans, the accountant would have bled to his death in the muddy ditch into which he had been pushed. When Robin *babu* comes to his senses and manages to speak, he cannot say with any certainty who the assailants were. Mr Roy Chowdhury calls his own doctor to look after the poor man. The ramifications of the attack on his innocent accountant have disturbed him no end: were the perpetrators *swadeshi* youths trying to pass it off as a heinous act committed by the wily and intransigent Muslims, thereby attempting to alienate any sympathy for them, or was it really Muslim anger boiling over and this cowardly deed its first expression? As *zamindar* of Nawabgunj, any action taken by him without establishing the incontrovertible truth could have serious repercussions.

Bimala stops attending lessons altogether. Miss Gilby doesn't write to Mr Roy Chowdhury again: the man is too burdened with graver matters to have the leisure to discuss his wilful and secretive wife's little obstinacies with her tutor. She waits for this sudden rain of madness to let up but deep down inside something tells her that she is not for long in the Roy

Chowdhury family. Something, some connection, thin as a strand from a spider's web, has been severed and there is no repairing it. The music has become subtly discordant.

ELEVEN

Saeed patters his stubby fingers on the faux-chrome top of the table to an invisible tune inside his head. It goes maniacally fast sometimes; at other times it reduces to the slow tapping of his index finger once every few seconds. Indeed, there is something manic about Saeed this morning; he has made the journey from Ganymede Road to Al-Shami, his favourite restaurant on Edgware Road, in fourteen minutes flat, zipping through the empty stretches and jumping most of the traffic lights on the way. He had kept drumming his fingers on his steering wheel, had fiddled with his rings and bracelets, and had spewed out an unstoppable stream of words at Ritwik during that quarter of an hour. The only noteworthy thing Ritwik managed to extricate from it was the fact that Saeed kept calling Zafar 'Sheikh bin Hashm' and, when asked by Ritwik if he was really a sheikh, he had replied, 'Yes, sheikh, sheikh, important person, VIP, very rich, lots money', with an accompanying gesture of rubbing the tips of his forefinger and thumb to emphasize the undeniable fact of Zafar's immense wealth. All this left Ritwik confused about whether Zafar was really a sheikh; Saeed could have been using the term loosely, in the way Italians call everyone 'dottore', regardless of their profession or level of higher education.

Now, Saeed sits smoking, waiting for the food to be brought to the table. The whole thing may be in Ritwik's imagination, but Saeed seems to be respectful of him, almost ingratiating in his holding open of doors, letting him enter first, asking him questions about his well-being, asking for permission to smoke, his over-solicitous concern about seat belts, restaurant tables, the food ordered. He assumes it to be the cachet that being friends with Zafar gives him. Ritwik is first baffled, then embarrassed; he finds it difficult to make eye contact with someone who has so unsubtly appointed him, Ritwik, his overlord.

'I speak with Sheikh. He tells me I give money, any money you ask. I have money with me. You want?' he says through a cloud of blue smoke soured by his breath.

Ritwik leans back, slightly alarmed at the possibility of Saeed unrolling and handing him soiled banknotes in such a public place. He says hastily, 'No, no, not now, it can wait wait until later.'

Saeed gives him another look of respectful reappraisal, as if he is seeing the real Ritwik for the first time.

'You work for Sheikh.'

Ritwik decides to treat this as a statement, not a question, so he doesn't answer.

'I work for him many years. Ten, maybe, maybe twelve.'

'What do you do for him?'

'I am . . . how you say last time . . . going middle? No?'

'Going middle?' Ritwik asks, puzzled.

Saeed makes a gesture with two hands placed at two opposite sides of the table and then removes one hand to do a walking figure with two fingers while repeating, 'Going middle, heh? Going middle.'

The penny drops. 'Ah, go-between.'

'Yes, yes,' Saeed nods like a happy child. 'Go-between, I forget, go between. I go-between for Sheikh.'

'But between what?'

Saeed takes some time to understand the question so Ritwik mimes his gesture and asks him to name the points on the table between which the to and fro of the go-between happens.

Saeed hesitates before answering. When he does, haltingly, Ritwik immediately understands that he is either lying or evading. 'People. Big people. Business, lot money. Business clients.' He repeats the word 'clients' several times as if it were a new word he has only recently acquired.

Ritwik wields his newfound power, if it is that at all, and pushes ahead with the questioning. 'What business?'

Saeed gives him an intensely quizzical look. At that moment the waiter arrives with the first of their dishes. Ritwik watches Saeed's dogged determination to please and flatter slow down over the sharing out of food – this time, Saeed heaps Ritwik's plate before serving himself – as he tries to work out the nature of the connection between Zafar and Ritwik, but the blip is thankfully short. Whatever he has deduced, it seems to be in Ritwik's favour for he reverts to his enervating solicitude.

'You eat. You too thin. Eat all this food.'

'I'll certainly try,' says Ritwik, smiling. 'I love this food, you know that.'

Saeed takes this as a personal compliment and preens. Ritwik seizes the opportunity. 'So, you never said, what business is it that you do with Zafar?'

Saeed takes a long time to spear his kebab, put a piece into his mouth, follow it with a forkful of buttery rice and another of salad, and then a morsel of vinegared chilli, chew it, swallow and address the question.

'You know. Business. Money. You do same for Sheikh.'

Once again, Ritwik cannot determine if this is query or statement; each has a radically different meaning from the other. His mind is thick with questions: does Saeed know the nature of his contact with Zafar or does he think that he is another of Zafar's business clients? Surely, given how Saeed has helped him in the recent past, he cannot think Ritwik to be anything other than an illegal immigrant scrabbling to feed himself one meal a day? Has Saeed ever asked himself, or even Zafar, for what services Ritwik is being given a blank cheque? What did Saeed and Zafar talk about? And, noisiest of them all, what work did Saeed do for Zafar? Did he look after Zafar's money in London? Was he just a low-level handyman for his interests here? *What interests?*

The air in the restaurant is dense and swooning with smoke. There are blue swirls of it everywhere, barely moving. Ritwik concentrates fiercely on eating and hopes Saeed will not demand a response. The waiter comes with more food and moves plates and bowls around on their table to make space for the new arrivals. He and Saeed talk for a while in Arabic, the waiter laughs, looks at Ritwik, says something to Saeed and leaves for the kitchen.

'What were you saying to each other?' Ritwik asks.

'He say you eat like little bird,' Saeed replies, smiling, and shows the size of the bird with his hand: it could be a sparrow in the nest of his palm.

The asymmetry of any relationship between Saeed and Zafar strikes Ritwik for the first time: what was a poshly spoken, educated, filthy rich sheikh doing with a criminal who had a line in a mild version of people trafficking and wanted to break out into more serious aspects of it? The chasm that separates the two men seems vast, unbridgeable.

Seems. They have obviously managed to have a long and functional relationship across class boundaries. Clearly, Saeed is no fool if he has managed such a thing with a man who strikes Ritwik as cunning, shady, powerful and disturbing.

'You still think what I do for Sheikh. Work, I tell you. No worry for you. You don't think of it.'

Ritwik is surprised at having his mind read. He gives a faint, false smile and asks, 'Are you saying it's none of my business?' He hopes the smile takes the edge off the question.

Saeed plays the same hand. 'Yes, yes,' he smiles, 'not your business, not your business.' Affable, even friendly, but Ritwik gets the sense that he has just been warned off.

'How much you want?'

Ah, business again. Ritwik decides to test his limits. 'How much can I have?' he asks.

'Any money. Two hundred, five hundred, you say.'

Ritwik looks steadily at the bright green parsley flecked sparingly with light beige grains of bulgur, the orange oil from the sausages, the broken ball of a falafel, and says, without lifting his eyes, 'Four hundred now, let's say. If I need more, I'll call you.' He pauses to look up and adds, 'Not here, please, in the car.'

For some reason he doesn't go into, Saeed refuses to take him to Ganymede Road and drops him off on Acre Lane, a three-minute drive away from where Ritwik lives. Ritwik reads this too as a sign and tries to keep his voice bleached of any interest when he asks Saeed, 'Does Zafar know Mr Haq?'

Saeed looks out of the window, spits, counts out four

hundred pounds in twenty-pound notes and hands the wad to Ritwik. His jaw muscle throbs under his pale skin. He bares his teeth in what is meant to be a smile, says something under his breath in Arabic then leans sideways to open the door and says, 'Goodbye', once in English and again in Arabic.

Ritwik gets out and walks the quarter hour to Ganymede Road, the dirty wad in his pocket an unsightly square bulge chafing and burning his skin. Everyone in the teeming crossroads of Brixton seems to be staring at him. A young, bespectacled man, wearing a white shirt too small for him, stands in the concrete garden in front of the Ritzy cinema and shouts, 'The Lord said, Come unto me and I shall give you everlasting life. Friends, Jesus has given me a peace I have never known before. Jesus has saved me. Jesus has shown me love above all.' He clutches a small Bible in his hand and paces an invisible perimeter of about twenty square feet. His eyes are fixed in the middle distance. He repeats the words over and over again, unchanging in tone and delivery. By the time Ritwik leaves the voice behind, he is ready to scream.

There is a message next to the phone in the living room one day: 'Gavin called'. When he asks Anne if Gavin had left a number, she says no. There is no way he can get in touch with him. But he has figured out a way to send letters to Aritra. He writes to his brother and asks him to address his envelopes to Anne Cameron, without any mention of his name anywhere in case the immigration people trace him back to Ganymede Road and throw him out of the country. Of course, he doesn't mention the reason for this subterfuge to Aritra and fobs him off with a lie about bureaucracy and quirky rules of the British postal system.

Zafar doesn't call or write. Ritwik doesn't dare to call Saeed and ask for information about him: he doesn't want Saeed to get the faintest whiff of himself as either a pining or a nosey rent boy. Of one thing he is certain – Zafar has lied to his handyman or has evaded the entire issue. The questions, double-guessings, doubts, all paralyse Ritwik and keep him from getting in touch with Saeed. Then three weeks after his first four hundred pounds, he calls Saeed again.

'My friend,' says Saeed, 'you need more money, I give you.'

In a split second Ritwik decides to say yes because he can use their meeting for news of Zafar. 'Why don't we meet at Al-Shami?'

'I too busy now, this week, next week. You meet me this night, Marble Arch tube, I give money, OK?'

'No, wait, Saeed, I just wanted to ask if you had any news of Zafar.' The question is phrased wrongly and Ritwik regrets his haste.

There is a pause before Saeed replies, 'OK, everything OK. You don't have news of Sheikh?'

Forced into this strategic ping-pong again, he tries to lob the question back to Saeed. 'Is he in Saudi Arabia?'

'Saudi Arabia?' The disbelieving tone is followed by a long pause. 'No, Sheikh in many countries. He travels now, business travel, lot of business travel. Africa, Sudan, Syria, Paris.' Another pause. 'I not know where Sheikh now.'

Ritwik swallows the flat contradictions and the seamless jumps between all those seemingly irreconcilable points on the map. A new question rears its dark head: is Saeed Zafar's eyes in London?

Saeed marks the silence and asks Ritwik, 'You in trouble, my friend? You need help?'

Ritwik says, somewhat more sharply than he intended, 'No, what do you mean by trouble? What sort of trouble?'

'No, my friend, I just ask. Your voice is . . . how you say . . . far, your voice is far, you know?'

'I'm fine. I'll come and pick the money up. What time is good for you?'

Slightly over three weeks after Saeed gives Ritwik his second installment, Zafar calls him to say he is in London for ten days; would tomorrow evening – late, say around half ten – be good for him, same place, Dorchester, that is, and then he could drive Ritwik to his new house. Ritwik says yes politely, with a slight tinge of formality, even; in this gradual illumination of someone else's life, the words 'new house' hold a little corner of surprise. The question why Zafar chooses to stay in a luxury hotel if he has a house in this country is not asked, of course.

It is well past midnight when Zafar and Ritwik set out on the drive to Surrey. Zafar tells him the name of the village – Hincksey Green – and promises to take him back to Brixton before three. Ritwik sits in the car, the metallic taste of Zafar's semen still in his mouth, and feels anxious about Anne, left alone in the house. When asked about what he did while he was away from London – did he see his wife, his children, what about the son whom he had mentioned last time – Zafar brushes the questions aside with a curt and condescending 'Oh, the usual stuff, boring, don't bother your pretty little head with it.'

Ritwik lets the first half an hour of the drive soothe the rage this condescension fires in him. Halfway through it, he asks, in a tone slightly more highly pitched than normal, 'But, Zafar, you cannot forever evade such questions. It's not just empty formality. I might be genuinely interested in your life elsewhere. I know practically zilch about it.'

Zafar gives his irritating, non-committal laugh. 'That's even scarier than empty formality.'

It is meant to be half a joke but the other half goes through Ritwik like a blade. He stares out of the window, watching the deserted, orange-lit suburbs of south London slip by smoothly and fast. He rolls down his window and a rush of cool night air, smelling of petrol fumes, grass and night vegetation, blows in. There are a lot of trees, green spaces and gardens where they drive through. After Peaslake, Ritwik loses interest in keeping track of places; he certainly doesn't want to keep on asking Zafar where they are. The houses thin out after a while. Ritwik feels Zafar's hand on his thigh and the tension in the car begins to fade away with his drowsiness. The cool air makes him shiver a bit so he rolls up the window.

'Don't you think there's something reductive in associating every Arab man you meet with oil?'

More than this abrupt fracture of the nearly companionable silence Ritwik is jolted by the meditated and carefully studied quality of the question.

'I don't meet Arab men,' he answers, as indirectional and evasive as Zafar.

'But it was one of the first things you asked me, did I have anything to do with oil,' Zafar insists.

'Well . . . you said . . . you said you were from Saudi Arabia and . . . and . . .'

'And so, with charming stereotyping impulses, you thought, ah, Saudi Arabia, therefore, oil.'

'Well, you're not wrong. I was being a bit . . . insular,' Ritwik says, very sheepish now.

Zafar returns his hand to his thigh and gives it a squeeze. 'My father made his fortune in oil. But it's not going to last forever.'

'What, the oil or the fortune?'

'Neither. Do you know anything about Saudi Arabia?'

'No, apart from . . .' he stops, trying to phrase sentences that won't smack of camels, oil or harems.

Zafar rushes in. 'Apart from thinking that everyone in that country is afloat on a fortune of oil.'

Ritwik tries to protest but Zafar gives a short, joyless laugh and continues. 'Do you know who runs the country? Do you know what the oil revenue is used for? Who gets that money? Who owns the oilfields? How oil multinationals are run?'

'No, Zafar, of course, I don't know. But why don't you take me through these things? I'll be glad to be enlightened.' Ritwik immediately regrets the last sentence: it could so easily be read as acid-soaked.

'OK, little by little.' There is no sign that Zafar has taken it as sarcasm but he clams up for a while.

'It's a one-resource economy. How long will that last you think?' Zafar has started talking again but Ritwik gets the impression that he is thinking aloud. 'In the next twenty or thirty years, that country is going to need nearly half a trillion dollars, yes, trillion, to upgrade oil pipelines, refineries, transport, the whole bloody infrastructure to keep the oil industry and its economy running. It's living in a bubble. Oil money is an illusion.'

'Where's the money going to come from?'

Zafar doesn't answer. Ritwik looks out of the window again and watches the fast glide of trees and houses and road signs. He is baffled by Zafar's sudden outburst. He takes a left turn at a sign and the roads become narrower. They drive past open country with sudden battalions of brooding Lombardy poplars and hedges huddled in the dark. Zafar seems to know where he is going: he takes more turns, each taking them down a narrower road. Suddenly in front of them, skulking in the dark, is a huge house, a mansion made of darkness, hiding cunningly and willing itself to remain undiscovered. There is a long crunching of gravel under the tyres as the massed shadow moves closer and closer until Ritwik can make out a façade broken up by unlit windows, scores of them, and cornices, a doorway, chimneys, bussoirs. They get out of the car and Zafar leads the way to the front door. He takes out a giant bunch of keys and fumbles around, the keys clinking and jingling, till he finds the right one. They enter and Zafar turns on a light switch.

The sudden light hurts Ritwik's eyes. They are in a huge hallway. The floor is wooden, with exquisite Persian and Afghani rugs on them. There is a mirror, in its heavy and intricate golden frame, reflecting them. There is wooden furniture everywhere – a slim table with curved and ornate legs, a heavy cabinet, two beautiful chairs with red silk upholstery; to Ritwik's untrained eyes, they all look very expensive and classy. These are the objects for which words such as nonsuch chest, davenport, card table with floral marquetry, veneered cabinet are used, Ritwik thinks; if only he could unite name with thing.

'What do you think? Come, come along, I'll show you the rest. Are you interested in antique furniture at all? It's something of an obsession with me,' Zafar says, moving ahead.

Ritwik is too struck by the sheer magnitude and opulence of the house and its heavy English furnishings and objects to respond. He follows Zafar to an enormous room that borders on the vulgar in its excess – cabinets and a huge chest of drawers against the walls, tables and stands, a gateleg dining table so huge that the twelve identical chairs around it look distantly placed from each other. The light from the two crystal chandeliers will not allow any dishonesty, any evasion. Zafar keeps up a running commentary, most of which doesn't reach Ritwik, apart from words and phrases here and there.

'The chairs are all Louis Quatorze . . . I had the rugs shipped to England . . . the only bit of the house that's fully furnished . . . Queen Anne, by the way . . . it's almost ready . . . Grace Carpenter in the village . . . you look a bit gobsmacked, if you don't shut your mouth, you'll soon start catching flies.' It is the laugh on which this ends that makes Ritwik pay attention to what he is saying. He shuts his mouth and says, 'This . . . this is amazing. How many rooms does it have?'

'Twelve bedrooms, on three floors. There are reception rooms, drawing rooms, morning rooms, smoking rooms, a billiard room. I think if you add the bathrooms, kitchens, breakfast rooms, and all that sort of thing, maybe forty?' Ritwik can hear the pride of ownership in his voice.

'But what are you going to *do* with . . . with this palace?' He cannot keep the incredulity out of his naive voice. 'You're not planning to live here, are you? It looks like a stately home, something English Heritage looks after. Do you really own it?'

'Yes, I do. As of last year. Do you want to have a quick tour around the other floors?'

'Zafar, you must be joking, you cannot own this thing. It's like saying you own Audley End or something. You cannot *buy* this sort of thing, can you?'

'Of course, you can. You can buy anything you want.'

Ritwik thinks he catches a moment of truth, a brief flash of the inner, real Zafar, in this last statement and, for some intangible reason, it makes him feel both small and sad. He shakes it off and asks again, 'But will you live here? In all of it? You could . . . you could house ten, a dozen families here.'

'Well, I wanted to buy something in this country, do it up, maybe have a place here when the family wants to travel.' His voice becomes hooded again. 'Besides, I work with important clients. It would be nice to have a place to entertain them, you know, have meetings, that sort of thing.'

'Does it have a garden?'

'A huge one. And an orchard. But it's too dark to see them now. There's even a gardener.'

Ritwik feels dispersed in this new world; in a strange way, it makes *him* feel dishonest, besmirched.

'What time is it?' he asks, feeling leached of interest and energy, as if it had all flown out to create the unremitting shower of attention the house so imperiously demanded.

'It's about half one. Time to go?'

'Oh my god, it's very late,' says Ritwik, a bit too promptly. 'Zafar, I would love to see the rest of the house but I must leave now.'

'All right then, let me turn the lights off.'

'I'm a bit paranoid about leaving Anne on her own. I keep thinking I'll go back home one day and find her lying in a heap at the foot of the stairs or in the bathroom. She's very, very old and frail. I've also recently discovered that she's a little gin fiend.' Ritwik keeps on this patter. 'You'll bring me here in the daytime one day, won't you? I'd love to see the garden and the orchard and the whole house in the daylight.'

'Yes, some time.'

'Come to think of it, I've never seen *you* in the daylight.'

'I might be a vampire, beware,' Zafar says, making a lunge for his neck with bared teeth. Ritwik starts laughing and holds him away. In an instant, Zafar envelops him in his arms, lifts him off the ground, carries him to the room with the chandeliers and sets him down on the table on his back. He kicks out of his way a couple of chairs, unbuttons his fly, rubs himself against the seat of Ritwik's jeans while he lies, knees up, on the table, then lifts him up again and pushes him down to his knees on to the floor. It is over in an instant, before Ritwik has even had a chance to tumesce. Saliva and semen drip off his chin on to the floor; he cannot banish the thought of the stain it will leave on the expensive wooden floor. He stands up, reaches into his pocket, pulls out some crumpled and frayed tissues, bends down and rubs the bit of the floor where he thinks the drops might have fallen: his dark-adapted eyes cannot make out anything much in this room.

They leave the house and begin the drive in total silence. There is no traffic and the redbrick houses behind their privet hedges and shielding trees all look abandoned. Even the streetlights add to the spectral effect.

'Do you want to live in that house?'

Ritwik isn't expecting a question like that; he turns his head sideways, in a flash, to look at Zafar. Zafar's eyes are steadily fixed on the road unrolling in front of him.

'What do you mean?'

'You could live there. If you wanted to, that is,' he says in an utterly detached tone, as if he were reading regulation 4.2 of the Highway Code.

'I can't leave Anne on her own.'

A brief pause. Then, 'It's not as if she's going to live for very long, is she?'

'Zafar!' Ritwik shouts. It's a reflex action he immediately regrets and tries to turn into mock-admonishment, not with great success.

'You had no compunction leaving her alone when you were working fields or factory warehouses.'

He starts disputing this – 'That's not true at all, I always returned home at night but . . .' – when, halfway through, there is a brief, illuminating flicker of light. It doesn't come in a blinding flash; only a slow, unsurprising discovery of how much Saeed has told Zafar about him that makes him nod his head with a calm realization, yes, they know this.

Zafar is too shrewd to miss the sudden, midway halt. He laughs and says, 'I'm just suggesting you might want to stay there, say, when I'm around in the country. But, of course, there's your old lady to think of.'

He lets Zafar understand he has taken his words at face value by remaining quiet. But the game is too far advanced for him to let be. 'Which bit of Africa were you in?' he asks, looking out of the window.

'Sudan, Sierra Leone, Côte d'Ivoire,' comes the answer, prompt and pat, throwing Ritwik completely: Zafar will certainly not give him the satisfaction of letting him hear the clicks inside his head.

More silence and the slipstream of trees, hedges, houses in its silent flow. Then another move in the game: Zafar asks, with as much disinterest as his voice can muster, 'Why do you ask?'

'Nothing, just wondering.'

They are now well inside suburban London. 'Saeed's given you money, I expect.'

'Oh, yes, he has, thank you. He's very eager to please.'

'You mustn't attach too much importance to him. I retain

him out of old loyalties but he's really very' – a ticking pause, one two three four five six – 'peripheral.'

Ritwik makes an effort to ignore the last word; he counts twenty backwards and then asks, 'What old loyalties?'

Zafar doesn't bother to respond. Instead, he says, 'We're in Streatham already. That was quick, wasn't it?'

'Thank you for dropping me off.' The armour had parted, only a tiny bit, for a tiny fraction of time; it has become impenetrable again.

'I'm off to Gloucestershire in a couple of days' time. For a night, maybe two. I was going to ask you to come with me but I know you can't.'

'Oh. What's happening in Gloucestershire?'

'Business stuff, meetings, prospective clients. Work.'

Only after Ritwik has shut the passenger door and Zafar has made a three-point turn to leave Ganymede Road does Ritwik notice the open curtains and the lights blazing in the living room. He lets himself in. Every single light in the house seems to be on.

'Anne, Anne,' he calls out.

There is no answer. That is not unusual but something about all these burning lights makes his blood pound hard in his heart, his ears. He runs into the kitchen and notices that the door to the garden is wide open. He rushes out but his pupils take a few seconds to adjust to the dark outside. He sees a pale shape, not even a ghost but the residue of one, under the horse chestnut. He advances with immense strides.

Anne is standing under the tree, her nightdress clinging to the bones of her frame. She has one hand cupped behind an ear, as if she is trying to focus on some very distant sound, and a finger on her lip asking for total silence. Regardless of the fright he has had, that gesture overwhelms everything else: he doesn't speak and listens out for what Anne might have heard.

After several moments of this silence, Anne whispers, 'Listen.'

A minute of waiting then the silence of the cold spring night shatters with manic laughter from up high, an eked out cackle and bray that curdles his blood. It is followed by another, then another, and Ritwik realizes with a flash that it is the call of an animal.

Anne hobbles closer to Ritwik and whispers in his ear, 'Kookaburras. A pair of them.'

They stay rooted under the tree, Ritwik suspended in a miracle he neither comprehends nor welcomes. After an eternity, he touches Anne's arm and steers her towards the house. He doesn't think they'll hear the birds again.

Anne witters on, '*Dacelo gigas*. It's one of the largest members of the Alcedinae, the kingfisher family. Alcedinae. The family name must be from the story of Alcyone, don't you think? Do you know the story of Ceyx and Alcyone, how one of them went to sea and was lost, and bereft of her love . . .'

XI.

On one of these nights of unrest outside and swelling anxiety inside, when she cannot sleep, Miss Gilby writes a short note to her brother, asking him for any information he might be able to glean from his wide range of acquaintances on Ruth Fairweather, but avoids mentioning what is happening in Bengal; chances are, he has a far greater, if removed, familiarity with these developments. She writes a longer letter to Violet apprising her of everything – Bimala's infidelity, her own growing interest in Indian birds, the tension caused by Mr Banerjea's presence in 'Dighi Bari', the village poised on the knife edge of communal riots. By the time she finishes, the dawn chorus has begun. She puts on her riding attire and decides to take Pakshiraj out without waking up the *saees*: a long ride, she thinks, will blow the cobwebs away from the increasingly dark and cluttered corners of her mind.

She reaches the paddy fields and directs Pakshiraj towards the Tulsi river, now a thin, bright ribbon in the winter, with large stretches of sandflats and wet riverbed around it crisscrossed by meandering, silvery threads of water. The morning breaks all pale gold and orange and before long settles into the white light of day. She has become a stranger in a family of strangers. The only person with whom she can converse is so busy and harried that she hasn't seen him for weeks, except that brief meeting in the verandah; even at a time like this, his natural courtesy reminded him, first and foremost, to be solicitous of her welfare and safety. The very thought makes Miss Gilby's eyes sting with tears. How noble and unselfish, how manly; such men are forever doomed to bear the slings and arrows of fortune with silent patience and grace. The haggard look, those lacklustre eyes, which were wont to shine with gentleness and warmth – could they be not only for the fires raging in his village? Could he have an inkling of what is going on between his wife and his closest friend, no, no friend, but a viper, right inside his very house? Does he know the full story? Has he let Bimala know that he knows? Or does he know and suffer in silence, like King Arthur in the tale by Malory? Miss Gilby had been taken by surprise when she had reached the end of the story to find out that the aged King had known of his wife Guinevere's adulterous relationship with Sir Lancelot for long but had kept quiet in the interest of the unity of the Round Table. A sudden memory gives this view the seal of certainty in Miss Gilby's mind: she remembers the anguished whisper of Mr Roy Chowdhury – *I cannot send my friend away, Miss Gilby, I cannot* – when she had asked him why he didn't arrange for Mr Banerjea to leave Nawabgunj and go away to Rungpoor, something he had been meaning to do for a long time.

Or was it some native code of honour, of loyalty to friends, which she doesn't comprehend at all, some time-honoured custom sanctioned by centuries of practice by people of this unreadable nation? So preoccupied is she with these unwholesome thoughts that she misses the track looping back to the village. She stops for a while to reorient herself and instead of turning back, presses forward and then turns right at a field; she is sure if she continues down that road it will take her downriver to the village.

She is not wrong. A few minutes later she notices a few men and has a mild sensation of relief that she is nearing Nawabgunj. She reaches the rail track, crosses it and continues south: she must be somewhere in between Nawabgunj and its north-neighbouring village, the name of which she cannot remember. The place looks slightly more inhabited than the open country through which she had been riding earlier. She gets off her horse and decides to walk to the nearest gathering of people and ask for directions.

Suddenly her back is hit by something hard and heavy. She turns around, letting go of Pakshiraj's reins. There are four men a few yards behind her. Two of them have *lathi*s in their hand and one of them is bending down to pick up another stone. Miss Gilby is so sure that a stone has been hurled at her in mistake or by accident that she advances towards them to complain and ask them to be more careful. Before she has taken half a dozen steps, the young man who had been picking up a broken brick flings it at her, his arm moving back and then forward in a sweeping arc. It misses Miss Gilby narrowly but she is no longer left in doubt that she is their target; she is also certain they have been following her for some time. Pakshiraj takes fright at the flung brick and runs away across the field, neighing. Miss Gilby cannot mount him and gallop away to safety or to the nearest police station – she is left to face them alone.

As the distance between her and the assailants decreases, she recognizes two of the young men. She used to see them often in the market square; they smiled and wished this exotic foreigner in their village 'Good morning, *memsa'ab*', 'Good evening, *memsa'ab*' every time they saw her. This is some terrible mistake, she thinks; if only she can talk to the two familiar men, everything will be all right. They will understand and go away to summon help. The men exchange a couple of words, another stone is thrown. This hits her forehead and she sinks down on to the muddy field on her knees, clutching her head in pain and shock. A warm trickle gets into her left eye, blinding it momentarily. She didn't know that her own blood could blind and sting her eyes.

The men gain in on her and before she has had a chance to look up, or hold out her hand in fragile defence, in protest, the *lathi* blows fall on her thickly, with a dull thwacking sound against her layers of clothing. She cowers and covers her head, cringing and squirming in the mud. She cannot see anything except moving feet, dark, dirty, shod in rubber sandals. She cries out in pain, in the vain hope that someone can hear her. And just as suddenly as they had arrived, they disappear, running off across the field, shouting *bande mataram*, *bande mataram*. We hail thee, mother goddess. After that, Miss Gilby doesn't remember anything.

TWELVE

Zafar says, 'I'll be back in half an hour. Just a quick drink at the bar. Let's see what he wants. You stay here, OK? I'll be back soon.'

Ritwik nods and watches him leave. An unexpected telephone call from one of his clients, he said; surprising that he should have come to the hotel within half an hour of the call, requesting to see Zafar, rather than let it wait until tomorrow. Must be something urgent, Zafar had said, although he added that he had no idea what it could be.

Ritwik counts one hundred, careful to space the numbers out equally, not rushing them, especially towards the end, and then leaps out of the sofa and goes to the table on which Zafar's briefcase, papers, laptop, filofax all lie in crowded confusion. There is no point in looking at the computer; he doesn't have a clue what to do with it, where to look. Besides, he might do something, in his ignorance, which will make it obvious that he has been snooping.

The filofax gives nothing away. There are a lot more entries in Arabic than he expected but then he forgets most of the time that Zafar *is* Arab. The English entries do not yield up their secrets either. Some names are followed by what appears to be clearly a name for a company or an institution: John Grimble,

381

Fender Care Naval Solutions; Jonathan Pacitto, Agusta Westland; Al Lilley, Accuracy International; Randeep Modi, William Cook Defence; Simon Newton, LM UKIS Ltd. Ordinary names, ordinary addresses, ordinary phone numbers, all unrevealing and silent. He puts back the filofax exactly where he picked it up from and looks through the papers, first gingerly, turning up corners and edges, then more boldly, lifting them up, leafing through them. Latest newsletter from British Aerospace Ltd. A thick tome: *SBAC Chain Directory*. Society of British Aerospace Companies. A folded printout, like a giant compressed Japanese fan, of the SBAC 'Members' Capability Matrix'. It is a beautiful thing, with randomly positioned red and blue dots and, here and there, ticks, an Arab character or two, a 'yes', a few crosses, dispersed across the unfolding concertina. Donna Tartt, *The Secret History*. His attention is held by the spanking-new hardback: the blurb intrigues him and he makes a mental note to buy it, now that he can afford such luxuries. Zafar has dog-eared the page to mark the point where he has stopped reading. There is an official-looking letter from the Defence Manufacturers' Association talking of strategic consultancies, cost-related improved efficiency, a forthcoming calendar of events, invitation to members' meetings. Ritwik has to read each sentence a few times over to understand the purpose and meaning behind the unfamiliar jargon. By the time he reaches the invitation to the Defence Systems and Equipment International Exhibition, he is so bored – and a tiny bit guilty about intruding shamelessly like this – that he is ready to take a catnap. Something in the invitation letter catches his eye and he reads it carefully to pin it down. In a minute he has it – both the date and the word 'Gloucestershire'. 13–15 May, Lydney, Gloucestershire. Today is the 12th.

A solid find at last, the secret of Zafar's disappearance to Gloucestershire, but it comes as an anticlimax and the boredom floods back in again. The ringing phone makes him start: he cannot make up his mind whether to pick it up, whether he should, and by the time he has decided not to, it stops. A minute later, it rings again; he picks it up. It is Zafar.

'Look, I have to go somewhere. Something's come up. You can stay here but I shall be back very late. Or I can get them to call a taxi for you to take you home.'

'I think I should go home.'

'OK, come down to reception in, say, twenty minutes? They'll have a cab waiting for you.'

'OK.' He is expecting something else, a brief goodbye, a 'see you later', or 'I'll call you when I get back from Gloucestershire.' Instead, there is the curt click of Zafar hanging up.

XII.

Montu enters the drawing room and announces that the car is ready and the boxes and trunks have been loaded. Mr Roy Chowdhury nods in acknowledgement and asks him to wait outside. His eyes are red-rimmed and small, he clasps his two hands together under his shawl to hide their stubborn shaking. Bimala hasn't stopped crying for the last week; now that Miss Gilby is really going away forever, now that it is no longer a faint possibility in the dim future but in the here and now, and happening right under her eyes with the truculence and irreversible tyranny of the present tense, she is inconsolable. She has given away all her books on Indian birds to her. On the fly-leaf of each she has inscribed in her childish hand, using her characteristic rounded and perfectly formed English letters, TO MISS GILBY MY TEACHER, FRIEND AND COMPANION, WITH MY LOVE. And below that, in cursive, 'Please do not go away.' Miss Gilby hasn't opened the books since the day she was given them.

The bandages around her head are still there, although now it is more of a bandage than heavy headgear. She still needs her stick to walk. She tries to get up; Mr Roy Chowdhury and Bimala are immediately at her side, trying to support her gently. She tries to concentrate on little, irrelevant things – the thin blue border of Bimala's *sari*, the terracotta horses from Bankura, which sit in the four corners of the room, the silver-tipped end of her walking stick that belonged to Mr Roy Chowdhury's brother. Her lips are pressed into a nearly invisible line. Judging by the copiousness of her weeping, Bimala is the one who needs support, she thinks.

She doesn't remember if she has spoken to them at all this morning. She opens her mouth to console Bimala but she can't think of anything appropriate to say, so she remains silent.

Montu toots the car horn. Shuffling and hobbling, she gets into the car, helped by Bimala and Mr Roy Chowdhury. The courtyard is a blizzard of circling pigeons: Bimala's *naw jaa* is scattering grains from behind the blinds. Only an occasional arm, disembodied, reaches out and the palm opens to fling down some rice.

Mr Roy Chowdhury gets into the car as well; he has insisted on accompanying Miss Gilby all the way to Calcutta, despite her protests.

Over the last week, Miss Gilby, foreseeing this moment, has talked herself into not looking out of the car window. She sits beside Mr Roy Chowdhury and busies herself with the difficulty of sitting in the back in her current state, with rugs, with finding a place for her walking stick. In the periphery of her vision, Bimala reaches out a hand towards the separating glass.

She remembers Mr Roy Chowdhury's voice breaking on his last words, ever, to her. 'Miss Gilby, I hope you will find it in your heart to forgive us.'

THIRTEEN

The meshes of the afternoon draw him in. He lies on the sofa looking at the sky framed by the window. Eventually, darkness falls like the sound of dew. The blinking lights of the aeroplanes traverse the windowpanes and he sometimes moves his head slightly to let the lights describe a perfect diagonal in the square of glass. At other times, he positions his head to have a line of those lights bisect two opposite sides of the square. There are occasions when two or three planes at a time crisscross against the dark panel of the sky. The geometric possibilities become endless, a whole bagatelle of distant lights remotely controlled from the darkness of the sitting room. Sometimes, Ugo sits on the windowsill, keeping an eye out for things. All lives have an onward flow, a beginning leading to a middle leading to an end; only his seems to be a swirling eddy in someone else's flow, destined to whirl round and round for a brief while till a change in current or wave pattern obliterates it. For that brief while, every day is today.

Ritwik discovers a tattered, termite-infested 1904 edition of *Mrs Beeton's Cookery Book*. He hesitates before showing it to Anne – who knows what tormenting history might jump out of this one like a particularly macabre jack-in-the-box – and leaves it lying on the kitchen table. After a day, Ritwik comments on it and Anne says, 'Good god, that used to be my mother's. Where on earth did you drag it out from?' Her tone is pleased, surprised.

Ritwik brews some tea and they sit at the kitchen table, gently browsing. He discovers a brown newspaper cutting between pages 72 and 73, in the section on soups. It says GLYCERINE – THE HOUSEHOLD FRIEND. There follow three short paragraphs on the uses of glycerine – making cake mixes richer, preventing crystallization of jam, as fabric softener.

'Anne, there's a recipe for mullagatawny soup on page 73. Do you think the cutting was to mark that? Did you cook it in India?'

Anne has no memory of the crumbling cutting.

'Oh my god, calf's head soup, sheep's head soup, ox cheek soup. Ughh.'

Anne cackles at his squeamishness.

'Anne, look, a "Useful Soup for Benevolent Purposes". Shall I make it for you tomorrow?'

On discovering that the first ingredient is an ox-cheek, they are helpless with laughter.

'And, pray, what may the benevolent purpose be?' Anne barely manages to say while dabbing at her eyes.

They ultimately settle on 'Pea Soup (Green)' – there are others: 'Pea Soup (Yellow)' and a 'Pea Soup (Inexpensive)' – and Ritwik spends a lot of time converting pints, pounds and quarts to more familiar measures.

'I can't taste anything or smell anything very much. Pea soups and mullagatawnies are all the same to me,' Anne says.

The levity suddenly fades from the kitchen. 'Do you ever have an appetite?'

'No.'

The short, clear truth of her answer has a sobering effect on Ritwik.

'You'll find out that when you reach my age, you need very little to live on. That's because you're not really living, but waiting, which requires a lot less, I suppose.'

Ritwik reaches across the table to touch her nearly naked carpals. 'As long as I'm here, you're going to be eating,' he says with enforced jollity. 'I shall watch over your meals like a hawk. Pea soup it is tomorrow for supper.'

The packets of frozen petits pois sweat on the kitchen table, the spinach soaks in the sink, the lettuce is shredded, the stock is a murmuring simmer in a broken-handled pot at the back of the cooker. Anne has insisted on having the television on. Ritwik has had to concede on this one; she said it gave her company, as if his were not enough or up to the mark, he had pointed out, to which she had replied that the television gave company of such a different sort that they should have a different word for it altogether. Ritwik is brewing some tea in Anne's old and chipped red teapot when she, in the middle of saying something about breadcrumbs to which Ritwik wasn't paying much attention, asks him with a bell-like clarity, 'Did you throw out all my gin or have you hidden it somewhere? I suspect the latter. In that case, we could reach a compromise: I'll let you keep your hiding place a secret and you let me have a bottle when I want. Rationing. By far the best solution.'

'On one condition,' he says. 'You tell me where you got it from.'

'No. Never reveal one's sources. Rule one. You should know.'

'What do you mean, I should know?'

No answer. Ritwik decides to spring his surprise, a pleasant one: he has discovered a stash of mouldy, curling, black-and-white photographs in the loft above his room, hidden away in the insulating material, while he was attempting to hide the bottles of gin. He had looked at all of them and realized, to his great delight, that they were photographs from Anne's days in India. Or perhaps not, because he couldn't identify Anne in any of the pictures, but it was undeniable that they were all taken in India while it was still under British rule. Maybe they belonged to someone else and Anne had forgotten all about them. He hopes that it will be a treat for her to rediscover these forgotten images.

He runs upstairs, brings them down and presents them to Anne. 'Look what I found. I think I'll agree to your deal if you tell me what they are. Let's go through each picture. Are you in any of them?' Ritwik is so excited, his recent wrongfooting so erased, that he babbles like a hyperactive child.

Anne takes one look at them and sits down on a chair. Ritwik pulls another one beside her and places the photographs between them on the table. He can hardly stop talking as he goes through the pile, passing them to Anne, one by one.

'Look, are these in India? What funny clothes. Did Englishwomen only wear these gowns all the time? And hats? God, they're so elaborate. And umbrellas, they always carry umbrellas.'

'Parasols. One needed to. It was a cruel sun out there.'

'And look, the men all have moustaches.' Ritwik is very amused. 'What's happening here?'

'That looks like tea on the lawns. I forget where.'

'And look at all these Indian servants in mufti, waiting on the lords and ladies.'

'Oh, yes, they were indispensable.'

'Why is everyone looking at the camera all the time? Anne, where are you? Are these from your days in India? Such a long time ago. Is this Simla, no, Dalhousie?'

Anne picks out a photograph, sepia with age, its edges spotted with a sprinkling of orange fungus. It looks like a tableau of an English family in a garden – a moustached man, sombre and grave; a lady smiling, her eyes in the shadow cast by her hat; a stiff boy dressed in his Sunday best; and a little girl, an infant really, in a floppy bonnet in the arms of her Indian ayah, reaching out with her little arms to the grass where she presumably wants to be put down. The ayah has a big, bright smile on her black face. There is a fiercely moustached Indian man in the background, a strap across his kurta, his turban too big for his head. There is also an Indian couple alongside him, looking startled, staring at the alien camera. They are in a garden washed with bright sunlight.

Anne points a moving finger at each figure and says, 'That's Christopher, here's Richard, here's Clare with her ayah, Savitri, that's Bahadur Singh, and I don't remember who the others are.'

'Where is this?'

Anne is silent. Sensing something, Ritwik looks sideways at her. She has shut her eyes and is trying to get up.

'Anne?'

'Savitri drowned Clare in the bath. She was two. It was an accident but Savitri was inconsolable. She killed herself the next week. She loved the children. *Chhota sahib*, Richard was, and when Clare came, *chhota mem*. Loved them more than her life. It was just as well she took her own, they would have hanged her, anyway. She could have killed for them. Such a fiercely loyal creature. Something broke inside her after . . . after the incident.

Christopher wanted all the Indian servants shot. Ridiculous, really.'

Anne manages to stand up, push her chair back and start walking towards the door. Some of the photographs spill in a fan on to the linoleum-covered floor. Ritwik looks down at them: they have fallen face down, he can only see their browning backs.

'You shouldn't have taken them out,' Anne mutters, more to the landing outside than to Ritwik, sitting behind her like an immovable rock.

The television continues to babble out its rubbish as Ritwik sits quietly after Anne has left the room, when some stray word or phrase seeps into his consciousness and stirs something. He looks up at the screen: there is a group of young men and women dressed in carnival costumes and a minor cavalcade of mock tanks and life-size armoured vehicles made of cardboard joyfully protesting against something. They are carrying CAAT banners; it takes a while before the running commentary decodes this for him: Campaign Against Arms Trade. They are trying to barricade a convoy of cars – the vehicles of invitees to the Defence System and Equipment International Exhibition at Lydney in Gloucestershire.

He sees a familiar car, a blue Bentley, in the held-up convoy before the heavy police presence disperses the protesters. But perhaps he imagines this flash of blue to accompany the words of the events coordinator of CAAT whose impassioned face appears on the screen and speaks out a new knowledge for him. '. . . *supply arms to the most detestable and repressive regimes in the world, arms that are used to crush democracy, kill people, extinguish their voices. If you look at some of the countries which have been invited to this fair, you'll be outraged. What are Burma,*

North Korea, Iraq, Sierra Leone doing here, countries with military juntas and ruthless dictatorships as governments, countries with a proven record of repression and torture? Some of the delegates here are brokers and fences: theoretically and officially we sell this to, say, Pakistan, or India, but where do they then end up? There are private buyers here, among the so-called delegates. This is just a legitimization of illegal arms dealing and it's being done in broad daylight, with the full knowledge, indeed, approval of the government. We are campaigning to reconcile a foreign policy with . . . '

He moves to the cooker and watches the peas agitated in the furious boil of the stock. A few seconds of staring into that roil and he is hypnotized by their movement.

He doesn't even know he is going to go out of the house until he steps out of the front door. The sky is the dark blue of an English summer night. Unerringly, he walks towards Brixton tube station. It is like sleepwalking, the motives and outcomes equally cloudy, the acts themselves unpredictable, zigzag. An old serpent inside him has begun to stir, awaking from a long, long sleep. He hasn't felt this hollowing out of his bowels, this insistent clenching and unclenching of his sphincter, since his cottaging years in university.

In the train, he keeps his eyes fixed on the ads over the opposite seats and the route of the Victoria Line, a blue, straight trajectory of sans serif letters from Brixton to Walthamstow Central. Despite a number of empty seats, a man stands holding the blue supporting rod in front of the doors and teeters precariously on the balls of his feet. He can barely keep his eyes open. At this hour, the carriages are littered with trampled newspaper pages, empty Lucozade bottles, McDonald's boxes, crumpled brown paper packets that had held chips, entire newspapers folded and left at the windows above the backrest of the seats. Only one headline is visible: BRITAIN TOPS ASYLUM SEEKER INTAKE IN EUROPE. *Daily Mail.*

By the time he gets off at King's Cross, the sky is still blue enough for the twin tower blocks of the Bemerton Estate to be silhouetted against it like two menacing gods presiding over their demesne of misrule and detritus. Once within the maze of alleyways, streets and culs-de-sac, the noise of traffic and human life on the bordering main roads fades away, leaving only an echo corridor of receding footsteps, the revving of an occasional car, the awkward shuffle of bodies disappearing into the dark, sometimes even the hissy whispers of haggling customers. Everything seems furtive and has the quality of noises off. Even the sound of trains entering the depot to the west, into sidings, has a faraway quality to it, something heard in a different, fairytale land, before a child's eyes close over with sleep.

His insides are fizzing fireworks of fear; it runs, thick and sluggish, in his feet, his calf muscles, his knocking chest, turning them heavy and light at the same time. Where does this end and hunger begin? Initially, he stays on streets from where running out onto York Way or Caledonian Road would be a short sprint, but the slowly diffusing smoke of the drug inside him obliges with its addictive hits only when he strays into the darker, more remote areas of the maze. The thought of those pimps with the acid bulb explodes in a delicious crackle-and-flash of fear in him. Tonight he will go with anyone and not ask for any money. Tonight it is faceless pleasure he is after.

He walks towards the stretch of water between Camley Street and Goods Way. It is the only way he can live with his fear, exorcizing it in the very place he was pinned down and threatened with the potent, disfiguring hiss of acid. He hasn't been in these desolate streets for well over six months; surely, the men who assaulted him have forgotten his very existence by now. Small change, that is what he was to them.

He hears footsteps in the next street and instinctively moves into the darker shadow of what appears to be a doorway to an abandoned warehouse. There are no streetlights here, only what meagre illumination reaches from the halogen lights of the Bemerton Estate; one could hardly count the change in one's hand in it. Two men appear at the end of the street. On instinct, Ritwik flattens himself against the door. One man could be a possibility, two men, almost always trouble: first rule of streetwalking. A few minutes later, he peeps: they are gone. He steps out and moves towards the end where he had seen the men. He moves fast because this area is slightly better lit than where he had hidden.

As if from nowhere, there are two men standing there. Skinny, young, pinched pale faces. One of them is smoking. Ritwik bends his head, concentrates on the road, and increases his pace. He can feel their eyes boring into his back, hears some whispering and then the punch of 'Paki cunt', not hurled at him, not yet, but just a casual conversational moment that exceeds and spills over the whispers. Whatever is invisible in the semi-darkness, colour obviously is not one of them. He tries not to panic, not to run, not to register any reaction, and keeps walking at the same pace. Thank god they are not those Albanian pimps at least, he thinks.

The men smell his fear, read his forced nonchalance easily, and gradually step up their abuse.

'Paki scum, hey you, Paki scum.' Tentative, even hushed, like a singer trying out his voice in a new venue, testing the acoustics.

'Fuck off to your slum you Paki bastard you Paki cunt fuck off.' Louder, bolder.

Ritwik arrives at a crossroads. If he takes a right and runs, runs very fast, he might be able to make it to one of the arteries feeding into the Caledonian Road. But the lane is so dark that he is scared to step in there. He hears running footsteps behind him. He wheels around: the men are within spitting distance. He has no choice; he makes his first mistake by turning into the street nearest him, thinking it will offer him a temporary sanctuary, the cover of darkness, or throw the men off the scent. Fear clouds his thoughts, and when he hears running behind him again, he blindly turns left, right, left, any turning that appears in front of him, desperate to lose himself and confuse the men. There are no niches and corners in the street he finds himself in, panting furiously, although it is darker than Camley Street. He has lost all orientation now. He is so scared that even the slow clang-and-rattle of a train in the background doesn't give him back his bearings. He is deaf to it; his ears are now wholly given to catching the sound of pursuit.

He hears a low whistle, a short hollering, the sound of more running feet, another whistle, and then, chillingly, the sound of running swells. There are five men now, at least five that he can see, entering his street, summoned like dogs by some ultrasonic signal unheard by the human ear, by the scent of prey. He huddles against a wall, wishing himself invisible. If he could only walk a few feet and slither under the hedge in front of him, he would feel safer but he is certain any movement will give him away.

'Find the fucking wog. You two run over to that end, we'll wait here for him. Let's see where that scum can hide.' The words are so loud that it seems to Ritwik all perspective, all distance, has been warped and shortened to pack this street and the five men into a little closed chamber. He finds himself shaking all over. He decides to risk it to the hedge – invisibility will save him – and in stepping out of the shadows he makes his second and final mistake.

He has hardly taken two steps forward, intending to crouch down and roll over the distance that separates him from his hiding place, when someone shouts, 'There he is. Jim, to your left.'

In an instant they are on him. Someone trips him up: he breaks his fall using the palms of his hand. He doesn't feel the skin scraping off them as he manages to save himself falling on his face, only the pure lucidity of his terror, like some clear afternoon light. They kick him while he is lying down, random kicks, aimed nowhere in particular. One catches him in his groin and he doubles up in pain. There is one on his ribs that takes all his breath away; try how hard he may, he cannot breathe anymore. As he chokes, he feels little popping explosions of light, a thousand lights, of dull, unnameable colour, behind his eyes.

'Send the fuckers back send those Paki scum away.' They are almost chanting it now, like a mantra at a ritual, their words resonating in some deep way to the blows they throw out in such aleoritic concord: a kick, a punch to the face, a sickening sound of cracking and crunching of bone. He tries to shout, but the scream is soundless. He doesn't know whether he should shout for help or beg for mercy. Just before he loses consciousness, Ritwik is granted not the diorama of his entire life flashing past his eyes in an instant but two unrelated moments of clarity: he is struck with wonder at the sheer rage these men are expressing; where is its wellspring? How can one small human harbour a sea of such anger inside him? Why do they not drown under it? The last light is the awareness of the fact that at some point during the chase or the assault, he had wet his jeans. Then he passes into the warmth of darkness.

He doesn't hear the sharp, cold flick of a metal blade emerging from its sheath, cries of 'No, Dave, no, don't be so fuckin' stupid, let's fuck off quick, no, Dave, no', doesn't feel the swift entries and exits of the knife, doesn't hear the desperate cry of 'You daft cunt, what the fuck have you done' repeated over and over, the sound of five sets of running, escaping feet, as his thin blood trickles out onto this dark corner of a back street that will be forever England.

XIII.

Miss Gilby sits on the terrace of the bungalow with a blanket drawn over her knees and soaks up the welcome warmth of the midday sun. It is so quiet that she can almost hear the wheeling of the brown eagle – Ruth would immediately reel off its scientific name, habitat, reproductive habits, nesting characteristics if she were to see it – in the middle distance, against the backdrop of the gleaming ranges of the Garhwal, their tops tipped with white snow that turn flame orange in the afternoons and then blue, an unfathomably dark blue, moments before the silent nightfall.

Ruth has gone inside to ask Mohun Singh to rustle up some lunch. She briefly appears at the door and calls out, 'Maud, there's a letter for you. I think it's from your brother. Shall I bring it out to you?'

Without looking behind her, she answers, 'If you will be so kind.' She is intent on watching the gliding arcs the eagle is describing in the clean, thin air. It gives Miss Gilby a vertiginous feeling inside her, as if she were in free fall. Part of that, she thinks, with her characteristic rationality, might be because the terrace of Ruth's bungalow is poised right on the edge, with nothing between it and the graceful bird but a steep valley of air reaching out over the tops of hills and ranges to the distant might of the Garhwal.

Later this afternoon, she is going to watch Ruth draw the next three birds for her new book – finch-billed bulbul (*Spizixos semitorques, did you know, Maud, some of these are really good songsters?*), hoopoe (*Upupa epops*) and the eared or snow pheasant (*Crossoptilon crossoptilon, really too low for it to be here in Almora, how strange, it usually lives in Tibet and northern China, this really is very unusual, I shall have to write off to Mr Elliot immediately*). Miss Gilby especially likes the hoopoe, and Ruth tells her quite a charming little story about how these birds had been given crowns by God for sheltering Solomon from the sun but they were killed for these crowns so often that they appealed to Solomon, who in turn prayed to God, and the crown was changed to the crest of feathers we see on their heads now. Miss Gilby is going to help Ruth with the accompanying illustrations of various individual feathers and vegetation, mostly leaves and flowers from the particular birds' native habitats. They have collected some specimens of flowers and leaves from their rambles in the hills so that she can have them in front of her while practising the sketches. It still gives her an excited shiver of delight to think that she has a hand, however minor or marginal, in helping Ruth Fairweather create her glorious ornithological survey of the Indian Sub-Continent.

Ruth comes out, gives the letter to Maud, and takes her place in the chair beside her. It is indeed from James and feels quite substantial. She decides to open it now and only skim it, reserving the proper reading for later. Five sheets of close cursive hand. Local gossip, new governor of Madras, North Arcot politics . . . she grazes inattentively . . . shipping taxes,

Mysore growing restive, Lady Ampthill's latest. Then the name 'Nikhilesh' on page three makes her halt and retrace her eyes over the relevant area of the paper.

You might already know this but I thought there would be no harm in repeating that Nikhilesh, your zamindar in Nawabgunj, died in the Hindoo-Mohammedan riots, which erupted in his village very shortly after you left. (Thank the good Lord for that.) Apparently, a stray bullet got him while he was out trying to stop a riot. Must admit to feeling rotten when I found out about it. My first thought was . . .

Miss Gilby neatly folds the letter and puts it away in a pocket. Ruth asks, 'Everything all right?' politely, perhaps because she has noticed the slight tremor of her friend's hands. Miss Gilby nods and reaches for the binoculars on the little stone table between them. She looks through it and tries to find the brown eagle but it is gone. She can only see the snow-scarred slopes of the distant mountains, brought so close now by the glasses that she could reach out her hand and almost touch them.

A NOTE ON NAMES

Bengalis, as indeed most Indians, address each other relationally. An older brother is called *dada*, while someone who stands in such a relationship to the speaker would be addressed by his first name with the suffix *–da*. An older sister, similarly, is *didi*, and someone like an older sister is called by her name with the suffix *–di*. *Mama* is maternal uncle, *mashi* maternal aunt and *dida* maternal grandmother. *Jamai* is brother-in-law, *jamaibabu*, a respectful way of addressing an older brother-in-law, so *didi*'s husband would be called *jamaibabu*.

ACKNOWLEDGEMENTS

It would not have been possible to write Miss Gilby's story without Sumit Sarkar's *The Swadeshi Movement in Bengal 1903–1908* (People's Publishing House: New Delhi, 1973, 2nd imprint, 1994). For those interested in the period and in the particulars of this chapter of colonial history, his still remains the most magisterial account: lucid, exhaustive, and deeply intelligent. I feel privileged to have taken some bearings from his work in writing my own.

Permission to quote from Cynthia Ozick in the epigraphs from author through David Miller at Rogers, Coleridge & White. Every effort has been made to obtain necessary permission with reference to copyright material. The publishers apologize if inadvertently any sources remain unacknowledged and will be happy to correct this in any future editions.

The Seas

by Samantha Hunt

ISBN: 978-1-84901-393-2
RRP: £7.99

**Award-winning debut novel from an
Orange Prize Shortlisted writer.**

The narrator of *The Seas* lives in a tiny, remote, alcoholic, cruel seaside
town. An occasional chambermaid, granddaughter to a typesetter, and
daughter to a dead man, awkward and brave, wayward and willful,
she is in love (unrequited) with Jude, an Iraq War veteran thirteen years her
senior. She is also convinced that she is a mermaid.

What she does to ease the pain of growing up lands her in prison.
What she does to get out is the stuff of legend. In the words of writer
Michelle Tea, *The Seas* is 'creepy and poetic, subversive and strangely
funny, [and] a phenomenal piece of literature.'

**'One of the most distinctive and unforgettable voices I have read in
years. This book will linger . . . in your head for a good long time.' Dave
Eggers**

Visit www.constablerobinson.com for more information

The Privileges

by Jonathan Dee

ISBN: 978-1-84901-405-2
RRP: £11.99

From acclaimed author Jonathan Dee comes a lyrical novel about the ways wealth can change and fortify a family over time, forcing them to re-examine what really matters.

Smart, socially gifted, and chronically impatient, Adam and Cynthia Morey are so perfect for each other that united they become a kind of fortress against the world. In their hurry to start a new life, they marry young and have two children before Cynthia reaches the age of twenty-five. Adam is a rising star in the world of private equity and becomes his boss's protégé. With a beautiful home in the upper-class precincts of Manhattan, gorgeous children, and plenty of money, they are, by any reasonable standard, successful.

But the Moreys' standard is not the same as other people's. The future in which they have always believed for themselves and their children – a life of almost boundless privilege, in which any desire can be acted upon and any ambition made real – is still out there, but it is not arriving fast enough to suit them. As Cynthia, at home with the kids day after identical day, begins to drift, Adam is confronted with a decision that tests how much he is willing to risk to ensure his family's happiness and to recapture the sense that, for him and his wife, the only acceptable life is one of infinite possibility.

The Privileges is an odyssey of a couple touched by fortune, changed by time, and guided above all else by their epic love for each other. Lyrical, provocative, and brilliantly imagined, it is a timely meditation on wealth, family, and what it means to leave the world richer than you found it.

Visit www.constablerobinson.com for more information

The Three Weissmanns of Westport

by Kathleen Schine

ISBN: 978-1-84901-571-4

RRP: £11.99

**Sense and Sensibility moves to Westport, Connecticut, in this
New York Times bestselling homage to the classic novel.**

*When Joseph Weissmann divorced his wife, he was seventy eight years old
and she was seventy-five...*

*He said the words "Irreconcilable differences," and saw real confusion
in his wife's eyes.*

*"Irreconcilable differences?" she said. "Of course there are irreconcilable
differences. What on earth does that have to do with divorce?"*

Dumped by her husband of nearly fifty years and then exiled from their
elegant New York apartment by his mistress, Betty Weissmann is forced
to move to a small, run-down beach cottage in Westport, Connecticut.
Joining her are her middle-aged daughters Miranda, an impulsive but
successful literary agent, and Annie, a pragmatic library director, who
dutifully comes along to keep an eye on her capricious mother and sister.
As the sisters mingle with the suburban aristocracy, love starts to blossom
for both of them, and they find themselves struggling with the dueling
demands of reason and romance.

Visit www.constablerobinson.com for more information

Crazy Heart

by Thomas Cobb

ISBN: 978-1-84901-512-7
RRP: £7.99

'Thomas Cobb's marvellous first novel doesn't just play on your
heartstrings, it breaks them.' *San Francisco Examiner*

At the age of fifty-seven, Bad Blake is on his last legs. His weight,
his ticker, his liver, even his pick-up truck are all giving him trouble.
A renowned songwriter and 'picker' who hasn't recorded in five years,
Bad now travels the countryside on gigs that take him mostly to motels and
bowling alleys. Enter Ms Right. Can Bad stop living the life of a country-
western song and tie a rope around his crazy heart?

The stunning novel that inspired the film, *Crazy Heart*, starring Jeff Bridges
in the Golden Globe and Oscar-winning lead role (Best Actor, 2010)

Visit www.constablerobinson.com for more information

To order other **Corsair** titles simply contact The Book Service (TBS) by phone, email or by post. Alternatively visit our website at www.constablerobinson.com.

No. of copies	Title	RRP	ISBN	Total
	The Seas	£7.99	978-1-84901-393-2	
	The Privileges	£11.99	978-1-84901-405-2	
	The Three Weissmanns of Westport	£11.99	978-1-84901-571-4	
	Crazy Heart	£7.99	978-1-84901-512-7	
	P&P			£
	Grand Total			£

FREEPOST RLUL-SJGC-SGKJ, Cash Sales Direct Mail Dept., The Book Service, Colchester Road, Frating, Colchester, CO7 7DW

Tel: +44 (0) 1206 255 800
Fax: +44 (0) 1206 255 930

Email: sales@tbs-ltd.co.uk

UK customers: please allow £1.00 p&p for the first book, plus 50p for the second, and an additional 30p for each book thereafter, up to a maximum charge of £3.00.

Overseas customers (incl. Ireland): please allow £2.00 p&p for the first book, plus £1.00 for the second, plus 50p for each additional book.

NAME (block letters):_____
ADDRESS: _____
_____
_____ POSTCODE:_____

I enclose a cheque/PO (payable to 'TBS Direct') for the amount of £____
I wish to pay by Switch/Credit Card
Card number:
Expiry date:_____ Switch issue number:_____